A TALE OF TWO CITIZENS

A TALE OF TWO CITIZENS

A NOVEL

Elyce Wakerman

YUCCA

Yucca Publishing books may be purchased in bulk at special discounts for sales promotion, corporate gifts, fund-raising, or educational purposes. Special editions can also be created to specifications. For details, contact the Special Sales Department, Yucca Publishing, 307 West 36th Street, 11th Floor, New York, NY 10018 or yucca@skyhorsepublishing.com.

Yucca Publishing® is an imprint of Skyhorse Publishing, Inc.®, a Delaware corporation.

Visit our website at www.yuccapub.com.

10 9 8 7 6 5 4 3 2 1

Library of Congress Cataloging-in-Publication Data is available on file.

Cover design by Yucca Publishing

Print ISBN: 978-1-63158-014-7
Ebook ISBN: 978-1-63158-035-2

Printed in the United States of America

For Jeff, Juliet, and Bobby
and in memory of Jacob

There are two ways of spreading light:
to be the candle or the mirror that reflects it.
—Edith Wharton

PROLOGUE

1976
Finding Fathers

Charlotte sat on the bed regarding the Florsheim shoe box with equal measures of anticipation and resistance. She had noticed it over the years, up on a high ledge of her mother's closet, and may have wondered every now and then while she was growing up why it was there: a man's shoe box was singularly out of place in their female household. But she never asked about it. It would be like finding a bottle of aftershave in the medicine chest, something that just did not belong, but whose explanation for being there she really did not want to know. Besides, her childhood trips to the closet while her mother was away at work caused jittery nerves enough without adding the shoe box to her concerns, for what brought Charlotte to the inner sanctum of her mother's life was a book she knew she would be forbidden from knowing about—much less handling.

Damp with guilt, Charlotte would methodically slide each of her mother's *Reader's Digest*s to the side as she slowly got closer to the object of her search, the sin-laden fruit whose grown-up secrets she and her invited schoolmates had gathered to pluck: *Over Sexteen*, the orange-and-yellow book-jacketed home to pages and pages of off-color jokes and shocking cartoons that Charlotte couldn't possibly imagine her mother's eyes gazing upon.

Her hands trembled slightly as she closed in, and always there was that moment of dismay to find that the book was still there. Yet she'd wrap her fingers around its spine and hoist it like a trophy before her wide-eyed friends, the select group who had either studied it with her before or heard of its existence at school and now stood at the dock of their maiden voyage among its treasures. A man with a wedge-shaped gap in his chest the size and contour of a woman's bosom occupied one page, eliciting uncontrollable giggles, rolling-on-the-floor hysterics from her and her friends, but could her mother's eyes ever ever have beheld something so indecent? Charlotte had long ago convinced herself that her mother didn't even know that the book was there, that it must have been left by the previous tenant.

And a faded, fraying shoe box? Too high to reach, anyway? Of passing interest, at most.

Even as she graduated from junior high school, high school, college, grad school, Charlotte never mentioned to her mother the pornographic hardcover that had brightened so many a winter afternoon of her early adolescence, and at some point, when she had looked for it just to see if her mother could still possibly own the licentious little volume, sure enough, it was gone.

Now, she sat on one of the twin beds in her mother's bedroom regarding the shoe box. "You are old enough to know," her mother had tersely announced moments after Charlotte had come upon it. She was staying at her mother's apartment for a few days before heading for teacher training in Connecticut, a job she was thrilled about because a) it would require a certain amount of traveling, which meant b) she could save money on rent and stay with her mom between assignments.

She had been going in search of a sweater when the unexpected object on the bed stopped her in her tracks. Of course, she didn't have to think for even one split second about what this was: it was the Florsheim shoe box that had sat high on a ledge in her mother's closet for the entirety of her childhood, and which, whatever it might contain, the least likely possibility was shoes.

But why was it here? What was she supposed to do with it? It was at that puzzling moment that her mother had appeared in the doorway and made her terse statement: "You are old enough to know." The declaration contained four words more: "It was your father's." She left the doorway as silently as she had materialized inside it and, oddly, closed the door behind her.

"Old enough to know." Charlotte was twenty-seven. She had a master's degree in art history, a boyfriend, a job she was looking forward to, and a pretty optimistic little attitude. Her confidence wasn't based on anything in particular, it was just the way she was. Some might consider her annoyingly sunny; one of those people would be her mother, who tended toward a more cautious worldview.

The box had no cover, yet its contents were comparatively dust free. Had her mother gone over the envelopes, documents, photographs with a cloth before handing them to her? Did she go through them occasionally herself, thereby keeping them from collecting dust? Sit at the kitchen table and pick through her deceased husband's papers as a way, perhaps, of feeling that he was with her?

Charlotte sifted through the papers and pictures warily. Her father, who had died of a sudden heart attack when she was a toddler, was firmly entrenched in her imagination as a hero. Worshipping his memory and what a perfect dad he would have been comprised the entirety of the relationship she wanted to have with him. Though a naturally inquisitive person, she really wasn't all that interested in learning things about her father that might tarnish the idol. He was dead, she had had to grow up without a father, who was dead; didn't she deserve to keep his image sacrosanct?

Photographs. Who were these people? A pretty young woman and a small boy.

One piece of paper was so delicate it nearly crumbled between her fingers; a government document of some kind. A congressional hearing?

Other sheets of paper, similarly fragile, were written entirely in Polish.

Really. Sunny Charlotte couldn't help but feel irritated. What was she supposed to do with all this stuff: sit down, now, at eight o'clock on some random night in September and learn the ins and outs of Harry Himelbaum's life story? Well, she didn't feel "old enough to know," not just yet.

And so, after her cursory perusal, she shoved the box away from her, grabbed her cardigan, and opened the bedroom door.

It would be years before she revisited the box, organized its contents according to date, found a translator, and put together an understanding of the road her father had taken to give her life.

~ ~ ~

PART ONE

1929
A Path to Citizenship

April

Wlodawa, Poland

Hope and sorrow mingled as travelers and those who had come to say good-bye gathered at the train station. Standing in his straightest posture among the mothers and uncles and neighbors, and people from the village who might not even know anyone leaving, but for whom these departures marked a noteworthy event, a ruddy young man of twenty gripped his visa protectively. Every few minutes, he tapped the pocket of his jacket to feel the reassuring outline of the precious steamer ticket. He squared his shoulders more broadly; he was really here, really doing this! Owing to his father, who had already been there for seven years, Yankel Himelbaum was going to America. His legal classification for entry as the minor, unmarried son of an American citizen was stamped right there on the visa he held so proudly.

Tugging at his overcoat, which Yankel wore on top of his jacket because there was no more room in his small suitcase, his little sister, Rifka, looked up at him with adoration. She laughed and sobbed simultaneously, her face busy with the effort, and, as always, she chattered: "Don't forget us, Yankel. What will we do without you? You will send for me, you will, won't you?"

Yankel's older brothers, already married, looked on skeptically. *What was the big deal with this America?* they wondered. First their father, now Yankel, the one everybody counted on. Even though he was the youngest, it was he who oversaw their small dairy farm. He kept the books like a real businessman and never shied from getting his hands dirty, either, working in the barn and fields by day, and long into the night with the figures and accounting. If something was broken, he fixed it; the two sides of the ledger didn't add up, he made the appropriate financial adjustments until they did. Where the neighbors had hungrily anticipated problems, resentment in the family—the third boy in charge?—none had materialized, for young he might be, but always Yankel knew how to act like a real *mensch*. Any of the three hired laborers who helped out on the small farm, located a kilometer outside of Wlodawa, would attest to this. Now—the Himelbaums heard the gossip and couldn't entirely disagree with it—who knew what would happen? Yitzak, the eldest son, was spending more and more time in Warsaw, saying he was expanding the family's business opportunities, though he was short on specifics; and Hershel spent half the day in the kitchen with Elke, their mother, kneading, baking. He never looked so happy as when he pulled a perfect challah from the oven. And cakes: he had one for every occasion; he invented occasions so that he could produce one of his "light-as-a-cloud" creations.

The locomotive blared its melancholy call to board, eliciting cries and gasps of separation from the gathered crowd. Yankel had never seen so many people at the station. It must be like the old days that his parents talked about, when it seemed that everyone was fleeing the pogroms, and countless thousands had left. Since that time, in the years immediately following the World War, life for the Jew in Poland had become more acceptable, thanks in large part to the minority-protection clauses that had been added to the peace agreement. A Polish Jew could make a living. He was entitled, at least on paper, to political and civil rights. Lately, though, the anti-Semitism that most gentile Poles seemed to be born with was bubbling to the surface, arousing its equally accessible counterpart: Jewish anxiety. Bolshevism was in the air, and Jews were getting the blame for spreading its subversive message. Jewish poverty was sneered at, Jewish affluence resented. The handsome and capable young man whom everyone admired for his ability to fix what was broken saw that perhaps Poland itself was broken for the Jews. Perhaps, all of Europe—one heard rumors about Germany, and the growing popularity of the Nazi party. So it made sense, the long line of people that had wound around the block the day he'd gone to the American consulate in Warsaw to apply for his visa, and all these people here today, waiting for the train.

But where was Reizel? He'd been looking for her all morning, craning his neck trying to catch sight of her. "Here, Rifkele," he said, momentarily leaving off looking for his girlfriend to take a piece of candy from his pocket and hand it to his distraught little sister. "Here," he said, "when you come to America, all the time I'll give you." Rifka, sniffing back her colliding emotions, peeled the wrapping eagerly.

Was it possible that Reizel wouldn't come? She had promised, but then again, she hadn't kept her feelings about this day a secret. How, in the face of their love, could he leave her? Start a new life without her on the other side of the world? Though their relationship was too respectful for arguments—their lovemaking a driving burst of nature inside an otherwise easygoing compatibility—Yankel never wavered about going to America, at least in front of Reizel. Perhaps in private, he might have second thoughts about pursuing the dream he'd held since his early teenage years—he was in love with his girl, running a reasonably successful business; why should he leave?—but he would quickly dismiss these thoughts. To Reizel's quiet protests he responded with gentle reassurances about the beautiful life he would build for them in a land without prejudice or turmoil, and the promise that he would send for her, soon. And for the moment, at least, she would seem to see the sense of it.

Greatly relieved, he spotted her, walking purposefully and looking straight ahead. Her face showed no emotion; she might as well be making her way through a busy market. Such a little person amidst the throngs, yet she held herself tall with pride, her carriage belying her petite stature. Grabbing Rifka's hand, Yankel nudged the two of them through the crowd toward his sweetheart.

Seeing him, Reizel looked down. It was a gesture to which Yankel had become accustomed, this bending of Reizel's head when they came upon each other. Beside her now, he crooked his finger under her chin and lifted it so that their eyes met. How pale she looked, and such strain in her gaze.

"I'm so sorry, Yankel," Reizel said, looking at him intently. "I am late, there's nothing I could do about it." Where moments before, her face had been a study in stoicism, her eyes now brimmed with tears. His fingers dabbed them lightly.

"Don't worry, Reizele," he said, "we've got a few minutes yet before the train leaves. I'm just so happy to see you. I was afraid for a minute…"

"No," his girlfriend said, "it's not the train I'm talking about." With uncharacteristic impatience, she brushed his hand from her face. And her head did not lower now. Instead, she looked straight at him, almost defiantly.

"Reizel, will you braid my hair this afternoon, after, after Yankel goes on the train?" The last part of Rifka's sentence came out haltingly, the words themselves reminding her of why Reizel was even here, and so early in the day. Yankel's girlfriend lived with her parents in Lukow, and came to Wlodawa only rarely. But whenever she did come, Rifka loved spending time with her brother's sweetheart, admired her unabashedly, as a sisterless nine-year-old might be wont to do. As for her other brothers' wives, Chava and Leah, they seemed more like her mother, old and old-fashioned. Reizel knew about and spoke of modern things, cities and cinema, and she knew how to be playful. Rifka loved it when Reizel braided her hair and told her stories about the latest fashions from Paris. Paris! Could there be such a place? Where people drank wine with lunch, out of fine crystal goblets?

At the moment, though, it was as if the younger girl hadn't spoken, as though she didn't exist, so intense was the gaze between Yankel and Reizel.

"I'm late, not with the train." Reizel spoke quickly, yet enunciated each word.

Yankel took a minute. "You're…?"

"Yes," she sharply cut him off.

"You're . . ." Yankel heaved a deep breath. "You're sure?"

Now his Reizele allowed her head to fall.

His own head felt disengaged from his surroundings. He might as well be standing in total isolation on a desolate piece of land, surrounded by silence. Time might just as well have stopped. Yankel held the visa in his fist, squeezing it into a wad. The steamer ticket sat like an empty book of matches in his pocket. Useless.

"All aboard," the conductor called. But Yankel knew he wasn't going anywhere today.

Iowa City, Iowa

"You may kiss the bride."

Will Brown, earnest by nature, regarded his bride. He had to lift his head slightly, for in her high-heeled shoes, she stood nearly a head taller than the groom. But they'd rehearsed this moment, worked out how Barbara would lower her head, just so, and he'd raise his so that their lips could meet without the necessity of Will having to get up on his toes. Barbara—Barbara Brown as of this moment—yes, she was very pretty. Will could not recall a time in his life when this face had not produced in him anything short of gladness.

A murmur passed over the room, the chapel filled with people Will had known all his life. Everyone was waiting, he knew, for the ceremonial kiss. Ah, well. Barbara subtly bent her neck as they'd practiced, and Will lifted the veil. He placed a small peck on Barbara's friendly red lips, and the onlookers sighed with pleasure, and perhaps a touch of relief.

Will looked around and almost wanted to pinch himself. Everything had gone according to plan. He didn't like surprises, and here at the Rotary Club, where his father had been a member for two years, a man could find respite from the general air of "anything goes" that had permeated the country, insinuated itself even here, in comparatively staid Iowa City.

Thankfully, Barbara had never fallen prey to the wild shenanigans of the U.S. female population during the so-called Roaring Twenties. She'd kept her hair and her hemline long, and her priorities straight. Even the dress she wore today reflected her commitment to tradition: it had been her grandmother's, and her mother's after that.

As they, he and Mrs. Brown (oh, how he liked the sound of it), hurried up the aisle collecting congratulations, the future, like the wedding, looked firmly in his control. Yes, everything was going according to plan: he had his law degree, an exciting new job, and now, a wife. Will had worked hard all his life, his father had taught him the virtue of hard work, and now everything was paying off.

"Mom, Pop," Will greeted his parents with a kiss and a handshake, respectively, as they joined the reception line. It seemed that everyone in Iowa City was there to greet them, owing mostly to the high regard in which his father was held. Nicholas Brown's popularity, Will reluctantly suspected, was the result not only of his warm heart and big smile, but what Will considered the overly generous allowances he extended to so many customers who walked into the store. With the stock market in perpetual flux these days—hitting the roof one day, plummeting the next—a lot of the people they'd known all their lives, many of them farmers, were hanging on to their finances by a thread, watching their savings steadily erode under the weight of surpluses. But spend, spend, spend, the government kept shouting, keep everyone in business, keep the farmers producing. So what if the money isn't there with which to buy? It will be, soon. The message to business owners, even the owners of small Midwestern dry goods stores, was clear: accept the good intentions of your neighbors, extend them credit, and before we know it, everything will be right again. Well, how could Will argue? Even Herbert Hoover, the solid Iowa native recently installed in the White House, had promised a return to prosperity. The "triumph over poverty" is at hand, he'd said. This was the promise of the United States of America, after all, and Will, a proud Republican, well, he couldn't argue with that.

Sure, he knew the facts, he saw the coffers shrinking every day as his mother tried desperately to balance the books, but if there were two forces of nature he had to acknowledge as stronger than himself, they were the country that he loved, and the father he idolized. If Hoover said give 'em credit, and his father, large of stature and stout of heart, went along, and if the key to American prosperity was just for everyone to go shopping, well, maybe that was the ticket. Will could only hope so.

But if his father's largesse and the national economic roller coaster defied Will's power to control circumstances, at least the job he'd secured for himself would put him right in the middle of a situation he could control. Ever since the military exemption he'd been granted during the World War—not, thank heaven, owing to his mortifying five foot five stature (he'd gratefully learned that a man need only be five feet tall to be called to active duty), but because of his father's heart attack in 1916, and the fact that, as sole offspring of Nicholas and Electra Brown, he'd been deemed to have "indispensable duties at home"—ever since he'd been relieved of having to serve in the military so that he could oversee the store while his father recuperated, Will had vowed to himself, and to Barbara, and to his parents, and to anyone who would listen, that he would find an alternative way to serve his country; indeed, he would dedicate his life to upholding America's freedoms. The Red Scare of his early years in college provided just the issue to which his patriotic fervor could adhere.

It was right after the war that labor unions started to run rampant over the tenets of free enterprise. Informed by the revolution in Russia and fueled, it was widely believed, by Bolsheviks, workers were demanding ever-higher wages and ever-shorter hours, and this anarchy must be stopped. Clearly, the tides of incoming aliens were at the root of this antiprofit, anti-American surge, and Will Brown, along with thousands of other God-fearing patriots, pledged to stem the tide. Thus, he'd decided to go to law school and, once enrolled, concentrated on immigration law, with an eye toward tightening restrictions on entering the country, or before anyone knew what had happened, the nation would be taken over by Communists and anarchists, Jews and other "free-thinking" types.

That the country had been settled by immigrants, that his own parents had been the children of immigrants, did not disturb Will's convictions for even one moment. Quite the opposite, for when his grandparents had changed their name from Dambasis to the all-American "Brown," and turned their backs on Greek Orthodoxy to join the Protestant faith, they'd steered the very course of his philosophy: if people didn't want to fit into this country and its ways, well then, no one had asked them to come.

To Will's vast satisfaction, he'd secured an important position at Ellis Island, the belly of the beast. The Island of Hope, some called it; others referred to it as The Island of Tears. Will had worked there as a legal inspector during a summer off from law school back in the early twenties. Back then, the island was overrun with immigrants, and it was all the government could do to keep it staffed. Law students eager to serve were a good fit for the long hours, middling pay, and demanding work expected of interrogators.

Hour after hour, sometimes seven days a week, Will would sit atop his wooden stool at a high wooden desk in the Great Hall, looking out onto the many long, penned-in rows into which the hopeful newcomers had been corralled. As a legal inspector, he knew he was the final obstacle these people had to face before being admitted into the country. They'd gotten through the preliminary questioning and medical inspections, and now his interrogation was the end of the line— exactly where his desk stood.

One by one he'd call up the eager arrivals, sometimes as many as 500 a day. Most of them wore clothing meant to make a favorable impression, but the carefully draped shawls and proudly perched caps struck Will, more often than not, as costumes from another time.

"Name? "Point of origin?" "Birth date?" "Married?" "Race?" "Destination?" "Do you have a job waiting for you?" Will asked the questions countless times each day, the tedium offset by the importance of doing the job honestly, conscientiously. This was a rigorous process, as well it should be, gaining entry into the United States of America, not like hopping over some border fence, for goodness' sake.

Not so easily overcome were the panoply of languages with which the young inspector was confronted. The majority of the people he interacted with spoke little to no English. They'd been on a boat for at least a week, Will would grouse to himself, couldn't they have picked up in that time even a smattering of the language of the country they'd *chosen* to come to? Yes, they were entitled to speak through interpreters, but locating the staff member to match the language took up valuable time, and then, all the back-and-forth, back-and-forth, it was just plain tiresome.

Then there was the odor. Frequently, Will would have to lean in to make sense of what an immigrant attempting to speak English was saying, and the experience had taught him how to breathe without smelling. Why didn't the steamship companies distribute chewing gum or breath mints before disembarkation? The Great Hall, high-domed and 200 feet long by 100 feet wide, still wasn't spacious enough to diffuse the acrid odor emitting from the mouths of these people.

But on he'd go with the work of weeding through them. He'd learned to pay special attention to whether or not the person standing before him claimed to have a job waiting. If the word on the ship's manifest under occupation read "laborer," Will knew he'd have to take his time with this particular foreigner.

While the United States frowned upon immigrants who had no means of income and who might therefore "go on the dole," the country simultaneously made it unlawful for a person to have arrived under the auspices of an American company that had promised him employment. Too many companies were taking advantage of people desperate to leave their homelands, footing the cost of their ocean passage in exchange for a job for which they could pay a ridiculously low wage, a wage that no bona fide American citizen would ever accept. The double bind continually played itself out at Will Brown's desk when he asked the question about whether the immigrant would be employed. If the person standing before him appeared too sure of himself as he asserted his upcoming employment with this or that company, or, on the other hand, if he dodged when asked the name of the company he would be working for, Will, in his position as legal inspector, knew what he had to do. Without hesitation, and because it was his responsibility to follow the protocol, he'd pin the man with an SI tag. Special Inquiry.

Tags, there were so many tags. The aspiring Americans wandering the hall looked like so many pieces of merchandise, drifting aimlessly, squares of paper pinned to their shirts. And everyone, even the

11

least literate, knew what this particular tag meant: detention. Anyone wearing that S.I. tag would eventually be hauled into a cell, and held on the island for however long it took to be seen by the Board of Special Inquiry. On more than one occasion, Will's heart went out to these uneducated aliens, lured to America by the cunning promises of big companies. But then he'd remind himself of the true victims of this unwitting alliance between unethical businesses and foreigners willing to work for nothing: average American working people, the people whose interests Will was here to represent, and who didn't deserve unemployment and poverty because non-Americans would take their jobs.

Detention, of course, was what every newcomer to Ellis Island dreaded, short of deportation itself. Even though they'd be fed, at the expense of the steamship company, and housed in a dormitory, at the expense of the United States government, immigrants placed in a detention cell, whether for medical or legal reasons—and for all to see—had to endure palpable humiliation. On top of that, they knew what waited at the other end of detention: an encounter with the board. A negative encounter loomed as an understandably terrifying prospect.

And Will did understand. Most of these people had divested themselves of whatever meager worldly goods they possessed in order to come here. Many had traveled with their spouses and children, and a verdict of no entry could mean a heartrending separation, and a forced return to a homeland that held no future, no loved ones. Thousands of deportees, Will had heard, had jumped overboard to their deaths rather than go back to the void that their homeland had become. He took no pleasure in making the kinds of decisions that might lead to such a miserable outcome, and he approached the responsibility as fairly as he knew how, ever mindful, though, of his patriotic obligation.

Will had heard that the island was less congested these days, not as many people trying to get in, which meant a less hectic schedule for the staff. But it wasn't the lightened workload that stirred Will's anticipation about his new job; as a fervent defender of the American way of life, he'd be willing to put up with any number of unpleasantries, and felt that he had certainly proven this about himself. No, what really had Will exuberant about going back to Ellis Island was his new position. He wasn't going to be a mere inspector this time. Thanks to his previous experience and his law degree, he'd been hired to sit as a member of one of the Boards of Special Inquiry—a big step up.

Will received the call about the prestigious appointment just weeks before the wedding. As validating as it was, however, and as promising for a career in immigration law, he had had to temper his excitement in light of breaking the news to Barbara. The job meant the two of them would have to relocate, and he knew he'd have to broach the subject gently.

Aware of her fiancé's ambitions, Barbara had anticipated that a move to New York might be necessary, but preoccupation with the wedding, and the not-unusual tendency to put off thinking about unwanted changes that for all anyone knows won't happen anyway, had swept the possible relocation from her mind. A simple Midwestern girl with modest aspirations, Barbara was loath to leave home and everything and everyone she knew, except that one of the main things she knew was that a wife had to stand by her husband, and, of course, if what Will wanted was an important job that entailed moving to New York City, well then, that's where she'd have to be, by his side in all that he wished.

Will had been prepared to persuade her gently, but it hadn't taken very much coaxing, nor, when he thought about it, did this really surprise him. Barbara had always been the one person on earth, aside from his parents, that he could count on. She had waited for him through college and law school and studying for the bar, waited until they were both thirty years old for him to propose, so that he could "have something solid" to offer as her husband. Barbara believed in him, and her sweet acquiescence in the face of leaving home was really nothing more than he should have expected. Still, it did make him feel even more keenly his divine good fortune in having her as his girl.

Of course, Will's imminent departure for the East Coast weighed somewhat heavily on his parents, who still relied on him, but he'd given the first thirty years of his life, minus that one summer on the island, to them, been a dutiful and devoted son, and now, they knew, they must learn to get on without him. Hadn't this been, after all, what they'd worked for: that Will should succeed in the world, and have everything he wanted?

"I hope you will give me the second dance." Nicholas Brown beamed at his new daughter-in-law. Nicholas was a tall, strapping man, of whom it was hard to believe a heart condition. "The first, of course," he said, "is for you and William."

The bride smiled up at the handsome man she'd have to learn to stop addressing as Mr. Brown. "I'd love to dance with you, Pop," she said, the last word coming awkwardly. "I'll try not to step on your toes," she giggled. Will found Barbara's nervous giggle, a habit she'd been prone to since childhood, endearing. He cherished the ease with which she lapsed into unembarrassed girlishness. It connected her, and them, to their roots, to the fact that, somehow, they'd both known since grammar school that this day would come. Everything as it should be. Well, everything, perhaps, except when she'd suddenly shot up to be taller than Will in eighth grade. By high school graduation he'd stopped waiting for the "growth spurt" his parents promised he too would enjoy, and resigned himself to his diminutive stature. Barbara seemed not to mind at all that she was the taller one.

"Come, Nicholas," Ellie, as Will's mother was known, nudged her husband. "Everyone is inside, and it's time for them to introduce the new married couple. Come." She took her husband's hand and led him into the large social hall, which had been decorated with crepe paper and balloons for the occasion. Will knew it wasn't as elegant as it could be, but times were hard, and the Rotary board had insisted on covering all expenses.

"Are you ready for our waltz?" he asked his wife, crooking his arm for her. He had tried to get this particular tradition struck from the program, ruing the spectacle of the short groom twirling his stately wife around the dance floor. But Barbara's eyes had filled with tears

14

when he'd broached the subject of not sharing the customary first dance, and the fact that they danced well together appeased his vanity.

"Ladies and gentlemen, I give you Mr. and Mrs. William Brown," the master of ceremonies announced from inside as the double doors opened, and to the accordion's strains of "I'm Always Chasing Rainbows," the young couple with the well-planned future made their way into their wedding party.

~ ~ ~

June

Yankel and Reizel had been married almost immediately after the aborted trip. They'd moved into her parents' apartment in Lukow, and now, once again, he was preparing to leave for America. Trying not to look at her lest his resolve melt in the face of her sorrow, Yankel packed his small suitcase. During the many conversations they had had, Reizel had agreed that Yankel should proceed with his plans, but now that the day of separation had come, she had been crying all morning, bent over in a chair and weeping into her hands, not something a person could easily ignore.

In the months since they'd been married, Yankel would frequently prop up on his elbow in the morning while they were still in bed and Reizel slept, her black curls puddled on the pillow, and slowly circle the area just above her stomach with his outstretched palm. If only he could feel it somehow, the life inside her. He was going to be a father! Shouldn't he, for the sake of the child, stay?

But then he'd think of his own father, how he'd emigrated for the very purpose of establishing a decent life for his family. Even if Yankel couldn't quite locate within himself the pull of fatherhood—he himself was only twenty—he knew he was doing the right thing.

He had married Reizel and stayed with her. Made himself part of her family by helping out in her parents' millinery shop. Wasn't it now acceptable, even more essential than ever, that he continue with his plans? Behave like a real husband and father, and sacrifice the short-term comfort of physical nearness to build a life in a country that would embrace them well into the future?

With each garment that he folded and placed in his suitcase, Yankel went through his litany of reasons for leaving and swept from his mind anything that might impede his going forward. The separation was necessary, the adult and correct course of action. Reizel might not be aware of it, but from the beginning, she had been the agent of his adulthood. For the year since they'd been dating, spending every Sunday together, he'd known it. Every week, after *Shabbes*, on the three-hour train ride to be with her, he'd known; drifting off to sleep by himself in the small sewing room behind her parents' store, and dreaming of the ravishing promise of the next day—each step of the way, he'd known it: she had made a man of him.

At first, Reizel had been happy to spend time with him in Wlodawa, where they'd met at the home of her uncle, an acquaintance of Yankel's family. Yankel had recognized immediately upon seeing the girl with the hat pulled low over her brow—fitted at just the right angle to simultaneously protect and beckon one toward the lightest green eyes— that this is what it meant to be a man attracted to a woman. The way she lowered her head when their eyes met, she must feel it, too. After a month of courting in Wlodawa, Reizel asked that he come to Lukow, the larger city, so much more cosmopolitan than his "old-fashioned" town, and he'd readily agreed. With a girl like this, older and sophisticated and beautiful, how could he refuse? If she wanted the two of them to spend time in her own hometown, he was happy to come after *Shabbes* each week, spend all day Sunday together with her. Not that they availed themselves of her "cosmopolitan" town. Shops and restaurants and commercial centers were closed on Sundays in Poland, where Catholicism held sway even in villages, like Lukow, with a large Jewish population. Instead, they would pack a picnic and hike into the countryside, knowing as they set out that their destination was each other's arms. Yes, they'd talk quietly, about their parents, the latest political developments one or the other might have read about in the newspaper; they'd laugh over tidbits of gossip, and carry the basket of sandwiches, but what drove them forward was a fierce desire to get to this tree or that field, where they would find "just the right place for a rest," and fold onto the ground hungrily. His hands on her skin, feeling its smoothness; her fingers stroking, his probing; her wetness, his hard core.

As they lay beside each other afterward, holding hands, looking up at the sky, even in the rain, or on a mattress of powdery snow, he would bask in the magnificence of all that she had given him. After a while, they would ravenously eat their sandwiches, laughing at their shared openhearted gusto, and then he'd walk her home, exchange a few friendly words with her parents, and return to the train station for the three-hour ride back to the farm. Now, since April, he'd barely left her side. He certainly hadn't made any attempt to take the train back home, for his parents mustn't know about the marriage.

He must keep it from them, that the facts stated on his visa no longer matched the truth. But face his mother in a lie? That he could never do.

That morning three months earlier at the train station, he'd told his brothers that Reizele was ill, that his trip must be postponed and to please explain to Mama and get in touch with their father in New York. At first, it wasn't hard to perpetrate this deception, for Reizel, anyone could see that day, did indeed look pale. He himself had noticed it, for weeks in fact, but he'd attributed her recent pallor to his upcoming departure. Whatever the fault in his character this selective blindness might suggest, there could be no question, once he knew the truth, of what he must do. And so, after his brothers and Rifka had headed back to the farm, he'd taken his sweetheart Reizel's hand and gone with her to find Rabbi Braun, the rabbi of Wlodawa, sworn him to secrecy, and obtained a *ketubah*, a Jewish license of marriage. To serve as witnesses, the rabbi found two strangers who had just finished praying.

It looked as though everything was taken care of: Reizel's parents, and Reizel herself, gave thanks that the relationship was sealed and that the child would be legitimate in the eyes of God. But a few days after the issuing of the *ketubah*, it was Rabbi Braun himself who came to the Lansky apartment in Lukow, all the way from Wlodawa, a noteworthy event since no one had ever known the rabbi to leave the small

19

village. Seeing him at the front door of the Lansky apartment, Yankel's heart sank. Something must be terribly wrong.

"This is a *shande* for the *goyem*," the rabbi had said, getting right to the point. "Anyone can see the girl is expecting." *Anyone but her boyfriend, now husband,* Yankel thought—*and hopefully my brothers.* "You must do the decent thing," the rabbi was saying, "and get the civil certificate. Period."

"But my papers," Yankel had tried to reason with the spiritual leader. He even took the visa from his jacket pocket in the closet and showed it to the rabbi. He had pressed it between the covers of a heavy book, so the all-important document had more or less straightened out from the crinkled wad he had squeezed it into. "You see here: it says, 'unmarried.' That is the only way they will allow me in."

"I don't know what it says or doesn't say," the rabbi insisted, waving off this piece of paper from a land he deeply suspected would be the ruin of the Jewish people. "You will do the right thing by your wife. And . . ." He paused to convey the magnitude of the words he was about to speak. "Your child."

And so, against his better judgment, and fearing that he might be digging the grave for his plans, digging a grave in the name of marriage and birth, Yankel was shamed by the rabbi into making his marriage official, legal.

"Okay," he said, beaten, but careful to return the visa to his jacket pocket. "Go, please, ask Yitzak to come, he and Chava will stand up for us. Reizel's parents, it's better they shouldn't be there, they're happy with things as they are. They'll wonder why my mother didn't come. But my parents, they must not find out, about the child, about the marriage, anything. They would be so disappointed, and frightened, knowing I have to lie to get into America." Visions of immigration officials filled Yankel's head, all the questions he knew he'd have to answer. The nonquota visa was clearly made out to the *unmarried* son of Icko Himelbaum. *Unmarried.* The word was pressed into his mind like a government stamp, an official rebuke of his every deed. He knew he was doing the right thing, but this right thing at the very same time became criminal the moment he stepped foot in America. "The baby I won't tell Yitzak about, he and Chava don't have to know. They're expecting their own child, that's enough. Just, I'll tell them . . . well, I'll tell them I want to marry my sweetheart before I go away."

And so, three days after he'd been forced by circumstances to turn his back on the train that would take him to his new life, Yankel, in the company of his brother and his brother's wife, a provincial woman who would obey her husband's demand that no one know of this, Yankel Himelbaum married Reizel Lansky in the eyes of the Polish government, and prayed to the God he had honored by so doing that no one would find out. After the brief ceremony in the small government office in Lukow, he folded the official paper, the civil marriage certificate, and asked his brother to hold it for safekeeping.

Why was it, he wondered, that he trusted Yitzak more than his own wife to guard the wedding papers? Perhaps he felt that he had now joined with his older brother in an act that Yitzak was very good at: deviousness. "Chava," Yankel couldn't resist imploring his sister-in-law one more time, "you know it would upset Mama very much, that I should get married like this, without telling her. That I should get married in the first place," he tried to seem lighthearted. "I'm the baby, after all."

Chava waved him off diffidently. "You say it's a secret, so *nu*, I won't tell no one. So *nu*, you're married, *mazel tov*, and I won't say a word." Chava's plain features were hard to read, but Yankel suspected that, in addition to obeying her husband, Chava had her own reasons for holding this secret: Mama paid a lot of attention to her now that she was carrying the first grandchild. Why disrupt the pretty picture with news that would inevitably cause a stir in the household from top to bottom?

So here it was, two months later, and the day of his departure had finally come. He could put it off no longer, even if he wanted to.

"You know I have no choice," he told his wife, as he placed a Polish-English dictionary at the top of the suitcase so that he could get to it easily. "If I don't leave today, that's it. On July first, they close the borders altogether in America. Two weeks I have."

Yankel wasn't entirely correct, but he was close to the facts, for in its ongoing efforts to limit the number of immigrants allowed into the country, the United States had recently inaugurated its strictest quota law yet. In 1917, the country added a literacy test to the legal inspection; in 1921 and 1924, increasingly rigid laws were passed to limit the percentages of various nationalities allowed in (based on populations already there, the new legislation clearly favored northern Europeans as more acceptable newcomers), and very soon—as of July 1, 1929— America would only admit 150,000 newcomers per year. Period.

"As soon as I'm settled," he continued, clamping shut the suitcase, "the very minute everything is ready, I'll send for you. You know I will. Meanwhile, you stay here, here with your parents. Have the baby, care for him, while I start a life for us."

Reizel only wept.

"Would it be easier if you didn't come with me to the train station?" Yankel asked as gently as he could. From the closet, he took his suit jacket and overcoat. In what had become an oft-repeated ritual, he reached into the pocket of the jacket and found that, yes, the visa and steamer ticket were safely tucked inside. Placing the jacket and coat on top of the suitcase, he sighed deeply and turned toward his wife. With an ache in his heart, he knelt beside her. "Please, Reizele, you know this is best."

He took a handkerchief from his pocket, gently moved her hands from her face, and blotted her tears. "You know this is best, that I go ahead. My father has made all the arrangements; another steamer ticket he sent me. He's expecting me; I can't disappoint him a second time. And soon, as you know, the visa will be no good. Once I turn twenty-one, *physsht*" (he made a ripping sound), "it's no good anymore." Yankel never enjoyed alluding to the difference in their ages—Reizel was three years older—but he felt that this reminder was necessary. Lying about his marital status was an act he'd persuaded himself he could manage, but his birth date was clearly stamped on his passport, and he would no longer qualify as the minor son of Icko Himelbaum once he turned twenty-one.

As Reizel seemed to be listening, he continued. "You always say how much you like a big city. You think here in Lukow is as big as it gets? I am going to set up a life for us in New York—New York, New York! My father already has a job for me."

"But it will be months, maybe years, until we see each other," Reizel was able to say, wiping away fresh tears that had fallen and sniffling back others. "Your son, if it is a son, please God, will grow up not knowing his father. Not knowing that he has a father."

With these words, Reizel's eyes threatened to once more spill over, but Yankel spoke quickly to stop them: "Not know he has a father? What are you talking? I'll write to you, both of you, send pictures. And before you know it . . ."

Reizel emitted a short laugh. "You think he'll be so smart he can read your letters? He'll be only a baby." Her delicate features lit up at the image of the infant.

So fine and dainty she was, that even now, Yankel thought, with the baby due in just three months, one would be hard-pressed to see that she was pregnant. Maybe that was why the reality of the situation continued to elude him, and why he could get away with telling his brothers that Reizel's "illness" had passed. Of course, Reizel's parents knew about the baby, and, while not pleased with the circumstances as a whole, they couldn't help but give thanks that at least the two had been married.

As for his own mother, she was so excited and thrilled with the upcoming birth of Yitzak and Chava's first child that she accepted at face value the reason for Yankel's delaying his trip to America. It was kind of him, she thought, just like her Yankele, to rearrange everything just because his girlfriend had a little cold. But while she might not concern herself with Reizel's health, Chava she looked after as though she were the first woman on the planet to be with child. A real *balabusta*, she was, Yitzak's wife; she knew that the kitchen was where a woman belonged, and she never complained. She kept busy, always helpful, quiet, just doing the things that needed to be done. Kneading the bread, stirring the soup, a good woman she was. Even Chava herself would easily assert that she was a homebody, an old-fashioned girl, who was lucky to have married into a family that cared so much for her. No, she had no complaints about helping Elke and Hershel and Leah in the kitchen, it was no inconvenience at all. But she did wonder, couldn't help wondering, about Yitzak's increasingly frequent trips to Warsaw. Well, he said it was for business. *Nu*, what did she know of business? Maybe he was doing something important there in Warsaw, it was just hard to see any changes here on the farm. Like always, they collected the eggs, fed the chickens. For what was he going so much to Warsaw?

Yankel, too, might have been curious about all the business meetings his brother attended, but he forced himself not to think about Yitzak and what he was up to, because, quite simply, there was nothing he could do about it. As long as his mother and sister were taken care of, as long as Hershel's cakes and Yitzak's mysterious "business" in Warsaw didn't get in the way of milking the cows, so that the farm continued to provide food and a decent living for all of them, well, he couldn't worry about the particulars. Soon, he'd send for them, the whole family, because in America, he'd make his fortune, learn the ins and outs, and be able to get all of them settled.

"I will go with you to the station," Reizel said, standing up and straightening her dress. A noticeable tummy protruded from inside the fabric, but it was nothing more than one might observe on a woman given to enjoying her bread and potatoes; nothing more, in other words, than one would see on most of the women in Poland.

Still, even though the summer weather didn't call for it, she put on her coat. Somehow, despite their vows to each other, despite her parents' acceptance and their legitimacy as a married couple in the eyes of God and the state, still, Reizel regarded this pregnancy as a source of shame. And Yankel, seeing her put on the coat and feeling the full measure of what he had caused her, did not object.

Emerging into the street, Yankel planted a kiss on his mother-in-law's forehead. She was taking a break from the store, where she and her husband, and their daughter, had made of their modest millinery shop a successful business, designing and sewing the most fashionable hats in Lukow. Seeing Yankel's suitcase, she said nothing, only gazed up at him with the unmistakable plea that he make good on his promises to her daughter.

Once again, Yankel found himself at a train station teeming with hope and sorrow, travelers trying to smile through their doubts, those left behind making no such effort. With a swoop, he lifted Reizel off the ground and hugged her to him, kissing her ears, her cheeks, her eyes, and lips. "An American family we will be," he said. "And when I see you next, you'll be one person again, and our son, another." Carefully, he set her down. He noted that she didn't bow her head, nor emit even one tear. She looked at him stoically, her face giving no indication whether she believed him or not.

Yankel embraced her once more, holding back his own knot of tears, and boarded the train. By the time he found a place to sit in one of the third-class cars and looked out the window to wave good-bye, he caught sight only of the back of her, her head held high as she walked away from him and disappeared from view. The smile Yankel had meant to offer her faded into pinch-lipped resignation. Well, what did he think, that she would stand there on the platform weeping? This was his Reizel, as strong and determined as she was delicate. She would be all right. They would be all right.

He settled back on the hard bench and looked around at the drab surroundings. The train spat and lurched. Wedged between strangers, he began his trip.

Yankel had ridden the third-class cars many times, so that the physical discomfort of the accommodations was not new to him. But almost immediately upon pulling away from the Lukow train station, he felt a different type of discomfort. From out of nowhere, the confidence he'd been talking himself into dissolved, and a sense of incompetence washed over him.

Accustomed to functioning as the person in charge on the farm, and more recently, trying to behave and believe in himself as a husband and soon-to-be father, Yankel suddenly felt as though the roles he'd been playing were a charade, the pretensions of a person hardly older than a boy. He wasn't headed now for Wlodawa, where his family counted on him to balance the books and oversee inventory, nor bound for a passionate tryst with his lover. Now, he sat on a hard bench inside a bumpy, rumbling train, riding into nothing less awesome than the future. And that blank broad vista, vast and alien, loomed in front of him, pitiless.

Was this plunge into anxiety, he wondered, caused by the falsehood he would have to tell about his marital status? No, the questioning and lies were a long way off; in fact, he wouldn't mind at this moment being able to recapture his identity as a person who had just left his wife and unborn child, to find within himself the confidence of a grown man. He struggled to do so, but failed.

Looking out the window as the greening fields of early summer swept past, he tried to calm the onslaught of fear and self-doubt with rationalization: it was good, this sudden awareness of his own youth. He was entering America as a minor, and this designation he surely felt. Yet, when he thought about his mother, the picture was blurred; he felt disconnected from her, and from his brothers and sister. He tried to conjure images of the people he loved, but he felt severed from them, stripped of all context.

Perhaps it was inevitable, he mused, that at this moment he felt like a child alone in the world, for everything in the world was about to crack open new to him. It was as though he was about to experience his own birth.

He thought of the Talmud and his other books of study. Surely, he would find within their pages words of comfort. He wished he had them with him now, those books filled with wisdom to hold in his hands. He remembered the dictionary.

Crowded on his seat, knocking knees and elbows with the family and three old men shoved next to and opposite him, Yankel managed to unclasp the suitcase sitting on his lap, and extract from it the volume of English vocabulary. Opening it, he felt a returning glimmer of optimism. This would keep him busy on the twelve-day journey to his new life—on this train to Warsaw; the connecting international train to Paris, and then the one to Cherbourg; and finally, on the ship that would take him to America. Studying this dictionary and memorizing it cover to cover, this would calm and prepare him.

Thus he sat, head bent over his new "bible" until a few hours later when the train pulled into Warsaw. Glimpsing the vibrant dynamism of the city from the window, and then emerging into it, Yankel forced himself to regard with indifference the tramways and tall buildings, the people hurrying purposefully, carrying briefcases, packages. He'd been terribly impressed that other time, the one and only time he'd been here, when he'd applied for his visa at the American consulate. Now, he must not allow himself to feel the excitement of the town, or think of it as a place that had any connection to him.

Following signs printed in Polish—for the last time, Yankel realized—he found with little trouble the correct platform for the train to Paris, got in line early, nearly at the front, and waited for his papers to be checked. Stories abounded of querulous officials going through passports and visas, finding reasons why papers weren't in order for the mere sake of harassing people and bribing from them a few rubles or Polish marks. Learning from all the stories about intimidation and bribery he'd heard over the years, Yankel was traveling as well with deutsche marks and francs in case he had to pay off an unfriendly conductor; but for whatever reason, the Polish officer here didn't seem to be giving anyone trouble, and Yankel boarded the international train without incident.

Being one of the first to enter, he was able to secure a seat near a window. Again, a hard wooden seat, but conditions in this train seemed to be slightly more comfortable, with only three to a bench. Maybe he'd even be able to get some sleep on the three-day journey to France.

Gradually, however, the car filled to capacity, crowded with even more travelers than the one he'd ridden to Warsaw. Everywhere he looked there were people, strangers whose manner and way of dress looked foreign to him, people speaking languages he could understand in only the most rudimentary way. Smatterings of German struck his ear, and Russian. (He could pick up no English.) Everyone going, traveling, leaving. Everyone with their satchels and their dreams. Were all these people going to America? Could one country accommodate so many?

An old woman sat down opposite him, her legs thankfully short, abnormally short (her legs stuck out from the seat, like a child's). She seemed to be traveling alone, until four men, looking to be in their thirties and very well fed, dispersed themselves between Yankel's bench and hers, and spoke to her in a manner that suggested they were together. Her sons? She didn't look at them, only barked a few words at them in German, but rather she pinned her eyes on Yankel, in a hard, pointed stare, as though she suspected him of grand larceny at the very least. He tried to communicate a formal yet friendly greeting in Polish, but she'd have none of it. She only stared, occasionally squinted, but stopped not for a moment fixing him with her insinuating gaze. Yankel reached once again for his dictionary, which he'd already placed in his lap, and resumed his study of the English language.

As the long dusk faded to darkness, the light in the car became very difficult to read by. Yankel dared not look up, though, for on the one or two occasions when he had wished to take a break from his reading—to give his neck a rest and run over in his mind the words he had learned—there she sat, still staring at him, prompting him to immediately resume his study posture.

Unaware of any fatigue except in his neck, he yet must have dozed off, for the next thing he knew, his shoulder was being rudely poked, and the train, lit by the thin strands of dawn, had come to a stop. They must have crossed the border into Germany.

Yankel rubbed the sleep from his eyes and raised his head, his neck painfully stiff, to see the staring woman squinting at him as she sidled from her seat and past him toward the aisle. "*Juden,*" she sneered, nodding her head as if her suspicions had indeed been validated and at last an official authority, in the person of the train conductor poking him, might take appropriate action. She continued her unwavering visual hold as she made her way to the exit, keeping Yankel's gaze similarly pinned on her even as he tried to get his bearings and find for the indignant conductor the passport he was demanding.

"Passport. *Mach shnell, mach shnell,*" the shrill conductor snapped, each syllable reducing Yankel's ability to function, or to think where he'd placed the all-important document. Because of what had happened with Reizel, because he'd had to rearrange his travel plans, it had become necessary to take this international train instead of the one that would have simply taken him to the port in Gdansk. It had become necessary to travel through these countries, where he didn't know the languages, where he must maintain his composure in the face of people who clearly saw in his face something objectionable.

His father, while praising Yankel's kindness for staying with his girl-friend while she was ill, had only been able to find a ship leaving from France, which required, in turn, this singularly unsettling journey. Yet, as was his way, Icko had found the good in the rearranged plans: "So," his father had written, "you're coming to America, you'll see a little bit of the world first. I've worked hard all these years, why shouldn't my Yankele travel like a *mensch*? Like a *mensch* you'll come to America." Was this what it was to be a *mensch*? From the first lurch of the train out of Lukow, and with each ensuing mile and each encounter, Yankel had struggled to maintain a sense of himself as a man, much less a *mensch*: a person deserving of respect. At least he'd been able to persuade his father not to send him anything more costly than a steerage ticket. The second-class cabin Icko had been so proud of when he'd put together the earlier plans, Yankel had persuaded him to forego. He couldn't accept both a more expensive steamship ticket and a cabin. For a week he'd survive, he'd insisted, even if it was rocky belowdecks. He was strong, he'd live.

"Here, here is everything," he said to the conductor in Yiddish, the language of his soul, the language he fell to when such acts as thinking and translation loomed beyond his capabilities, when, for instance, an indignant German in a uniform was snapping orders at him.

Hearing Yankel's words and perusing his papers, the conductor echoed the absent woman's appraisal with a disgusted curl of his lip. *"Juden,"* he said, the syllables emitted like so much phlegm from his throat. He foisted Yankel's visa and passport back at him as though they must truly carry disease and continued to the next traveler.

Yankel's heart beat loudly in his chest. He was covered in sweat. He must remind himself to speak Polish at the border crossings. He must force himself to stay awake.

It was late at night when the train crossed into Belgium, but Yankel, though dizzy and exhausted, handed over his papers immediately when asked for them. To the already cacophonous mix of languages, Flemish was now added, the train ride yielding whispered conversations in so many unintelligible languages, rolling and jerking his body like a limp string of *lokshen,* he might as well be a senseless particle of dust on the Tower of Babel. But the papers were working, Yankel reminded himself, the papers would get him there, to France, the ship, America, and his father. He longed for his father as he could not remember yearning for him before. Papa's warm eyes and quiet ways, the understated resolve with which he'd made his decision and his plans to emigrate, promising the family that it wouldn't be long before they, too, would join him. That had been seven years ago, when Yankel had just turned thirteen, a *Bar Mitzvah.* Soon afterward, right after his youngest "became a man," Icko Himelbaum had set out. Yet for Yankel, the journey was reversing time, dissolving him from a man, back into a boy.

Well, at least he would be an educated boy. Though there was barely any light coming into the car, Yankel bent his aching neck to the dictionary. "*Brata,*" he read, "brother." In his mind he rehearsed *brother* with a hard *th,* the two letters unknown to him except for the important English phrase, "Thank you."

At the end of three days, even the filtered light of a rainy Paris morning blinded Yankel's eyes as he stepped from the train. Every joint in his body ached, he could barely move his neck. He was weak from eating just the two sandwiches Reizel's mother had prepared for him, and he was dirty. Knowing he had less than an hour before he must board the train to Cherbourg, and confronted with arrows and printed instructions he didn't begin to understand at the large and stately depot, he followed the line of men making their way to a door that read LES HOMMES, and once inside, went directly to the sink. He filled his palms with water and before even relieving his thirst, brought the water to his face. And then he did it again, rubbing his face this time, smacking the water onto his skin to revive himself, feeling the cool life-giving strength of water. Taking the slim piece of soap sitting on the sink, he washed his hands, his neck, and dried himself off with the rough paper torn from the dispenser.

Though he didn't understand their words, Yankel knew that several men behind him were telling him to hurry up, let them get to the sink. Lifting his suitcase, which felt ten times heavier than when the trip had started, he took a moment to regard himself in the mirror. The momentary antidote of the water evaporated as he beheld the haggard, shabby person in the wrinkled suit of clothes. His collar was yellow and damp with sweat, his chin pocked with stubble, his blond hair matted on top of his head. The sickening image made him feel his thirst. He was desperate for a drink of water.

"A minute, a minute," he said weakly in English, not only the words, but his voice coming out foreign to him, thick and barely audible from his tightened throat. He knew he must drink something, or collapse on the spot. Quickly, he palmed a handful of water into his mouth, the shock making him gag, and somehow he made it to the urinal before vomiting.

Maybe, he thought as he once again decided to follow a stream of people carrying suitcases because he couldn't read the signs, *maybe I'm feeling sick like my Reizele told me she was in the beginning. Maybe this is how we stay together, the two of us and the child.*

But no, he mustn't think about that. He couldn't allow himself. He was the unmarried son of Icko Himelbaum, unmarried.

"Married?"

Following people with suitcases had proven a useful tactic, for Yankel had located the train to Cherbourg, made his way to the steamship, and stood before it now, its hull gleaming just beyond the gangplank. His trip had not been the sightseeing opportunity his father had envisioned for him—he hardly took in the worlds of Germany, Belgium, or France; rather, he tried desperately to get through these locations with a modicum of deportment as each geographical crossing brought him closer to the ship. Finally, he was here, and if he succeeded in boarding, he was as good as safely arrived in America. This he knew from his father and others who had made the trip more recently: decisive aspects of the interrogation process had been shifted from Ellis Island to the point of departure.

The change in policy sat well not only with the overburdened immigration authorities in New York, and indeed the immigrants, who enjoyed smoother sailing knowing that it was tantamount to being accepted into the country once they were allowed onto the boat, but it was especially appreciated by the steamship companies themselves. Why, they reasoned, accept a person on board if they would just have to turn around and subsidize his return trip in the event he failed to pass inspection in America? It was much more sensible, and economical, to apprehend an unfit émigré in the first place, without the unnecessary expenditure of time and money to take the poor soul on a fruitless journey.

Yankel had known about the new dockside procedures and had prepared himself for the questions; what he hadn't anticipated until mere weeks ago, however, was that he would be lying.

"Married?" the inspector repeated, fixing him with stern appraisal.

"No," Yankel responded, wincing when a stab of pain pinched his neck as he looked up at his interrogator.

"What is wrong with you?" the inspector asked suspiciously, his question translated from French to Polish by the required interpreter.

"Oh, I'm not sick, it's nothing," Yankel told the interpreter, smiling to convey an air of lightheartedness as he massaged his neck. "I'm so excited looking at everything, I guess maybe I stretched too much my neck." Somehow, he didn't want to say that he'd been bent over a dictionary studying English, for fear of underscoring his foreignness—a ridiculous idea, he realized. He certainly wouldn't mention the glowering woman on the train whose accusing looks had caused him to ride for hours with his head bent down. But as the two men discussed the situation between themselves, and Yankel waited with a forced grin for the inspector to decide whether he believed him, he couldn't help but notice the ease with which falsehoods had tripped from his tongue. Since learning of Reizel's pregnancy, he kept finding himself in situations where it was necessary to lie, and he was getting good at it, disturbingly efficient, and he thought this was a shame: that to claim a place in America, he must sacrifice a portion of his character. With all his heart, he hoped this would be a temporary sacrifice.

"He says if you are sick, you are coming right back," he heard the Polish interpreter say. Apparently not concerned about holding up the rest of the line, the inspector stood staring at him for what felt like endless minutes. And then, to Yankel's alarm, he saw the man wave over another official, this one with a stethoscope hanging from his neck. The medical inspector pulled him aside, those who had been waiting behind him eyeing him derisively.

Once again, Yankel felt a well of nausea gather in his chest, but he mustn't reveal any weakness. With every ounce of what strength he had left in him, he smiled. "This is silly," he said, "there's nothing at all wrong. But I understand, of course, the importance of only healthy people . . ."

The French doctor cut him off with commands Yankel couldn't understand, but understood well enough. Following a coughing gesture the doctor made, Yankel coughed, and over the cylinder of agony his neck had become, he followed instructions to turn his head this way and that, his smile acting as a taut shield against the pain. The stethoscope probed his chest, searching fingers pushed at his neck while he coughed some more, and then, the doctor writing something on a piece of paper, Yankel waited as the medical expert brought what he had written over to the initial inspector, who stopped what he was doing to read the doctor's findings, gaze once again upon Yankel, and then back at the sheet of paper. He scribbled something on the ship's manifest, and without even looking at him this time, gestured for Yankel to hand him his steamer ticket and board the ship.

Walking as proudly as he could, trying to hold his head up tall, but moving quickly, Yankel crisscrossed the ship's endless passageways looking desperately for a bathroom.

He didn't take the time to acknowledge the vast waters, a stark contrast to the serene Bug River beside whose narrow, wending path he had grown up, or to look back at the crowds on deck and gathered onshore to say good-bye to loved ones. No, he must make it to a bathroom, and pray that he would find no one else in there, so that he might relieve himself in private of the wretched sickness in his throat.

As though he had reached the Promised Land itself, Yankel beheld with limitless appreciation the bathroom door. He pushed inside just in time to throw up into the sink. Afterward, he heaved a deep sigh, straightened up, and once again caught sight of himself in the mirror. *Nu*, better he had looked in his life, and it had gotten a little scary there for a minute; that, he couldn't deny. But here he was, he had made it to the ship. Next stop, America. Maybe, he had a feeling somehow, things would work out.

Opening the bathroom door and finding his way to the railing that overlooked the sea, he felt a freshening spray of ocean kiss his cheeks.

Ellis Island

Will Brown scrubbed his body vigorously, taking his third shower of the day. As a Special Inquiry inspector on the island, he divided his time between the increasing numbers of candidates for deportation and the arriving immigrants, and the very intensity of his responsibilities found relief under the force of the water's spray. True, the Great Hall wasn't as noisy as it had been back in the early twenties, when there'd been thousands of immigrants talking in what seemed like thousands of different languages, talking but more like yelling, many of them crying, shouting. Now, at the end of the decade, there may be fewer of them, but the volume of sound had been replaced by a thick volume of tension.

The quota acts of 1921 and '24, with their percentages based on nationality, had eased the numbers of those trying to get in, so that the Port of New York was handling most of the incoming flow. But that left Ellis Island primarily a center for deportation, making Will's duties that much more significant and his interactions with the people whose fate he was deciding that much more sensitive.

He must listen carefully for attempts to defraud the requirements, conduct his inquiry precisely, and listen carefully for any slipups. In the case of the incoming alien sent to Ellis Island because of questions aroused by the ship's manifest, was he as young as he claimed? Truly unmarried? Really expecting to be met by a relative? The answers to these questions were crucial for fulfilling nonquota status. Hundreds of thousands of men had left their loved ones behind in the first decades of the century, with the idea of establishing themselves and then sending for their families. Now, one must be vigilant to catch the fraudulent "minor," the woman swearing she was to be met by a husband, a brother, a father. For obvious reasons, women were not allowed into the country by themselves. Just this morning Will had tagged two women with a *D* for detention, and warned them that unless and until they were met here at Ellis Island by a male relative, back they'd go—to Czechoslovakia and Hungary in this case. Yes, they'd looked miserable and frightened, but what was the United States supposed to do: admit unaccompanied women who would surely become public charges, unable to take care of themselves except in the most questionable ways? He couldn't allow himself to feel sorry for them; he had a job to do, and it was a job that was no less in defense of his country than if he held a military post.

And so it was here, in a dormitory shower room on Island Number 2—Ellis Island was really three islands connected by covered passageways—it was here that Will found respite from the daily assault, and where he felt most like himself and most at home. Even at the actual home that Barbara had found for them, Will felt out of place. When they'd first arrived in New York, staying at an inexpensive midtown hotel, he had granted her the wish of choosing an apartment for them as a way of making it up to her that they'd had to relocate, and her bright mood over the "cutest little place" she'd found on a tree-lined street just "a tram-ride from the ferry" had at first delighted him. Then they'd moved in and lived there for a few weeks and he'd had a chance to take the full measure of the neighborhood. Greenwich Village, with its broad array of undirected, unwashed souls, bearded riffraff, and alleged artistes made Will himself feel like an alien. It was bad enough that he spent his days surrounded by the aura of poverty, did he have to come home as well to an atmosphere of indigence, where he didn't even enjoy the compensatory benefit of being an authority figure?

For Barbara's sake, he made the best of it. The apartment itself, a one bedroom on Eighth Street, was nice enough, and it was true that public transportation to the ferry couldn't be more convenient. Barbara felt intimidated by the hustle and bustle of New York City, Will could understand that, and it would be she, after all, who would be spending most of her time here. So, while the Village, as it was called, may be a disturbing amalgam of speakeasies and miscreants, Will had to admit that it was quieter, more reminiscent of Iowa City than anywhere else in Manhattan that they could afford, and if it was tree-lined Barbara wanted, well, at least this wasn't Brooklyn, another area that she'd spoken highly of. Will would under no circumstances even contemplate living there. Why, he might as well settle in Poland or Russia, ship himself off to eastern Europe as begin his married life or consider living any part of his life in the likes of Brooklyn. The Village might be filled with vagabonds and ne'er-do-wells, but at least they were American.

It was three in the afternoon, and Will toweled off. He'd have to hurry to make his three o'clock deportation interview. Rushing past one of the dorm rooms that housed the women awaiting hearings, he could make out the familiar moans of fear and bewilderment emanating from that area. He heard the sound so regularly, it'd just become a part of the place, a part of the ambience of his workday.

From the corner of his eye, he glimpsed a bare-chested woman nursing a baby as she rocked back and forth, whimpering. No attempt at modesty among these people, Will recoiled. They knew the island was staffed mostly by men, didn't they have any sense of shame? Here they arrived without a penny to their name, their pasts sold for the money to come over, their futures highly doubtful, couldn't they at least hold on to their shame? He wanted it for them.

Grabbing a cup of tea from the staff dining room, vast and just about empty at this hour, Will made his way through the breezeway that connected Island Number 2 to the Main Building, where interrogation areas had been set up. The penned-in rows that had once comprised the hulking center of the Great Hall had, owing to lower numbers of immigrants, been removed, and replaced by benches, most of which at this moment were filled, and cubicles for questioning. More and more, Will's job as a Special Inquiry inspector involved deportation interviews, and his assignment this afternoon was to determine whether a certain Reva Lansky was making trouble over at her dressmaking plant. Like the majority of potential deportees, she had been on the island for weeks, awaiting her hearing.

So many problems in the garment industry, Will made the familiar observation to himself, *so many demands.* Why couldn't people just be satisfied that they had work? Well, he was doing his part to clean up the mess, and for that opportunity he was grateful.

There she was, sitting by herself in the cubicle allotted for the examination. "Miss Lansky," Will said by way of greeting as he scraped the chair from behind the desk and sat down. "I see you have foregone your right to legal counsel."

"You should be ashamed, the conditions here," the heavyset woman with the gaunt face accused, by way of her greeting. Will, leafing through her paperwork, did not respond. "You treat people like animals, if you ask me. Bars on the windows, for God's sake, you got it set up like a jail."

Without even having posed a question, Will could ascertain that the woman sitting before him was no friend of the United States. As for her manners, well, her manner offered no surprise.

"We have the largest medical facility in the world, Miss Lansky," Will said without looking up. He had his drill well prepared for all the complaints he heard. And it was true, the hospital on Ellis Island was not only commodious, but offered its services free of charge. Same with the dining room, which could feed 1,100 at a sitting. Everything was paid for by the steamship companies or the federal government; these people dared complain?

Will remained focused on the document:

```
Reva Lansky.
Age, 31.
Arrival, from Ukraine, 1925.
Occupation, seamstress.
Marital status, single.
Home address, 346 Kings Highway, Brooklyn.
   with two sisters and uncle.
Education, undetermined.
Suspected of: incitement to overthrow the
government.
Inspector's Recommendation _____
```

"You choose, Miss Lansky, to represent yourself at this hearing?" Will asked again, this time for the record.

"You choose, mister whatever your name is, to ask obvious questions?"

Well, one thing was obvious: Miss Lansky had no compunctions about antagonizing her interrogator.

"I'm William Brown," Will said.

"Glad to make your acquaintance." Reva shifted in her seat.

Could she be enjoying this, Will wondered. Didn't she know what was at stake? Maybe she wanted to go back. He'd heard of people "converting" to anarchy so that the United States would pay for their passage home. The land of milk and honey was serving up a lot of gruel lately, the shaky economic situation being what it was; maybe they thought things would be better back where they came from. Will was vigilant: schemes to defraud the United States of America came in many guises.

"You've been here how long?" he asked.

"What, can't you read? Maybe you should be deported," Reva shot back.

Will cleared his throat. "All right, Miss Lansky, there's no need to make this any less pleasant for yourself."

"What is that, a threat?"

"Just answer the question." Of course, Will did know the answer, but if this woman had been singled out after nearly five years of residence, the limit at which a person could be deported "for cause," she must have some serious strikes against her. He hadn't read the entire file as yet; he perused it as they spoke. But he wouldn't be surprised if she was an agitator, one of those Bolshevik union infiltrators.

"Four, almost five years. I came because they, the Communists, don't like the Jews any more than the czar did. So I came, ha, to the land of fairness and opportunity."

"And what exactly are your complaints against the United States government?" Will asked, finally looking up at her. This was a central point: anyone suspected of faithlessness, of a desire to undermine the system, was an immediate candidate for deportation.

"Complaints? How long have you got, Mr. Inspector Brown? Hey, is that your real name? You don't look like a Brown to me."

"I'll ask the questions, Miss Lansky." Whether she did it intentionally or not, the woman's reference to his swarthy skin tone and possible ethnic appearance did nothing to help her case.

"That's the problem over here, if you ask me. Freedom of speech it says all over, but seems to me a person says what they believe they can get in a whole lot of trouble. Especially if what they believe don't match the program."

"The program? To which 'program' would you be referring?"

"The take-advantage-of-the-greenhorn program. The work-their-fingers-to-the-bone program. That's what program. We come over believing the streets are paved with gold and then, bango," (she clapped her hands), "you stick us in dark rooms, squeeze us together like sardines, and hand us a needle. You see that buttonhole on your fine shirt?" Will looked down at his shirt despite himself. "Yeah, any one of those buttonholes. Are they wet, Mr. Inspector Brown, wet with tears and sweat, because that's what they're made of. That's the thread we use."

Will wrote something down. "So, you take issue with the conditions of your employment?"

"Yeah, issue I take." Reva's voice had lowered, her toughness instantly punctured by the image she'd just described, of the sweatshop conditions she and her sisters and her neighbors and every female she knew endured day in and day out. Supposedly, the unions changed everything, and of course things were better than thirty years ago. So? So, big deal, things were still rotten. Twenty-four dollars a week a dressmaker made, less than they made in a slaughterhouse. The unions, too, were rotten, with gangsters and infighting; the workers didn't know which way to turn, who to believe. But the union at least was better than nothing.

Of course, from Will's perspective, these people had a hell of a nerve complaining. There wasn't any place on earth as prosperous as his country (the very country, he had no way of knowing, that in a few short months would see its entire economic structure collapse).

"Tell me about New Year's Day, Miss Lansky," Will read, and homed in on the charge against her. "New Year's Day of this year."

"What, you think I had a hangover? I don't drink, mister."

"You know what I'm referring to."

What Will was referring to was the Needle Trades Industrial Union, formed on New Year's Day, 1929. And clearly willing to be led by Communists. Communists, who had infiltrated and tried to take over just about every other garment-related union in New York. Lengthy and disastrous strikes had created hostility toward these extremists in most of the unions, but not this Needle Trades group, apparently. To his chagrin, he'd read where a few hundred Greeks, furriers, had taken part in some fisticuffs on behalf of this new group. Another reason to be grateful for his grandparents' decision to distance themselves from their ethnic ties.

"So I joined a union, so what?" Reva picked at her nails, already bitten almost to the cuticle.

"And you are aware that this is a so-called 'revolutionary' union?"

"Who cares what it's called? They help us make more money, make better our working conditions, let them call themselves what they want."

"Are you interested in overturning the United States government, Miss Lansky?" This, of course, was the nub of the interrogation.

Reva had to laugh. It's not that she wasn't aware of the leadership and its Communist affiliations, but she, barely putting two cents together, was she going to overturn America? *Vey iz mir.* What was wrong with this country, that this man could sit here and say such a ridiculous thing? Well, she knew why she was here, the accusations against her.

"You laugh, Miss Lansky, but these are serious charges." Will got to the point, the answer to which must determine his decision. "Are you willing to disavow your membership in this treasonous organization?" He looked at her squarely, his pen poised to record her answer.

"I been in this hellhole for three weeks, almost four. And always the same question."

"This is the last time you'll have to answer it," Will said darkly, "I assure you."

"You'd send me back." Reva met his gaze.

"You know the law." But Will repeated it to her, anyway: "'Any immigrant in the country for less than five years can be deported for cause.' We in the United States government believe that a person in sympathy with revolutionary Communist ideas has given us cause, ample cause."

Reva's voice became dry and quiet. "I left the Ukraine when the Communists took over. That Stalin is trouble. You think I want to go back?"

Will said nothing. Though he could have pointed out that thousands of Hebrews had done so, gone back to Russia after the Revolution, so enamored were they with the Bolshevik line about "power to the working man." If this woman insisted on remaining affiliated with a Communist-led union, maybe she had had second thoughts.

"You're good at what you do," Reva said to him. "I been questioned many times, but I can tell you are serious. You would send me back. You'd sign that paper ordering my deportation without blinking. What made you so hard, Mr. Inspector Brown?"

"I'm a patriotic American, no more, no less." Will waited for her answer. "Well?"

Reva had had plenty of time to go over her options. She believed in the new union, applauded its no-nonsense approach to improving working conditions. Look at the furriers, who were a big part of this new Needles Trade Union: led by Communists, they'd won the first forty-hour workweek in the garment industry, with a pay increase, to boot. Reva had signed on wholeheartedly right after New Year's, encouraged her coworkers to sign up.

But what would she have at home? Nothing. Nobody. Her parents were dead, her sisters were here.

Still, she wouldn't give this bastard the satisfaction of backing down so easily.

"You drive a hard bargain, Mr. Inspector Brown. Maybe you should be in the union, with your talent for bargaining. Ever thought about that?"

"What will it be, Miss Lansky?" Will pressed. He tapped his pen impatiently and sighed to drive home the urgency of her situation.

"I can't go back," Reva answered quietly.

"And you're willing to sever all ties to the Needle Trades Industrial Union?"

It was Reva's turn to sigh. "So I'll sever."

"You'll sign a document to that effect?"

"I told you. I'll sever. I'll sign."

"You understand this will be a legal document. You will be signing under penalty of perjury. If we find that you've remained active with this union, you will have lied to the government of the United States of America."

Reva tried to conjure her previous defiance. "*Nu?* So it's against the law to lie?"

"Oh, yes. It certainly is." Will Brown couldn't have spoken more clearly. "It's a very serious offense to lie to the United States government."

Owing to notes regarding the stiffness in his neck that had been recorded on the ship's manifest—a stiffness induced by an old woman whose unremitting gaze had made him feel complicit in something evil, causing him to keep his head bent down toward the dictionary for three days straight—Yankel Himelbaum was required upon arrival at the Port of New York to take the ferry ride to Ellis Island for further inspection. What was the cause of his difficulty moving his head? Was there an illness? The authorities didn't even allow him to find his father before ushering him to the ferry. They did, however, assure him that they would tell his father, who was waiting for him at the pier, that he must now meet his son at Ellis Island.

Yankel's stiff neck had long since eased and he made it through the medical inspection quickly.

He passed the literacy test handily, as well, reading twenty words of the U.S. Constitution in the language of his choice, English. Now, he'd been sitting on a bench for three hours, waiting to go through the legal inspection. When he finally heard his name called, he walked with head held high and placed himself before the interrogator. One by one, he answered each question.

Age? Twenty.

Point of origin? Cherbourg, France.

Nationality? Polish.

Race? Jewish.

By whom was passage paid? Father.

Planning to join a relative if granted entry? Yes.

Nature of relation? Father.

Proposed place of residence? Bronx, New York.

Married? No.

~ ~ ~

PART TWO

1932

Climate Change

March

New York City

Harry sat on the elevated train looking out the window as the streets of the city clattered by. It seemed he spent a lot of his life on trains: back in the old country, going back and forth to Lukow; making his way from Poland to America; and, now that his work took him to the opposite end of Manhattan from where he and his father lived, he found himself "riding the rails" morning and night, five days a week. *I'm like one of those hobos,* he smiled to himself, thinking of all the young men he read about in the newspaper who were hopping trains, mostly in the middle part of the country where the farms were not doing so well. From what he understood from Yitzak's letters, the farm in Stawki had seen better days, too, but he allowed himself to be comforted by Yitzak's reassurances that there was no need to worry—they were making out.

Across the aisle from where he sat, a man read the *Daily News* blaring a headline about another hoax in the Lindbergh kidnapping. The country was riveted by the story, which Harry believed was certainly a very sad thing for the family, but which he also thought might be serving as some kind of distraction, helping everyone keep their minds off the serious economic situation. Just this morning, on his walk to the subway, he'd seen a pile of furniture stacked in front of a building, the evicted tenants crying on the street. How could this be happening in the golden land of America? He'd witnessed the unhappy scene moments after marveling at the majestic expanse of the newly opened George Washington Bridge. It was a breathtaking sight, the graceful sweep and symmetry of girded steel spanning the Hudson River, enough to persuade a person of the great things that were possible, and keep him going with the daily grind that had become his life. Then, not two blocks past the grandeur of the bridge, the stacked-up belongings of a dispossessed family. The wailing and crying and looks of utter desolation. It had been like this since he'd arrived: the grand open arms of America, generous and promising, side by side with the wringing hands of misery; the inescapable disparities between the haves and the have-nots; the apparently unbridgeable chasm between the truly embedded citizens and those struggling to prove that they belonged here.

He'd noticed a small boy sitting behind one of the chairs on the sidewalk, sucking his thumb and looking gravely into space. It was so young a face to hold such hopelessness. His little Yakob came to mind when Harry knelt beside the boy to show him a magic trick. He'd learned it from a fellow apple vendor.

"Here, you want to see a penny from out of nowhere?" he'd asked the child. Maybe the boy would have relinquished his solemn stare and become engaged by the trick, but from the corner of his eye, Harry saw two policemen approaching and he quickly took the penny from his sleeve, placed it on the boy's knee, and hurried away. Officers of the law had that effect on him, unless he had cultivated some kind of a relationship with them (another trick he'd learned from apple vendors). A person never knew when he could get into trouble, and that was the last thing Harry needed, to be hauled into a police station, authorities demanding to see his papers. Who knew where that kind of investigation could lead? Harry certainly didn't want to find out. Well, at least he'd left the penny for the boy, that was something.

Although he rarely boarded the subway without a newspaper under his arm, Harry didn't unfold his own copy of the *Daily News* just yet, for he knew that at the 125th Street stop a crowd of passengers would board and he'd want to give his seat to someone. Ever since that mysteriously judgmental woman in Warsaw had unnerved him with her withering stare, causing the stiff neck that had nearly had him shipped back to Poland, he was vigilant about avoiding the wrath of women on trains. Women on trains and policemen, *nu*, there were things a person had to protect himself against.

Along with his fellow New Yorkers, Harry was adept at hanging on to the overhead strap, which he did now that a well-dressed matron had accepted his seat. Manipulating his newspaper and folding it into quarters, he maintained his balance as the train lurched its way downtown. About his commitment to reading the paper he was adamant. Just as the dictionary had once been the object of his devoted study, the *Daily News*, and on Sundays the *Times*, comprised his ticket to becoming an authentic American. Every waking moment, this was his goal: to earn his right to citizenship by becoming as learned, informed, and fluent in English as possible.

A man had to hold on to his determination, Harry told his father every night, when he'd come home from another day on the street with aching legs and back throbbing. But Izzy, the man whose own determination had brought him here, the father whose longed-for companionship had carried Harry to America as surely as the boat he'd boarded in France, would only sit, his arms resting wearily on the kitchen table, shaking his head. His father had become the picture of a man defeated.

It hadn't been this way at first. As soon as Harry, still Yankel at the time, had gotten through the interrogation at Ellis Island, he'd run downstairs to a maze of rooms—the Money Exchange, baggage room, railway and ferry ticket offices—and found his father easily. A bit grayer, perhaps, than when he'd last seen him, but Icko was even more handsome than Yankel remembered, his eyes as warm and welcoming as every letter of encouragement he'd written over the years. Icko clutched Yankel's shoulders, bathed him in approval and hugged him fiercely, and he repeated these gestures several times before accepting that it was all right to let go. Yes, he could believe his eyes: his son was here.

Those early years in the coal cellar, the only place Icko could find work when he first arrived, and the terrible cough he'd developed from the cold, dank atmosphere before his brother-in-law had finally found him a job at a fruit stand, every hardship was worth it now that he had his Yankel here with him.

The whole ferry ride into Manhattan and then in the subway and then the bus that brought them to the Bronx, Icko fought back the tears of amazement that threatened to overcome him by assuring his son over and over that he'd secured a job for him with the fruit vendor on Fordham Road, also from the old country; that his aunt and uncle, Mama's sister and her husband with whom Icko lived, had made up so nice the room they would share; that he had for him comfortable shoes, he shouldn't worry, although, the way he'd grown, who knew, maybe they wouldn't fit. On and on he went, covering his emotions with his words, but his very excitement contained all the information Yankel needed to affirm the decision that had brought him here. How good it felt to be the son of a loving father!

Starting with that trip from Ellis Island to the Bronx, Yankel repeatedly found reasons not to speak of his marriage and imminent paternity. *Why dampen Papa's happiness?* the reasoning went at first. Then, mere months after he'd settled in, the Fordham Road fruit stand closed down along with most of the banks and businesses in the country. The Himelbaum men—now Izzy and Harry—were out of work: why add to his father's troubles?

In the fall of 1930, Harry managed to find work for them. Crossing from the Bronx to Manhattan well before dawn, he'd wait in a long line of other out-of-work men to pick up apple crates that the International Apple Shippers Association was selling at a dollar seventy-five a crate. On his own, he could hoist two of these crates from the delivery truck onto a wagon, and then, maneuvering his load carefully so as not to lose any of the inventory, he'd make his way to the corner he'd established for his father and himself on 186th Street and St. Nicholas, where Izzy would be waiting. Together, they stood all day selling those apples, five cents apiece, so that, on a good day, when it wasn't freezing cold, or when enough people in the neighborhood had received their relief check to afford the luxury of buying an apple, maybe even several to take home to the family, they would between them come out with as much as a four-dollar profit.

By this time, by the time they'd been reduced to selling apples on the street and established themselves on the Upper West Side corner, Harry's son was a year old. Yakob. Reizel had written to him soon after the baby was born, sent him pictures. Harry spent countless silent hours gazing at the East River, thinking about the child, yearning for him even as he strained to feel a sense of connection to him. Maybe if he told his father, the generational thread would provide the yearned-for attachment. But what would be the point of telling Izzy, whose shoulders stooped with the shame of unemployment, and now the humiliation of selling apples out of a wagon?

According to President Hoover's strident protestations, the public demonstration of need personified by the apple vendors was a national disgrace. Was it any wonder that Izzy's eyes had lost their sparkle? The light went out of them altogether by the winter of 1931, when Hoover's aggressive disapproval translated into teams of law enforcement officers banishing the vast majority of apple vendors from the streets. Six thousand in New York City alone lost their one source of income, and it was then that Izzy had taken up his place at the table. Why, by revealing his deceptive entry into the country, should Harry add to his father's shame? His marriage, his son, must be kept from him. Even as the continued secrecy kept Reizel and Yakob from feeling altogether real to Harry, himself, especially now that, in an effort to sound more American, his wife had changed her name to Regina. He was now married to a woman named Regina, but it was for the precious intimacy with his lovely Reizel that his heart longed. Sometimes he thought his heart would burst with the longing. And the secret.

To make good on his promise to her, Harry did not allow himself to be deterred by Hoover's tactics. He had to earn enough money to save for his family, didn't he? He and his father had to eat, didn't they? Thus, despite his trepidations about an encounter with the police, and after fleeing from the uniformed men on several occasions, as they waved their batons and barked orders to disperse, Harry returned to the corner without his apples, furtively, and studied the situation. Did the policemen appear at a specific time each day? And why did they leave some of the vendors alone? Something was going on here, some kind of mutual agreement. It took Harry a little over a week to recognize that it was the same three or four officers working the area. Listening to their banter after they'd succeeded in clearing the street of all but a few of the vendors, he memorized the officers' names and observed that they accepted bags of apples from the men they'd allowed to remain. Why couldn't he similarly ingratiate himself? He was friendly, a good *kibbitzer*. True, the prospect of giving away free merchandise did not sit well with him, but it would be better than living with the constant anxiety of being bullied from his livelihood.

Harry's investigation paid off. He befriended the officers, charmed them with the magic tricks he'd learned from the vendor on 188th Street, gave away a few apples "they should take home to the missus," humbly accepted reports of their wives' gratitude for the crisp McIntoshes, and soon the law enforcement officials would even warn him when other officers would be on duty the following day. Thus, with most of the competition scared from the streets and this mutually advantageous understanding with Officers Cole and Muldoon and their deputies Perry and Dean, Harry found himself the proprietor of a reasonably dependable business, even adding oranges and then pears to his inventory. With his brimmed cap perched on his thick, wavy blond hair, and wearing a turtleneck, trousers, and corduroy jacket, the amiable and attractive young man and his crates of fruit became a welcome fixture on the 186th Street corner. When the economy took a turn for the worse, when the New York banks failed and people saw their savings accounts disappear, Harry still sold enough to support himself and Izzy, and even send a little extra back to his Reizele without his father noticing. To compensate for the somewhat diminished business after the New York bank failure and its ripple effects, he found a modest apartment for the two of them in the Upper West Side neighborhood of Washington Heights, just a few blocks from his corner. That way, he had his crates all set up by the first ray of dawn, and it took the onset of darkness itself to initiate closing. Everything considered, Harry couldn't complain. Nor did he want to do anything to taint his father's one source of satisfaction. Why burden him with the fact that his beloved Harry, whose stomach for hard work and head for commerce were keeping a roof over their heads and food on the table, was here illegally? After all his other excuses, Harry's very success now became the reason for keeping his marital status a secret.

Toward that end, not a day went by that he wasn't grateful for his cautious decision, made in Lukow, to have Reizel get in touch with him through her cousin: the sheer volume of her mail surely would have aroused Izzy's suspicions. Maybe because she had not that much to keep her busy, or because she missed him, or maybe even to make sure he didn't forget about them, his wife wrote to him frequently, occasionally enclosing photographs of their son's progress from infant to toddler. She wrote to Harry through her cousin, Reva, a woman in her thirties, who lived in Brooklyn. The dress factory on the Lower East Side of Manhattan, where Reva worked, made for a convenient meeting place (only several blocks from a train station) and it was through his weekly rendezvous with her that Harry became familiar with that part of the city, and came to recognize it as a promising location for expanding his business. Particularly on the west side of lower Manhattan known as Greenwich Village, a mecca of tourism through which Harry walked to meet his secret cousin-in-law, pedestrians and casual strollers filled the streets. The area was unusually leafy, homey—and singularly conducive, Harry decided, to a friendly, hardworking guy with a quantity of fruit for sale.

It had taken quite a bit of his persuasive powers to convince his father to maintain the uptown part of the business—he played heavily on Izzy's mortification at the prospect of collecting relief— but persuade him he did, so for nearly a year now, Harry, his father ensconced uptown, had been a staple on Fourth Street, the crates of fruit he collected at the port transferred to a food display cart he'd purchased. To avoid thinking of himself as just another greenhorn with a pushcart, Harry referred to the conveyance as a kiosk—a more professional-sounding structure from which to do business. And in a further effort to authenticate his entrepreneurial endeavors, he painted the name *Himelbaum and Son* on the awning. When he brought the twin kiosk he'd purchased uptown for his father to sell from, Izzy's face lit up with a long-absent smile. But it was just a temporary glimmer in the downcast manner that had overtaken him. A few hours a day on the 186th Street corner were all the older man could tolerate, what with the occasional hounding by police (which Harry, downtown, handled as he had the uptown harassments) and the vicissitudes of weather nipping at his stamina. The coughing brought on by his years in the coal cellar had thankfully abated, and the last thing Harry wanted was for his father's health to be compromised in any way. As for the beggars that habitually tried to grab merchandise without paying, Harry had suggested that Izzy let them have an apple or two, as he did, to discourage confrontations, but this was a notion completely antithetical to Izzy's fiber; he just couldn't do it. So, instead, they'd agreed that at the first sign of coughing, or thievery, or the appearance of a police officer to whom Harry had not introduced him, Izzy would immediately close for the day, and wheel the unsold merchandise to the alley in back of their apartment building for Harry to dispose of when he got home.

Thus, on this brisk morning in March, as Harry rolled his "kiosk" to Fourth Street, his path to belonging—approached with all the good intentions of an earnest young man—had been planted with tricks, watered with bribes, and paved in falsehood. Yet, with the same concentration he extended to displaying his produce—oranges here, apples over there, and pears in between—he managed to compartmentalize his circumstances. If the wife and child in Poland formed the impetus behind his labor, even as their very existence rendered his presence here illegal, he must not allow these troubling truths to blur his focus. He must save enough money to send for a wife that he had sworn did not exist, and the only way he knew to sweep this contradiction from his mind was to work all the harder. With a proficiency that he could depend on, the workday itself provided the means by which to reach his goal and the surest escape from thinking about its complications. Here on Fourth Street, it was the display that mattered, and the numbers of apples sold, and the congenial exchange or two he might enjoy with a customer.

A line of expectant shoppers had already gathered. Harry heard them chattering about the false lead in the Lindbergh case. It seemed a rich man in Virginia had claimed that the kidnapper had contacted him, this same man confessing just one day later to a lifetime of hallucinations, and imploring the authorities to commit him to an asylum. Harry had read the story in the newspaper, and now he smiled and waved over the first customer. Always, she was the first, this nice-looking redhead, and her reliable warmth and friendliness had become a wonderful way to start the day.

"Can you believe it, Mr. Himelbaum, the lengths some people will go to just to make it into the newspapers?" the woman asked. "I mean it's obvious the man was crazy: why would the kidnapper be in Virginia if the Lindberghs live in New Jersey?"

Harry sidestepped the geographical *non sequitur.* "*Nu,* there's phonies all over," he returned.

"Yes, I suppose," the woman said. She was nearly Harry's height, a gorgeous woman, but utterly unaware of her beauty as she clutched her overcoat against the wind. She went on, "I love that '*nu*' thing you always say. What is that? What does it mean?"

Harry held out an apple to her. "You see how beautiful they are today? Shiny and red like your hair. Here, take it." It pleased him to give away the occasional piece of fruit to a customer, made him feel successful, and more important, he felt it conveyed an air of success. "'*Nu?*' It means everything, and nothing. It means, 'What can you expect?' And, 'So, do you have anything else to say?' It's just an expression, that comes in very handy, believe me."

The woman bit into the crispy apple and smiled her appreciation. How old was she, Harry wondered. She was so elegant, but at the same time, she exuded innocence, a girlish quality. "Mm, delicious," she said. "Can I have three?" She fished in her pocket and extracted fifteen cents. "Almost as good as back home. We have the best apples in Iowa."

Her cheerfulness instantly faded into the shadow of homesickness. "Mr. Brown says he has no idea when we'll be able to go back for a visit," she said. "But, you know how it is, what with the Depression and all, and all those people coming and going on Ellis Island. That's where he works. An immigration inspector. He works so hard, night and day."

Harry swatted away the sting of "those people"; he knew the last thing in the world she meant to do was offend. While there was no doubting that trace of sadness in her face, it was easily eclipsed by the more prominent openheartedness that she brought to each of their morning encounters.

"Well, I guess I'd better move along," she said gamely, her apparent need to linger and chat giving way to her natural sense of fairness. A long line of women waited behind her.

"Tell your husband he should enjoy the apples." Harry smiled, and he turned his attention to the next customer.

"*Nu*, Mrs. Yates, how are the children? They enjoyed last night the oranges? All the way from Florida they came."

"Oh, yes, and I'll have a half dozen more. I'm telling you, Mr. Himelbaum," she said as Harry filled her canvas sack with oranges, "I'm just a nervous wreck about this kidnapping. I'm terrified to even send them to school."

Harry continued his exchange with Mrs. Yates as he momentarily looked over her shoulder to see the beautiful redhead disappear into the crowd of early morning commuters and the unemployed making their way to the nearest soup kitchen.

Barbara jostled past the usual throngs of people toward home, knowing she'd just enjoyed her last social encounter of the day. She'd have to figure out a way not to be the first person in line each morning, but Will liked to see her up and out of the house early, and she had no desire to burden him with the truth of her loneliness as she watched the hours crawl toward evening each day. The few pleasant words she exchanged with that Mr. Himelstein, such a friendly fellow, comprised the highlight of her days, but maybe if she could get there just a little later, she'd meet some of the other women in the line and even strike up a friendship. Back home, she had lots of friends; she couldn't understand why it was so hard for her here in New York.

The smell of alcohol infused Barbara's nostrils as she walked up Mercer toward Eighth Street. The bar on the corner of Sixth was opening up, even this early in the morning, and despite Prohibition, which everyone agreed would be repealed soon. Law enforcement certainly seemed to look the other way when it came to these downtown bars; what with all the unemployment, you couldn't really blame people for wanting to spend their days among familiar faces and drowning their frustration. Even Barbara enjoyed a little sip of brandy before starting on the day's chores. Her cousin Suze had given them the bottle of liquor as a wedding present. Will had never approved of Suze—referring to her always as "that flapper"—and he definitely wouldn't have allowed Barbara to keep the unlawful gift had he known that it existed. But when they'd moved to New York, he'd left the opening and sorting of the presents to Barbara and, while she'd been mildly taken aback when she'd unwrapped the bottle of golden alcohol, she'd nonetheless tucked it away under the sink, where she was sure Will wouldn't come across it, and in fact she hadn't even thought about it until months later.

At first she would save the brandy as a reward for after she'd gotten everything done—the marketing and the laundry and such—but lately that early morning drink was just what she needed to get her started. The hours passed a little more quickly that way, with just a few little sips of brandy in between chores, and the endless afternoons could be endured more tolerably as the time drew toward dusk and that wonderful *Amos 'n' Andy* program that she so enjoyed. The radio show started at seven and how it made her giggle as she put the finishing touches on dinner, even if it meant that soon Will would be home and she'd have to adjust to whatever mood he happened to be in. Oh, she knew he loved her, he was crazy about her; but sometimes, it was just the pressure of his work, of course, but he could be so critical.

Mr. Himelman had complimented her on her hair color today, not the first time he'd compared it to the redness of his apples, but Will, oh, he had hated it when he'd come home that first night and she'd surprised him with her "new hue." She thought he'd get a kick out of the rhyme, he used to love her poetry in high school, but instead he said it made her look cheap and that he was confident that she'd let it grow out. Which she was doing. Soon she'd have to wear a scarf, her roots were coming in so quickly.

"Please, lady, can you spare some change?" Barbara thought of herself as a giving person, but she'd long since learned to look straight ahead and ignore the many panhandlers that lined the streets. She and Will were doing very well, and at first she had always kept some spare change in her pocket to hand out to the increasing numbers of unemployed as she'd made her way through the Village, but Will convinced her of the danger of stopping to give people money. You didn't know who was walking the streets; these beggars could be crazy, most likely drunk, and it wasn't good for the character of America, giving money to people who hadn't earned it.

Iowa City

"Well, you can't say I haven't given you fair warning," Officer Forbes told Nicholas as the dry goods merchant straightened and dusted the shelves, closing up for the night. "I won't charge you but practically nothing for my time."

For weeks now, Tom Forbes, retired from the force and probably in need of a little extra cash, had been trying to persuade Nicholas to hire a man nights to watch over things. The local farmers were "finished playing nice"—he told Nicholas those were their very words—and if the government wouldn't help them, they were ready to "take the gloves off."

"You know it's not the money, Tom," Nicholas said, "and I appreciate your concern. But I hire a night watchman, what am I telling my neighbors? That I don't trust them. You know I can't do that. And the fact is, I do trust them. How can I not?" He hung the duster out of sight behind the counter.

"Well then, I'll mind my own business," Tom said good-naturedly as he opened the door over which Nicholas was pulling the closed sign. "But at least invest in some grates for those plate-glass windows, will you?"

"I'll think it over, Tom," Nicholas said with a friendly squeeze of Forbes's shoulder. "Hello at home."

He locked the door as always, and with a last, satisfied visual sweep of the premises, retired upstairs. "You got supper on, Mrs. Brown?" he gave the customary call.

A few mornings afterward, as he sat at the kitchen table finishing his coffee, his wife's shrill cry echoed up the stairs.

"Ayyyy, Nicholas, Nicholas, come quickly!"

What in heaven's name?

"Come, Nicholas, come."

As quickly as he could, Nicholas grabbed his apron from the hook behind the kitchen door, and ran downstairs.

The sight that greeted him made his knees buckle, so that he had to grab the wall to remain standing. It'd been over ten years since his heart attack, but as if by reflex his other hand went to his chest. How could this be? What was this?

It was as though a tornado had stormed through. The front plate window was smashed to pieces and everything, everything that was left, was overturned: cartons, cash register, the buckets where the dry goods were stored. Shelves hung from their walls by a nail, every surface strewn with bits of rice and coffee beans. Whatever grains were left covered the floor like so much sawdust, smeared with the incriminating footprints of hurried escape.

Without being conscious of it, Nicholas had slid down to one of the steps, where he found himself when Ellie ran over. "Your heart, Nicholas," his wife knelt beside him, "is it your heart?"

"I'm all right," he spoke very slowly. "Don't worry."

"Thank God," Ellie said, and she, too, slumped onto the floor. Unaware until this moment that she could contain such misery inside herself, she broke into wracking sobs. They seemed to originate from deep in her abdomen and come with such insistence that she felt as though they might crack her in two.

Nicholas stared at the wreckage that had been his life's work, and reached over to stroke Ellie's head. The shock he'd felt upon coming downstairs was draining from him as he realized that the destruction he beheld was the unavoidable outcome of what Tom Forbes had been warning him about and what he'd known but staunchly refused to admit had been brewing for years. How long could the farmers hold in their fury as surpluses deprived them of ample pay for product, so that they could not afford to buy the very corn or grain or bread that their labor had provided? With their mortgages overdue and beyond their ability to pay, and their families going hungry, men Nicholas had known all his life couldn't be expected to feel loyalty toward their dry goods merchant, no matter how long they'd been neighbors and friends. He'd heard of things like this happening all over the country, honest citizens breaking the law if that was their only way to put food on the table.

Not six months ago there'd been a story in the newspaper about a situation down in Arkansas where the Red Cross had held off an angry mob of farmers who'd shown up about five hundred strong in front of a grocery store to demand food for their families. A full-out riot was averted only when the relief agency agreed to subsidize the grocers for whatever food they handed out. He and Will had talked about it, his son appalled by the image of homegrown American farmers making such a sorry spectacle of themselves: to Will, no less than to the president he idolized, nothing was quite so un-American as asking for any kind of handout. "Protect yourself, Pop, get a gun if you have to," Will had advised, "but don't you fall victim to these people wanting something for nothing. Don't you go giving away merchandise to folks you've been extending credit to all these years. And for God's sake, let me keep up the insurance payments, will you? This is no time to let the insurance lapse."

Father and son had gone back and forth on Will's attitude, Nicholas pointing out that up there in the big city things might not be quite as bad as they were in Iowa, where the combined effects of surpluses and economic depression, impossible enough, were now being multiplied by the drought that wouldn't let up. It'd been years since the Midwest had seen rain in any meaningful amount, and all that topsoil that had been cultivated within an inch of its life during the ballyhoo years of the twenties, was being blown around, useless, by the dry winds that gusted unremittingly. With all the grass and topsoil gone, the land couldn't hold any planting.

All the more reason, Will had observed, to exercise caution. "Those excess bushels of grain and corn are just sitting there for the taking. It's a sad situation, Pop, but it's not your fault, is it? You bought that merchandise fair and square, and it's not your fault the customers can't afford to buy it from you. You've got to hold on to what's yours, even if it means protecting yourself with a firearm."

"These are my neighbors, William," Nicholas had reasoned with his son, whose voice was taking on that fervent patriotic tone that most of the time filled him with pride. "I grew up with old Mark Jenkins, Pete and Lester Smith, the whole bunch of them. We raised our children together, belong to Rotary together. It's a darn shame what's happening to them after all the hard work they've put in. I'm not going to pick up a gun against them, and it's just plain foolish of you to even suggest that they'd do anything to hurt me."

"I don't know, Pop, when people are hungry . . ." Will hadn't finished the sentence, probably because he agreed with his father about the unlikelihood of these neighbors, whom they'd known all their lives, doing anything to harm his well-respected and highly regarded parents. Now, the sentence had been finished.

Nicholas sat ruminating and stroking his wife's hair. Obviously, the lack of any kind of organized rebellion in town, at least that he could see, had given him a false sense of security about where things stood. About where his own finances stood, he enjoyed no such sense, of course, he and Ellie just getting by with the additional income Will sent them, the boy was doing so well. But even with all the foreclosures occurring around them—a handful of people even being forced to leave Iowa for other parts of the country—he'd counted the many who'd stayed as his friends, and felt sure that they'd all stick together through this dry spell that would surely pass. When it came down to it, though, Rotary was no substitute for home, and that's where charity began, even if it was at the expense of the local dry goods store.

"Let's clean up," he said to Ellie, and he lifted himself from the stairs to begin the daunting task.

Ellie looked on as her husband walked slowly toward the supply closet and extracted a broom. His helpmate in every endeavor since the day they'd been married and taken over his parents' store—the business had been their wedding present—washing his apron by hand each night to make sure he had a freshly starched and pressed one every morning, even when the number of customers they could expect on any given day had dwindled to practically nothing, she could not find it within herself at this moment to come to his aid. What was the point? Clean up the store: for what? For the customers that wouldn't come? For the customers who had done this to them? No, it was time to leave. Like the Bertrands and the Converses. It was 1932 already, this had all started years ago, and things weren't getting any better.

The swish of the broom, the clinking of the shards of glass, entered Ellie's hearing like a sour lullaby. Yes, it was crazy in the face of this upheaval, but she felt sleepy. After thirty-five years of marriage and work, saving and planning, she was weary, bone tired. She just couldn't find it in herself to help.

Yet, she wondered, as she pulled herself up from the step and looked at her husband, if she'd ever seen anything quite so lonely as the sight of Nicholas sweeping.

Stawki, Poland

"Here, *tateleh*, taste the challah, it'll melt in your mouth." Hershel carefully sliced a thin sliver from one of the cooling braided breads he'd prepared and handed it to his nephew; but the boy, clinging to his mother's skirt, blanched. "Here," he handed the slice of bread to Chava, "your mama will give you." Affectionately, he patted the boy's head.

Hershel was never so content as when preparing the evening meal for *Shabbes*. As had been his fondest dream, his baked goods were becoming so popular in the village, so much in demand, that soon his modest bakery business would overtake the money the family brought in from the dairy farming. Oh, they still needed the income from the eggs and the milk, but neither of the brothers had the interest in the family business that Yankel had had, and now, three years since he'd gone, they were down to only one employee to help out. Leah, God bless her, was expecting (Hershel knew the neighbors had been buzzing about his wife's persistent childlessness) so they were being very careful with her, and Chava, well, Chava could do very little these days without Moishele clinging to her skirt. Even now the child wouldn't sit down at the table unless his mother sat beside him. Which, of course, she did. Tearing a piece from the bread, she fed it into her son's mouth. He ate happily.

"You know he shouldn't eat before mealtime." Yitzak strode in carrying several pails of eggs. "You spoil him like nobody's business. The way he hangs on you, you'll lose the baby." Chava, like Leah, was expecting, and it was true, as her husband said, that the weight of the chubby three-year-old did sometimes cause a worrying strain in her back, which, to keep her husband quiet, she never mentioned.

"What? You want the child shouldn't eat? Then you'll be happy?" As always, she took her son's side. No one on the earth loved her like the boy, certainly not her husband, whose trips to Warsaw in recent years had only increased. Sometimes, he'd be away for a whole week, coming home only for *Shabbes*. But that was the important thing, after all, the proof of his primary loyalty: always he was here for *Shabbes*.

"Hungry, he won't go," Yitzak grumbled.

"What, you want he should be hungry?" Chava returned.

"I want," Yitzak said, wiping the boy's mouth somewhat roughly with a handkerchief, "that he should at least eat like a *mensch*."

Moishe started to cry.

"There, now you're happy," Chava said, her face wrinkling into misery on her son's behalf. She grabbed him to her and picked him up, leaving the large kitchen area that was the center of the family home. "Always you make him cry. That's all you know."

Elke Himelbaum, the matriarch of the growing family, wiped the table meticulously and inspected it for the slightest imperfection. This she would always do before laying out the white linen tablecloth that she and Icko had received on their wedding day and treasured ever since. "*Nu*, it looks all right," she said. And with that pronouncement, Hershel stopped arranging his challahs, Leah paused from stirring the *cholent*, and even Yitzak's irritated demeanor smoothed into tranquility. With a broad and forceful upswing of her arms, Elke flung open the tablecloth, and all watched as it gracefully made its floating descent onto the table. The weekly ritual accomplished, each member of the Himelbaum family resumed activity, for there was not much time until sundown: Hershel had his breads to get out to the customers, and Yitzak similarly must disperse the eggs, while Leah, breathing in the scent of the slow-cooking stew, reassured herself that, indeed, it would be ready.

Amidst all the industrious preparations, only Rifka sat impassively in her customary corner on the floor near the window. God only knew how many times she had leafed through the issue of *Illustrated Week*, the Yiddish magazine with pictures that Yankel's girlfriend had given her years ago. She studied it as learned men studied Torah, folding it carefully each night and tucking it under her pillow, lest it disappear. Of course, the cost of a new one would be much too expensive to even consider buying, but Rifka was content to believe that the photos of golden-haired movie stars and svelte beauty contestants kept her up to date, at least in relation to her outmoded family. Even yellowed by age, the periodical was the height of modernity compared to Mama and Chava.

"Go, Rifkale, get ready," Elke instructed her daughter. "Your dress is clean?"

"Yes, Mama," the twelve-year-old muttered. "It's too small and ugly as sin, but it's clean."

"Shah, what a way to talk! You want I should wash your mouth with soap? Go!"

As Rifka went to retrieve her *Shabbes* dress, Elke confided in her daughter-in-law: "*Nu*, without a father, she's grown into a hussy. I don't know what to do about the girl. She was only two when he left, what can I expect?" As always, thinking about her husband, whom she hadn't seen in ten years, brought a huskiness to Elke's voice and tears to her eyes.

Leah comforted her. "She's a good girl, Mama. Don't say such things. Soon he'll send for us, you'll see, and she'll make you proud, there in America."

"*Nu*, if all the girls in America are like that, proud I won't be." But of course, her daughter-in-law's words soothed her. It was true what she said, soon they would all go.

Elke said these words to herself regularly—*Soon we will all go*—but the thought was no more than an abstraction, a set of syllables that somehow assured her eventual reunion with her husband, but had no basis in reality. Yes, she knew that thousands had left, even some of her neighbors and her own sister, before the World War, when conditions for the Jews here were so terrible, and afterward, too, when bitter experience still prompted many to leave despite the so-called minority-protection clauses. The Second Polish Republic, a sovereign government since 1918, talked like they wanted them, but the majority of Poles, everyone understood, would just as soon be a Jew-free nation. Everyone knew that. Icko certainly did, and so, soon after the Polish-Soviet War in 1920, in which Polish Jews had fought and died for their country's independence, and after which they were still greeted with suspicion by their gentile compatriots, her husband had left the farm in the able hands of three sons and a strong wife and followed the call to a better land, where soon, he promised, they all would go.

Yet here in Stawki, where Icko had bought the land and Elke had established a family in the small thatch-roofed house, well, here was home, and "soon they all would go" aroused just as much apprehension as hopefulness in her mind.

Coaxed from her musings by the tapping on her shutters of the *Shabbes klopper*, the man who came each Friday like clockwork to signal that it would soon be time to stop everything and observe the Sabbath, she wondered if they had such a personage in New York, and then took off her apron to get ready for evening.

Hours later, the candles flickered in their golden holders as the family finished dinner. The kitchen, redolent with the fragrances that gather after a carefully prepared meal, glowed quiet and peaceful. Even Yitzak held his tongue as his wife fed their three-year-old, each tendered forkful peppered with her soft-spoken encouragements: "Here, *tateleh*, take a piece meat"; "You like the *cholent* on the challah, *tateleh*?" It irritated him no end, to see his boy babied so, but it was the Sabbath meal, after all, never the time for squabbles, and, too, he had a surprise for everyone. What good would it do to upset the mood?

"Ahem, ahem," Yitzak cleared his throat. "Maybe before the sponge cake, you all want a little news?"

"News": it was the magic word, sure to provoke from Elke a gasp of anticipation, an eager flush on Rifka's face, and a general sense of excitement around the table. Even young Moishe understood from the quiet hubbub around him that a letter was to be read, and he reflexively scampered onto his mother's lap and thrust his thumb into his mouth to settle in for the communal listen. "It's like a story from another country," Chava had told him when explaining what a letter was.

Taking from his shirt pocket the onionskin envelope, Yitzak tore it open and unfolded the crinkly pages covered in Yiddish. Clearing his throat once more, he began:

> *My dearest family,*
>
> *Forgive me for the many months that have passed since I wrote to you. I am sorry to say that things have gotten worse here, not better. Do not worry, the coughing is no longer bad, thanks to our Yankele, who works so hard at the fruit stand that I only have to be outside a few hours a day. I didn't want him to tell you about the coughing, but I know that he did, and, believe me, it's no longer a problem. So, Hoover, the president, put a stop to selling apples on the street, so now what we have is a city of people living on relief. Almost a million, the papers say, lining up at the relief offices getting maybe eight dollars a month since the Depression. I'm telling you, here in New York, it's really bad, everywhere you look there's lines, for money, for soup,*

worse even than Warsaw during the war, the breadlines. Your sister,
Elkele, and her husband, send to you their love.

At the sound of her husband's endearment, "Elkele," and hearing
Yankel's name, and picturing her beloved sister, Elke cried quietly into
her napkin.

"'The bums on the street are something terrible,'" Yitzak continued reading.

Not that I can blame them, everyone is out of work, but it's no fun,
I can tell you, having to fight them off up here, I'm alone. Yankel,
downtown in that Greenwich Village, like they call it, he manages
to keep them away. Maybe, I don't know, he gives to them some fruit
so they leave him alone. I don't have to tell you the head on his
shoulders he's got.

"Why does he keep calling him Yankel?" Rifka groused. "He's
Harry now, why is Papa so old-fashioned?"

"Shah, Rifkale," her mother scolded.

"Leave it to Yankele," Hershel said, "even in New York, he figures
out how to do things."

Chava shifted in her seat and sighed, silently bristling. Always
Yankel got the praise from the family. Little did they know he was
hiding there in Lukow a wife. What the big secret was, she still didn't
know.

But for me, in the cold, it's hard. A few pieces of fruit I sell in the
mornings, but then, between the thieves and the weather, that's
enough for me. Himelbaum and Son he has on the pushcart. He
calls it something else, but to me, it's a pushcart. And down there,
downtown, he's selling. Sometimes fifteen, twenty dollars he brings
home in a week. Not that it's home as far as I'm concerned, but a
place we have, near 186th Street where I stand with the pushcart
in the mornings.
Well, to make a long story, I'm coming home.

Yitzak stopped reading, his objective role as reader halted by the words he had just spoken. A general air of disbelief spread around the table, followed by a chaos of questions—"What? What is he saying?"; "Does Yankel know? Is he coming, too?" "Coming home? What about us?"—and urgings that he continue.

His brow furrowed in bewilderment, Yitzak went on:

> *Yankel I haven't told yet because I know he will not be happy. He will try to convince me to change my mind. But I'm not doing any good here, and I miss all of you more than I can even write. You know, I don't have to tell you. With the money he brings home, I am slowly saving, that's why you won't find any dollars here this time. I'm saving so I can be there with you.*
>
> *Yours, with love from New York,*
> *Icko*

Moishe looked around in confusion. This was different from how Papa's stories usually ended. Everyone was so quiet. Bubbe always cried, but her crying was different this time.

Finally, his mother spoke. "*Nu*, so he's coming back. So it's not so wonderful there in America. I'm not surprised."

"You don't know what you're talking." Yitzak broke the rule against arguing on *Shabbes*. "The Jews from Germany are pouring into Warsaw like you've never seen. These Nazis, I'm telling you, they're up to no good. Telling everyone it's the Jews' fault everyone is out of work. Always, everywhere, it's our fault. You know, they have a Depression there, too, in Germany. So whose fault is it? Of course, ours."

"*Nu*, so the Jews from there are coming here," Hershel said, starting to gather the dinner plates to make room on the table for dessert. "What do the Nazis have to do with us? The Jews are coming to Poland because here it's safe."

Rifka sat quietly, all color drained from her face. "Now, I'll never get to go," she said.

"Help your brother with the dishes," Chava chided her.

New York City

Harry gazed with wonder at the two faces staring out at him. Yes, he knew they were looking into the camera, but the expressions in those eyes were meant only for him: the husband; the father whom the boy had never met.

The child was blond, impossibly blond, his hair white and fine as corn silk, combed into short bangs above the probing gaze. He stood behind his mother, who was seated in a chair. Her left hand, displaying the wedding ring Harry had sent her, reached up to hold her son's, which rested on her shoulder.

He wore a sailor suit, his Yakob, probably provided by the photographer. In her letter, Regina apologized for spending the recent money he had sent on a photographic session, but surely he would want to see them at their best. Her lips pressed firmly into an inquisitive smile, her expression seemed to say to him, "See? Do you see what pleasures you are missing? This gorgeous son and devoted wife?" The letter was signed *From your most loving Regina.*

At moments like these, Harry had to fight an impulse to end everything and race back to them. His Reizel's arms, his Yakob's serious gaze, to clutch them to him and never let them go.

Standing next to Harry, Reva Lansky peered over his shoulder. "A beautiful picture," she said. "A beautiful family you got there." In a brown paper bag, she held the apples Harry had given to her.

"So . . . so it's your family, too," Harry said, still looking at his wife and son.

"You must miss them something awful."

Harry tucked the photo into the envelope Reva had handed him and slipped the piece of mail into his breast pocket. "Miss them." He shook his head. "Sometimes, I feel like I don't even know them. That's what I miss: knowing them. He's a beautiful boy, no?" From his trouser pocket, he withdrew a few dollars. "Here, I had a good week. Please, take."

Somewhat uncomfortably, Reva accepted the money. They were, in a way, family, though she had never actually met her cousin Reizel, and the handsome young man standing next to her, who came with the apples and money, and with whom she'd been meeting like this, on this very corner on Avenue C, for years now, well, it might be hard to think of him as family, but she couldn't think of anyone she'd met in America who was kinder, more generous. He was barely more than a boy himself, yet so dependable, responsible. A real *mensch*. "Thank you," she said. "You know I hate to take from you, but things are bad, I'm lucky I have a job. They cut our pay again, I'm making less now than before, but something is better than nothing, like they say. At least I have a job."

"Soon, maybe we'll get rid of this Hoover," Harry said, "and get in Washington a better man."

"From your mouth to God's ears," Reva agreed, and then the two, having exchanged the goods and meager conversation that always accompanied their weekly meetings, shared the few awkward, silent moments that were also customary before acknowledging that they'd see each other again the following week and said good-bye.

On the way to the subway station on Fourth Street, Harry picked up the afternoon edition of the *Daily News*. The cover of the tabloid was emblazoned with a headline about yet another fraudulent lead in the Lindbergh case, but inside he knew he'd find something about Roosevelt and his bid for the presidency. As a future citizen of the United States, he must stay informed. In a couple of years, please God, he'd be eligible for naturalization, and then, with citizenship, he'd be able to vote. Imagine that: he, Harry Himelbaum, an American citizen, voting! He'd go first, of course, first thing, back to Poland to get his family, his wife and son. How he would tell Mama and Papa, he still hadn't figured it out. But as a U.S. citizen, he was sure he'd be able to bring Regina and Yakob over. During his years and years of dreaming about emigrating to the United States, this hadn't been part of the picture—a wife, a son, whose photograph sat in his pocket—but from his arrival, their very absence was a presence in his life, as though America and his secret family went together. Along with denial. Of the myriad problems that lay ahead, and the legal trouble he might get into—and of any kind of attraction. Other women must be ignored, avoided; he mustn't notice or think about or linger in their appeal for even a moment. He was a married man. For all of this, he must thank his curly-haired Reizel. The truths of his life, and its lies. She would be very surprised, Harry thought with a wry smile of affection, to learn of her power.

Hanging on to the subway strap on the uptown train, he saw in the paper that Governor Roosevelt would fly to Chicago to accept his party's nomination at the Democratic Convention should he be chosen as the candidate. Such an optimistic person, Harry thought, and such energy. That's what America needed, a shot of optimism; enough already with the doom and gloom.

In Germany, he read, not for the first time, there was also a Depression, and bands of tough guys, they called them in the paper "brownshirts," were roaming the streets harassing people for no reason. Brownshirts, what a name. It'd been a whole week now since Mrs. Brown had come to buy anything. That face on her. The last time, he had asked her why she was wearing a scarf, covering up her beautiful red hair. Maybe he shouldn't have said that, too friendly maybe, too personal. Had he scared her away? *Nu*, maybe it was better.

Harry forced his attention back to the newspaper. They'd be having there, too, an election soon, he read, in Germany.

His father was sitting at the kitchen table looking at the *Daily Forward* when he got home. "Anything good, Pop?" he asked, bursting into the room with the high energy he always mustered for his father's sake. "Any good *mises* in the "Bintel Brief" today?" Harry teased his father about the popular column of dramatic stories the newspaper printed, about missing husbands, betrayed sisters-in-law, broken families: thank God the paper was written in Yiddish, so the whole world didn't have to know what scoundrels the Jewish people were. Of course, Harry himself didn't mind reading the column after dinner each night, amused by all the troubles suffered, and perpetrated, by his *landsleit*.

"*Ich hub foon Polski ein brevela,*" Izzy said as Harry looked through the icebox for the chicken and potatoes from the night before. "*Vilstoo layenen?*"

Harry blanched at the mention of a letter from Poland; it made the one sitting in his pocket weigh that much more heavily, like a stone of guilt whose outlines must not protrude for his father's notice. "English, talk in English, Papa," he said more forcefully than necessary, covering guilt with accusation. "You want to sell more apples, you have to speak English, talk better with the customers." He placed the leftovers in a pan on the stove.

"*Nu*, most of the customers like that I talk with them Yiddish," Izzy said.

Glad to have turned the subject away from letters, Harry stayed with the argument he'd started. He rarely criticized his father, wanted nothing less in life than to hurt or upset him, but at the moment it was that letter in his pocket, and the photograph, that were dictating his words. "But there could be other customers, too, that don't speak Yiddish," he said. "You think only Jews want an apple for the table?"

"*Nu*, you want to read?" Izzy asked, clearly not interested in being drawn into Harry's rebuke. "It's from Rifkale."

Making sure that dinner was simmering at the right heat on the stove, Harry wiped his hands on a kitchen towel, and then looked at them. They were red and calloused from the cold and lifting, stained by all the coins he'd handled. "First, I'll wash," he said, "then I'll read." He strode past his father and into the bathroom.

After cleaning his hands and face and rubbing his scalp and fluffing up his hair, which had been flattened by the cap he wore all day, he walked quietly into the small bedroom he and his father shared. He tossed his cap onto the straight-backed wooden chair that sat next to the bed, and carefully hung his jacket in the closet, taking from the pocket the clandestine piece of mail. Reaching behind the folded linens on the upper closet shelf, he extracted the shoe box in which he kept Regina's letters and placed that day's envelope on top. "I did today a very good business," he called to Izzy, as if there were any possibility that the old, tired man might hear a piece of paper being placed inside a box. "For next week, I'll buy a pot roast. Enough already with the chicken."

When he walked back into the kitchen, his father seemed riveted by something he was reading in the *Forward*. "This you gotta hear," he said in English. "But it's okay with you *ich redn* Yiddish?"

"Go ahead, Pop, talk in Yiddish if that's how the story is written."

The newspaper item that had so fascinated Izzy pertained to a young man who had recently decided to emigrate to Palestine. His parents, having settled in New York and raised him here, were beside themselves with grief at the prospect of losing him.

"*Nu*," Harry asked, "so what does the editor advise?"

Izzy looked up at his son with a serious expression, and recounted the advice, which he had memorized, in his best attempt at English. "The editor says your son is an adult and you should trust his decision."

Catching the intensity in his father's eyes, Harry asked, "What are you looking at me? I'm not going anywhere."

"Not you," Izzy said.

"Not me, so *vos redn?*" His confusion caused Harry himself to lapse into Yiddish.

"I'm talking about me," said Izzy. "Here." The old man slid Rifka's letter, which had been sitting on the table, toward his son. "Your sister isn't happy about it, and you won't be, either."

"What are you talking about?" Harry asked, picking up the letter.

"There's no use talking," Izzy said. "I've thought it over and my mind is made up. You'll read, you'll see."

Harry didn't have to read Rifka's words to understand what his father was saying, but at the same time, seeing it in black and white, the news came as a shock. Izzy had written home to announce that he was returning to Stawki. Harry turned off the stove and sat opposite his father, never taking his eyes from Rifka's letter.

She begged her father to reconsider, expressed in florid detail how her every waking moment was devoted to coming to the United States, how her very life depended on getting out of Poland. Harry felt terrible for his beloved little sister, but for the moment it was his own sadness that consumed him. New York without Papa? It was almost impossible to contemplate. Even with his Yiddish and his old-world ways, the slow pace he had adapted and his chronic misgivings, Izzy, for most of his son's conscious life, had been the very symbol of coming to America. Izzy Himelbaum, here, was what it meant to be an American.

"So you wrote to them already? I live here with you under the same roof and you don't even tell me?"

"I'm tired, *tateleh*, I don't feel good. *Tut mir vey in holdz, oon yedn tog ich hob a kop-veytik.*"

"So we'll go to the doctor about your throat. They don't have doctors here? The best. So I'll hire someone to help you at the fruit stand. Better yet, you won't work at all; you'll sit, read the *mises*, *redst* with the neighbors." Harry was so upset, his words, like his thoughts, were a jumble of language.

His father looked at him with quiet resolution. "Are you listening, or just talking?" Izzy sighed. "Long enough I'll stay to send for Rifka. You'll help me, we'll try to arrange it. With the quota system, it won't be easy anymore, but at least maybe with her father here a citizen, it can be arranged. Yitzak will help. He knows people in Warsaw, he'll..."

"So, you have it all worked out," Harry said. "I live here every day with you, and you have everything worked out. You live with a person, day in and day out," he shrugged his shoulders, "and you don't even know what's going through their head."

"*Nu*, so I'm the only one with secrets?" Izzy asked, his head tilted in almost playful inquiry.

The gesture threw Harry, confused him. His stomach tightened, and he could feel the red heat of mortification wash over his face. His father knew?

"You think I don't know," his father continued, "you have someone? Once a week like clockwork you come home late, you think a papa doesn't put two and two together that you've got down there a *maidel*?"

Despite himself, the sweet, troubled face of Mrs. Brown flashed into Harry's mind; he quickly erased it. How nearly right his father was, and yet how thoroughly wrong. "No, Papa, there's no one downtown," Harry said, greatly relieved that the "secret" Izzy referred to had nothing to do with his marriage—he hadn't been apprehended— yet disconcertingly aware, as well, of the trace of regret he caught in his own voice. No, there was no *maidel* downtown. To steer his father away from suspecting anything along the lines of a romantic attachment, he added, "Sometimes I stay a while on the corner, I give to the hobos if I have extra. I *kibbitz* with them."

Izzy merely nodded his head, conveying that his son would tell him about the girl when he was ready.

"You hungry?" Harry asked, getting up to dish out their meal. Whatever moisture might have been drawn from the warmed-over food had long since congealed.

"So maybe instead of to the hobos, you'll save for your sister. We'll put together a little each week, send to Yitzak for the steamer ticket." Izzy dug into the food Harry set before him with hunger, as though something had been settled.

Harry's appetite was as dried up as the chicken. Money. His father didn't know how much he was able to save, or that he sent a few dollars to Regina every month. How could he suddenly stop? He couldn't; it was that simple. Her parents' hat store was making out well, but he knew that the money he sent helped. Rifka, he'd find a way to save for her, too. Soon, they were opening a new subway station closer to the apartment. He'd leave earlier in the morning, open up the fruit stand earlier.

"Don't worry," Izzy was saying, "I'll stay longer outside, now the weather is getting warmer, I'll sell more. Together, we'll get our Rifkale on the boat. You'll see."

"Sure, and you'll be going the other way. She'll never know her papa." With all the worries going through his mind, Harry didn't bother to soften his reproach.

"*Nu*, she'll have Uncle Sam," Izzy said. "She won't need her father." Although he said the words with a smile, his voice was clogged with emotion. He coughed a deep, wheezy cough to clear his throat. "*Oy*," he sighed, "*tut mir vey in holdz.*"

When Will arrived home, his arms loaded down with files that wouldn't fit inside his briefcase, he could see Barbara examining the roots of her hair in the bathroom mirror. Because he found the scratchy noises of the radio irritating, and the supposed humor of the program she was listening to even worse, he switched it off before plunking down his paperwork on the neatly arranged rolltop desk in the foyer.

"Will, I was listening to that," Barbara called.

"Well, listen to this," Will said as he came up behind her, and encircled her waist, pulling her toward him. "Your husband is home and I'm starving." He kissed her neck, which invariably made her giggle, and regarded her reflection. "I'm so glad it's growing back, Barbara," he said. "You've got such beautiful blonde hair, I don't know what you were thinking." He snuggled closer. "Mm, you smell nice."

Before *Amos 'n' Andy* came on, Barbara always took a bath. She wanted to smell good for Will when he got home, and get rid of any traces of alcohol.

"Oh, I suppose once it grows back it'll be all right," Barbara said. "But it'll be weeks before I look like anything other than a clown. I'm positively two-toned."

"Well, you're the prettiest clown in New York," Will said, pulling her closer.

"Pop called again," she told him, referring to Will's father. She'd long since gotten used to thinking of Mr. Brown as Pop. "Things are bad." Maybe she hadn't done it on purpose, but the report had the effect of loosening Will's grip on her. His face immediately soured.

"I spoke to Ben Sills about it," Will said. "He assured me that the insurance will take care of everything, put them back on their feet."

Will had been crushed by the attack on his parents' store, and in the weeks since, had been on the phone with the Iowa City Attorney's Office countless times to facilitate reparation. Hell of a thing, the way the farmers were behaving, like common criminals, but they were struggling like so many others in the country, and the drought out there just made everything seem that much more hopeless. Will knew the situation was terrible, all those people unable to pay their mortgages; still, it broke his heart to think of lifelong friends of the family taking it out on his father, or, at the very least, turning the other way when the break-in was planned.

Barbara gave him a peck on the cheek. "I'm sure things will work out, Will," she said. She edged past him and went into the kitchen to set dinner on the table. No use telling him again how poorly his mother was doing, how she barely got out of bed, and when she did, according to Pop, and her own mother when she visited, Ellie just kind of dragged around all day in her housecoat, no help at all anymore. Pop was worried, but saying anything further on the subject would just upset Will, and she'd worked so hard today on the lamb, she wanted everything to be perfect.

Maybe after dinner.

They talked as they ate about how nice the new wallpaper looked, how it brought out the gleam in the white stove and cabinets, and Will told her how much it meant to him to come home to a cheerful atmosphere after spending his days in the dingy half-light of Ellis Island. They ate and they talked about pleasant things and then, within minutes, it seemed, the meal was over, after all those hours of preparation.

Barbara's mother had once pointed out to her that that was the unique thing about the art of cooking: the better the product, the more quickly it disappeared.

"Delicious," Will said as he dabbed his mouth with his napkin and leaned back. "I'm a lucky man."

"Luck hasn't got a thing to do with it, William Matthew Brown, and you know it," Barbara said. She was feeling magnanimous, what with all the compliments Will had given her, and pleased with the way the stewed apricots had added just the right flavor to the meat, just like the magazine had said.

She sometimes felt guilty about the extravagance of her orders when she went to the butcher shop or phoned in to the market. With so many people out of work, waiting on breadlines for something to eat, it embarrassed her that she could purchase just about any ingredient from the latest recipe she'd found in *Redbook*. "You've worked hard, very hard, your whole life to get us where we are," she said to Will, and to reassure herself.

Routinely, when asking for the two pounds of lamb, or paying the grocery delivery boy a fifty-cent tip, she would thus find solace in justifying their good fortune. She could afford an even bigger tip on Will's nearly four-thousand-dollar-a-year annual salary—three thousand more than the national average, she'd read in *Life*—but then there was also that timorous indecision between wanting to be as generous as she could afford to be and seeming like a show-off.

"My parents have worked hard, too," Will said quietly, appreciating Barbara's acknowledgment and wishing, quite fervently, that it were that simple. His whole life, his work and philosophy were pinned to that simplicity—hard work yielding its just reward; want representing a failure of zeal and character—but his own father, reduced now to restarting a business he'd devoted his life to, was calling into question the beliefs Will had learned at that very father's knee. It wasn't anything Nicholas said to him, per se, but didn't the situation speak for itself? All the bootstraps stuff and the importance of individual responsibility, well, here was an instance where one couldn't deny that the hardships of other people were having a direct bearing on one's own economic viability. Leave it to his father, though; even in the face of what had happened, he was cleaning up the mess, trying to restock the inventory, doing what had to be done to reopen for business.

But why was he calling so frequently? What did he expect Will to do?

He pushed away from the table and patted his stomach. "Delicious," he said again.

"Don't you want some coffee?" Barbara asked, thinking that it was a shame to end the conversation before she'd had a chance to broach the subject she'd been determined to bring up since getting off the phone with his father. She knew how Will hated handouts, but certainly in this instance, it wouldn't be a handout to help his parents until things back home got back to how they used to be. Now that Pop himself was calling so often, in the middle of the day, which suggested to Barbara that he meant on purpose to speak to her, well, it was obvious they needed money, and she and Will could certainly afford to be sending them a bit more, at least until the insurance money came in.

"I've got a lot of work," Will said. "Maybe you could bring my coffee over?" He indicated the side table by the easy chair, and Barbara decided she'd talk to him about Pop first thing in the morning.

As Will leafed through his files, a blast of trumpet and garrulous laughter blew in from the street. He dropped the stack of folders and strode over to the window. It was bad enough that Greenwich Village was a hotbed of so-called nonconformists and artists and all manner of deadbeats; now the neighborhood had become famous for these characteristics, adding congregants of tourists to the once at least reasonably habitable streets. The place was a circus, and Will couldn't wait to get out.

He shut the window and pointedly drew the curtains, the heavy ones he'd made Barbara buy just months after they'd moved in. He didn't want to make her feel badly after the lavish meal she'd prepared, so he held his tongue about the neighborhood. She knew how he felt about it, and besides, she really was being a good sport about her hair—the blond growing in after the red did look ridiculous, even if it was her own doing. So Will just heaved a sigh and got back to his files. He'd made a concerted effort tonight not to criticize Barbara, to compliment the wallpaper and all, and he'd leave it at that.

He squeezed her hand affectionately as she placed the coffee cup on the side table and turned his attention to the stack of work he'd gathered on his lap. Tab upon tab of foreign names greeted him, each file containing paperwork relating to why this or that immigrant thought the United States should pay for their fare home. The poor economic situation was inducing more aliens to leave the country than enter it, which was fine with Will. But even if Ellis Island had turned from a clearinghouse for immigrants into a deportation center, Will's task remained essentially the same: to weed out the phonies from the honest ones, and keep a keen eye out for fake claims about being a Communist or anarchist in the interest of having the United States foot the bill for passage back to wherever they'd come from.

The muted strains of music and laughter seeping in from outside did nothing to allay the headache brewing in Will's temples. He sipped thirstily from the coffee cup, the caffeine sometimes working to ease the pounding. All these names ending in "sziak" and "witz": the letters became a jumble of nonsense syllables, defying Will to comprehend the business at hand. Maybe it would be a better idea, he thought, to wait a while with these deportation claims and look over some of the files of ongoing surveillance. It'd been a while since he'd perused these reports, each of them representing a person he'd interviewed and allowed to stay in the country with the proviso that there be diligent follow-up. There might be something requiring his attention here and at least the reading was a bit more interesting since he'd had personal contact with these people and could find a picture in his mind of each one. The material here also had the advantage of being typed by his various agents, as opposed to the handwritten, tortured scrawl of the deportation requests.

At least twenty of the reports he read contained evidence of once-earnest immigrants who had sworn they'd break all affiliation with their unions now taking part in the latest form of protest: sit-down strikes. Instead of walking out of plants purported to be practicing "unfair working conditions," the dissatisfied employees would just stop work and stay right by their machines. This stymied the owners more effectively than picket lines because it became trickier to bring in replacement workers. Of course, there was nothing illegal about striking, but these sit-downs were so well organized, with workers setting up miniature "cities" in their shut-down factories, that Communist organizers must have been the ones to dream up the idea.

Will red-flagged these reports, encouraging continued observation of these characters. Unions! They would bring down the country if something wasn't done to stop them.

He red-flagged, too, the file of a woman he'd interviewed years ago, when he'd first started working at the island. Reva Lansky was the name. Like so many others, she'd sworn up and down that she'd sever ties with any union that might have even a hint of Communist influence, and the truth was that the garment workers had suffered salary cutbacks along with everyone else in the country, and, understanding the national situation, hadn't fought the pay cuts with nearly the fervor they'd once demonstrated. But he had to agree with the agent assigned to her case—there was something suspicious here. Miss Lansky continued to meet with a young man on a weekly basis, right in front of her dress factory, and seemed to be passing some kind of communication to him. They'd talk for a while, he'd hand her a paper bag, sometimes cash, and then be on his way. What was going on here? Will wondered.

Remain vigilant, he wrote at the bottom of the report, scribbling his initials with a flourish. *Keep an eye on this.*

No sooner had his headache seemed to abate than Will heard the click of Barbara's radio. He knew she liked to listen to some kind of pops music while she cleaned up after dinner and, in her considerate way, she always kept the volume down, but between the merrymaking on the street and now these crackling sounds coming from the kitchen, he felt like a thin spread of cream cheese between two pressing hunks of bread. "Barbara," he called, "will you . . ."

But before he could utter his perfectly reasonable request, the volume went up on: "rupt our programming with this special announcement. Miss Amelia Earhart has announced her intention to become the first woman to fly solo across the Atlantic. We repeat—"

"Barbara, turn it off! Please," Will called from his chair. A woman flying an airplane. What *was* going on? From the kitchen, he heard the obedient click.

~ ~ ~

August

Iowa

Gale-force winds turned day into night as soil that had been plowed, planted, and reaped useless split from the ground in great gusts of powdered earth. Tons of it, acres of pulverized dirt, hurled horizontal in whirling masses of darkness before blowing skyward. Children cried in terror; they couldn't see. This was blacker than night, more blinding: pupils could not adjust themselves to this kind of opacity, nor could eyes stay open without flinching from the shards of fractured farmland. And the howling, deafening sound of it, splintered and broken ground raging through shattered windows, nearly muted the children's' cries, cries earned at the cost of breath itself, each inhalation filling the mouth with filth too thick for the lungs to accommodate.

Fathers sat at dust-laden tables, clutching to hold on, their lives sucked and swirling beyond will or know-how.

Women gripped children, photographs in frames, the hardened pieces of bread that passed for sustenance.

Silent and wailing, sightless and perceiving, storm-tossed and stalwart, the farmers of the Midwest held on as best they could to what had become of their land: a black and merciless cloud.

New York City

Every Sunday since they'd moved into Manhattan, Harry and Izzy rode the bus to Jack and Malka's apartment in the Bronx for a midday meal. On this brutally hot afternoon, however, Harry had begged his father to break with the tradition and stay indoors. A horrid stench filled the air with the dust that had blown in on the jet stream from the west, and the humid conditions of the city kept the filth hovering, making the day so dark that streetlamps burned. But to every gentle rebuke about his health, Izzy only responded, "They're expecting us," and so, after the usual stop at Cushman's Bakery—they shouldn't walk in empty-handed—father and son made their way slowly through the thick, dusty heat to the bus stop on 181st Street, their shirts soaked with sweat. After a while, the bus huffed and wheezed within earshot, its headlights just discernible through the fog of Iowa's wind-tossed farms.

If the air outside was hot, the interior of the vehicle, with its windows closed against the airborne particles, carried its passengers in an atmosphere so sweltering that it burned to breathe. Thus, Izzy and Harry inhaled sparingly as they rode over the bridge that connected the two boroughs. At least from their exit, it was just a short walk to Tremont Avenue.

As they crossed the street toward Malka's building, Izzy doing his best to stifle the coughs rumbling in his chest, they could see silhouetted through the clouded air a small group of people standing on the sidewalk. They were gathered around a burly-looking man, talking and laughing convivially.

Unlike everyone else who had ventured outside on this inclement afternoon, when short-sleeved shirts and blouses were the only bearable manner of dress, the man at the center of the circle wore a jacket and tie and seemed not in the least disturbed by the sweat beading his forehead and temples.

"Let's rest a minute, Pop," Harry said. "See what's going on."

"*Nu*, I don't need a rest, but if you're interested," Izzy allowed. As they drew closer, they could see particles of dust clinging to blouses, shoulders. A woman brushed a tickling dot of debris from her forehead.

"Like I always say," the husky man was telling the crowd, "I may not be of your faith, but you can place your faith in me." He paused, knowing the line went over well with these Jewish constituents, who smiled and nodded their heads approvingly. "With Tim Barkley, you have a friend in Washington."

"Especially now with Roosevelt, maybe you'll have a friend, too," one of the men called out. His high hopes regarding the upcoming fall election met with handclaps and whistles.

"Who have we here?" Barkley inquired, his keen eye never missing the arrival of potential voters. He put out his hand to Izzy and Harry, who somewhat shyly sidled past a few bystanders to accept the proffered handshake.

"Tim Barkley, Seventeenth District," the man introduced himself. "What's in the box?" he asked Harry, who explained that he was carrying a cheesecake in the white bakery box, the customary gift he brought for his aunt and uncle each Sunday.

"A cheesecake in this weather?" Barkley quipped, "I hope it doesn't melt." He pumped Harry's hand vigorously, his strength palpable even in the casual pat on the shoulder by which the handshake was accompanied.

Somewhat flustered, undeniably impressed to be speaking to an actual congressman, Harry tried to hold his own: "Well, if it doesn't melt, I hope it won't turn sour." He introduced himself and his father. For a split second afterward, he regretted the possible mistake, giving out his name to an official from Washington. But surely, this man wouldn't get him into trouble with the authorities, he was all smiles and backslaps.

"So, what do you say, Mr. Himelbaum," Barkley addressed Izzy, "I'm running for reelection here in the Seventeenth; can I count on your vote?"

Izzy cleared his throat to make his voice less scratchy. "We're only visiting," he said. "But if we lived here, you could count."

"I only wish I could vote for Roosevelt," Harry volunteered, getting caught up in the spirit of this singularly American street-corner campaign. "In a few years, when I'm a citizen, I'll vote for him for reelection." The brash prediction drew a hearty endorsement from the crowd.

"Your English is very good," Barkley observed. "How long you been in the US of A?"

Harry blushed, receiving the highest compliment he could wish for, but rueful, again, that he had brought up a potentially dangerous subject. Why had he even mentioned citizenship? "I'm here a few years," he said haltingly. "First my father came, then me. I was just a kid then. But always I read English, I make it my business. Nothing is more important to me, nothing."

"So, your father's a citizen?" the aspiring three-term congressman inquired.

"Sure, I am," Izzy volunteered, "but his English, I can't say no, is better than mine."

But Barkley was more interested in voting pools than language skills. He addressed Harry: "What makes you think you're not a citizen? Wasn't your father naturalized by the time you came over?"

The crowd by now was listening intently, clearly admiring their congressman's talent for engaging and finding the personal story in even the most casual passerby.

Harry shrugged, "Well, sure, he was by then naturalized. How else you think they let me in?" The scrutiny and apparent interest of a public figure, a Washington, DC politician moreover, threw his English as well as his equilibrium off kilter. What had he been thinking, calling public attention to himself, announcing in front of a crowd that he was an immigrant? Now all these questions; questions were the last thing he wanted to elicit.

But then, Barkley's examination took an unexpected turn. "Well," the congressman buoyantly declared, "your father's a citizen, you're a citizen! Roosevelt doesn't have to wait for his second term, my boy, you can help him win his first." Barkley thumped Harry's back with his beefy hand. "You are twenty-one?" he asked, to which Harry, his head swimming with this new, astonishing information, managed to indicate that yes, he was. "So, you can vote right now, sir." Barkley thrust out his hand once more. "This very November. *Mazel tov!*"

And with that, Harry found himself the focus of enthusiastic applause and handshakes of congratulations. It would be hard to say whether he was more delighted at the news of his sudden citizenship or abashed by the hot summer-afternoon spotlight, as the robust congressman drew him close to explain. "You come over as the minor child of a citizen, you automatically derive citizenship. That's the law. You can look it up: May 1928, we passed the statute."

Could this really be true? He wasn't in trouble; he was a citizen of the United States! Harry stood there trying to take it in.

His shirt even more soaked with sweat than it had been earlier, he found the composure to speak. "Pop, I think we should move back to the Bronx so we can vote for this man. He just made me a citizen." Was he dreaming this? He thought he knew the rules, the regulations. But it was true, he didn't keep up with all the laws and congressional goings-on like he should. And in 1928, besides, he hadn't even been here to read the newspaper. Pop had waited five years to be naturalized as a citizen, so he always assumed that that's what he would have to do, what everyone did.

"Who you here visiting?" the congressman asked.

"My wife's sister and her husband," Izzy said.

"Their name?" Barkley inquired.

"Lazar. Jack and Malka."

"Give them my best," Barkley said with one more politic backslap before noticing a young couple that had just strolled over. "And tell them to vote in November." And then he was welcoming the new-comers, finding their story, their votes.

Up in Aunt Malka's apartment, welcoming with the homey aroma of the matzoh meal pancakes that Harry savored more than just about any other dish, and which, therefore, his aunt prepared for them each and every Sunday, Harry placed the cheesecake in the icebox as he and Izzy shared the unbelievable encounter they'd just had right downstairs on the street.

"That Barkley is something," Jack agreed, Izzy sitting down next to him at the kitchen table. Harry, too excited to sit, crossed his arms and stood in the kitchen doorway, still trying to digest what had just happened. Nipping at his euphoria over the incredible turn of events, was the private annoyance he felt with his ignorance: how could he, who took such pride in his conscientious study of current events and all things American, have been so uninformed when it came to his own citizenship? It was an odd sensation: learning that he was a citizen he felt less deserving of that status for not having known he deserved it.

"He's an Irishman, you know," Jack was saying, "but the way he's so good to us, he might as well be a Jew. I'm telling you, the man's a saint. Always helping people, whether it's finding someone a job, talking to a landlord about an eviction. Whatever comes up, he doesn't forget who put him there, in Washington."

Izzy nodded his head in agreement, the gesture, perhaps, bringing on a fit of coughing, dry insistent coughs, which Harry answered with a glass of water hurriedly poured from the tap. "You okay, Pop?" he asked.

"Fine, I'm fine," the older man said as everyone watched him. He sipped from the glass, and the coughing subsided.

"Here, I have cold in the icebox." Malka opened the door and handed Harry a pitcher of ice water. He refilled his father's glass.

Even with the reassuring and fragrant comfort of Malka's kitchen and the momentary distraction of his father's coughing spell, Harry's mind was busy: with statutes (were they the same as laws?); with the rules of citizenship (was Regina now a citizen? Yakob? Was his son now an automatic citizen? Should he send for them?); with how suddenly everything had changed. His plans, his timetable: everything was different now.

Yet here was Malka, standing at the stove in the same flowered housedress she wore every Sunday, patiently tending the frying pancakes.

"On a day like this," Harry said, "in this heat, you could have made something else. Something you wouldn't have to use the stove."

His aunt just waved her hand to dismiss the very idea. "What are you talking? I know how you love, so I make." Gently, she lifted a pancake from the pan and slipped it onto a brown paper bag to absorb the fat. "I don't like how he's coughing, your father. He shouldn't have gone out today. Jack, too, from that job they had in the cellar shoveling the coal, all those hours breathing in that filth. But, thank God, it's not so bad with him. Your father, though? That's another story."

"I tried to tell him," Harry said.

"I know, you're a good boy. A better son, I'm telling you . . ."

"Shah, already," Izzy piped in from the table. "I hear what you're talking. I'm fine, I feel fine. And look at it this way: you see what would have happened if I listened to him? We wouldn't have come today, met this congressman downstairs, so a greenhorn he'd still be. Believe me, a father knows best. So now, my Yankele, my Harry, a citizen they made him."

The truth of Izzy's words did not go unappreciated, and Malka announced they should everyone wash their hands, it was soon time to eat.

As the two older men pushed away from the table and walked toward the bathroom, Jack said, "You believe how hot it is in here? But she doesn't want to open up a window, who can blame her, with this heat?"

Harry took the opportunity, alone with his aunt in the kitchen, to take some bills from his slacks pocket. Without a word, Malka slipped the cash into her housedress pocket, and shrugged helplessly. "It embarrasses me, you know, every time. But we need. If Jack knew." She raised her eyebrows. "*Nu*, but we need. Eight dollars a month we get from the relief, who are they kidding? Who can get by on that?"

Harry kissed her forehead. "I'm doing well, and look how you helped Pop all those years. Please, not another word about being embarrassed."

"But you need it. I know you're saving to bring them over."

Harry knew she was referring to the rest of the family in Stawki, but this didn't prevent a pang of guilt as he thought about the objects of his other secret saving.

"Rifkale, your mama writes me," Malka said, setting the food and dishes on the table, the sour cream and drinks. "She's blossoming into quite a lady. So excited she is to be an American girl. Icko will take one look at her, believe me, he won't want to go back. We should all be here together. There's nothing to talk about."

Of course, Harry agreed with his aunt, but he'd given up trying to talk his father out of going back to Poland. To steer the conversation away from the frustrating topic, he, too, quickly hit on another one that he realized almost instantly was better left avoided. "And Lannie? You hear from him?"

Malka's kind and friendly face soured. "He's still drinking. He's out of work, so who's gonna hire a man smells like alcohol? I told him, come, stay here with us. Have you seen him? God knows where he sleeps. I'm telling you, Harryleh, when a mother's heart breaks . . ." She searched for words to name the unnamable, but only gazed outside at the cloud of alien soil. "You believe what's doing out there?" She forced herself to think of brighter things, an innate characteristic, and her face smoothed out again to its usual loveliness. "Who knows, maybe with Roosevelt, everything will be different. 'A new deal for the American people,' he said. Sounds good, no? Come, let's sit."

Harry looked at his aunt's pretty face and thought of his mother. He missed her. Sometimes, he wished he'd spent more time being a boy. But from the date of his father's departure for the United States, he always found himself in the role of person in charge. For a brief moment, when he had first left Poland, he had felt the total vulnerability of a child, and the truth was, he hadn't liked the feeling at all. Well, a person couldn't fight his nature, Harry decided. Maybe he was lucky even, to have been given shoulders sturdy enough to carry the responsibilities that always seemed to come his way. Maybe, owing to his makeup, he invited responsibility. Only now, trying to figure out how to get his Reizel and Yakob here, he wished he had the know-how to match the shoulders.

"God willing, they'll all come over soon," Malka was saying. "Hershel will open a bakery; Yitzak, who knows, maybe a lawyer he'll be, the way he loves to talk. And Rifka, Rifka will be a movie star."

Izzy's cough rattled from the next room as the brothers-in-law returned to the kitchen, and they all sat down for the Sunday meal.

Izzy lifted his glass of hot water and lemon: his preferred drink even on a day that sweltered. "*Nu, mein zun*, the American."

Cabs and sleek limousines lined the curb outside the recently opened Waldorf-Astoria, reputed to be the largest hotel in the world, and surely the most elegant. The swoosh and rustle of women's gowns nearly rivaled for aural eminence the ubiquitous honking horns blaring their importance and right of way. Yet, if one looked closely, a distinct feature of this particular night of arrivals included the repeated and subtle attempts of the well-turned-out women to brush from their shoulders and meticulously coiffed hairdos the particles of dust that had been swirling around the city all day and were now landing on them, tainting the yardage of white silk and gold lamé they'd so assiduously kept pristine for the occasion of arriving here.

Barbara had made her dress, buying reams of white crêpe de Chine and following a pattern that closely mirrored a gown cut on the bias that she'd seen Katharine Hepburn wearing in one of the ladies' magazines. She'd laughed off as silly her mother's earnest warning about wearing white to such an important event. Though Barbara maintained a light and open air of small-town innocence, especially in the eyes of New York neighbors and the occasional business associate Will brought home for dinner, she herself couldn't help but note the provincialism that marked those who had formerly comprised the parameters of her world: her friends and family back in Iowa City. She and Will had been back only twice—most recently in May, when his mother died—but each time she had been struck by a reluctant awareness that she didn't belong there anymore. The quick rhythms and easy familiarity of New York had, without her noticing, permeated her expectations. It was sadly true that she could claim no friends in her new home, nor, after three years, did she even really think of New York as home, yet the pace and attitude of city life had become part of her bones, the Iowan neighbors she'd known all her life giving off, through their broad smiles and proffered pies, an off-putting insistence on reserve. Maybe it was the endless horizon, the wide-open space itself that produced in Iowa's citizens their distance and cool remoteness. Oh, they were friendly to be sure, much friendlier than most of the people she'd met in New York, yet an invisible hand seemed to emanate from each of them, warding off anything that might be construed as intimacy. Barbara couldn't say when or how exactly she'd developed her affinity for real honest-to-goodness contact with people, even if that contact came out as a sort of rudeness, and probably wouldn't even have been able to identify it as something she appreciated until, back in Iowa, she discerned in its absence a valued quality missing.

Of course, his mother's death had come as a blow to Will. For months, he'd been on the phone with his father, reassuring him, reminding him of Ellie's sturdy backbone and resolve. The break-in had just slowed her down, was all, and probably, well, after years of hard work, maybe it required something like this to get her to take a rest. She'd be back on her feet in no time, Will predicted, week after week; Pop just needed to be patient, take good care of her. But then, one morning, she simply failed to get out of bed. Her presence there beside him when Nicholas awakened was all he needed to realize that a troubling situation had become a catastrophe; even on her most lethargic days, Ellie rose from bed before him, prepared the coffee, and pressed his apron. Hearing her comforting industry in the kitchen had been Nicholas's wake-up signal for the entirety of his adult life. Now, with her presence in their bed well after dawn, he didn't need to bolt to a sitting position or insistently shake her or say her name over and over (although he did all these things) to know that his Ellie, his partner, his love of loves, was beyond his reach.

The doctor would cite heart failure as the cause of death, and the neighbors point out that it was a blessing going like that, so peacefully in her sleep, but Nicholas was barely consolable, his naked anguish hardly the stuff of stiff-upper-lip Iowan fortitude.

It was only after he didn't know how many discussions at the kitchen table those days after Ellie's death that Will persuaded his father to keep the store open and go on with his life, as Mom surely would have wanted. In truth, his father's weeping through the funeral service and at the graveside discomfited Will, the public display yet another nail in the coffin of everything Nicholas had taught him. "Those thieves back in March stole more than grain and rice if you sell, Pop," Will exhorted repeatedly. "It'll look like they stole our backbone as a family. Is that what you want?" To which Nicholas would respond, "They took your mother, that's all I know."

The hours of back and forth, however, did eventually lead to Nicholas's acquiescence: he'd keep the store open and even accept Tom

Forbes's offer of help. Will would continue to send money, as he'd been doing for months, which would help out with Tom's salary, and then, it couldn't be long now, the economy would pick up and, with it, the daily exchange of cash for merchandise that had established Brown's Dry Goods as a reliable business in the early decades of the century and would, Will felt sure, return the store to its rightful and profitable status. "Everything as it should be, Pop, if we just hold on a little longer."

The way everyone was talking, it sometimes seemed to Will that the only other person in the country who felt as sure as he did that this Depression situation would blow over was the president himself, hardly known for being an optimist. And if you believed the newspapers, increasingly socialistic in Will's opinion, it looked like President Hoover was going to take quite a beating in November; this Roosevelt fellow, with his "New Deal for the American people" (which, Will could read between the lines, really just meant more handouts, more relief) this Roosevelt seemed to be gaining in popularity as Hoover's principles of individual effort and stick-to-itiveness came to be blamed for everything that was going wrong.

Here on Park Avenue, all that naysaying seemed worlds away. Will certainly wasn't going to think about his father tonight, or the store, or the American economy, or even the upcoming election that could quite possibly put a veritable Socialist into office. He and Barbara were being taken to dinner at the Waldorf-Astoria, and, he suspected, appraised for a possible promotion to Washington. Why, it was his man Hoover himself who had marked the reopening of this grand hotel back in October with what even his critics had hailed as a stirring radio address. Maybe Hoover would surprise everyone. Bigger surprises than a second term for Hoover had upset speculation before. Meanwhile, let everyone else air their doubts about the country and its recent stumbles; it would take more than a few hard times to shake Will's confidence in the basic capitalistic tenets that had founded this great land and brought him as an invited guest to the doorway of America's most lavish hall.

Barbara did look beautiful tonight, like one of those movie stars. The neckline of her dress dipped a bit low for Will's taste, but looking around, he had to admit to himself that her immodesty was shared by most of the female contingent. Wiping a smudge of ash from her shoulder, he suggested that she wear her wrap instead of carrying it on her arm. She thanked him for the advice, and, adjusting the navy-blue satin cape she'd purchased in compliance with her mother's counsel about the practicality of dark colors, she fluffed her once-again blonde hair, which she wore curly and shoulder-length as was the fashion. Will took her arm in his, and into the Art Deco palace they strode, the door held open for them by a man in full livery.

A man similarly attired offered to accompany them to the bank of elevators, one of which would take them to the eighteenth floor, and the storied Starlight Roof, "the jewel of décor and dining" as it was described in the magazines, and the spot where Joseph Connelly, Director of the DC Board of Review, had said to meet him and the others. Following the formal but friendly Guest Services man, Will and Barbara silently marveled at the opulence of the hotel lobby, with its giant crystal chandeliers and marble floor. Neither had ever seen, nor even imagined, such abundance; why, the enormous vase that led to the entrance of the lobby held more flowers than all the Iowan fields put together that they'd ever scrambled through as children. Barbara fluffed nervously at her hair, straightened her cape, and tried not to think about the one aspect of the evening that had above all others caused her forehead to dampen with anxiety: she had never been in an elevator. The eighteenth floor!

Taking several deep breaths to stay calm, she smiled graciously as their escort gestured toward the small mahogany enclosure that would beam them skyward. "Eighteen," he said to the elevator operator, and the doors whooshed closed on the Browns and several others dressed in their evening finery.

"Clever of you to wear your cape," a sophisticated matron wearing white winked at Barbara. "I can't abide what that farmers' dust has done to my gown." Barbara tried to eke an appreciative acknowledg-ment toward the woman, but there was no doubting the moisture she could feel accumulating on her brow, or the sickness gathering in her stomach. If she didn't grab hold of herself, breathe deeply as she'd promised herself she must, there'd be more than "farmers' dust" (what a derogatory phrase!) soiling her outfit. And, of course, she'd rather die than embarrass Will on this so important occasion.

But the tubular glide of the elevator proved too much for her. Breaking from Will as soon as the doors slid open, she was lucky enough to find and follow the restrooms sign and burst inside before the paltry contents of her stomach (she'd purposely fasted all day, allowing herself only the tiniest sip of brandy to steady her nerves) gushed from her mouth and onto the hemlines of both cape and gown. A bit even caught in her hair, which had fallen over her face as she'd bent forward. "Oh God, oh God," she kept saying through the hand that covered her mouth. "This is terrible, terrible. Oh God, what am I going to do?"

"Oh, I've seen worse, honey," came the deep tones of what sounded to Barbara like nothing less than a fairy godmother standing nearby. "We'll clean you right up, don't you worry."

A dark-skinned Negro woman dressed in black with white cap, apron, and cuffs gently but purposefully led Barbara to a chair more lushly upholstered than any she'd ever sat in, and somehow, miraculously, applying sweet-smelling fluids from various bottles, restored the young woman's clothing and her hair, washed her hands, even, and, as the finishing touch, instructed her to look in the mirror and freshen her lipstick. "See? You're better than new."

When Barbara emerged from the ladies' room, smelling every bit as sweet as when she'd dressed that evening, there was Will, talking pleasantly with the woman who had made the observation about her cape in the elevator, and the man to whom she was obviously married.

"There you are, my dear," the woman said, graciously pretending that there had been nothing unusual in Barbara's bolting from the elevator, and advising her to take off her cape, "the better to make an elegant entrance." Barbara could only conclude that one really did meet fairy godmothers in palaces, and that everything was beautiful and serene in such places, even in the face of the most unthinkably mortifying eventualities. She could feel herself glowing with relief.

Helping her with her cape, Will introduced Mr. and Mrs. Connelly, but was immediately interrupted. "Oh, we're Joe and Martha to you," Mrs. Connelly said. And smiling toward Barbara: "She's perfectly charming, Will. Yes, I think we're all going to get along splendidly." Thus anointed, the Browns followed the Connellys into the Starlight Roof. The famous Waldorf supper club was bathed in a golden light and twinkling with elegance. "You never know when you're going to make a silk purse out of a cow's ear," Barbara could hear her mother saying, as she had in all manner of situations while Barbara was growing up. Whenever the young girl cried over being too tall, or too thin, or too thick to figure out her arithmetic homework, her mother's reassurances always lifted her mood. "God throws hurdles in our path to see what we can make of them." Well, somehow or other, the necessity of running to the ladies' room had endeared her to Martha Connelly, and Barbara had to smile to herself. Mama was right: you never did know what a silk purse might be made of.

Of course, in the back of her mind, Barbara wondered whether it might be that tiny little sip of brandy (on an empty stomach) that had exacerbated her sickness in the elevator; but no, she wouldn't even allow that thought one more moment of her time.

Never in all his imaginings, as Will had anticipated and worried over this dinner, had he thought that it would be Review Board Director, Joseph Connelly himself, who would be introducing him to the other board members, but that's exactly what was happening. As Will shook hands with a Mr. Hannah and a Mr. Forsythe, a Mr. Pearson and Mr. Waverly, and smiled politely at their wives (each of whose garments or hair held a fragment of residue from the dust storm) and saw from the corner of his eye how radiant Barbara looked as she similarly greeted this important group of Washington immigration officials, he had a very good feeling about his prospects. And he had her to thank for the ease with which everything was going. It had been her inexplicable dash to the ladies' room, which, as it was happening, embarrassed him no end, that had actually engaged the Connellys, and moved them to approach him in the vestibule and try to abate his concern.

What nice people, Will had thought, until Mr. Connelly put out his hand and identified himself, causing Will's insides to shrink into a ball: this was Mr. Connelly, the very person he was here to impress?! Whatever had possessed Barbara to make such a spectacle of herself? Why did this have to happen in front of Mr. Connelly? But Will's alarm lasted only moments as the older couple eased his misgivings, graciously (miraculously, Will thought) finding the humor in the situation. "Well, Mr. Brown, may I call you Will? I'm sure this isn't how you pictured your arrival at the Waldorf, ay?" Mr. Connelly had said. "I instructed my secretary to time your arrival a bit after the others, to make sure the table was well set up and so on," he continued. "Shall I go in to see what's wrong?" his wife asked. "No, that would only embarrass her," she immediately corrected herself. And as they breezily talked about Will's duties at Ellis Island, Will trying to match their unexpectedly light conversational tone even as he strived to convey the seriousness with which he took his work, Barbara had reappeared and apparently discerned immediately that her unfortunate retreat to the restroom had enhanced rather than ruined the evening's purpose, winking at him ever so subtly as the introductions were made. Yes, Will had to hand it to his beautiful Barbara: she was the perfect helpmate, just like Mom.

"You know, of course, that we're reorganizing down in Washington," Connelly addressed Will now that they were seated and enjoying the famous Waldorf salad. He spoke over Barbara, seated in the honored position to his left. "We'll remain inside the Labor Department, but early next year, whoever becomes president, the idea is to consolidate the two bureaus: so instead of one for immigration and another for naturalization, well, we're going to be the Immigration and Naturalization Service: the INS. I've already been tapped as deputy commissioner," here, he winked at Barbara, "so it falls within my purview to appoint new members to the review board, which we're going to be expanding."

"Don't worry about a thing, dear," Martha Connelly assured Barbara from Will's left. "Oh, I know how difficult relocating can be, but we've lived in Washington since before the World War. I know everybody and I'll introduce you around."

Barbara blushed; the older woman, nice enough, talked as though Will had already been offered the job. "That would be wonderful," she said, trying not to sound hesitant on the one hand, or presumptuous on the other.

"Well, it looks as though my wife has already appointed you," Connelly laughed. "And I learned a long time ago not to rub her wrong. So: interested?"

"I'm more than interested, sir." Will was beside himself with excitement. "I can't think of a higher honor."

"Well, let's shake on it, then." And they did. "With those Roosevelts coming in, well, I want to surround myself with right-thinking Americans. I like your pedigree, I like your background. Nothing like a hardscrabble life in the Midwest to teach a man what matters in this world. President Hoover himself attests to that."

"Yes, we're very proud of him back in Iowa," Will agreed. He felt like he'd landed on a soft bed of sympathy and reason.

Barbara only picked at her salad.

"That Roosevelt's an elitist and a showboat, I'll tell you that much," Mr. Hannah or Mr. Forsythe put in, "don't you think, Will? Flying to the convention to accept the nomination. Only a man born to luxury would think of such a thing."

"I agree," Will said, "and that's why I'm not as sure as you are that he'll win the election. People have a nose for phonies."

"Oh, I'm afraid he's all too real," Martha Connelly said. "Before we know it, we'll be living in a Socialist state, the way he's talking about helping the needy. What the needy need is more gumption, don't you think, Barbara?" She didn't wait for a reply, assuming Barbara to be in full agreement. "And what we need is a stricter immigration policy, so that Americans can get the jobs."

"I'll drink to that," Will said. He raised his water glass, and they all clinked heartily, Mrs. Connelly displaying her gumption by predicting that pretty soon there'd be wine in those glasses, as the Twenty-first Amendment promised to be a thing of history within the year. "Even

President Hoover backs the repeal," she noted, thereby lending a moral imprimatur to her prediction.

"So, tell me Will, how long before you and Barbara can wrap up your affairs here in New York, make it down to DC permanently?" Mr. Connelly got down to cases. "Any chance you'll beat Roosevelt to it? Assuming he's elected, which, sorry, my boy, looks to be what we can expect, the inauguration won't be until March. Think we'll be able to count you in by then?"

"You bet, sir. I can't imagine anything that would hold us up. Right, Barb?" Will took her hand and squeezed it. He knew she looked beautiful and all, but beyond that, something about Barbara had absolutely captivated Mrs. Connelly, and he was grateful to her.

"You'll come down as soon as the weather cools off, Barbara, stay with us," Mrs. Connelly said. "We don't want you getting a taste of the heat, Washington gets ungodly hot and humid in the summertime, turn you off to the whole idea. But then in the fall, when the leaves are turning, why you can come down by train, I'll meet you at the station, and we'll look around together for just the right place. How does that sound?"

"You're being too kind," Barbara said. Everything was happening so quickly.

"Oh, not at all. I'm thrilled to help out," the older woman assured her. "And don't you worry about Will. He'll get by for a few days without you, won't you, Will?"

Bathing in the satisfaction of just having been offered a position he'd aspired to for a lifetime, sitting in the grandeur of this splendid gold-hued room, Will forced himself to flick away the momentary hesitation: *Get along without Barbara?*

Iowa City

Nicholas knew that Will meant well, and he was very proud of his son and all that he was accomplishing, but the new Dodge parked at the curb in front of the store only drew attention to him and the family's relative prosperity. Ellie's illness had garnered a certain amount of good will among their old friends and neighbors, some of the wives of men whom Nicholas suspected were involved in the break-in coming to sit by her and comfort her when she'd taken to her bed. With word of her death, a steady stream of neighbors came with casseroles, pies. Pete Smith and his brother, Lester, well, Nicholas hadn't seen them until the funeral, but their hangdog faces read like a confession. And sure enough, a little over a week later, back in May, they started coming into the store to pick up small amounts of flour, Nicholas extending them credit as though nothing had happened.

But that car, he might as well put up a sign saying he didn't need anyone's business. Will might be a good lawyer—this new job down in Washington came with an unheard of five-thousand-dollar-a-year salary; even the mayor of Iowa City didn't make that much!—but Nicholas sometimes wondered whether his son knew the first thing about people: what they might be feeling and how to adjust his actions in the light of that. When the truck stopped in front of the store a week ago, and the driver came in with papers asking for Nicholas's signature, he thought there must be a mistake. "Nope, no mistake," the driver had said, "this is the right address. You Nicholas Brown? It your birthday or something?" And even as he signed the receipt, Nicholas knew that all the reinstated good will in the world was about to ooze away, like the ink leaking from his pen and staining his fingers.

Sure, it was true he needed a better car; the old Ford had been giving him trouble for months. It barely started up when they'd set out for the cemetery to bury Ellie, which had irritated Will no end. "How you going to go visit her, Pop?" Will had said once Nicholas had succeeded in turning over the engine. "It makes no sense you chugging along in a car like this. With what I earn, I could at least help out with the down payment." Then Will got that new job offer, and his ability to "help out" exceeded even his own expectations. "I'm not down there yet, Pop, but it's as good as money in the bank," he said to explain his largesse when Nicholas called to thank him a few hours after the car had been delivered. And, of course, in spite of his discomfort with the whole business, Nicholas didn't have the heart to do anything but thank his son in the most gracious tones he could muster.

But a vehicle that must cost six hundred dollars if it cost a dime? Most of his farming customers didn't make that much in a year. Even two, these days. But it sat on the curb, nonetheless; what was he supposed to do with it? And Nicholas believed there must be some campaign, for every time he looked outside there was someone walking by and spitting on the sidewalk, right in front of him, in front of the store and that ostentatious automobile.

"Well, you could sell it," Tom Forbes recommended one morning as Nicholas stood looking out at the albatross Will had inadvertently hung around his shoulders. "It is a mighty awkward situation."

"I'll go out and talk to them," Nicholas decided. "Drive out to their homes and explain the situation. Talk to them, like friends."

Tom only blew a skeptical whistle. "I don't know," he muttered.

"Tomorrow morning, first thing, that's what I'm going to do," Nicholas said. "You'll keep an eye on things here?"

"Well," said Tom, "I guess you might as well drive the thing."

The following morning, Nicholas set out, and the car did drive like a dream. The engine started right up, the ride smooth as anything a man could want from a vehicle.

The day was going to be a hot one; even in this early morning Nicholas could feel the heat emanating off the pavement. But to show his respect, he had put on his Sunday suit, the one he'd worn to Ellie's funeral and to Will's wedding and to his Rotary Club inauguration, back in the days when the very people he was going to visit now were his friends. Once and for all, he had to make peace with them.

It was hard not to feel conspicuous in the gleaming vehicle as he drove past the breadline in front of the Red Cross storefront. Making his way out of town, he saw a family of six gathered in front of their run-down pickup, sitting on crates. Some wore shoes. Some not. FOR SALE signs seemed to come closer and closer together the farther he drove into the dry acreage that had once filled the eye with the gaudy show of crops. Every now and then, he'd pass a man pushing what must be the entirety of his worldly goods in a wheelbarrow, his wife and kids not far behind. Nicholas's shirt was soaked through, but he didn't stop to take off his suit jacket; he couldn't take the chance of coming face-to-face with one of the displaced, homeless farmers. The parched land stretched out in front of him, an endless vista of hopelessness. Tom was right: how could he pull into Mark Jenkins's place or the Smiths' in this car that rode smooth over their misery, dressed up like some showoff undertaker? Nah, it was a dumb idea.

But Nicholas didn't turn the car around. For some reason he couldn't explain, he just kept driving.

Will, of course, had a barrelful of theories for how the breadbasket of the world had become a wasteland. And he shared these views not only with his colleagues at Ellis Island, over lunch or waiting for the ferry, but also with his father. Basically, Will argued, the farmers had sown the seeds of their own destruction with their hostile plans and activities. And it was an embarrassment to end all, he said, that the most virulent group of so-called protestors had organized a national convention right in Iowa. They called themselves the Farmers' Holiday Association, and they meant to do nothing but cause trouble. This misguided group of "revolutionists" was led by some minister or other named Milo Reno, a fact that made Will recoil. Was it possible that this radical troublemaker, like those furriers in New York, was of Greek heritage? Just another reason to file his ethnicity under ancient history, a private play on words through which Will could occasionally find amusement.

"Stay at Home—Buy Nothing—Sell Nothing," that was what the Farmers' Holiday group advocated, a sure formula for failure if Will ever heard one. How could farmers, men whose very livelihood depended on selling, come up with such an ill-begotten strategy? And then they blamed the banks and the government for the foreclosures dotting the landscape? Oh, they had a clever scheme for getting around the foreclosures, Will had to hand it to them, but it only worked at a few dozen places, not nearly enough to save the vast majority of wiped-out properties.

These so-called "penny auctions" depended on word-of-mouth when a neighbor's land had been foreclosed and was up for auction. A few beefy-looking men (fewer and further between as the farmers' ill-conceived tactics yielded less and less to eat and thus fewer imposing physiques) would show up and start the bidding, for a piece of machinery, say, way down at ten cents, the next fellow upping it by maybe a nickel. If someone dared to put in a serious bid, he'd quickly be "reminded" by one of the thickset unionists on the scene that that was a little high. Will had heard that more than one farm managed to stay afloat on the six or ten dollars handed over to the bank at the end of the auction, but what good was a plow or even a few chickens that a farmer might manage to hold on to if he went along with the idiotic revolutionist idea of refusing to sell his goods? As for the hand the drought played in the farmers' situation, well, were they going to blame the banks for the weather, too?

Will had it all figured out, Nicholas ruminated, but the desperate men banding together to somehow create a united front against their wretched circumstances were no more "revolutionists" than Will himself. These were Iowans, and Texans, Oklahomans and Kansans, conservative Americans, whose hunger had turned to anger as hard and dry as the land that refused cultivation, the land Nicholas found himself aimlessly driving through in his brand-new smooth-as-silk automobile on this hot and desolate day.

The Farmers' Holiday Association, blinded by dust and poverty, wasn't selective in its choice of victims, for misery is wanton in its quest for company. One family whose future would be altered by the farmers' promiscuous wrath had once changed its surname to Brown.

As Nicholas continued his smooth, sweat-soaked and thought-filled drive along the parched roads of rural Iowa, he was shaken from his listless musings by an inexplicable jostle. The car rattled and swerved, and then the whish of escaping air.

He turned the steering wheel furiously, hard to the right, the left, only to feel another tire blow underneath him, and then another.

He lost power to control the car, the wheel a circle of straining tonnage in his hands. Finally, the vehicle thumped forward a few feet, and then came to a lifeless halt.

Will didn't hear about this particular Farmers' Holiday Association tactic until days after his father's maiden drive in the brand-new Dodge ended on a deserted road with its tires slashed by spikes. The idea, he learned with disgust, was to put a stop to commerce. "No Way In and No Way Out" was reputed to be the group's slogan, as these proud Americans-turned-protestors hammered sharply pointed pieces of metal into logs and telegraph poles, installed them on roadways, and thus succeeded in halting the travel of their intended targets, milk trucks. Collecting what they could from the stymied vehicles in buckets to feed their children, they simply got rid of the rest. Sure, these men were aware that blockading the highways was illegal, but so, too, they would defiantly assert to the authorities, had been a certain tea party in Boston.

Sitting in his useless vehicle, Nicholas finally removed his suit jacket. It wasn't until deep into the night that Tom Forbes found him slumped behind the wheel, staring out into the endless starlit horizon.

Another family into whose future the tentacles of Midwestern wrath would extend had, for as long as it could remember, called itself Himelbaum.

Warsaw, Poland

It's like a different world, Yitzak thought as he dodged honking cars and pedestrians hurrying to their destinations. He, too, was in a hurry, as he always was, to get to his Ava. For nearly four years now she had been his sweetheart, but each time, approaching her apartment on Styrska Street, he could feel his pulse quickening and a smile spreading across his face. Ava, her name translated to laughter and gaiety, so different from his wife and the world at home. *Like two different worlds,* he thought again.

There are Jews here, he considered, so it's not that. Plenty of Jews, maybe almost half the population of Warsaw, so, no, that wasn't the explanation. But here, the sun shone, people moved with vitality and purpose. Children played in the courtyards with gusto and shrieks of joy. Not like his Moishele, pinned to his mother's apron, terrified, it seemed, of the very air if she wasn't breathing it alongside him. Yitzak tried to engage the boy in play, but it never amounted to more than a few moments, his son reacting to him like a stranger, worse than that, a stranger who meant him harm. And Chava was hardly friendlier to his attempts at intimacy. Sex with her felt like a medical procedure, a necessary evil to perpetuate the race. And that, they seemed to be doing.

The girl, Sarah, at first he had hoped that maybe things would change when she came along. A roly-poly little angel. Of course, at first, even her birth itself had thrown Moishe into hysteria. For hours, while she was in labor, he had to be separated from his mother, an intolerable situation for the boy. In this instance, even Chava agreed he couldn't be in the room with her. What an agony.

Allowed into the room after the hours of separation, Moishe stared with horror at the sight of his mother cradling another child. And Chava herself, propped up on the pillow as he entered, seemed to withdraw from the girl, as though feeding her, even loving her, was somehow a betrayal of her son. "Come, *tateleh*," she said weakly to the boy, "see the sister I give you." The whole family, surrounding Chava's bedside, cooing over the baby, had refocused its attention to await Moishe's response. "For me, Mama?" The boy wiped his tearstained face. "Sure, for you," Chava said, and with that Moishe slowly approached his new sibling, from that moment joining his mother in the nurturing of their shared project.

Yitzak had to admit that Chava had acted wisely in handling the potentially volatile situation, but the triumvirate that had been established between her and the children, calming the fears of the boy, assuring loving attention for the girl, had served as surely to leave Yitzak outside the circle they created. For a few passing moments, gazing at his daughter as she breathed her first breaths on earth, he had thought that maybe, perhaps, a new life could start for his family, too. He had once been in love with Chava, after all, her slender form and quiet ways enticing him as a young man. But her quiet had turned to silence, pinched and unyielding, to the point where it was hard to say whether it was her intransigence that had led him to his infatuation with another, or vice versa.

Watching the children play tag in front of Ava's apartment house, Yitzak observed again that yes, here in Warsaw it was the twentieth century, a different world. Jews and gentiles, everyone together.

Ava worked as a clerk at a local school. Now, during the summer months, she could see him more often, only needing to be at her desk a few hours a day. They had met as a result of a business scheme Yitzak had persuaded Yankel would be worth at least a try, and his younger brother had agreed. Why not approach the schools in the large cities, offer their dairy products at a cut rate? It was that simple and although he failed to sell the discounted milk to any of the administrators with whom he met, the warm dimpled smile of the receptionist at the third school he'd gone to for an appointment changed his life. The young man certainly hadn't gone to Warsaw with the idea of finding a lover, despite his fallow circumstances at home, but the easy banter, and the openness of those blue eyes had charmed him immediately. Bewitched him, actually, and Ava Szumanski seemed from the first to be equally ensnared. "I can't predict how this milk idea will impress my employer," she said, "but I myself make a beautiful cup of tea," and she'd handed him her name and address on a small, white piece of paper. Climbing the stairs to her doorway, these four years after that first encounter, he could already smell her perfume.

They never talked until afterward. Even that first afternoon of the proffered tea, the insistence of their attraction preempted all other relations. They were drawn to each other without reason or explanation, not wildly so much as naturally, softly, inevitably. And then, in bed, naked, words spilled from them just as easily.

Mostly, they talked about politics: the Polish situation both internally and externally, with the Socialists, the Zionists, the Bundists and Bolsheviks; the Russians and the Germans, the Depression in the United States and how it had rippled into Germany. Ava was particularly worried about the Reichstag, and the recent electoral success of the Nazi party. They talked about everything in the world that had any significance, it seemed to Yitzak, except the one subject Ava refused to address: his life in Stawki. His wife, his children, his attempted promises of a divorce, none of this would she listen to or entertain. Here in her bed, there was room for everything, the entire world with its conflicts, but not his family, the single entity, in Ava's eyes, that tainted the purity of their devotion. Yitzak, of course, did his best to comply, to respect Ava's edict that by its very nature demanded a relationship that exacted no demands.

The two lay entwined on her bed trying to catch a draft from the open window. "They are going to be reducing the quota of Jewish students for the fall term," Ava said, her fingers gently twirling several hairs on Yitzak's chest, where her head rested. She herself was not Jewish.

"Quotas," Yitzak said lazily, stroking his lover's shoulder, "can you believe there is no Yiddish word for it? We live and die with quotas, and yet. So, they're increasing, they're decreasing, who can keep track?"

"You think you have a friend in the government, but you lie to yourself. Is there a word for self-deception among the Jews?" The two spoke in Polish, and Ava certainly meant no harm by her question; she worried that a storm was gathering in Europe and that the Jews would be the brunt. "Every day when I walk to and from work, I hear someone yelling to a Jewish passerby, 'Go to Palestine.' Even today I heard the nasty words coming from a child."

"Words," Yitzak dismissed her concern. "You think after all we've suffered, we're worried about words? They wash off us like so much dust. The world seems to need a common enemy and so, maybe that's us. We call ourselves the 'chosen people,' maybe this is for what we were chosen."

"You think that's funny?" Ava asked. "Okay, if it helps you to ignore the situation, go ahead."

"Look at me," Yitzak said. "Come on," he tussled her hair, "turn around and look at me."

Ava lifted her head and turned to him.

"You say it is me who is ignoring a situation?" he asked.

Her kind blue eyes glazed over with the nuisance of his question.

"If they didn't need me on the farm, I'd never go back," Yitzak pressed on. "You are my Palestine."

And again his Ava's eyes transformed, this time into a lake of softest blue. With his fingertips, he patted away her tears, and slowly placed them on his tongue. "We are the same," he said.

Stawki, Poland

Chava by now had grown used to Yitzak's absences, even welcomed them. She and the children lived inside a little world that felt safe to her. Let his whore satisfy his needs, the *shiksa*. What, did he think she didn't know? She had found the piece of paper years ago, stinking of perfume in his shirt pocket. A business contact, he had told her, and she went along with the pretense; even Yitzak wouldn't abandon her for a gentile. Szumanski, this was not a Jewish name. But a blind eye is not closed. When he was home, she would sometimes have relations with him, more to make a sibling for her Moishe than anything else. His touch made her wince. That was some cruel joke God had played, devising such a way for people to have children. A test, it must be, to see how badly they wanted to reproduce themselves.

She sat off by herself in front of the house mending socks while Moishe solemnly watched the baby sleeping under the cottonwood tree.

They were all the same, the brothers. Well, Hershel maybe wasn't so bad, at least the way he treated his wife. But the way he worshipped that other one, the American (she cut the thread with her teeth), just like the rest of them. He was gone and never coming back, what did he need a wife for? A wife no one was to know about. It ate at Chava, the way the family talked about Yankel with so much respect. A letter came from him, it was like a national holiday. Not even the father knew, from what she could tell from Icko's letters. He, maybe, was the smart one, wanting to come home. But even him, how smart could he be, not even realizing his precious "Harry" was a married man. Well, she'd make of her Moishele a *mensch*, he wouldn't be like the rest of them.

"Mama, she's sweating," Moishe called.

"Shah, Moishele, you'll wake her up," Chava said in a projected whisper so that her son could hear. "Come, give your Mama a hug."

Moishe raced to her. "But she's hot," he said, snuggling to her bosom.

"Well, she's asleep, right?" The boy nodded. "So, she doesn't know she's hot." He smiled to show that what his mother said made sense. "There," Chava concluded, "finished the business."

New York City

In the weeks since the Waldorf dinner—the crowning moment of his professional life, as far as Will was concerned—things were going sour at home. Sure, the city was in the grip of a terrible heat wave, which didn't help anybody's mood, but Will knew better than to attribute Barbara's uncharacteristic orneriness to the weather. She was an Iowan, used to dramatic climate changes. Will had known her practically their whole lives and never had he seen her like this.

If the phone rang and Will was home, she'd throw down what she was doing and instruct him to tell the caller she wasn't there. The problem, of course, was the frequent phone calls coming from Martha Connelly. She seemed to have found in Barbara a baby bird to take under her wing, and Will had to admit the constant phone calls must get irritating. But the woman was just trying to be nice, befriend a young couple moving to the nation's capital, where they didn't know anyone. Every day, to hear Barbara tell it, sometimes several times a day, Martha called with a new apartment she'd heard about or seen advertised in the newspaper. Should she "swing by" and take a look at it? She heard the view of the Capitol building was "unparalleled." And Barbara was "not to worry about a thing," everyone was "just dying to meet her." Reporting their conversations to Will, Barbara mimicked Mrs. Connelly's phrases with open scorn.

The move was still months away, Barbara pointed out, genially, at first, to her self-appointed patroness (and she did remain grateful to the woman for her kindness that night at the Waldorf). But as the calls multiplied, she found it increasingly difficult to keep the curtness from her voice, because the truth was that things were happening very quickly, too quickly, and the woman's friendliness had come to feel much more like badgering, imbuing the move to Washington with not less, but more cause for anxiety.

As a young bride, Barbara had accepted the idea that marrying Will meant leaving home, and in the ensuing years she'd done every possible thing she could to support him in his endeavors: that's what a wife did, after all. She never complained about not having friends here in New York, for example, never. She just made the best of things. But not having any friends to talk to was beginning to look preferable to having someone foist herself on her, as though she didn't need time to adjust to moving, as though she were no more than a weightless twig following where the ocean took her.

All this Barbara explained to Will, and he tried to understand. It got her goat when he chuckled condescendingly at the twig analogy, and even then he was sympathetic, coming around to apologize for not taking her seriously. But really, since when did a woman not jump for joy when her husband got a promotion? Wasn't this what they'd been working toward ever since they'd left Iowa? That's what married couples did, looked out for each other, helped each other. Look at his own mother, rest her soul. The conversation usually stopped at this point, though, neither of them having the heart to articulate the glaring truth that Ellie Brown's untimely death hardly recommended a lifetime of unquestioning wifely support. Will's mother, like all the women back home, had been a model helpmate, asking nothing for herself but the continued opportunity to be of service to her husband. She kept his books, raised his son, adopted his philosophies, cleaned his house, cooked his meals, ironed his aprons, and then one morning, when the outside world burst in to overturn the day-in-and-day-outedness of her existence, she just stopped. And Nicholas, ever since, well, he wasn't the same man.

None of this stood as a glowing illustration of the virtues of selfless womanhood, so calling up Ellie as an example was usually where the conversation ended. Either then, or when the phone rang.

On this particular Saturday night, the last in August, Will was home to answer it.

"Yes, Martha, just a couple of weeks now, right after Labor Day. She's looking forward to it," Will said into the phone. "I can't tell you how much we appreciate all you're doing. My best to Joe."

When Will hung up, he went over to Barbara, who was standing by the window, fanning herself with a magazine. Outside, the usual assortment of tourists and ne'er-do-wells milled around, their numbers during the summer months cramping the streets so that a person could hardly walk without brushing against the sweaty body of another.

"I know they say it's humid and hot in DC," Will said, putting his arms around Barbara's waist, "but at least we won't have this to contend with."

"Did she find something 'just absolutely perfect'?" Barbara asked sarcastically.

"She's still talking about Georgetown as 'the' place," Will said, hoping his mildly sardonic tone would mollify his wife, put them in the same camp.

"I'm going to miss it," Barbara said.

"What?"

"The neighborhood. The people."

"Oh, please." Will withdrew, went into the kitchen to pour himself a glass of water from the tap.

"I know it's your life's work to keep America pure," Barbara said, venturing into territory on which she'd never before trespassed.

Will smashed down the glass, nearly breaking it on the counter. "What the hell's that supposed to mean?"

"Nothing." Barbara knew she had gone too far, and retreated.

"You think what I do is wrong?" Will wouldn't let it go. He strode up to her by the window. "You think it's okay to have all those people unemployed, waiting in lines to get fed, nearly a third of the country, while people who don't belong here, who lie and cheat to get in, take the jobs for a fraction of the pay?"

"No, of course not," Barbara demurred.

"Well, that's my life's work, Barbara."

She fingered her temples, escaped his closeness by walking over to the easy chair, folding into it. "I know, Will. I'm sorry."

Things had been so much simpler, so much more tolerable, before she'd finished the contents of the bottle under the sink. She'd made it last as long as she could. That morning after the Waldorf, though, while Will had been showering, she'd mixed what was left with some water, and that was it. She wondered if these headaches were a symptom of withdrawal. She wondered whether she'd ever work up the nerve to walk into one of those bars and order a drink. When *would* the law be repealed? It would make things so much easier. Surely, she'd feel less guilty, the day she could walk into a bar or a proper liquor store and purchase something. She'd just say it was a wedding present. Like Suze must have done.

"I'm going out for a walk," Will said. Barbara had no response. "Want to come? Buy a soda or something at the candy store?"

"Sure, Will," she said. "And I really am sorry about what I said. I know that what you do is best for the country. Important work."

The stagnant humidity of the evening seemed to lean against the wrought-iron door as the young couple pushed out into the city. People dressed in rags, people who certainly didn't live here, dirty and unkempt, blocked their path down the stairs of the brownstone stoop, and they gingerly stepped around them.

"Amelia Earhart flies transcontinental," a newsboy's piercing tenor cut through the thick heat. "First woman pilot flies coast to coast in nineteen hours, five minutes."

Inching their way through the crowds toward the soda shop, or candy store as they called it here in New York, Will and Barbara held hands. "I really will try to be more patient about Martha Connelly," Barbara said. "I know she means well."

Will pulled her to him and kissed her on the cheek. "That's my girl. Hey, want to share an ice-cream soda?"

"Mm, that sounds good," Barbara said. "But I'm not sure I want to share one."

Will squeezed her hand, winked at her. And just at that moment, Barbara caught sight of a familiar face among the crowds, a man moving with a throng of people getting out of the subway station. "Oh, look, Will. There's that nice Jewish man I used to buy the apples from," she said. She didn't call out to him, though; in fact, she'd forgotten his name. He carried a newspaper under his arm.

"Whatever happened to those apples?" Will asked. "They were good."

"Oh, I just got tired of apples," Barbara said. "They're never very good in the summertime." The truth was, once her blonde hair started to grow in, she'd been embarrassed to face the apple vendor. He'd always admired her red hair so much, maybe she was afraid she'd hurt his feelings, telling him that her husband didn't like it. She knew that was awfully foolish but, well, for some reason she couldn't really put her finger on, it had been months since she'd stood in that line in the mornings. What a friendly person he was, and he was looking very well, kind of handsome, in fact.

"You know, I heard a good one on the island," Will said. "A lot of people are calling Roosevelt's plan the 'Jew deal.' You know, because he seems to have them in his pocket, talking about all the relief he's going to give out, and all."

Barbara smiled wanly. It wasn't very funny, Will's "good one." Outright prejudiced if you asked her. But they'd argued enough for one evening, and her headache had finally eased up.

Even though it was an unusually hot evening, Will and Barbara readily found a seat at the candy store counter; not that many people had the money to treat themselves to an ice cream. A fan whirred ineffectually overhead. "Vanilla?" Will asked. And Barbara smiled that'd be fine.

By the time they'd finished and come out onto the street to walk home, darkness had fallen. Still, the heat hung heavy, and the crowds slowly threaded their way. Especially at night, one had to walk carefully, never knowing when someone might be set down right in the middle of the sidewalk. Sometimes, two people might be huddled together there. It seemed that these impoverished souls had long been part of the landscape, but that didn't make it any easier to get used to.

"I'm glad it's the weekend," Will said. "I've got all kinds of paperwork to catch up on."

"Mm," Barbara said. She'd been hoping they might be able to take in a movie, but Will's work, well, that always came first. "Isn't it exciting about that lady pilot, Will?" she asked.

"Sure is," he agreed. "But now, don't you go getting any ideas."

She tapped him playfully. "What are you talking about, William Matthew Brown? Me fly an airplane?" She giggled in that way he loved.

"Oh, you know I'm just teasing." He was so glad to have Barbara acting like her old self. Walking on the street together like this, her arm in his, well, even with the inconvenience of the masses of people, he felt like a lucky man. "It just sometimes makes me nervous, that's all, when you start talking about needing time to adjust and all that. Like you weren't proud of me. Oh, I don't know. Forget it. I'm just, oh, never mind."

The way Will was tripping over his words made Barbara, too, feel the pull of old times, when he'd come to pick her up for a date, all nervous and jittery. Here he was, about to be an important man in Washington, DC, behaving like the boy she remembered back home. It was endearing. Whatever else a person might say about Will, he did love her.

"Ready to make the climb?" he asked as they approached their brownstone. Thick clusters of silhouetted heads suggested that the number of people camped out on their front steps had grown.

You'd think they'd be ashamed, Will thought as he took Barbara's hand and guided her around the accumulated thighs and peeling shoes. Of course, he kept his gaze averted; the last thing a person would want to do is meet their eyes. Someone tugged on his trousers, and he pulled away. The gall!

"You okay, Barbara?" He turned back toward his wife, still holding on to her hand.

But she was standing there, openmouthed. Staring at one of the people on the steps. When Will pulled her hand to keep going, she pulled back, so forcefully that he nearly lost his balance. What was she looking at? What was she doing, standing there like that? Was this another one of her acquaintances, like that Hebrew apple salesman? What was she doing?

"Will," she said softly.

She didn't need to say anything else, for the man who had pinned her to the spot where she stood turned to face him. It was his father, Nicholas Brown, dressed in his Sunday suit, all rumpled and damp.

"Pop!" Will exclaimed. "What in heaven's name? When did you get here? What are you doing here?" He quickly grabbed his father's elbow to extricate him from the huddled, faceless mass, and lifted him up. "Come on, let's go upstairs. Come on, Barbara."

In his hand, Nicholas clutched a worn piece of paper with Will's address printed on it. "There's nothing left for me in Iowa," he said, "I can't go back." He talked all the way up to the second-floor apartment and continued talking as Will fished for his keys and opened the door. "It was a very nice idea, son, the car, very thoughtful. But things are different from what you remember. And the store, well, now, I just can't go back." He told him about the incident on the road, and how he didn't know what else to do but come here, but mostly he went on and on about the store, and how he couldn't go back there.

"You heard me. I want you should work for me here at the store. You'll start at twenty dollars, maybe more in the summer. We'll see, if business is good." Ralph Weiss stood with his hands in the pockets of his white apron, waiting for an answer. He had work to do, customers. He didn't have all day, standing out here on the sidewalk.

Harry knew the man to say hello, they'd been crossing paths for years. Back when Harry had first arrived in the country, they'd met in the line waiting for apple crates, amicably agreeing to set up respective corners five blocks apart on St. Nicholas Avenue and, slowly but surely, the older man's corner had grown to a very steady business, the competition one of the reasons Harry had decided to travel downtown while his father remained on 186th. Harry didn't begrudge Ralph's success, turning his fruit stand into a small fruit and vegetable market in a storefront he'd rented right here on the same corner of 181st. He accepted that Ralph had been here longer and was more Americanized than he and Izzy put together. So now Ralph was offering him a job. He had just gone outside to take a walk on a warm Saturday afternoon, and suddenly the world was turning upside down, a job he was being offered.

It would mean the end of Himelbaum and Son, the pride of trying to set up his own business, but would he mind working closer to home, being free of the daily trips downtown, loading and *schlepping* the kiosk? Working for Ralph, he'd clear just about the same amount of money. And with his father planning to go back to Poland, it added up. Maybe he'd learn something from Ralph.

"I make now twenty a week," he said. No harm in seeing if he could get a little more money.

"Yeah, and you spend on the subway and give inventory away. I know how it works with the stand on the street. I can't go higher than twenty. Take it or leave it."

Harry narrowed his eyes and considered a moment longer. Finally, he put out his hand, and the two men shook on the deal. "*Zein gezunt*, you'll start Monday morning, five sharp," Ralph said. He patted Harry's shoulder and walked back inside the store. Harry stood looking at the place for a few minutes, the black-and-white-tile floor covered with sawdust, the scales suspended over the neatly arranged produce. *Nu*, in the wintertime, he thought, it wouldn't be so bad having a roof over his head. Since he'd arrived in the country, he'd never worked indoors.

"Sure, he's a very nice man," Izzy said when Harry told him the news. He sat at his usual place at the kitchen table.

"I'll have to run downtown, sell the kiosk, and also the one up here. Between the two of them, we should make a little bit of money."

"Good, because I have to buy my ticket."

"What about Rifkale? You said you wouldn't go back until she got here." Harry knew that he was just trying to put off what had already been decided. Mama, everyone back home, was looking forward to Izzy's return. As for Rifka, she had already written to say that her bags were packed. Yitzak had gone with her to Warsaw to get the visa. All she needed was the ticket for passage.

"That was before the congressman made you a citizen," Izzy managed a chuckle. He still couldn't get over it, that until the encounter with that congressman a few weeks back, his English-newspaper-reading son hadn't known that by virtue of his citizenship, the boy, too, was naturalized. That's how he thought of his Yankel: as a boy. Harry understood this, and treasured it, that here sat the one person on earth who felt protective toward him, who glowed with the pride of a grown-up regarding his child whenever he accomplished something, however inconsequential, and whose withdrawal from his life would mean the final relinquishing of that cherished status: someone's child. "So, you don't need me," Izzy was saying, "you can meet her at the port."

Harry sat down. "You're talking like this is happening very soon."

"Why not? What is there to wait? I sit here like a lox, I'm costing you money, you think I don't know? I'll buy my ticket, finished the business. Believe me, hard they make it to come into America, not so hard when we want to leave," Izzy said.

The prospect of being here without his father saddened Harry. But there was no disputing that Izzy had aged beyond his fifty-three years; he looked and moved like a much older man, too fragile to put in a day's work. His lack of employment coupled with his adamant refusal to collect relief, well, Harry couldn't argue with him: he was depleting rather than contributing to their finances. He hated calculating his father like an item on a balance sheet, but an ongoing fact in Harry's life was that he had to be calculating: he, too, was a father, and the additional savings would hasten the day that he could at long last meet his own son.

"Okay, later I'll go downtown, see what I can get," Harry said.

"So you'll be working on the *Shabbes*?" Izzy asked. "Ralph, I see he's a real American, keeps the store open Saturdays, closed on Sundays. They might as well make from us Christians. Look at you, you made a business arrangement on the *Shabbes* with him. I don't blame you, it's just how it is here."

"I don't know, Papa," Harry said. The truth was, the question of whether he'd have to work on Saturdays hadn't even entered his mind while he and Ralph were talking. He couldn't attribute the lapse to having been taken by surprise by Ralph's offer; working on the *Shabbes* simply wasn't something Harry worried about. Sure, he didn't work on Saturdays now, but that was only because it was understood between father and son that that wouldn't happen. *Nu*, his father was probably right, he probably would be expected to work on Saturdays. Maybe this was another advantage of Izzy going home: they would both be spared their competing ideas on the subject.

Harry was eager to get downtown to see what he could make on the kiosks, but he decided to wait until after sundown to get on the subway. Traveling on *Shabbes* was just as bad in his father's eyes as working on the so-called day of rest, so why upset him?

He didn't know what the Torah had to say about making telephone calls on the Sabbath. Obviously, there were no telephones thousands of years ago when the rules had been written, but neither were there subways or automobiles, now understood as forbidden on Saturdays, so the logic of the religious edicts had long since escaped him. But to be on the safe side, so as not to aggravate his father, he went downstairs to the phone booth in front of the house to make some necessary arrangements. Tomorrow, like every Sunday, he and Izzy would be visiting Jack and Malka in the Bronx, and with work starting Monday—five o'clock sharp, Ralph had said—Harry hoped he could settle a few things while he still had the time and freedom to do so.

Frank Accompare, the guard who dispensed the kiosks at the warehouse on Mercer Street, said on the phone that he'd wait there for him as long as it didn't get too late. He had a "hot date" that night, the gruff but amiable Italian said in his gravelly voice, so Harry had best not keep him waiting.

As he traveled downtown that night, the train inexplicably stalled at Fifty-ninth Street, Harry thought about all the changes that were gathering in his life, and the pressing change he must set in motion. With his citizenship, he had unequivocally ascertained, his son, too, was a citizen of the United States. It was his duty as a father to send for them, Regina and Yakob, to do everything in his power to reunite his family as soon as possible. Yet, when he was being completely honest with himself, he acknowledged the part of his mind in which the prospect terrified him. Would the government catch on to his lie? What procedures should he follow? What papers would he need to sign? Lurking as well, haunting him, was that other, heart-wrenching fear: Would he love her? Would he be able to locate inside the unquestioned responsibility he felt toward her the tender feelings that had prompted it?

For goodness' sakes, why didn't the train move, already?

To get his mind away from his impatience and his disquieting thoughts, Harry opened the newspaper he'd found on a nearby seat. It seemed a woman pilot had crossed the entire country (With everyone starving, who could afford an airplane? Harry shook his head) and some kind of antiwar congress was convening in Amsterdam (He didn't know this word, *convening*, but anything against war must be good; hopefully, the word meant meeting, not breaking up). He couldn't stay focused on the stories though. It was nearly dark outside, and Frank wouldn't wait around for him, not with that "hot date" of his.

Finally, the train squealed into West Fourth. Harry tucked the paper under his arm and ascended the stairs slowly, locked inside the crowd climbing with him. Reaching the sidewalk, he surveyed the street, trying to figure the quickest path through all these people to the warehouse. That's when he saw Mrs. Brown, no mistaking her, so tall and stately and, look at that, she had become a blonde.

He wondered if he should make his way over, say hello, ask why she hadn't been coming to the fruit stand. For her, he'd make Accompare wait a few minutes. But then, he quickly looked away. Mrs. Brown wasn't by herself. She was laughing and talking and holding hands with a man—Mr. Brown, it must be. Oh, she shouldn't see him.

Harry took what little solace he could as he kept his head bent toward his chest: plain as day he'd seen it, her husband was shorter than her, by at least a few inches.

Imagine running into her. Better yet, that he actually hadn't. Just seeing her from a distance stirred feelings that were forbidden to him. It was just a crush he had on her, like a schoolboy, that's all. He swatted away the attraction as adamantly as he had his doubts about Reizel.

"That's my best offer," Frank said a little while later. He looked almost unrecognizable in his tie and button-down, short-sleeved shirt, but his manner was the same, as he and Harry stood just inside the sweltering warehouse. "Remember, I gotta rip down the sign, put up another one. The wear and tear, what am I haggling? Twenty dollars, that's the best I can do. The other twenty when you return the other cart."

Harry had paid seventy-five dollars for the two kiosks, an additional ten just for the signage. The businessman in him balked at the loss he was being asked to take. But for the second time that day, actually the third, if he counted Mrs. Brown, he accepted what was on the table. Sure, he could probably get more for the kiosks, just as he could have held out for a better salary from Ralph, but Frank was in a hurry, and Harry, too, had somewhere to be.

Allowing himself a moment of regret as he looked at the Himelbaum and Son sign on which he had hitched the dream of establishing a concrete place in America for himself and his father, he accepted Accompare's two ten-dollar bills, put them in his pocket, and headed to the east side.

On the phone that afternoon, he'd asked Reva Lansky if she could possibly meet him at eight o'clock on the usual corner on Avenue C, and she'd said okay. He said that when he saw her he'd explain why he was asking her to meet him on a Saturday. But meanwhile, it was so nice of her to come out on a Saturday night, maybe he could buy her a cup of coffee? "What else I have to do?" Reva had said, but sure, she'd agreed, there was a coffee shop they could go to, not far from their meeting place. "Two letters for you I got," she told him.

Once he and Reva had walked over to the coffee shop, settled in a booth, and placed their order, she handed him the envelopes from Lukow.

Here we are, standing in front of the store. You see what a beautiful child you have? Your loving Regina. The words were printed on the back of a small black-and-white photograph. His son, his Yakob, looked like a regular mischief-maker, sticking out his tummy and patting it, standing next to his mama on the cobblestone street. Regina gazed into the camera as if asking the very question she posed on the back of the picture, as if asking a million questions Harry was not yet able to answer: When will we see you? How much longer? The woman and little boy wore ankle socks and sandals; it must be a warm day.

Reva glanced out the plate-glass window next to their table. "Well, at least we outsmarted them, meeting on a Saturday," she said.

Harry, lost in the photograph and its questions, looked up at his wife's cousin, hearing but not quite comprehending her words. "What? Outsmarted? We outsmarted someone?"

"Nothing," Reva said, taking a bite of her egg salad sandwich. The crusts that she'd stripped from the edges of the bread sat in a mound beside her plate.

Harry let her mysterious statement about outsmarting someone go. This wasn't the first time Reva seemed to be looking around, for what Harry had no idea. She was an unusual woman, not particularly warm or friendly, yet always reliable, obliging. Unlike her cousin, she never asked questions about anything, just brought the letters and accepted the fruit and small amounts of cash Harry always made it his business to offer her. Tonight, he'd give a few dollars, too, and pay, of course, for the dinner she seemed to be enjoying. He took a sip from his coffee cup.

"So, I've got a new job," he said, tucking Reva's letters into his shirt pocket. "That's why I asked you to come meet me." He told her about Ralph's fruit and vegetable store, and about his father going back to Poland, and that as much as he thought it was a mistake and that he'd miss him terribly, at least, without Izzy there, he'd be able to receive his own mail at his own address. As soon as the date for Izzy's departure was set, he told Reva, he'd write to Regina and let her know that she could address her mail straight to him. In the meantime, since he'd be working uptown, their usual weekly meetings would have to be more up in the air.

Reva didn't question, as she never had, why the marriage must be kept secret. As far as she was concerned, it was none of her business. As far as she was concerned, that was part of being an immigrant in America: secrets. But did they have enough saved up for his father's passage back to Europe? Money was an issue that everyone in America shared, not just greenhorns.

"It won't be easy, but not impossible, either," Harry said.

In fact, he and Izzy had opened a savings account at a bank on 188th Street. With the money they sent to Poland—and the amounts he sent to Regina, that his father didn't know about—and living expenses and keeping up their independent business, it was true they hadn't managed to put away very much. But still, the couple-hundred-dollars passage they could probably scrape together.

"I hear talk at the factory," she told him, "people make it look like they're anarchists, Communists, you name it, any type the government doesn't like, they put together a confession. And what do you know, even with all the questions and hearings and whatnot—you know what's doing there on Ellis Island—every once in a while, it works: somebody pulls one over and the government pays to ship them back. I'll tell you: I think they get a kick out of deporting people, some kind of feather in their cap, like they say." Finished with the sandwich, she was nibbling now on the crusts. "They must be very happy, the government. With the Depression and everything, I hear more people are going than coming in."

"Well," Harry said, sighing, "soon my father will be one of them." He watched with Reva the people streaming past the window until the waitress came and put the check on the table.

As they walked out onto the street, Harry gave Regina's cousin a few dollars from the ten he'd just broken in the restaurant, and thanked her again. He told her how much he appreciated her willingness to see him on different days, that they'd arrange their meetings by phone as they had tonight, until it was safe for Regina's letters to be sent directly to him.

"It's fine by me," Reva assured him. "Maybe better. Confuse them a little bit. They think I don't know they're following me? I see him all the time, the man with the paper, taking notes. I didn't want to tell you, get you worried, but this is better, believe me."

They said good night and walked their separate ways to their respective subway entrances. Harry thought Reva might be a little crazy, the way she talked: about a man, notes. But more information about this he certainly didn't want. Sometimes a person had just enough on his plate to wave off any more food for thought.

The following afternoon, Harry stepped off the bus near Jack and Malka's apartment carrying the cheesecake in the Cushman's bakery box, as always. He didn't know how many Sundays he and his father had taken this bus to this stop with the same objective, carrying the cheesecake in the white box wrapped with the thin red-and-white string. They'd made the trip in the rain, the heat, only a blizzard had once prevented a visit: they'd arrived at the bus stop and waited nearly an hour holding their heads down and their overcoats against the wind, until a man walked by and told them the buses weren't running.

This day was different, though. Their conversation on the ride over had utterly altered the Sunday mood. At least, Harry had started it as a conversation, but their exchange had quickly become something far less amiable.

They had been discussing the benefits of working at a salaried job right in the neighborhood; how, even though they sometimes made more than twenty dollars a week, they also sometimes made less, and this way there wouldn't be any more guessing. And the subway rides, Harry said, he could also do without. Izzy said he felt better about leaving, knowing that Harry wouldn't have to carry on the business without him. He felt a little badly about taking money from their savings in order to go back home, but after all these years, and with the way he'd been feeling lately, he was sure this was what he wanted.

At this juncture, just as the bus approached the bridge that connected Manhattan to the Bronx and after Izzy apologized for taking money out of their account, Harry mentioned, just making conversation, that a friend of his, someone he ran into sometimes downtown, had told him that a lot of people try to get the government to pay for their passage back. That they pretended to be against the United States so they could be deported.

He turned to look out at the East River. He always loved how it sparkled in the afternoon sun.

"This a friend of yours told you?" Izzy asked. "What kind of friend?"

Something in his father's voice compelled him to turn around.

Izzy's face was gray with anger. He looked straight ahead. What kind of friend, he repeated. To trick America, this was amusing? This land that gave so much to so many should be lied to, its standards made fun of? He sat stiffly, his face hard.

Harry tried to lighten the moment, assure his father that it was just something he'd heard, that he didn't agree with what these people were doing, just mentioned it to make conversation.

But Izzy sat immovable, as though he had just heard from his son's lips the most abominable proposition, no trying to make light of which could erase the hateful idea now that it had been aired. Lying to the czar, to the Communists in Russia, to these Nazis he was reading about in the *Forward*, this he could see, but lying to America? What kind of people was Harry associating with?

Harry shared his father's high regard for their adopted country, although his attitude didn't quite reach the reverence Izzy clearly held. He'd seen too many beggars on the street, hopeless and unemployed, too many tossed-out piles of furniture cried upon by their hapless owners. The system was the best in the world, Harry believed, but it was not perfect.

He restrained himself from challenging his father—if America was so wonderful, why was he leaving?—because he understood that wonderful it might be, but home it wasn't. In fact, his father's stern expression forestalled any further response, and in a way, Harry was glad of this, because what he was really thinking about, and feeling the full weight of, was Izzy's condemnation of lying. Once again, the thoughts that haunted him returned.

His admission into the country was based on a lie, his citizenship, a lie; his schedule and secret meetings and clandestine phone calls: everything, lies. His marriage itself, weighing on him heaviest of all, this marriage to Reizel, Regina, whose face he couldn't even conjure except for the photographs sitting in a shoe box high in the closet where his father wouldn't find them, this marriage was the biggest lie of all, as long as he was here, so far away from her.

Maybe he should go back with Izzy, back to Poland and the only relief from all the lies. Be a father to his son, an honest son to his own father, and finally put a stop to all the pretending.

Wracked with the magnitude of three years of deception— tomorrow, the twenty-ninth of August, was Yakob's birthday—Harry emerged from the bus carrying the Cushman's cheesecake.

Walking toward Tremont Avenue, the father and son locked in silence observed on the corner up ahead a man addressing a small crowd. As they drew closer, they saw that it was Congressman Barkley. The people gathered around him applauded some of the things he said and laughed with delight at his quips.

Stepping from the curb to cross the street, they heard Barkley call out: "Mr. Himelbaum, Izzy, Harry. Enjoy the cheesecake. Give Jack and Malka my regards," and father and son, despite the hard feelings pulling at them, waved hello.

"You see?" said Izzy when they reached the other side of the street, still looking straight ahead. "This is the country your friends lie to. A country where a congressman remembers your name."

~ ~ ~

PART THREE

1937

Child Welfare

February

New York City

Harry pulled down the awning on another day's work. It was Saturday just before sundown, and he had a special evening in store for Irene. Business, thank God, was good, despite the scare a few years back when the initial excitement over FDR's New Deal had burst as quickly as many of the programs the new president had put in place.

Roosevelt had bound into office with all the good will, good intentions, good ideas, and good people to execute them that he had promised, creating relief agencies that utilized every variation on letters of the alphabet for which a hungry nation had voted him in; but the voracious appetite for change had proven harder to satisfy than even the most well-meaning recipe could muster, and more expensive than the business community could stomach. As the national deficit soared, the courts weighed in, the Supreme Court ultimately striking down the subsidies of the Agricultural Adjustment Administration (AAA) and the workers' protections of the National Recovery Administration (NRA), leaving Roosevelt only temporarily bowed as he prepared for reelection in '35 with a slew of new ideas—among them, the National Labor Relations Act, the Works Progress Administration, and the Social Security Act—that not only secured his place in Washington, but put hundreds of thousands of the unemployed to work and gave them the confidence and dollars with which to buy fresh produce at the neighborhood fruit and vegetable market.

So, Harry ruminated as he bundled up against the windy cold of dusk and made his way toward the apartment on 181st Street that he now shared with his sister, he was making out good. Ralph was paying him thirty dollars a week now, and soon, very soon, he'd finally have enough saved to go back, and bring his family over.

Typically, Irene spent her Saturdays with Ralph's son, Saul, a nice enough fellow, but, personally, Harry thought she could do better. Of course, she was young yet, barely seventeen and a very conscientious student at the nearby George Washington High School, and nobody was talking yet of anything serious as far as their relationship was concerned. But the boy had energetically pursued Irene ever since she'd arrived a few years before, until she'd finally just fallen into becoming part of the couple that Saul had obviously envisioned since the moment he'd laid eyes on her. Harry thought his sister was too young to limit her horizons, to become committed to a relationship before exploring life as a young woman in a new country. Perhaps blending her situation with his own, he didn't think she should rush into adulthood before enjoying the carefree possibilities of youth.

Somehow, he had managed to persuade her to separate from Saul for this one night and go downtown with him. He wanted to spend time with her, just the two of them, at one of his favorite spots in the city: the still-under-construction Rockefeller Center. Harry didn't know why he loved it down there so much, but whenever he had some time on his hands, he found himself taking the subway to Fifty-ninth and walking the Fifth Avenue stretch to the site. Through the months of loneliness after Izzy had left, it provided him company; and through the economic turmoil and worry of the mid-1930s, the very construction reassured him, the boldness of it. There was hope in this place, and the essence of America: the strength of its skyscrapers, the openness of its possibilities, the elegance and style with which it persevered. Looking down at the ice-skating rink, once it had been completed, Harry would picture coming here with his son, the two of them gliding across the ice, laughing and holding hands, and getting to know each other. Maybe tonight, he and Rifkale would take a spin on the ice. He remembered from when she was little what a good skater she was.

They'd all watched her doing her little jumps and pirouettes on the frozen river behind the house like a regular ballerina. Sometimes, he'd skate with her. They always had such a good time together, he and his sister, back in Poland.

Rifka's trip to the United States had been postponed by the untimely death of their father. "He came home to die" is how the family, after its shock, would record Izzy's passing, mere months after he returned home to Stawki. And the girl would forever hold a little patch of guilt for how she'd pressed him so relentlessly during his brief time at home. In the initial weeks, just becoming acquainted with the father she'd never known had distracted her from her lifelong pull toward America, but soon it was: "Tell me all about New York, Papa," "When can I go, Papa? I have my papers," "Tell me about the apartment, Papa, and the street. Is there a movie house nearby?" She rode him with entreaties, riddled him with questions, announced to one and all that she would call herself Irene once she got there—but when, oh when would she ever get to go?

Izzy's cough, exacerbated by the ocean voyage, was as insistent in its refusal to quiet as were Rifka/Irene's questions, until the family came to realize that the joy of having Papa at home was just a fleeting thing that must give way to the more permanent intention for which he'd come.

By the time Izzy had been removed from his bed to the burial ground and Elke and her children had moved beyond the rawness of their initial grief, Rifka's visa had expired, and any talk of leaving for the United States seemed little more than the most base frivolity. It was only thanks to Harry's letters—steeped in misery and his own swatch of guilt—that Yitzak once again took up the paperwork and logistics of sending Rifka off to live with her brother in New York. Izzy had put away money specifically for Rifka's emigration; clearly this is what he would have wanted for her. As for the rest of the family, they saw no compelling reason to leave. Especially with Icko "here," Elke wouldn't even consider it.

Now, on this frosty night in February, as Harry and his sister made their way along the Rockefeller Center promenade to the line at the skate-rental booth, neither of them could imagine a time when they hadn't been together in this wonderful city.

"You remember the first time I brought you here?" Harry asked.

"Remember?" Irene's face broke out in a smile. "I had to pinch myself that this place was real, that I was real. That it was really happening. When you told me that they broadcast the radio shows from that very building," she pointed toward the seventy-story RCA Building, "that Jack Benny and all those movie stars I heard about might be inside at the very moment we were standing outside, I thought I'd faint. I still think I might faint. You think maybe Kay Thompson is up there right now? Or Loretta Lee? Getting ready for the *Hit Parade?*" Irene craned her neck to gaze at the magical recording tower and started singing, "Red sails in the sunset, doo doo doo-doo doo."

"You sing very nice," Harry said, guiding her forward in the line.

"And you're very nice," Irene said, suddenly throwing her arms around him. "You're the best brother in the world. Always." Her head buried in the folds of his jacket, she said, "I only wish . . ." But then she stopped herself.

"What? What do you wish?" Harry asked.

"Nothing. Here, look, it's almost our turn. I'm a six," Irene said, indicating her skate size and hoping to have changed the subject.

The two found some space on a bench and squeezed in to lace up their skates. It was cold outside and they had to blow the stiffness out of their fingers to perform the intricate procedure.

"So, you gonna tell me what you wish?" Harry asked.

"Um, can we get hot chocolate after?" Irene sidestepped.

Harry swatted her playfully with his glove. "What, you think so easily you can fool me? Huh? Huh?" But he let her unnamed wish go as they clutched hands and made their way onto the ice.

Anyone observing the pair would have seen two attractive, if slightly out-of-practice skaters, with honey-colored hair, hers cascading in waves from a blue woolen hat, his plush under a well-worn, brimmed tweed cap. The two seemed to enjoy each other, to laugh a lot, even when spilling onto the ice, which they did with less frequency as the music-accompanied evening deepened into night. Having, after an hour or so, found her skating legs, the young woman glided backward holding her partner's hands, so that the moving picture became one of grace and ease. Somehow, the cheerful collaboration suggested a relationship that was not a romantic enterprise, two people learning each other, and enticing each other to learn more. Here were a brother and sister, whose intimacy was rooted in birth.

Red-cheeked and slightly out of breath, Harry and Irene sipped cups of hot chocolate while the rink was cleared for maintenance. After congratulating each other on the loops and spins they had succeeded in executing, the subject turned to Saul. How could it not? The relationship was very much on Harry's mind and, while he hadn't explicitly planned this time together as an opportunity to probe the extent of his sister's involvement with the boy, this was in fact a rare opportunity to speak with her alone, for when Irene wasn't doing homework or setting her hair or doing all those other things females did behind closed bathroom doors, Saul was generally around. As often as not, and even though he'd already eaten, he was there at the kitchen table when Harry and Irene had their supper; he was there by the time Harry came home from work on Saturdays, and he was there on Sundays, too, giving Irene one excuse after another for not going with Harry over to Jack and Malka's for the weekly visit. Saul would help her with her algebra, her chemistry, her social studies. He would walk with her to New Jersey over the George Washington Bridge. Always, he colored their meetings with some necessary or quasi-educational function, which, for Harry to question, would seem unappreciative and uncaring. Now that he had her to himself, and as much as he felt reluctant to taint in any way the convivial time they were sharing, the older brother had no choice but to broach the situation.

As red as her cheeks already were, a flush overtook Irene's face. And this was only at the mention of Saul's name, when Harry noted what a good worker he was at the store. "Maybe," he postulated, "Ralph is grooming him for manager. Sure, he's young yet, but he is, after all, the son; it makes sense. He has a high school diploma, he's obviously very good at mathematics, he helps you so much with your homework."

"We don't talk about the store that much," Irene said, placing her cup on her knees and holding it there with her hands and gaze.

"So, what, you only talk about algebra?" Harry hadn't been going for sarcasm, but there it was.

"He's helped me very much. I don't know how I would have passed any of my math courses without Saul's help."

Harry, feeling an inferiority her comment had not meant to elicit, shrugged diffidently. Saul was, if lacking in other ways, American-born, and certain unquestionable advantages came with that status, an American education being high on the list.

"You know he thinks the world of you," Irene's remark hardly pulled Harry from his thoughts. Was there an element of jealousy, he wondered, in his disapproval of the boy? Here he'd worked so hard for five years, from dawn to closing six days a week, and Ralph's kid comes in and, sure, it made sense that he'd want his own son to be manager. Harry brushed the troubling suspicion of jealousy from his mind, as he did whenever it threatened to materialize, like a phantom insect one senses before it lands. In this instance, Irene's voice helped to swat it away.

"His father, too," Irene continued, "they both admire what a businessman you are, and how much the customers like you. Don't think otherwise for one minute, Yankele; they know how much you've done, how hard you work."

But Harry hadn't begun the conversation to have it focus on him. To decisively establish that fact, he leapt, too abruptly he realized, to the question at hand: "So you love the guy?" He fixed his eyes on her down-turned head. Perhaps their heat was perceptible through her cap, for she turned to face him. "Love." That was all she said.

"Love," Harry repeated. But he had his answer.

"I know I'm young," Irene said. "I never thought that this would happen. I didn't plan it. At first, when he started coming over, well, you know, I was just a baby, a greenhorn off the boat. I didn't understand. I thought, a friend of Harry, a nice person, a smart person who . . ."

Harry broke in on her gush of truth telling: "And now you're not a baby? You think you've experienced America? Enough to make a decision like this? What, you're going to marry him already? What do you know of men or dating? You're hardly out of pigtails."

"I never had pigtails."

"You know what I mean."

"Ladies and gentlemen, you may return to the ice," the voice came jocular and scratchy from the speaker system. "Grab your partner and . . ."

"So he asked you? He proposed to you?" Harry ignored the announcement.

Again, Irene lowered her head. "The subject came up maybe once or twice. A formal proposal, no, I haven't let him. I change the subject always because . . ." She paused. "I wish . . ." There it was again, that unmentionable wish of hers.

Harry didn't say anything. He knew she would finish this time.

"I don't understand why you don't go out with anyone. Look at you: you're handsome, a nice living you make. You don't know the women at the store who come in just to buy one apple at a time so they can see you. You think I don't know? Saul tells me. They laugh about it, him and Ralph. 'God forbid they'd buy a bag of apples. No, one apple at a time they come in for, just for another chance to see if maybe Harry will ask them for a date.'"

"They don't know what they're talking about," Harry demurred, although, of course, how could he not be aware of the pretty brunette who came in three, four times a day, always with the excuse that she forgot this, just remembered she needed that? A dainty little thing, just his type. And the tall one, also with brown hair, they *kibitzed* over the cucumbers, the asparagus. Quite an off-color sense of humor on her. Well, tall he liked, too.

"You know I can't see anybody," Harry said. It was his turn now to look down at the ground. Puddles of melted ice dotted the wooden planks beneath the benches. "Reizel and I, I promised her, you know, before I left. We write to each other."

"That's eight years ago, Harry. A long time. How can you hold so long a promise like that? Aren't you entitled to a life?"

"She is in that life," he could only say.

Between them for a while there was silence, while just a few feet away, the piped-in strains of "The Music Goes Round and Round" blended with the scratch of blades on the skating rink.

"You write to each other?" Irene finally said.

"Of course, we write. We're sweethearts, you know that."

Without having to confer, they were both unlacing their skates. Neither felt much like ice-skating anymore. Irene breathed a heavy sigh.

"What? Why are you sighing?" Harry asked. "You were always so crazy about her, no?"

"That was a long time ago, Harry. I was a baby. Sure, I liked her, but did she come to see me even once after you left? I asked her uncle, you know how many times? Shmuel, you know, where you met her that first time? He said he and her father weren't talking anymore, some kind of fight they had; who knows? It's not bad enough the whole world is against us, we have to fight among each other? It makes no sense to me, but anyway, that's neither here nor there."

Harry eschewed the philosophical possibilities in her question, putting on his galoshes and returning the skates to the rental booth. They walked quietly past the gaiety and swirling colors of the skating rink, turning left on Fifth Avenue toward the subway.

"So anyway, I had a letter from Mama, maybe a week, two weeks ago, and to make a long story short," Irene sighed once again, "maybe you should forget about Reizel."

"She calls herself now Regina," Harry said, ignoring Irene's ridiculous, if well-intentioned, advice. Whatever Mama had said in her letter could have no possible relevance.

"Regina, Reizel." Irene stopped walking.

Harry took several strides before realizing that his sister was no longer beside him, and looked back at her, puzzled. Slowly, she caught up to where he was standing, and fixed him with a serious expression. "She has someone. Someone else."

Irene's eyes probed her brother's face for some response: the hurt she'd dreaded since reading Mama's words; some sign of bewilderment, confusion, anger, even. But instead, he only looked at her as though she didn't know what she was talking about.

With all the tenderness she could gather to speak the words aloud, she said, "She has a child."

Responding to the pained effort with which Irene had made her announcement, Harry lingered with her in the seriousness of the moment—and then he just erupted, bursting out in full, throat-drenching, bent-over hysterics. He just couldn't stop laughing. Tears spilled from his eyes, his rib cage ached with heaves of hilarity, as though every fear he had repressed, every doubt he had strained to smother, every shred of guilt he had stifled lest he shatter under the sheer, enormous weight of his secret, was now free to explode in a torrent of relief and utterly unfettered emotion.

Irene's eyes burned with humiliation. Why was Harry acting like this? What was he doing? He leaned a heavy hand on her shoulder, as though the weight of his emotional exhibition left him weak. He pulled her to him and hugged her, his breath coming gradually under control.

"The child is mine," he finally whispered. "You have a nephew; his name is Yakob."

On the walk to the subway station, on the platform waiting for the train, and throughout the ride uptown, Harry told his sister about the marriage, about keeping it a secret to protect Papa from being complicit in the lie he'd told to enter the country, about Reva and the letters, about his keeping the mailbox key from Irene so that she wouldn't come across the envelopes from home marked "photograph enclosed." He told his sister, as he had told no one until now, that he was married and a father and that before the year was out it was his intention to go back to Poland and bring his wife and child back with him to America. He had, at long last, saved the money to bring them here.

Interspersed with Harry's revelations, Irene, her recently sanguine features bleached with pallor, recounted without emotion the contents of their mother's letter: the apparent reconciliation between Reizel's uncle and father; the rumors that had followed Reizel's recent visits to Shmuel in the company of a young boy, who must certainly be her son. When she'd read Mama's letter, Irene said, it started to make sense, Reizel's disappearance, her failure to get in touch with her after Yankel left: she must have married someone else. Irene had felt so terrible about the news, she said, that she didn't have the heart to tell him, only decided that she must urge him to go out and enjoy himself, find himself a girl.

"So now, you see I have one," Harry said as they climbed the narrow staircase from the subway out into the cold night. He couldn't understand quite why, but a kind of dread pervaded him. After the initial relief and subsequent confessions, he felt ashamed, exhausted, exposed. Having spoken the truth, at last, his situation became real.

"It will take me a while to get used to this," Irene said. "I can't imagine what it's been like, keeping a secret like this for so long."

As they entered the apartment, Harry went reflexively to remove his cap; it was just what he did every time he came in from out-side—he reached for the cap he wore every day, the cap he'd worn for years, whatever the weather, to place it on the entrance table. But tonight, there was no cap, it was only his hair he pulled. Where was the cap? Somewhere along the way, it must have slipped off, somewhere between the ice-skating rink and home.

Irene tossed her coat into the living room that had been converted into a bedroom for her and turned the light on in the kitchen. "Come, I'll make coffee. It's early yet."

"No, I lost my hat. Maybe it's down in the street, the subway. I'll go take a look."

Harry knew it wasn't right, leaving Irene by herself so late at night, especially after what he'd just told her; she shouldn't have to sit alone with it. But he simply couldn't face the brightly lit kitchen, or the dim shadows of his bedroom. And he really did hope to find his cap. Everything had changed tonight, but please, he thought, *not also the hat I've worn all these years. Let me have that one thing the same.*

He stopped before closing the front door behind him. "You'll be okay here alone? Maybe give Saul a call. Call up your boyfriend, he'll come."

Walking through the cavernous lobby to the front door of the building, he thought to turn around: maybe he should tell Irene not to say anything to Saul if he came over. But he thought better of it, for this was the very threshold he'd crossed tonight: his marriage was no longer a secret.

Tomorrow, first thing in the morning, he'd sit down and write a letter, tell Mama he was coming home for a visit. With the news itself, about his wife and son, he'd wait. The big news, that he'd tell her face-to-face.

Irene he'd have to tell not to write about it, either. He'd also write to Regina in the morning. They had already agreed that he would come for them this year, but now, tomorrow, he'd set a definite date.

And of course now there was no reason for Irene not to have a mailbox key. He'd have one made up. And he'd show her the pictures, yes, in the morning, he'd show Irene the pictures. The boy, Yakob, his face was thinner now, and serious, he looked like maybe there was a sadness there. Did Regina tell him bad things about his father? Could he blame her?

She, herself, looked a little heavier, but always she had on the latest hat. With feathers, with peaks and brims: like here in America, and why not? Women everywhere seemed to be wearing their imaginations on their heads.

He had to laugh: that Alice, the one with the sense of humor, she'd put an iceberg on her head the other day and asked him how it looked.

So, why shouldn't Regina wear a different hat in every picture? That's what they did in the shop, she and her parents, hatmakers. But the boy, Yakob, he wore, like Harry himself, a brimmed cap. Perched on the back of his head, a white one, so cute it looked. And always with his arm around his mother, like a caretaker.

So tomorrow, he'd write his letters.

Thoughts and plans and reflections toppled around Harry's head as he went downtown in search of his hat.

He got off the train at Fifty-ninth Street. Couples walked arm in arm, but he looked downward, studying the streets, making his way back to Rockefeller Center, as if there were any chance at all that he'd find his tweed brimmed cap.

This summer he would go to Poland.

Irene knew she couldn't call Saul at this hour; the household was probably asleep. She paced back and forth in the small kitchen. Even the music coming from the radio jangled her nerves. She switched it off, but then the silence nipped at her. Ice-skating: she should have known it wouldn't turn out well. Whenever she thought of the sport, the image that came to her mind was that day she'd tried to manage on one skate, and the humiliation that followed, and the questions about her own character. The Bug River was beautiful and serene that winter morning, a frozen playground in their very backyard.

As a child, Irene had loved the feeling of freedom that came with skating, gliding along the surface of the river that turned silver and gave off a lustrous light in the winter months. Yankel, when he wasn't busy in the fields or the barn, or keeping the books, would watch her for a while, and then skate out onto the ice and grab her hand, making her go faster than she wanted to, but holding her in such a way that her legs felt stronger and she could tolerate the speed, even revel in it. Mama and Hershel, sometimes Yitzak and Chava, would watch from the banks, applauding their daring maneuvers. Why didn't she think of those days on the ice, and all the fun she'd known? No, in relation to ice-skating, the snapshot that popped from the darkroom of memory was that morning with Moishe. There was only the one pair of skates in the household, and Moishe cried that he wanted to go, too, and no one ever said no to Moishe.

She was thirteen at the time, Moishe a skinny little thing at four. He hardly ate unless his mother fed him and, finally, Yitzak had put his foot down. Chava was making a laughingstock out of their son, turning him into a baby for life, the way she hand-fed him every morsel. So the boy didn't eat, and Chava mumbled under her breath: this had come to be the customary dining experience at their table in Stawki.

On that particular morning, seeing Rifka grab her skates from the hook, Moishe had started crying that he wanted to go, too. Why didn't

Rifka ever take him? *"Nu, dos is ah frage,"* Chava had said, looking accus-ingly at the girl. "A good question." "I'd be happy to take you, Moishele," Rifka said, purposely addressing herself not to the mother, but to the boy, himself, "but you have to tell your daddy to get you some skates." The stern tone and the reference to his father only made Moishe wail louder, which set little Sarah off in the next room. Chava threw Rifka an accusing glance: Now see what you've done? Putting the skates back on the hook, Rifka went to pick up the baby and soothe her. "Why doesn't Daddy buy me skates?" Moishe kept crying. "I want skates." "*Nu*, she'll take you," Chava said. "Here, see how Mama can make for you?"

Rifka, bouncing the baby in her arms, returned to the kitchen to see her sister-in-law stuffing one of her ice skates with rags. "What are you doing?" she wanted to know.

"*Nu*, so now you both can skate. You'll hold his hand, he shouldn't fall."

"But . . ." Rifka was incredulous. "I can't skate on one foot," she protested.

"You'll each have one skate, one foot for balance. You'll teach him." And with this perfectly logical solution, Chava took Sarah from Rifka's arms. "Go, *tateleh*," she prodded Moishe. "I'll put Sarahle on a jacket, and we'll come watch. Go, go with your aunt Rifka."

With great reluctance, Moishe put his hand in Rifka's. As loath as he was to do anything without his mother, the little boy was perceptive enough to understand that with the fuss he'd made, he couldn't very well refuse. "You'll come?" he asked, craning his neck before the door closed, and he followed his aunt around the corner of the house to the back, and down the path toward the frozen river.

It was now Rifka's turn to mumble, as, above his residual sniffles and practically palpable fear, she laced on her skate, and then Moishe's. "There, does it feel all right?" she asked curtly. "It should be snug." He only nodded. "You see how lucky we are?" she asked, resigned to being her nephew's first skating instructor and, no denying it, enchanted by the soft light spreading from the sky onto the glimmering ice. The little boy certainly didn't look as though lucky was one of the things he felt, but Rifka held out her hand to him. Instead of taking it, he

141

began to run back toward the house, falling almost immediately on the awkward footwear of one boot, one ice skate. Rifka was equally unsuccessful as she ran to pick him up. So there they both sat, waist deep in snow and feeling foolish.

She lifted herself from the snow, its wetness seeping uncomfortably through her long skirt, and decided to give him one more chance. Again, she held out her hand. "I'll watch you first," Moishe said quietly, still sniffling. "When Mama comes, then maybe," he didn't finish.

"Okay, suit yourself," Rifka said, and she fairly marched in a kind of hobble toward the river.

It took but one glide for her to lose her balance and fall down hard.

An unaccustomed sound filtered through the thin air. Turning toward the riverbank, Rifka saw Chava's figure growing larger as she drew closer to them, running. But what commanded her attention, lit up with a glee the likes of which she'd never thought it capable, was Moishe's face. A sparkling gemstone on a frayed sweater, Moishe was laughing! Bending over and holding his sides, he laughed as Rifka's ribs and backbone throbbed with pain. His squeals slicing through Chava's hysterical concern that he'd catch a cold, sitting there in the snow, he laughed. Chortling with unbridled delight, Moishe laughed—at the spectacle of his hapless aunt Rifka, splayed out helplessly on the frozen Bug River.

From that day until this, Irene could not see anything positive in the prospect of ice-skating. It was an activity, she'd decided, that just did not bring out the best in people. Even at the time, she knew she should feel happy for her nephew. So what if his enjoyment came at her expense? His joy was such a rarity, shouldn't she gladly sacrifice her dignity to arouse it? Yet, an inexplicable and unreasonable resentment coursed through her, compounding her humiliation, and producing a sense of her own sheer gracelessness that she could easily recapture, just by reflecting back.

When Harry suggested ice-skating, she should have known the evening would turn out badly. Uncomfortable circumstances to which one had no appropriate response always reared their heads whenever that silly, slippery sport was involved. Who thought it up, anyway: the idea of sliding on a sheet of ice?

The following afternoon, Harry was not surprised when Irene declined to go to the Bronx with him. For a change, her excuse did not involve Saul. Instead, she had a date to get together with a girlfriend, she said, to talk about *Gone with the Wind*, a book Harry knew she'd been immersed in for weeks. He might have pressed her, as he did most Sundays, to come, but today he was relieved that she wouldn't be there with him in Jack and Malka's kitchen. It was better that he go alone so that he could control the conversation, not worry that it might veer somehow to matters of which his sister was now apprised.

According to conventional wisdom as well as biblical injunctions, speaking the truth was supposed to lighten a person's burdens, but the confession of the night before continued to weigh heavily on Harry, adding more of a complication to his life than an easing of conscience. As disheartening as it was for him to acknowledge, the simple truth was that duplicity had become a state of being to which he had grown accustomed. Knowing that his marriage was no longer a secret was like having to adjust to a new pair of pants that were the right size but just didn't feel as comfortable as the old ones. His lie hadn't been a virtue, surely, but Harry had grown familiar with the fit.

Earlier on Sunday, while Irene was still asleep, Harry had sat down over a cup of coffee and a toasted bagel to write his letters. To his mother, he wrote in Yiddish, regretting that he couldn't follow his night-school teacher's stern advice to stick to English when writing. But this was for Mama to read, not third-hand through Yitzak, a letter between the two of them, and the Yiddish writing would immediately make that clear to her. And so he began:

> *My Darling Mama,*
> *Are you sitting down? I'll get right to the point.*

He crossed this out and reversed it to read:

I'll get right to the point. Are you sitting down? After eight years, who can believe it's finally happening, I'm coming home. In Stawki I'll be this July. Is it cold now by you? Think of me and how warm it will be once we're together. Me? I can hardly wait. When I know the exact date, you'll hear from your loving, Yankel.

Harry looked at the letter and saw that it was very short. So he added:

P.S. Rifka, she sleeps like nobody's business. On the weekends, don't ask. But don't worry, not when she has to be in school. Then, she is up early and is doing very well. I'll take soon a picture of her and send it to you. Like a movie star she looks. Say hello to my brothers and tell them, too. That I'm coming this summer for a visit.

After reading over what he had written, and deciding that the letter contained ample information, Harry took a clean sheet of paper and began his letter to Reizel. To her, as per her determination to become fluent in the language, he wrote in English.

My Dearest Regina,
I know you like to hear first what's new with me in America, so I'll start with your cousin Reva. I went a week ago to see her and you'll never guess where—backstage in a theater if you can believe it. She is helping out with a play, in the back sewing costumes and the funny thing is that the play is about garment workers. Pins and Needles they call it and it's a riot. Reva got permission for me to watch a rehearsal. Whether the audience will come remains to be seen. The country is funny about the labor unions. On the other hand, try being a working man without joining one, it's impossible. Even me, I think I told you, I had to join the Vegetable and Grocery Clerk's Union. So a little bit I give to them in dues each month, there is no way to avoid it.

But here's my big news, darling, we really now can count the days because I'm coming to get you this summer. In July. Imagine. Finally, at long last my darling, we will be together. Tell my son.
Your loving, Harry.
P.S. To Rifkale, I told everything, but please, my dearest, wait just a little longer so we can tell my mother when we're together.

Harry folded his onionskin airmail letters, tucked them into his jacket pocket for mailing, and set out for Malka's. Carrying the Cushman's cheesecake, Harry went over in his mind the afternoon he could expect, and the picture reconfirmed his feeling that it was just as well Irene wouldn't be there. Lately, Jack and Malka's son, Lannie, was home for the Sunday lunches, and his behavior, cranky and demanding (hung over, Harry suspected) tainted the once easygoing visits. Harry knew it wasn't a nice thing to take solace in the unhappiness of others, but especially today, knowing how the afternoon would go formed a kind of relief: Jack would sit quietly at the table, injecting an occasional, "What are you talking?" and a dismissive wave of the hand as Lannie grumbled about the job market; Malka would be producing her savory matzoh meal pancakes as though a satisfying meal might dissipate the tension in the air; and he, himself, along with his aunt trying to lighten the mood, would make his customary contribution, comprised of stories from the fruit store, reports on Irene's progress in school, and today, he thought to himself, an account of Rockefeller Center and the night of skating he and Irene had shared.

The recent Sunday afternoons in the Bronx were like the deception he'd been living with for eight years: troubling, yet somehow comfortable in their familiarity.

This Sunday afternoon was no different, except that Harry arrived home with a terrible stomachache. He spent the entire night in the bathroom, wondering why his body should commit such a betrayal when everything he'd eaten today was exactly the same as always.

By the following morning, he was feeling a little better; empty, maybe, like on Yom Kippur, but well enough to rise before dawn, knock on Irene's door to wake her for school, and put on the coffee. He managed to keep down a piece of dry toast, and didn't even consider staying home from work. For the first time since yesterday at Malka's, he was even able to enjoy a cigarette.

"What's wrong with you? You look pale," Ralph Weiss made the observation as he and Harry neatly arranged the morning's delivery in the tiered produce baskets.

Harry had tied his apron a little looser than usual, his midsection still somewhat sensitive. "Oh, it's nothing. A little indigestion I had last night."

"From Malka's pancakes?" Harry had made them famous. "The way you rave about them, you should get a stomachache?" Ralph *kibitzed*. "And where's your hat? I don't think I've ever seen you without your hat," the boss went on. "Saul," he turned his attention to his son, mopping the floor, "there's *shmutz* over there by the bananas."

"Don't ask," Harry said. "I lost it the other night. I don't know where."

"With a *maidel*, maybe?" Ralph quipped.

"No, no *maidel*. I wasn't with a girl," Harry said, "unless you count Irene. I was with her when I lost the hat." He glanced over at Saul for some sign that he might know what else had transpired Saturday night. The boy just continued with his floor-cleaning duties.

The apples and onions and cucumbers and icebergs unloaded and attractively arrayed for the day's business, the black-and-white-tiled floor pristine until the first customer tracked in the detritus of the sidewalk on the soles of her galoshes, Harry took his position by the pears, Saul his as the greeter at the threshold of the store, and Ralph made sure everything was in order at the cash register. By eight o'clock, the first shoppers began to arrive.

Harry had become accustomed to Saul being the front man, the first person the customers encountered before coming in. He knew it was an important position, one that he had held in his early days of employment here, before Saul graduated from high school and became the heir apparent. Well, he was a good-looking boy, that Harry couldn't deny, tall and with a nice face. Even with the eyeglasses he wore, on him they gave a look of intelligence. Combined with the friendly smile and the father as rightful proprietor, Saul's future couldn't be more clearly spelled out. After Irene's veritable acknowledgment of their romance Saturday night, Harry would have to live with the probability that his sister was in that future, and how all this would affect his own—would he have to get used to working for this kid and could he ever get used to it?—time would tell. Ralph wasn't kidding anyone, having Saul mop the floor in the morning. As far as Harry was concerned, this was just further proof that the man was teaching his son the business from the ground up.

As always on a Monday, the store filled with a steady flow of customers and the time went quickly. Dainty Doris (as Harry privately thought of the petite brunette) had by noon already been in twice for her McIntosh apples and the celery she'd forgotten, and as he was ringing up a customer at about two o'clock, here was Alice the *kibbitzer*, looking at the bananas.

"They're very good, very fresh," Harry said as he approached her. "I've already had, for lunch."

He could see by the way she was handling the fruit where her humor would go, and the truth was that he found himself a little bit aroused. This wasn't the first time he thanked God for the apron when this woman was around.

"They feel maybe a little hard," Alice said, throwing him a mischievous glance.

"That's the best way." Harry winked. "What, you want a soft banana?"

And the two of them broke into laughter just as Irene walked in, carrying her books on the way home from school. The sight of her brother and this woman embroiled in an inside joke, laughing and clearly enjoying each other, would have pleased her enormously a short forty-eight hours ago, but everything was different now. She stood in the doorway transfixed, ignoring Saul's attentions as he ran over to her, asking how she was, gushing at the pleasant surprise.

"I just came to see how my brother was feeling," Irene said, not looking at her suitor. "Last night, he didn't feel so good. I see now he's much better." How could Harry behave like this? She stood there, miffed. No better than Ashley in *Gone with the Wind*, betraying Scarlett and her lifelong love for him.

"Yeah, he said something before, about his stomach," Saul said, all admiration for his sweetheart's sisterly concern. "Harry, Irene is here," the young man called across the length of the market.

As he caught sight of her, Harry's gaiety visibly transformed, first to simple gladness at her surprise appearance, then to awkwardness as he comprehended the sour expression on her face. A bit too abruptly, he shoved the banana he was holding into Alice's hand and approached his sister.

"You're feeling better, I see," Irene said, still staring at the tall, attractive woman.

"She comes in, we kid around," Harry spoke softly to his sister.

"No more stomachache?" Irene finally looked at him.

Harry put his hand over his stomach, then his heart. "Here it's better," he said, "and here it's fine, you shouldn't worry." Then, putting his hand on his hatless head, "Only here, I have to get used to."

Wlodawa

"Mommy, Mommy, please don't leave me," Moishe sobbed hysterically, hoarsely, like his heart was breaking. "I don't want you to go. I don't want to go to school. Please, Mommy, don't go." The eight-year-old boy had no shame, no concern for his dignity or pride; his entire being was misery.

He clutched at his mother's waist, buried his head in her bosom, looked up at her, pleading, his face washed in grief, despair, terror. He just couldn't imagine life on this earth without her.

With trembling fingers, Chava gripped his hands and eased them from her waist. "This is best," she said dryly, her own heart breaking, too.

The walk across the bridge in the morning, the little boy gaily skipping alongside her, unknowing, had perhaps been the hardest piece of the excursion for her. "What is the surprise?" he kept asking. "Where are we going, it's so cold today?" Chava was in agony over the imminent betrayal, but she had no choice. Ever since President Pilsudski had died, all pretense of tolerance for the Jews in Poland had faded into a laughable hope. A person heard every day of harassment and pogroms. In the universities, "ghetto benches" were set aside for Jewish students and, in Stawki, government subsidies for the school had been terminated. If Jewish families insisted, as the national-minority clause in the Treaty of Versailles mandated, that their children be taught in Hebrew and Yiddish, let them pay for it. Here, across the river, the Jewish school remained open, and of course there was no question that her son was to be educated, even if it meant tearing her heart into pieces. Chava had no choice.

"Every Friday, I'll come for you," she said. "For *Shabbes* you'll be home. And in the meantime, how smart you'll be, teaching Sarahle and showing off for Grandma everything." She didn't mention Yitzak, who barely made it home more than once a month since Rifka had gone to New York. She had lost him to another woman, he didn't even deny it. The *shiksa*—let her have him.

Still inside a pool of tears and unbridled howling, Moishe fell to the floor and grabbed the hem of his mother's skirt to weep into. She couldn't leave him here, she just couldn't.

Nearby, on a bench just inside the entrance to the school, a group of boys with visored caps and worn shoes tittered at the display. Only one of them looked on with anything resembling sympathy. His eyes intently glued to the spectacle, the solemn expression on his face momentarily distracted Chava from the dire scene of which she was the center.

Pulling her skirt from Moishe's grasp, she looked down at her son and mustered her ability to speak. "Be a good boy," she said. The voice came out low-pitched and hard, a sound she'd never heard before and, placing the satchel with Moishe's clothes and books beside him, she turned and left the building.

One kilometer away, Leah laughed merrily as she rode her bicycle on the dirt road leading to Wlodawa. Beside her, Hershel pulled the cart with his breads and cakes for the bakery. For several years, he had been delivering his baked goods to the merchant in the larger village, the arrangement with Feldberg providing a major portion of financial support at home now that Yitzak had found employment in Warsaw, and Elke had grown weary with the farm chores. Harry's money from America helped, of course, and between the three of them, no one was complaining, least of all Hershel, who felt blessed every day that the thing he loved to do brought in money for the family.

"I can't ride so slowly." Leah, bundled against the cold, balked playfully. "Can't you pull a little faster?"

"You want to trade places?" Her husband smiled. As the dirt road turned to cobblestone at the edge of Wlodawa, his task only grew more arduous. Leah got off the bike and walked it the rest of the way into town.

Outside the baked goods shop, a crowd was gathered. A lot of customers this morning, Hershel thought, standing up a little straighter to look more like a professional.

As the couple approached Feldberg's, though, they saw simultaneously that the people outside the shop were not women in shawls who had come out to buy household provisions. Rather, an unusually large assembly of men stood out front, some in silent awe, others raising their voices in indignation. A few wept. The glass window of the bakery was shattered, and the Star of David on the front door, slashed through with a bold smear of black paint.

Washington, DC

Will Brown stood in the cafeteria line at the mammoth Main Labor Building with his friends Doug Pearson and Stan Waverly. It was all he could do to hold his tray and keep his place amidst the reaching hands and prodding elbows similarly jockeying for lunch. Thanks to the explosion of programs, agencies, and departments created by Roosevelt, DC had ballooned from a comparatively sleepy southern town into a bustling metropolis of administrators, office workers, bankers, do-gooders, and the multitude of press people necessary to cover them all, and each day at around noontime, it seemed that every last one of them descended on this very space to feed their unquench-able appetite.

The din reminded Will of nothing so much as the Great Hall at Ellis Island, back in the early days of processing the hordes of for-eigners looking to call the United States home. It was a straight line from those days to these, Will felt, the writing on the wall even back then: open the floodgates, something's gotta give. What gave was the economy, the jobs and farms and homespun institutions of American life. No surprise, therefore, that now we had this: relief spelled every which way from Sunday.

Frances Perkins, Will's boss, and the first female cabinet secretary ever appointed—and a Communist if you asked Will and his friends—had, with her clout and Socialist ideas, practically single-handedly inaugurated a slew of these programs, from Social Security to the Federal Emergency Relief Administration and Civilian Conservation Corps, from minimum wage to maximum hours, and even the since-debunked National Recovery Administration. Yes, all this med-dling by the government into business and free enterprise could easily be traced to the conniving mind of Miss Perkins. But what really aggravated Will and his colleagues was the decisive role she'd played in limiting the Bureau of Immigration, which had been placed under the aegis of her Labor Department in '33. The special corps of invest-igators known as Section 24, whose job was to look into the unlawful residency of immigrants and build a case for deportation, Miss Perkins had insisted on disbanding on the grounds that the operation was too expensive and amounted to unseemly harassment. Then she had the temerity to cast herself as the champion of the unemployed, when it was the very illegal aliens that she'd shielded from the law who were eating into the job opportunities of born-and-bred Americans. The circular and self-serving reasoning and the administration's endorse-ment of it riled Will to no end. The only thing that got him angrier was the November election.

The country had had the chance to vote these left-wing social engineers out of office, with their brilliant ideas that had yielded nothing but a huge deficit and still millions out of work, but they had just gone and reelected them in a landslide! Alf Landon, who'd seemed exactly what the country needed: a head-on-his shoulders, likeable, Midwestern kind of fellow, lost every state but Maine and Vermont. It just made no sense at all.

Finding three seats together at a long crowded table, the three INS colleagues dug into their chicken potpies before beginning the day's observations. Like most of their coworkers at the largely diminished offices of Immigration, they found solace in each other's right-thinking, if nationally unpopular views.

"So I'm reading *Fortune* last night," Doug began, "and I nearly upchucked my supper."

"Elaine cook one of her Viennese specialties again?" Will teased. All their friends acknowledged that Barbara won the prize when it came to cooking—he was proud of her for it—and he knew that Doug wouldn't be offended by the reference to Elaine's ongoing culinary mishaps. When they'd last been over to the Pearson's for dinner, her *wiener schnitzel* had defied both knives and teeth.

"She made a very good meat loaf," Doug defended his wife. "No, it wasn't that. It was this article. Listen to this: Remember how last year they had this report about how over sixty percent of the country believes in birth control? Well, now it looks like almost a quarter of the country thinks that premarital sex is okay."

"Who are they asking?" Stan asked, astounded.

"I don't know," Doug said. "I assume it must be some kind of cross-section. I mean, what's going on out there? This is *Fortune* magazine I'm talking about, not some Commie rag."

"It's the twenties all over again," Will put in. He sidled away from a man next to him whose phlegmy cough was not only unappetizing, but sounded dangerously contagious.

"Well, see, that's the interesting thing," Doug said, swallowing a portion of soggy carrots and beans. "These same people? In this survey? They have nothing but praise for the family, family life, and so on. I'm telling you, it doesn't make sense."

"I just hope we can hang on, because the way things are going, I fear for this country," Will said, the most earnest of the three and, with his recent promotion to assistant commissioner in charge of the Warrant Division, the most senior. No one begrudged Will's advancement, even if he had come on board after they had. While most of the INS crew enjoyed themselves on weekends and took summer vacations, Will eschewed off-time, diving into the responsibility of overseeing deportations with a dedication that had won him the respect of just about everyone in the bureau. He deserved his promotion.

"Thanks to that madman Hitler, we have boatloads of immigrants coming in again," Will went on, "so naturally, morality is going to go down the tubes. Not to mention jobs, an upswing in unions, strikes every other week. It's a mess."

"Well, at least we're keeping them busy over at Ellis Island," Stan said. He and Doug were the chief attorneys for the bureau, in charge of filtering and acting on Will's recommendations. "There's waiting lists to get cases going in the hearing rooms." He raised his paper cup of milk in Will's direction. "You're doing a heck of a job."

Will nodded his appreciation and patted his lips with his napkin. "Thank you, gentlemen. And speaking of job," he checked his watch, "there's just time to call Barbara, see how Junior's doing before heading upstairs."

After years of disappointment, Barbara had become pregnant and given birth to a son a year ago. At first, when they'd moved to Washington, just taking care of Will's father and getting settled in a new town had been more than enough to keep her occupied. Thanks to Martha Connelly's persistence, they'd found a charming little house in the newly built, picturesque neighborhood of Woodley Park before real estate prices went through the roof with all the New Dealers pouring into town. Even Barbara begrudgingly acknowledged that it was Martha's foresight that allowed for their well-timed purchase. Of course, Martha's enthusiasm for socializing with the Brown family had visibly mellowed upon meeting Will's father. The once-upstanding patriarch walked slowly and with a stoop ever since his trauma on Iowa's roads and his subsequent relinquishment of his own custody to his son. The gay and attractive couple, so all-American, seemed far less the social asset now that they were encumbered by his somber and constant presence.

Not being part of the Connelly's cocktail circuit sat just fine with Barbara, but the more time she spent with Elaine Pearson and Betty Waverly—meeting them at the park with their children, getting together for family dinners—the emptier their pretty new house felt upon returning home. Nicholas slept in the downstairs bedroom, but it was a large room, surely designed for the growth and antics of a child. Nicholas himself said he was just "keeping it warm" for his grandson.

In their late thirties, Will and Barbara had just about given up hope of conceiving, when, lo and behold, her period was late and, sure enough, the test came back positive. Nicholas wept with the news. The tall, strapping man on whose composure Will had built the framework of his unruffled convictions cried easily these days, the old swagger and unstudied manliness hard to recall. Not that there was anything unmanly in greeting the pending arrival of his first grandchild with a tear or two, but did he have to bend forward on the couch and sob into his hands as though he'd never stop?

Will would never allow himself to think of his father as an embarrassment—he wiped the thought from his mind whenever it reared into consciousness—but in truth, he had fought Barbara on naming their son after him. "Nicholas": it was such a foreign-sounding name. Now that they were finally going to have a child, wouldn't Tim or Tom, or even William if it were a boy, speak more affirmatively of their proud American identity?

Barbara always tried to shush him when the baby-naming debate came up. Did he want his father to hear? But one evening she hadn't diffused the argument quickly enough, and when Nicholas, who moved so quietly these days—like a ghost—walked in on them, and Will saw the shame on his father's face, he had no choice but to acquiesce: Nicholas it would be. Calling the boy "Junior" appeased Will's preference for an Anglican-sounding name, and the future grandpa had nothing against it.

With the birth of his grandson, Nicholas started to come out of his depression, bouncing the baby on his lap and singing Greek rhymes that Will could vaguely remember, taking him for walks while Barbara saw to the household chores.

Feeling that it was only right to make personal calls on his own dime whenever possible, Will headed to the bank of pay phones in the massive lobby. He found the shortest line (there were always lines in front of the phone booths at lunchtime) and fished in his pocket for change. What with the wet, cold weather they'd been having, the baby had been sniffling for the last few days, broken into a fever the night before, and he just wanted to see that everything was all right. Barbara didn't do well when Junior was sick, drank more than her usual glass of whiskey with dinner, and could hardly sleep. Last night, he'd found her sipping a drink while doing the dishes; that was a new one. Will tried to tell himself that Barbara was just trying to be fashionable with her regular diet of highballs and whiskey neats. Everyone consumed alcohol in unnecessary quantity these days, probably in leftover defiance of Prohibition. As far as Will was concerned, a tall glass of seltzer made for a satisfying beverage after work, but he'd been the brunt of enough teasing on that score to realize that he himself was straitlaced and that Barbara's taste for the harder stuff was closer to the norm. Thus, he trained himself not to be suspicious of her, even as he couldn't help but notice the frequency with which their stock of alcohol needed to be replenished. He couldn't tell himself that his dad was contributing to the alcohol consumption, because Nicholas, ever since the repeal, had reacquainted himself with his taste for wine with a meal, specifically, retsina, of which there was always a bottle in the pantry. Retsina was the only drink Nicholas ever had.

"What is that you're drinking?" Martha Connelly had asked the first time she and Joe had come for dinner. She had regarded the colorless liquid as though it were some sort of exotic potion. Except in high society, or to those aspiring to identify with it, wine wasn't nearly as popular a drink as whiskey, and surely she'd never seen, or smelled, wine that looked like this.

"Would you like a taste?" Nicholas had offered.

"Oh, no, thank you." Martha had actually moved her glass as the swarthy older man tilted the retsina toward her, lest it contaminate the rim. "What a strong smell," she'd tried to sound merely observant.

"All yours, sir." A young woman whose wavy hair fell to the shoulders of her tailored suit jacket emerged from the phone booth, and Will stepped in. He looked after the woman as she sashayed toward the front doors. *Awful lot of women working these days,* he thought disapprovingly, and he turned to dial the number.

Barbara answered on the first ring. "Yes? Dr. Trackman?"

"Hi, honey," Will said. "You called the doctor?"

"Oh, it's you," Barbara said, clearly disappointed. "Yes, he has a hundred and three. Oh, Will, I'm very worried."

"Honey, it's just a cold. You should see it here at work. Everyone's sniffling and coughing."

"Will, a hundred and three," Barbara said, "and he's crying something awful. Dad's walking around the house, holding him, right now. He won't hear of being put in the crib."

"You and Pop baby him," Will said. "We don't want him to be spoiled."

"Will, he is a baby," Barbara said pointedly. "I should get off the phone. The doctor may be trying to call."

"Okay, well, let me know what he says. I'll call in an hour or so," Will said. "Maybe he'll come take a look. Set your mind at ease, anyway," and he hung up.

Making his way through the busy lobby and up to his third-floor office, Will hoped Trackman would come and see the baby. A hundred and three: that was high, even for a little one.

"You had several calls, sir." Will's petite and no-nonsense secretary, Annette, held out a piece of paper with his messages. "Congressman Barkley called several times, says he has to talk to you."

Will had no sooner taken the sheet of paper from Annette than he heard the office door swing open and the bellowing voice of Barkley himself.

"That's right, I need to talk to you," Tim Barkley said. He strode in as if he owned the place.

"Congressman," Will greeted his nemesis, toward whom he had never feigned anything more than professional tolerance. The man had been pushy enough during his early years in the House. Now that he had garnered Frances Perkins's praise as champion of all those immigrants in his district, his blustery self-importance was downright insufferable.

Without being asked, he walked right into Will's office, Will having no choice but to follow him in. It wasn't necessary to offer him a chair; Barkley was already seated.

"I've had complaints from three constituents this morning alone, and I'm telling you, I won't have it," Barkley said. "It may be your desire to deport every damn Jew in the country, but not in my district."

"I'm doing my job," Will said quietly as he sat down behind his desk. "And I take umbrage at your implication that we're singling out any particular race."

"I'm not implying anything. I'm telling you outright, Mr. Brown. Half the people in my district are Jews. They're the ones putting me in office. I promised them a fair shake and active representation, and I'm not going to let them down. These 'notices' you're sending out, these 'hearings' you're orchestrating are nothing short of harassment, and as far as I know Secretary Perkins put an end to that years ago." He paused for strategic effect. "She is your boss, as far as I know."

"There's nothing out of line about what I'm doing, Congressman," Will returned. "If your constituents are getting subpoenaed to appear at Ellis Island, there's good and thoroughly researched cause. They'll have a fair hearing and the opportunity to make their case."

Barkley leaned across the desk to within inches of Will. "These people can't afford lawyers. They can't afford to miss days of work while they wait in line for their case to be called. This is harassment, Brown, and if you don't call off your wolves, slow down with this, I'm going to bring the issue straight to the US Congress, you hear me?"

"Your threats have no bearing here," Will said. "Even if they are mostly Democrats, the congressmen I know are not in favor of keeping perjurers and Communists on our shores. My work will continue until I hear otherwise." He stood up to signal the end of the conversation. "Kind of you to drop by," he said.

The congressman squinted a determined look his way, then sauntered out. From the outer office, Will could hear him tell Annette how lovely she was looking, and her thank-you couldn't have been more coquettish. It made Will blanch: politicians!

Will resisted the urge to angrily pound a pile of papers on his desk and sat down to collect himself. What had begun as a reasonable enough day—a couple of decisive indications of immigrant fraud that would surely meet with Connelly's approval for warrants, nice lunch with Doug and Stan—had turned into one of those knotted-stomach afternoons against which his only defense was deep breathing and further study of the reams of paperwork in his inbox.

Damn that Barkley. Who did he think he was? But Will knew very well the sway the man held over Washington. The Irish king of the Jews up there in the Bronx was unbeatable, brash. And in this environment? This Rooseveltian, New Dealy do-gooder would hand them a welfare state if they weren't careful. Barkley was a force to be reckoned with, and he knew it.

Well, Will didn't recommend deportation warrants without damn good evidence. Strong, thorough investigation and reports. Let Barkley take his complaints to the Congress, or even Perkins. There wasn't one case Will wouldn't stand behind 100 percent.

He picked up the file he'd been going through before lunch. Here was a doozy. Bunch of union people in New York—where else?—putting together some kind of show. All about labor practices and injustices. A musical, no less. Very entertaining! Only in today's atmosphere could these people even dream of getting an audience to pay good money for this kind of anti-American rubbish. He'd perused the cast of characters, creative and backstage crew, involved in this travesty and, sure enough, there were some familiar names.

He pressed the intercom button. "Annette, can you get me the Lansky file? Reva Lansky." At least, she was out of Barkley's jurisdiction. If memory served, Miss Lansky lived in that other borough of troublemakers: Brooklyn.

His stomach really was cramped. God, the power that man had. Junior's temperature was eating at him, too.

Not only did Dr. Trackman come to her rescue in all manner of new-mother anxieties, but he was by far the most handsome man. True, he was starting to go gray, if one looked hard enough, but anyone could see he was the spitting image of Robert Taylor, with his soft, reassuring voice and thin mustache. He was tall and walked straight as anything, and Barbara sometimes joked that he was more her doctor than the baby's. Junior could be burning up, crying for Lord knew what reason, fussing, miserable, red in the face, yet sure enough, just opening the door for Dr. Trackman, seeing him with that little black bag of his and that nice overcoat, she could feel her jangly nerves just melt away.

The doctor diagnosed the cause of today's misery as an ear infection. Babies get them all the time, he told her. Makes them miserable. Wouldn't you be, Trackman asked, with pus plugging up your middle ear? Barbara nodded compliantly.

The baby howled as the doctor gently drained his ears with a rubber syringe, and didn't take too kindly either to the cold washcloth he placed on his forehead, with directions to keep the compress going until the fever went down. If the baby kept moving around or if he tossed off the washcloth, she should try placing him in as cool a bath as he would tolerate, the doctor said. With these instructions and a prescription, and a smile to dazzle her fears into ether as she saw him to the front door, Dr. Trackman disappeared into the gray afternoon.

"Isn't it something," Barbara said to her father-in-law, who was sitting in his rocking chair in the room he shared with Junior. "He just always has such a calming effect, don't you think?" And indeed, Nicholas Junior had already fallen asleep in his crib, not fussing at all. The cool washcloth sat undisturbed on his little forehead.

"He has the knack for healing," Nicholas agreed.

"You mind sitting here with him while I go out to the drugstore to fill the prescription?" Barbara asked. She wondered if a day went by that she didn't have to go to Connecticut Avenue for one thing or another. If it wasn't the marketing, it was a bulb that had blown out, or diapers, or shampoo. Well, she didn't mind. Going out gave her an excuse to visit the 5 & 10, just about her favorite spot on earth since they'd moved to Washington. Such a handy place, like the general stores they had back home, with the extra feature of the ice-cream counter.

Oh, she knew she still hadn't managed to lose the weight she'd put on with the pregnancy, and it said in the magazines that it was high time, Junior being over a year. But she'd been a good girl while she was carrying him, hardly had even a thimbleful of alcohol the whole nine months, and ice cream had somehow or other become her substitute, her reward.

Now, of course, she was drinking again and still having a dish of ice cream over at the 5 & 10 practically every day. Well, what was she supposed to do? She'd promised herself today that she wouldn't have any, but then the baby got this fever, Dr. Trackman had given her a prescription to fill, so even though she hadn't had any plans whatsoever to be on Connecticut Avenue, here she was, putting on her overcoat and galoshes, heading over to the drugstore, right next door to the 5 & 10 and, well, a dish of creamy chocolate ice cream sounded so very good. At least she didn't buy it at the grocery store and keep it in the house. She deserved some credit for that. At least she was trying to manage her cravings.

Before leaving, she went into the kitchen and reached under the sink, where she kept her personal stock of whiskey, just an old habit, and took a quick shot, just to keep her warm. It was cold out there.

"If he wakes up, just let him rest in the crib," Barbara called from the front door. "Unless he gets cranky, you know. Oh, and Will will probably call to find out what the doctor said."

"Don't worry, Barbara," the throaty voice of her father-in-law came from the bedroom. "We'll be fine."

"Thanks, Pop. I've got that ground beef defrosting for dinner," and then she closed the door behind her.

I don't know what I'd do without him, Barbara thought as she walked past the other row houses on their street. The way Will had tried to persuade him at first to go back to Iowa, it was positively painful to watch. Why, the man had had a heart attack before they were even out of high school; hadn't he gone through enough in his life? Those awful hooligans destroying the store, and then Ellie dying, and that horrible incident on the road. If that snobby Martha Connelly looked down her nose at them now that Nicholas was part of the family, well, that was just one more advantage Pop brought with him, saving them from endless evenings of her chatter. Of course, it was sad beyond words, the circumstances that had brought him to them, but even if it was thanks to those terrible things that Nicholas lived with them, well, God had his reasons, and Barbara was grateful.

"How are you today, Mrs. Brown?" the friendly boy at the counter greeted her. "The usual?" He didn't wait before scooping two mounds of chocolate into a glass dish.

"Oh, I've been better, thanks," Barbara sidled onto a stool and adjusted her coat underneath her until she was comfortable. "I'm just waiting for Mr. Gerard to fill a prescription next door. Junior's sicker than I've ever seen him."

Eddie was such a darling boy. Those pimples must worry him, but surely they'd clear up in no time. He had a beautiful smile, made a person feel good in her skin, and welcome.

"Just about everybody's come down with something," Eddie said, placing the long spoon in the ice-cream dish and putting the creamy confection on the counter in front of her. "Want a little whipped cream today?"

"Oh," Barbara hesitated for only a second, "why not? It has been a difficult day, so much worry and all."

"Well, don't you worry, Mrs. Brown," Eddie said, spooning some whipped cream on top of the chocolate scoops. "Look at how empty the store is; just about everyone's sick with something or other." He put an extra dollop on for her. "I can't wait till we get one of those dispensers I've been reading about. Would you believe it? Whipped cream right out of some kind of pressurized can. They've got 'em in Europe; just a matter of time before the good old US of A figures out how to do it."

"Mm, this is good," Barbara said, savoring her afternoon treat. "Don't tell Mr. Brown about that. He gets very cross about anyone believing that anything happens in Europe before here. American ingenuity and all that."

"Mum's the word," Eddie said, and he folded his arms and watched her, the nice, pleasingly plump woman who came in just about every afternoon. Always a smile on her face, always a friendly word. It was gratifying to see a person enjoy something so much. Not many people came in for ice cream these days, in the dead of winter.

Junior awakened with a whimper and then a series of sounds from his throat that grew into fierce screaming by the time Nicholas startled awake to see his grandson standing at the rail of the crib, red-faced. He bolted from the rocker and lifted the boy, who clutched the damp washcloth that was now quite warm to the touch. The boy himself was burning. Where was Barbara with that prescription?

"Now, now, sweetheart." Nicholas bounced the baby in his arms. "Ssh, ssh. Mama's coming soon." He bounced him in his arms, walking from room to room. Oh, he was a big boy, grown pretty heavy. The heat emanating from his little body, though, was something awful, almost made Nicholas want to cry.

Hadn't the doctor said something about a bath?

Nicholas carried the little fellow, burning up, to the upstairs bath-room. He had to go slowly, Junior was quite a bundle in his arms. "Here we are, sweetheart, I'll run a nice bath for you. Won't that be nice?"

Lowering himself and the baby to the floor next to the tub, he turned on the faucets. Cool, he remembered the doctor saying, it should be a cool bath to bring down the fever. "See your toys?" he asked Junior. "Oh, we'll have some fun." A tightening was gathering in his chest, probably from the stairs. Nothing.

There, he felt the water with his wrist, like Ellie used to when they gave Will a bath. A little on the cool side. Just right.

Junior squirmed as his grandfather took off his soaked-through pajamas. The diaper was sopping wet, hot. But the baby had quieted down a little, seeing his toys floating in the water. He loved his bath.

Oh, but he was heavy to lift up and into the tub. What a big boy. Nicholas lowered him slowly, the tightness in his chest gripping his insides. Sweat poured down his temples.

His bottom meeting the cool water, Junior's calmed demeanor wrinkled into distress. This was different from what a bath usually felt like. The water was so cold against his fevered skin.

Again, he started crying, whimpering, working himself up with short, rapid breaths.

Squeak, squeak, Nicholas squeezed the rubber tugboat and moved it through the water toward the boy. As he had hoped, it caught the little one's interest. Junior's face played between misery and fascination.

"See? Isn't it a big boat coming through the water?" Nicholas sucked in some deep breaths, hoping the oxygen would quell the pain in his chest. He mopped his face with a towel and smiled down at the beauty of this child. What a blessing. To know this kind of happiness again, he could never have expected.

"Qweak," Junior gurgled, splashing his little hands in the water and grabbing the boat. "Qweak, qweak, gampa."

Rrriiiing, rrriiiing. The phone sounded from Will and Barbara's bedroom. "That must be your daddy," Nicholas said. "He's worried about you, I bet."

Rrriiiing. The phone didn't stop, and the indecision about whether to answer it compounded the pressure in his chest, which had seemed to be abating. *Rrriiing, rrriiiing.*

Maybe the baby would be all right for just a second, if he quickly answered the phone. Will must be terribly worried.

Nicholas placed his large square hand on the rim of the bathtub to hoist himself up. But the effort was too great. He just didn't have it in him, he realized, to stand up. *Rrriiing.* Where was Barbara?

"Why doesn't she answer?" Will paced the floor behind his desk, clutching the phone. He'd told her he would call. Where was she? "Where's Pop?" he said aloud.

All kinds of thoughts raced through his mind as he let the phone continue to ring, twenty, thirty times. It was impossible that they'd both left the house, that no one was there to answer. He'd told her he would call. Could the baby have taken a turn for the worse? Had the doctor told them to get him to a hospital? No. Barbara would have called. Unless they'd left in a hurry, unless it had been an emergency.

He banged the receiver down and grabbed his coat. "Get me a car," he ordered Annette as he passed through the reception area. "A bureau car, right now!"

When he thought back on it, which he would every day for the rest of his life, Barbara's screams and the shrill cry of the ambulance as it shrieked from the curb in front of the house merged in his ears as one sound. Which had he heard first, he'd try to remember. What did he already know before running up the front steps and seeing his wife ashen, slumped at the foot of the stairs? Where was the baby? He knew that was his first thought. A small white paper bag from Gerard's Pharmacy sat next to Barbara. That white bag was always part of the picture, its presence there on the floor—folded at the top and stapled, unopened and unnecessary, like an afterthought—had told the story.

"Your father had a heart attack, Will," Barbara uttered in barely discernible syllables, as though shaping words required more ability than she had. Her voice was dry and cold.

Will could barely ask: "The baby?"

After an impossibly long stretch of silence: "He was in the bathtub."

Will threw his head back, his fingers clawing his heaven-seeking face, and a sound came from him, a low, guttural, primitive sound, that terrified him with its otherworldliness. He fell to his knees and sobbed, as though he would never stop, into Barbara's lap.

Warsaw

Yitzak hurried past the Nozyk Temple on Twarda Street as he made his way to Grzybowski Place, the central market where the merchants would be setting up their stalls and opening their small shops. He always walked quickly around the Orthodox Jews that tended to congregate at the doors of the synagogue. With their long beards and *payess*, their tattered, heavy coats and fur hats, they looked as though they had been transplanted straight from the Middle Ages, and there was no question they gave the Jews a bad name. It gave Yitzak no pleasure to think this way, to feel embarrassed by his own people, but what did he have in common with these darkly ostentatious characters? Just one thing, and that only made him more bitter toward them: he was the target of the same hatred. Anti-Semites didn't differentiate between Jews.

Yet around the corner from the Orthodox gathering place, like a scrappy assertion of Jewish modernity, the bustling marketplace burst into view. Enterprising businessmen worked purposefully to arrange their wares in the most attractive way possible, and well-dressed shoppers circled the area as they prepared to sift among the dresses, shoes, books, fresh-baked pastries, and the finest wines and liquors. For the past three years, Yitzak had been working at Grozky's Liquor Store, at the northern corner of Grzybowski Place, where the owner had more or less put him in charge. He made a good living managing the store, but what he especially enjoyed about the job was the proximity it afforded to the many writers and intellectuals who came in.

Warsaw had become a cauldron of freethinkers and political types, and from Yitzak's vantage point among the liquor bottles, alcohol seemed to be an active ingredient. Each and every day inside the wood-paneled premises of Grozky's Liquors, he'd eavesdrop on the arguments and revolutionary ideas: the Bundists with their calls for massive strikes and demonstrations representing the workers; the Zionists advocating relocation to Palestine; the Communists and Socialists, the anarchists and Trotskyites—everyone articulating a different plan for the perfect society and how to combat the increasingly irrefutable animosity toward the so-called "Jewish Nation in Poland." In the tradition of any enterprising businessman, Yitzak made himself agreeable to all of his customers, never taking sides, or questioning the conflicting ideas offered up for consideration. As long as the fractious clientele walked out of the store with bottles of schnapps under their arms, he stood happy to listen and offer perhaps the congenial smile, wink, shrug of the shoulders.

Even on this freezing-cold morning, he wasn't surprised to find a few of the regulars standing outside reading their newspapers and commenting to one another as they stood waiting for him to open. As he unlocked the wrought-iron grating that protected the front door, Yitzak heard Bloom, an aspiring poet who always stopped here on his way to the Writers' Club on Tlomackie Street, confront Friedman, a Zionist.

"You see what they got their hands on?" He held out a page from the newspaper. "You gonna run away to Palestine when we got this to fight?"

"I'm not running," Friedman said reasonably. "I'm joining my people in the one place on earth we can call home."

Bloom responded to the absurdity of Friedman's statement with a dismissive sweep of the hand. "What, you think the Arabs like us any better than the Poles? Listen to this," and he found the article that had recently incensed him.

"Straight from the Catholics, they got this letter, and reprinted it. From the Primate of Poland, no less, the chief guy. Here's what he writes: 'The Jews are fighting against the Catholic Church, persisting in freethinking, and are the vanguard of godlessness, Bolshevism and subversion.' That's from the Primate. And from a Jesuit periodical, they also quote. Listen to this: 'We must have separate schools for Jews, so that our children will not be infected with their lower morality.'" He slapped the page angrily. "Morality! One out of ten Polish citizens is a Jew, and they dare to propagate this filth. If this is how the big shots in the Catholic Church talk about us, you think it's going to be better in the Arab desert?"

By now the men were inside, blowing the cold from their cupped hands. "So go join up with the Communists," Friedman said, "you think they like us any better? They'll be the first to repudiate us. Go ahead."

"I'm not joining; I'm just saying."

The two men interrupted their ongoing argument to bid Yitzak a friendly greeting, and he smiled at them in return.

"*Nu*, when will it end?" a third customer asked philosophically. "Probably? Never." Having answered his own question, he walked over to a shelf of vodkas. "But at least, with so many millions of us here, there is strength in numbers."

"That's what I say," Bloom agreed. "Tell him."

"I see no reason to stay in a place where I'm not wanted," Friedman said.

"Well, in that case," Bloom threw a sardonic chuckle into his retort, "Himelbaum, you got behind the counter a gun? My friend Friedman here might as well shoot himself right now. Because in heaven, maybe, is where we're wanted. As long, that is, as we can count on God not being a Catholic."

Knowing that Bloom wasn't expecting a response, Yitzak just laughed along. Of course, he'd never acknowledge that he did in fact have a gun behind the counter. Ava had insisted, as much as she abhorred violence of any kind, that he not stand there alone in the store day after day with all the pillaging and bullying taking place. Just a few months ago, Jewish-owned homes and businesses had been torched in a town just outside of Warsaw during anti-Jewish riots. God forbid some Polish hoodlums should get it in their heads to come in and give him trouble. A liquor store, Ava said, that's just where they'd go.

Bloom and Friedman were still debating the pros and cons of staying in Poland versus the far greater calling of founding a Jewish homeland as they paid for their respective bottles and wished Yitzak a good day. "A good day," the philosophical customer whom Yitzak didn't know by name, muttered under his breath. He counted out the several *zloty* for his vodka and tucked it into his overcoat as he left the store.

While Yitzak found the spirited back-and-forth of his customers invigorating, he tried not to get involved in the political ferment nipping at the equilibrium of his country and his people. He didn't want to believe that the episodes of harassment, inarguably violent, posed a serious threat to Jewish existence in Poland. In Germany, yes, things were bad. This Hitler, from the moment he'd come into power he'd instituted laws stripping Jews of their work, their education, their dignity as equal citizens—in the country they had fought and died for during the World War, no less. He knew from reading the newspapers and his talks with Ava that the German Jews were pouring out of the country. Scientists and composers, lawyers, tens of thousands were leaving. But no longer were they coming to Poland. Did they know something? This troubled him. No, to Palestine and America they were going, the fleeing German Jews. Well, Yitzak quieted his anxieties, Poland had never been good enough for them. That's why they weren't coming here: they looked down on Polish Jews, that was the reason.

"You can find in your mind all kinds of reasons," Ava would say when he posited this explanation. "But however much one group of Jews hates another, I'm telling you, I hear it at work, nothing compares to how Hitler hates the Jews. And believe me, when he's through with Germany, we won't be far behind."

With increasing regularity, Ava was urging Yitzak to leave Poland. "There are too many of you here," she'd say, "it's too tempting for a madman like that. He'll march in, I'm telling you. Right now, he's probably sitting in the Reichstag studying the map."

"You're so eager I should leave?" Yitzak would say, pulling her hair playfully, or stroking her shoulder.

"I'm eager you should live," Ava would return, affectionately mocking his syntax even as she tried to convey her seriousness.

At her prompting, because she had heard that it would soon be the international language, they frequently struggled to converse in English, even debating in the foreign tongue. Perhaps it was this layer of needing to translate his thoughts that helped Yitzak remain a step removed from his true feelings.

In the liquor store and on the street, in Ava's bedroom and on the train back to Stawki for his monthly visits with Chava and the children, he tried to cast off his fears, to gaze around and persuade himself that life went on in its usual way: children playing, intellectuals arguing, merchants opening and closing their stores, lovers strolling in parks, farmers pulling their harvested crops behind them in carts, mothers baking, neighbors exchanging secrets.

About his feelings for Ava there was no ambivalence whatsoever. She was the love of his life, pure and simple, and he was devoted to her. Now that he had secured a good job in Warsaw, bringing home generous sums, his life here demanded fewer justifications. Chava knew what was going on, he denied it only halfheartedly, and as long as he could help to support the family and see his children every now and then, as long as Ava remained firm in her refusals when he suggested that they marry, the situation, if not ideal, was acceptable.

On the last Friday morning of February, Yitzak set out for the long trip home. He dozed on the train, startling awake a few times with the lurching motion, and clutching tighter each time the customary bottle of whiskey he was bringing. But when he stepped off the train in Wlodawa, the sight that greeted him made him forget the bottle; as he clapped his hands over his face, it crashed to the ground. Windows on the Jewish shops were shattered; anti-Semitic slogans covered front doors and sidewalks. It looked as though repairs might have begun, but *Shabbes* was only hours away, so the streets stood empty.

Thinking in Yiddish, Yitzak didn't have to overcome a language barrier to identify his feelings. A tight knot clenched his stomach. He walked quickly toward the dirt road that led to Stawki. Would he find everyone all right? God forbid, had there been a pogrom?

Running now, he felt vaguely reassured as the houses he'd seen all his life, on this road that he'd traversed for the same duration, seemed to be standing, uncharred by fire or damage. The children must be all right. And Mama, surely he would have heard if something had happened.

Out of breath, sweating despite the icy temperature, he reached home. He stopped and stood a few moments to catch his breath, rushing from his mouth in clouds of smoke. He wiped his brow, adjusted his hat. From the chimney came the sure signs of cooking and preparation.

When he opened the door, Chava greeted him with her usual indifference, Moishe at her side. Sarah ran up to throw her arms around his legs, and his mother wept, as she always did, to see him standing there.

"Come, sit down," she said, wiping her tears away with her apron. "We have from Yankele a letter. Hershel, he read already. Would you believe? He's coming home."

With her words, Yitzak understood clearly and for the first time the truth he'd been denying for months and years. The truth was that he lived on the constant cusp of terror. Yankel was leaving America? To come here?!

~ ~ ~

June – August

New York City

Standing in line among the other adult students in the classroom with its familiar musty smell and fraying charts on the walls, Harry waited to say good-bye to the night-school teacher. He tried to maintain a dignified posture for this privileged encounter, but two concerns weighed on him. First, there was the matter of Alice's invitation. For eight years he had been faithful to his wife and marriage vows, and now, with his steamship ticket in his dresser drawer and his suitcase packed, why had he now, of all times, agreed to go out on a date? From the moment he had said yes, he'd told himself that he would phone her to cancel, but that call did not take place. He and Alice were due to meet at the Nickalaus Coffee Shop on 181st Street at nine. Why had he made such an appointment? What could he have been thinking? But she would be there waiting for him; he had to go.

The second thing troubling Harry was what he should say to Miss O'Rourke when his turn came. "You have made magnificent progress," the slim, straight-backed teacher had told the group of immigrant intermediate-level English learners—mostly eastern-European Jews, with a smattering of Italians—at the end of class, "but don't allow our summer break to bring an end to that progress. Speak in English, our American tongue, as often and as confidently as you can as you enjoy the summer months." And then she had invited them to please have a private word with her before leaving.

Harry found some amusement in his teacher urging the students to speak English over the summer, when here he was practically on the boat back to Poland. But should he, in his private words with her, (he liked that expression: "a private word") should he ask what she would suggest under the circumstances? He couldn't decide whether to even mention that he was returning to Europe: wouldn't it make him seem a hopeless foreigner, so attached to the old country that he couldn't stay away? On the other hand, he sincerely wanted to keep up with his English and welcomed any suggestions Miss O'Rourke might have on how much to encourage his family back home to speak the language.

So Harry stood in the line beset by uncertainty: what would he say to his teacher? And once that was gotten through, would he proceed out the classroom door and take the bus to Nickalaus's and betray his marriage?

Generally, he didn't like waiting in lines very much, but tonight he was in no hurry.

Regina: her letters were always about the boy. As though she understood that he was their tie, that without him, there would have been no marriage. At least not before he'd left Poland. They had talked about her coming to America and getting married once he got settled, but they had been kids, dreamers under the spell of spring fragrances and an undeniable physical attraction. Who knew how things might have turned out? When Harry looked at her pictures now, a short dark woman, slightly plump, with burning eyes (they were a light green, he remembered) he barely recognized her. She was the mother of his child, Yakob appeared in every picture, but a woman he loved? Always when he opened the envelopes from Lukow, he would pray to find a picture that would rekindle romantic feelings, arouse tenderness, yearning, connection. But the connection was the boy, the three of them as a family, the object of his every effort: that was what connected them. And wasn't that a form of love? Nothing like the mysterious allure of that beautiful, tall redhead with the scarf all those years ago, the one who came every day for her apples. Mrs. Brown from Iowa. Nothing like the easy affection he felt whenever Doris came into the store, with her shy ways. Sometimes, he'd remind himself of Reizel's black curls under all those hats she wore in the pictures, and the day he would squeeze them in the palm of his hand as he drew her toward him. There was that. And he had been true to his wife, managing over the years, as a young man will, to satisfy his physical needs with the help of fantasies and magazines—the latter hidden from his father and then Irene with the envelopes up on the closet shelf. As for Alice?

Miss O'Rourke was holding out her hand to him, "Mr. Himelbaum?" This was an unusual gesture for a female, shaking hands, yet Harry admired it quite a bit, as he did most things emanating from his highly accomplished teacher. He noticed, as she congratulated him on his mastery of sophisticated terms and obvious interest in current events, that she looked younger close-up. "I can tell from the sentences you use and the questions you ask in class," she said, "that you must be an avid reader of newspapers. You really should go to the advanced class next term." Harry felt himself blush, a mortifying feature in himself that he could do nothing about, but her compliments emboldened him, so that he did indeed find himself asking her about Poland, and what language he should speak while he was there.

"You're returning to Poland, Mr. Himelbaum?" the teacher asked, her brow wrinkling with apparent concern. "You know there have been certain . . ."—it was odd to see the teacher searching for a word—"incidents. Not to concern you unnecessarily, but why are you going?"

Harry knew about the pogroms and harassment; though there was surprisingly little mention of these events in the newspaper, Yitzak wrote to him, and people were talking. He knew. "Family," he said meekly, feeling foolish, and very sorry that he'd made the decision to mention his trip to her. "It's been many years," he started to explain.

"Yes, but wouldn't it be better to bring your family here," Miss O'Rourke asked, "under the, well, under the circumstances?"

"I will, I will bring them," Harry said. "And in the fall, you wait, in the fall they'll be here, studying, like me."

"Best of luck, Mr. Himelbaum," the teacher said, and she reassumed her detached demeanor as her eyes searched for the student behind him.

As he left the classroom, Harry realized that, for all his previous indecisiveness and attempts at preparation, he had managed to ask the question about which he had been so torn, but the teacher hadn't answered it.

Or had she? Harry reconsidered as he took a drink from one of the water fountains. The thin, warm trickle was hardly refreshing. *Obviously, she doesn't think I should go,* Harry realized. *Well,* he said to himself, *that's not even a question.*

And a sundae at Nickalaus? That wasn't a question, either.

The night air was soft and balmy, and it was early yet, so Harry decided to walk the thirteen blocks. Even walking, he'd probably get there before she did, and probably, knowing Alice and her flirtatious ways, she'd be a few minutes late, to keep him waiting. Should he wait for her? How long?

He didn't know why he was thinking so much about that lady in the Village lately. It started the week before, when he'd gone to see Reva backstage at that theatre on Fiftieth Street. He'd figured it was only right, before going to see Regina, that he once more thank, in person, the woman who had enabled the relationship to continue. Maybe she had a message for her cousin? Something he should take with him to the old country? "What do I have that you should take?" Reva had laughed. Sitting on a folding chair in the cramped backstage area, one of many seamstresses with bundles of folded fabric on their laps, and a strand of thread poised between her lips, she had looked up at him and laughed. Well, that was something; he realized he'd never seen her laugh before. "You bring her back with you, that's all I can say," Reva told him. "You'll come in November, to the opening, if they haven't closed us down first. You think we don't know the feds are watching us? A bunch of unionists putting on a show?" But she looked utterly engrossed in what she was doing, barely worried about anything at all. Like a different person.

Reva wasn't the only sign of progress at the theatre. Since the rehearsal he'd attended back in the wintertime, this was starting to look like the real thing, and Harry couldn't help but be impressed. The costumes, the scenery, the high energy and bustle were undeniable. From the stage, he could hear a piano tinkling a spirited tune. "Ladies, come on," a young man in overalls called in. "I have to see how the dresses are going to look."

"You take care of yourself," Reva said to Harry. "It's a *shande* what's going on over there. I just hope you bring them all back with you, there shouldn't be a Jew left in Poland, God forbid, before that Nazi takes over."

"Sing me a song of social significance," the strains of a song followed Harry as he left the theatre. Always Reva talked about the "feds"; *nu*, it was in her makeup. It was nice to see her happy. Maybe he'd find for Regina a job on the show. She was a milliner, after all, and they must need hats for the costumes. He bet they did.

Maybe it was seeing Reva that set him to thinking about Mrs. Brown. They belonged to the same period in his life. The last time he'd seen her, she was walking with that man, probably her husband. Harry remembered, but for the first time acknowledged, that he'd felt jealous. Walking to the subway after seeing Reva, and tonight on his way to Nickalaus, he admitted it to himself: if things were different, he would have liked to know her better. Such a lovely, friendly person. On the other hand, would he have stood a chance with a woman like that? Even if they weren't both married? She looked a little bit older than him, but wasn't Regina also older? The stab of guilt. What was he thinking? Just some kind of self-inflicted torment he carried around in his head: Mrs. Brown with the red hair.

Alice was sitting and smoking a cigarette at a small, round table against the wall in the back of the narrow coffee shop. It wasn't even nine yet, but, he should have realized, this was not a girl who played hard to get. Through the ribbon of smoke streaming from her freshly lilac-lipsticked mouth, the message was all "come hither."

"You look even nicer than usual," he said, sitting opposite her. His short-sleeved shirt, slightly damp from the walk, filmed over with another layer of moisture. In her crisp, white, sleeveless blouse, her arms disarmingly smooth and tan, and her fingernails painted mauve to match her lips, Alice looked the picture of someone who wouldn't mind being ravaged. Her arm moved slowly as it led the cigarette to her lips for a drag, then lowered to pat an ash into the ashtray. The face before him and the dark brown eyes never wavering from their stare would not be considered beautiful—the nose was too large, the chin less defined than it might be—but the whole undeniably trumped its parts, and the seduction was on. Harry was twenty-eight years old and hadn't been with a woman in almost a decade. Why, when he would be with his wife in just a few weeks' time, had he chosen this late date to succumb to the needs he'd managed so strenuously to deny? What kind of a person was he?

As the waiter with the white triangular paper cap came to the table and asked what they'd like to order, and Harry asked for a sundae, Alice demurring that she'd only like coffee, and they exchanged the banalities of small talk while they waited and then indulged in the ice cream, the coffee, and then Harry asked if she'd like to take a walk, self-recrimination, and the matter of his timing, dissolved into so much nothingness. He only knew that he would have her and that she'd take him and that the grassy tree-lined area overlooking the Hudson River afforded privacy and that the feeling of her silky arms around his neck, and her mouth on his, the warmth of her breath, and the supple firmness of her breasts in his quivering hands, the hot moist entrance that spasmed ever so slightly as it yielded to his fingers and his entering there with the bone-hard center of himself overwhelmed words, questions, second thoughts. He only hoped it wouldn't be too qui—Eruption! Release! All of time and the cessation of time shuddering through his body at once. Alice, too, convulsed with pleasure.

Afterward, clothes rumpled, they lay side by side on the grass, looking into the starry night.

When his breath returned to a normal rhythm, Harry said, "You know I go back to Poland next week." He knew it was unnecessarily harsh, this sentence his first utterance following their intimacy; yet this was the thing he wanted her to know.

"I'll miss you," Alice said.

"I'll probably be there a while. A month at least, maybe more."

"I'm not sorry that we did this," Alice said, turning toward him, and snuggling her head into the crook of his shoulder. "You could tell, I'm sure, that it wasn't the first time, so you don't have to feel bad about anything."

What Harry was feeling, looking up into the night sky, came as a total surprise to him. After all the years of abstinence, the disciplined turning away from any woman he might find attractive, this act of indiscretion had reawakened his feelings for Regina. He found himself longing for her closeness, that way she had of lowering her head and then looking up at him when he tucked his finger under her chin. Her springy soft curls. Her eyes. He remembered the girl he had made love to and couldn't wait to be back with her, back home. Suddenly, with these thoughts, it was Alice he was betraying.

"You have someone in Poland, yes?" she asked.

Harry waited only a moment before acknowledging that yes, he did.

"I, too, have someone. We've been keeping company for two years, maybe longer. He wants to marry me. It's with him that I, well, you know." Alice rolled away from him, so that they were two parallel bodies gazing skyward.

"He's a lucky man," Harry said.

"Spoken by someone who doesn't wish to be so lucky," Alice said with resignation. They didn't say anything for a few minutes. "I think I may be pregnant," Alice broke the silence. "I have to marry him. I only did it with him because I hoped it would persuade me to love him. He makes good money, my parents beg me every day to accept his proposal. He's very good to me, but, you know, there's no spark with him. Not like, with you. Even the way we just *kibbitz* in the store," she laughed softly. "I figured you must have someone, but, well, before I say yes to Morris, I wanted to see. I wanted to see what it was like with someone, with, you know, someone with the spark." She turned onto an elbow to look at him. "So now I know."

Harry could only say that he was sorry.

"I told you, don't be sorry," Alice said. "Now I don't have to go to my grave not knowing what it's like to enjoy sex. I'll have children, a nice home, and that knowledge. No, I don't want you to be sorry."

Harry smiled and tucked a stray hair behind her ears. "We've had a good time together," he said. "You make me laugh all the time, and it's been very nice."

"We've had a good time, but tonight was the topper." Alice smiled. "Come, I should be getting home."

They straightened themselves out and walked slowly away from the river, down the 181st Street hill to Alice's apartment house. He kissed her forehead, and they said good night.

Harry, not wanting to believe that things would go as far as they did, hadn't brought protection with him. He felt like an idiot, a demon. A very, very lucky demon. If Alice wasn't already pregnant, he actually could have impregnated her. Gone to the boat with his ticket and his suitcase and learned right there on the spot that yet another woman was carrying his child just as he was about to leave her. The thought made him queasy, so that he had to sit down on the stoop outside his building before going in. He looked up to the heavens and with the deepest humility a man can know, he thanked God.

Upstairs, Irene and Saul sat riveted at the kitchen table as a scratchy voice from the radio described the recent marriage of the Duke of Windsor and Wallis Simpson. Between *Gone With the Wind* and King Edward VIII's abdication of the throne for the woman he loved, Americans had a spate of romances to distract them from a recent economic downturn, and in Irene's case the international spectacle provided an equally useful distraction from academics. This was precisely Harry's observation when he walked into the kitchen.

"I thought you were studying for your math test," he said, going straight to the sink for a glass of water.

Saul leapt to Irene's defense. "Not everyone stays so late at night with their studies." He looked pointedly at his wristwatch and threw Harry a conspiratorial wink.

"I stayed to talk with the teacher," Harry countered, not entirely untruthfully, but he was glad that Irene had agreed to keep his matrimonial status a secret, preferring the occasional teasing from Ralph and Saul about his, until tonight, imagined social life, to the ripple effect the truth would have. It was going to be hard enough explaining the deception to his own mother; telling his boss would be easier once he'd confessed to everything at home and, please God, been forgiven.

To divert attention from himself and his late arrival—it was almost eleven o'clock—Harry asked Saul whether the Dodgers had played that day, baseball having become an area of small talk the two engaged in with increasing frequency. When things were quiet at the store, Saul loved to talk about the game, its rules and intricacies, and they'd even thrown a ball around out on the sidewalk a few times.

"Yeah, they played. I don't know about those green uniforms, though," Saul said, referring to the change of uniform color introduced at Ebbets Field that year.

"Sshh," Irene scolded, "can't you two be quiet?"

"So," the radio voice summarized, "while the divorcée from Baltimore will never be Queen, Great Britain has its new Duchess." And with that pronouncement, orchestral music filtered from the radio.

"It's so romantic," Irene said as she gathered the loose papers from the table and tapped them into a neat pile.

"It's late. We should all go to bed," Harry said. He kissed his sister's head and told her he'd get her up extra early in the morning for the test. "You think she'll pass?" he asked Saul.

"Pass? I think she'll get at least a hundred percent. This is a very smart girl we've got here."

"Thanks for helping her out." Harry patted the young man's shoulder. Given his own situation, Harry no longer pressed Irene about her relationship with Saul. Clearly, they were smitten with each other, and there was no evidence whatsoever that the boy's intentions were anything but honorable. Who was he, after all, to pass judgment on male-female relations?

The discomfort Harry felt at the store the next day unequivocally supported the wisdom of remaining strictly uninvolved with women for eight years. Arranging the produce, interacting with the customers, ringing up sales, each and every moment he dreaded the arrival of Alice.

When she finally did appear, late in the afternoon to buy some potatoes and onions, there were none of the customary innuendos or even much gaiety. The two lovers of the night before treated each other with courtesy and thin voices, a dead giveaway to Saul.

"So you finally went out with her?" he asked when Alice left.

"Just some coffee, it was nothing," Harry said.

"She's a beautiful girl. It's been coming for a while, you two."

"I'm leaving in a few days. I don't know what you're talking." Harry regretted the sour tone, but things were much more complicated for him than Saul's well-intentioned single-man-to-single-man appraisal could guess.

"Well, you're coming back, aren't you?" Saul wasn't taking the hint. "I knew, when you were so late coming home last night. I should have known it was her. I'm glad it was, a woman from the neighborhood, always a smile on her face."

"Stop about it already," Harry said, irritated with Saul's harping. "She's got somebody, all right? And things will be different when I come back. That's it, finished the business."

He stood up on the stepladder to turn on the fan; it was getting hot in the store. As accepting as he'd become of Irene's attachment to the boy, and as much as it eased his mind to know that Saul would be a source of companionship for her while he was away—a friend of Malka's, just here from Poland, would be staying in the apartment with her in Harry's room until he came back in August—at this moment he wanted nothing more than for the kid to shut up.

As his day for departure neared, his anxiety over what had transpired with Alice had cause to dissipate. The potatoes and onions, she told him later in the week, had added to a delicious stew the night she'd accepted Morris's proposal. The wedding date was set for the following month, and they'd be moving to a luxury apartment on the Grand Concourse. "I'll miss your cucumbers." She gave him one of her saucy looks and, as if by reflex, he winked at her and smiled.

Unfortunately, the reawakened romantic connection he'd felt toward Regina required less than a week to dim. That very night of his tryst, after leaving Saul and Irene in the kitchen, he'd taken the box of letters and photographs from the closet shelf, anticipating the attraction that his wife's image would evoke. The woman looking out at him from the photographs, however, resembled only faintly the girl he had pictured earlier near the river, like she might be a distant relative. He managed, though, as the days accumulated, and as he had for the last eight years, to reassure himself. The upcoming reunion was with his family, his wife and son. The woman with whom he had started that family, this stranger in the photographs, held his Reizele within her, and together they would find her.

The following Sunday afternoon, they were all there—Irene and Saul, Ralph, Malka and Jack—to see him off. The pier bustled with travelers, and the sun shone brilliantly. Hugging his beautiful grown-up sister, Harry reached into his pocket to give her a piece of candy. "For that *A* you got in math," he said. "Be a good girl and listen to Sonia."

Through her tears, Irene scoffed. "You talk like I'm a child." She fiddled with the candy wrapping. "Don't worry about anything. Give Mama a hug for me. And, everybody, tell them I love them. Come back soon, Yankele. With, well, try to bring them."

Harry patted his breast pocket, which held the U.S. Passport declaring his citizenship, and with it, the concomitant citizenship of his son. Some, like his night-school teacher, might question his decision to return to a place where Jews were hardly welcome, but investigation and informed gossip had convinced him that this was the surest way to bring his family over. "Believe me," he said, "it's going to be very crowded in the apartment."

Stawki

At first, Chava found it ridiculous, all the fuss. You'd think the king of France was coming, the way everyone was carrying on. The painting, the scrubbing, the whitewashing, not even for *Pesach* did the family immerse itself in such preparation. But soon she herself got swept up in the excitement. After all, she concluded, Yankel was coming from America, he shouldn't think they didn't live nice. And it pleased her, too, to see Moishele so busy and helpful with his sister. The weekend Yitzak had come home with Yankel's arrival date—the brothers were writing now back and forth to Warsaw? Where did her husband get his mail: at that whore's apartment?—he had shown the boy how to make a broom from birch twigs, and never had she seen her Moishe so interested in any project not associated with herself. For hours at a time, he'd sit on one of the benches evaluating and selecting the twigs for their strength and suppleness, pulling away leaves and brush and then carefully knotting the twigs and tying them together. He was good with his hands, the boy, and to see his little eyebrows knit in such concentration, yet never uttering a cross word to Sarah as she babbled questions and tried to help, made a mother proud, and hopeful.

David, Leah and Hershel's boy, was more of a physical type. The same age as Sarah, he was twice her size and seemed never to be clean. A perfect job for him, then, adding water to the dirt Hershel dug up to make mud for recoating the floors. How such a young boy could lift those pails of water Chava didn't know, but Elke distributed her praise equally between Moishe's birch brooms and David's mud, so a sort of peace permeated the hectic activity and the inconvenience of stepping carefully on newly coated floors, keeping one's hands away from freshly painted walls inside and out, and vigorously scrubbing before touching the whitewashed stove.

The enterprise of preparing the house for Yankel's arrival went on for weeks, although no one had quite figured out where he would sleep. The two rooms on either side of the kitchen belonged to Yitzak's and Hershel's families, and Elke had for years been content that her "room" be located in the form of a bed in a corner of the modest entranceway.

Sanding and scrubbing the benches in the front yard after all the other tasks were gotten through and the place sparkled—"like a palace," they all agreed—and as the children grabbed fistfuls of discarded leaves and placed them in the pail for disposal, Hershel brought up the topic of Yankel's accommodations once more. "Mama, you'll sleep with us, and Yankel in your room. We've talked it over, Leah and I, and there's nothing more to discuss."

"What do you want an old lady in the room with you?" Elke dismissed the offer. Everyone knew she was concerned that Hershel hadn't had another child and that it was therefore a priority that he and his wife have privacy to repair that unfortunate situation. "He'll be here a whole summer, you want I should sleep with you in the same room?" The matter seemed indisputably closed. Accompanying the children toward the back of the house, where they would disperse the leaves near the river, Leah felt the lingering warmth of embarrassment on her face. She loved her mother-in-law, but wished that her private life were not a topic of family conversation. Hershel, equally embarrassed, had been effectively silenced.

Chava, with her husband gone most of the time, knew it was only logical that she offer her room for Elke to share, and that this invitation would stand a better chance of being accepted. It had been years since she and Yitzak had engaged in any activity that might be inappropriate in the presence of one's mother-in-law, yet to ask Elke to room with them seemed too overt an acknowledgement of that fact. Yitzak had indicated that he planned to be in Stawki more frequently while Yankel was home and that, as far as Chava was concerned, sealed her decision not to invite the *shviger*. Would there be intimacy between them? Chava sometimes allowed herself to wonder about this. But her prim mind didn't linger on the possibility for more than fleeting moments at a time. The children, while they slept soundly, would yet be in the room, and anyway, Yitzak had relinquished his right to intimacy long ago.

Adding to Chava's stubbornness regarding Yankel's sleeping arrangements was her knowledge that he was a married man. The wife and, rumor had it, her child, were in Lukow. No one in Stawki had the slightest inkling that the child could be Yankel's—in all likelihood the reason for that rushed and secret marriage—but surely all the deception would be cleared up as soon as he came home. Why else was he coming, Chava reasoned, but to reunite with his wife and child? Elke's little space in the foyer would hardly accommodate all three, and Yitzak had concurred in a rare moment of private conversation that Yankel would likely be spending most of his time in Lukow with Reizel and her family, with only occasional nights spent here. *Oy,* Chava could just imagine how Elke would carry on when she learned the news. *Nu,* everyone would probably treat them like royalty, all three of them. Morality? Decency? None of it would matter once the American marched in with his secret bride and their son. To suggest a sleeping arrangement closer to the actual needs of Yankel's situation, Chava said, "*Nu,* the Kaminskys next door have now an empty room since their daughter got married. His own room there Yankel could have, why should we squeeze together?"

Elke looked at her as though she had uttered a profanity. "He should sleep with strangers?!"

"Mama, Ruthie Kaminsky is like a sister to you, you've known her all your life. What are you talking 'strangers'?" And there the matter rested, unresolved, as Chava knew it need not be. Soon enough, he would be here, and everything would fall into place. She'd tolerate the summer and the status Yankel and his family would command as she'd learned to tolerate everything else. At least, she had to admit, the house sparkled like new.

Lukow

One hundred twenty kilometers from the farmhouse in Stawki, a town busy with commerce accommodated shoppers and those who had come merely to browse. Women pushed their babies in carriages along the cobblestone streets as older children tugged on their skirts asking if they could please have some chocolate today, and inside the stores, earnest seekers of just the right ensemble held fabric up to themselves making decisions on color and design.

With the coming of the summer season, men and women alike knew they'd need to protect their faces from the sun, so the hatmakers' shop at No. 3 Staropijarska Street served a steady stream of customers.

Even so, the proprietors, Mr. and Mrs. Lansky, forgave their daughter for not being there to help on this busy afternoon. She was upstairs in their apartment above the store understandably preoccupied with her own appearance. Finally, after eight years, her husband was returning to Poland.

"Thank God, it's like a miracle," Frieda Lansky, Regina's mother, had repeated countless times since the letter had arrived, clasping her hands and looking heavenward.

"What, you thought he was just going to leave her here?" her husband, the logical one, would counter, although he privately wept with relief and gratitude when he heard the news.

Upstairs, in the room she shared with her son, Regina studied herself in the mirror. This was not the first time she'd stood there feeling defeated, and her face wrinkled in disapproval. For a month she'd stayed away from bread and sugar, but still the figure was not what it once was. Obviously, he knew from all the pictures she'd sent over the years that she'd put on a little weight, but when she'd finally received word that he was coming, every ounce of her will had been dedicated to recapturing the lean frame that waited just inside these extra pounds. The results were meager. The belt on her dress closed maybe one more hole if she held in her stomach. And how could she talk to him if she couldn't breathe?

Yakob, on the other hand, she'd been trying to fatten up, he was skinny like a herring. She didn't want Harry to think she starved the boy. But most of all, as she tried to cinch the belt to just one more hole, she hoped he wouldn't be sorry about her.

She moved closer to the mirror and examined her face. Even that was heavier, she sadly acknowledged. Grabbing her tweezers from the dresser top, she plucked at her eyebrows; how quickly the hairs came in. They at least should be thin, like models in the magazines had them. With the right hat, maybe she'd be all right.

Nu, did she have any recent pictures of him? In the beginning yes, so the child could see what his father looked like, but since then? For all she knew, he'd gotten fat, too. Not likely. Her Harry would look just like always. Handsome like a movie star, hair thick and wavy, golden like a wheat field at sunset. He wrote as often as he could, she told herself and their son, and if no pictures of him came inside the envelopes, she certainly couldn't complain with all those other pictures he sent, of the presidents on the dollar bills. The years of being without him, raising their child by herself, had been long and not easy, but the money he'd continued to send, even as he saved to bring them to America, more than provided: she and her parents were able to employ a helper in the store now to keep up with all the orders. Women from as far as Warsaw came to get the latest designs.

As Regina searched through her closet to see if there might be a dress that would fit her better, Yakob came into the room. He wore a tan suit that his grandfather had bought him for the occasion. After many fittings, the suit sat on him perfectly, but his thin face wore an even more serious expression than usual. *"Mama, ich darf a por broyne sheekh oon zokn,"* the boy said.

Regina turned to admire her son. "Look at you, like a regular man you look," she said, and she took his face between her hands and covered it with kisses. Yakob's somber expression melted into a smile as it always did when met with his mother's effusive love, and he returned her affection with a peck on the cheek. "But in English, *bubeleh*, you have to speak, remember?" Yakob sat down on the bed sheepishly. "No, don't sit, the suit shouldn't wrinkle," Regina scolded, and he stood up quickly. "So we'll buy for you brown shoes and socks, they should match. Now, get into your work clothes and go downstairs. *Bubbeh* and *Zeydeh* expect you should be helping."

"Very well, Mother," Yakob said with mischievously exaggerated formality. He stood straight as a soldier. "But whom are *Bubbeh* and *Zeydeh*? Do you mean Grandmother and Grandfather?"

"Now you're talking," Regina said, always happy to see her son in a playful mood. "Practice those big words, your father should *plotz* with *naches*."

"*Plotz* with what?" Yakob asked as he left the room.

"Pride, *mein bubeleh*, your father will be so proud of you." Alone in the room, Regina sighed, "As for me?" She returned to the clothing rack in her closet and her fervent prayer that Yankele shouldn't be too ashamed of her to take them back with him to America.

Washington, DC

Dressed in mourning clothes, Will and Barbara sat in silence at the dinette table just off the kitchen. As they had promised, Betty and Elaine had taken care of all the preparations for the gathering after the funeral, and a perfectly sociable, while appropriately measured, DC lunch carried on around them.

Despite having suffered what the doctors called a "significant cardiac event" back in February, Nicholas had survived the calamitous death of his namesake, but his last months on this earth had seemed to be calculated by him to ensure a requisite time for penance. Since the baby's drowning, words among the three Browns came as scarce as smiles, joy, or engagement of any kind; sound itself seemed to have been sucked into another universe, where such things as the will to live resided. They moved around the split-level townhouse in a state of shocked silence, so that the telephone's ring or the thwap of the newspaper arriving on the doorstep elicited a startled exclamation of astonishment.

Had they done anything more than merely collect the newspaper just to toss it in the trash, they might have read that FDR, in a bid to find more sympathy for his programs on the Supreme Court, was proposing that the institution be enlarged from nine justices to fifteen; that a forty-four-day sit-down strike at General Motors ended in a contract with the United Auto Workers, spurring greater union membership, more strikes, and subsequent capitulation by Chrysler, Studebaker, and Cadillac; that Henry Ford's "Service Department," ordered to head off Walter Reuther and his band of "union trouble-makers," beat Reuther and his colleagues to a pulp as they posed for a photograph on their way to distribute leaflets; that Francisco Franco's forces were besieging Guadalajara; that the U.S. Social Security system paid its first benefit check; that the transatlantic flight of the German airship *Hindenburg* ended in an explosion of flames in New Jersey. If Will had even considered reading the newspaper cover to cover as he'd always done, he would have found that over 70 percent of Americans answered yes to the Gallup Poll question: "Do you think it was a mistake for the United States to enter the World War?" With Japan invading Manchuria, Germany in the Rhineland, and Mussolini's march into Ethiopia, with the economy on the home front still anything but secure, the citizens of the United States might be distracted from their daily cares by a dazzling array of Hollywood stars and entertainment the likes of which the world had never known, but they weren't forgetful of the catastrophe of world war and thus applauded unambiguously Roosevelt's Neutrality Acts, which assured against involvement in "foreign entanglements." The situation overseas threatened conflagration, the very reason that Will, like the majority of his countrymen, would have been heartened by the Gallup Poll, had he read about it. Had existence in the Brown household resembled its former aspect, he and his father would have exchanged vigorous and mostly concurring opinions about the country's resolve to stay neutral, but verbal intercourse remained as sparse as interest in anything that could be going on in the world. Because it wasn't in Will's nature to miss too much work, he did go into the office and carry out the duties of his job, but back at home each evening, the household, like the country, continued in an atmosphere of determined noninvolvement—until on a June morning, Nicholas, like his wife before him, simply failed to awaken.

The ambulance, the death pronouncement, the funeral were all gotten through in a quiet and emotionless way; both Will and Barbara had run out of tears. When the Pearsons and Waverlys volunteered to see to the arrangements, that was fine with them. It was nice that so many of their acquaintances came to pay their final respects to Nicholas, though Barbara doubted she'd be able to name half the people currently milling about in her living room.

Wearing an outlandishly ornate hat with some sort of barnyard scene on its brim and two feathers pointing skyward, Martha Connelly sat down at the dinette table to urge Will and Barbara, distraught parents and children at once, to eat something. "Can't Annette get something for you," she asked, "a sandwich, a drink?" Barbara word-lessly lifted her glass, indicating that she was fine for now.

"You take as much time as you need," Martha turned her attention to Will. "Joe and I can't begin to express how badly we feel for the two of you. What a year you've had."

The ice cubes in Barbara's glass rattled as she took a serious swig of rye. Remembering the hardly masked condescension with which Martha had treated her father-in-law, she could only marvel at the woman's hypocrisy. It may have been the strongest emotion Barbara had felt in months, gazing at Martha Connelly talking about the year they'd had. "Maybe I will have another," she said after emptying her glass.

"I'll fix us some sandwiches," Will said, rising slowly from the table. In the months since the baby, he'd spent more time with his wife than he ever had in the eight years they'd been married, so her fondness for alcohol was no longer something he could deny. At first, he attributed her overuse to grief, but she'd become terribly thin, and with the meager inclination he could find in himself to care about any-thing at all, Barbara's well-being was utmost. In the weeks following Junior's drowning—no one in the house could say the word *death* in connection with the child; the usual locution regarding anything fol-lowing his death was "since the baby"—Will had appreciated her silent kindnesses toward his father, the frequent visits she made to the hos-pital during his recuperation, and the three square meals she placed in front of him, following the diet prescribed by the doctor, once he'd come home. She walked around the house, as they all did, as though floating in an alien environment, but her ministrations kept them alive and functioning, so if alcohol fueled her heart-wrenching efforts, Will could understand. It was only recently that he began to worry about whether she had developed a dependency on drinking. Of course, he didn't want to accuse her of anything or confront her about it, but he did maintain what he hoped was a gentle vigilance.

"I don't think I can eat," Barbara said.

"Try," Will said as he walked toward the ample buffet in the living room.

"I'll get you some coffee," Martha offered, and she left Barbara blessedly alone, softly clinking the ice cubes in her glass.

A din of human voices, like a pillow of sound, greeted Will as he made his way toward the cold-cuts tray. Words like *unions* and *workers* and *what do they want?* filtered through the undifferentiated language, as did faces screwed into sympathy, coming in at him with mouths saying, "We're so sorry," "Condolences, Will," and then returning to their conversations.

At the buffet table, Will regarded the platters of thinly sliced meat, the bowls of tuna and chicken salad, egg salad, the baskets of breads, and nothing looked good. Neither did the tastefully arranged pastries whet his appetite.

"Won't you let me fix you something, Mr. Brown?" Annette was by his side, always looking out for him. In her black belted suit, she appeared even tinier than usual, one of the few people beside whom Will actually felt tall. Over the years, he'd teased her that that was why he'd hired her, and he couldn't even say for sure that her diminutive stature hadn't been the very attribute that had tipped the scales in her favor during the string of interviews he'd conducted when he first arrived in Washington. Why not hire a secretary who stood at five foot two in heels if she also came, as Annette did, with sterling references and exemplary typing and shorthand? His whole life Will had been the shortest guy in the room—even Barbara had inches on him in anything but her stocking feet—so when he finally reached a point in his career when he could hire someone to assist him, the young woman's petite size capped her credentials. Not for a moment had Will regretted his choice. Along with her stellar secretarial skills, outer-office friendliness, and sturdy at-her-desk competence, Annette's ability to anticipate Will's needs and satisfy them with a smile that sat like a bow on her efficiency made her a part of his work that he couldn't imagine doing without.

"Maybe, if you could put a few of the salads on a plate, for Barbara," Will said languidly, "that would be very nice."

"Of course," Annette said, reaching for a plate. "And you? What shall I make for you?"

Will just shook his head. "I don't know."

He felt a hand on his shoulder, and turned around to find Joe Connelly, highball in hand, regarding him with a paternal attitude. "Fix him a roast beef on one of those rolls," he said to Annette, and steered Will back toward the kitchen.

"I want you to take as much time as you need," he said, squeezing Will's shoulder with the hand that remained there.

"Yes, Martha already . . ."

"You came back to work too soon last," Joe paused awkwardly, lowering his eyes. "Last time." He waited another moment, then raised his eyes to look at Will. "I'm sorry, I hate to bring it up, but everyone in the department knows how much you contribute, what an important force you are for us. But for God's sake, man, for Barbara's sake, and your own, take a few weeks. We'll catch the bad guys without you."

The two men stood in a corner of the dining room, people respectfully walking past them. "They're the ones who did this to him," Will said. "The immigrants who started this whole union business, they're the ones who gave the farmers this idea about organizing. He was never the same afterward, after that godforsaken act of protest," he said the word disdainfully. "First, the store, then that contemptible outrage with the car." He shook his head. "It broke him."

"I know, a horrible thing, horrible," Joe agreed.

"You wouldn't have recognized him back then, what he used to be like. Tall, distinguished-looking, Pop was one of the most respected men in town, back home. People looked up to him. Everyone knew him, liked him. They crippled him, those farmers, sapped his lifeblood." He was quiet for a few moments. "And it's all connected. The immigrants come and take the jobs, no one has the money to pay for what the farmers produce, the farmers start a union. It's all a predictable, vicious circle."

Joe nodded in agreement.

"At least at work, I can do something about it," Will said matter-of-factly. "Sitting at home, well, what's the point?" Will hadn't heard himself put so many words together in a long time. He felt spent by the outpouring. "I'll stay home a week, maybe two," he said quietly.

"Be here with Barbara." He looked over at her, sitting at the dinette table, listlessly poking a fork into the lunch Annete had prepared for her. He patted Joe's shoulder and walked over to resume his position on the chair next to hers.

As they sat silently picking at their food, Will went over the things he'd said to Joe Connelly. He knew everyone at work thought he'd come back too soon after the baby, but going through the files on his desk, matching interrogation reports with visa information, visa information with union memberships, while he hadn't approached the work with anything like his usual zeal, the very rote manner in which he could get it done—the reading, examining, and matching—acted as a tonic to the biting agony of his loss. Numbness, not feeling things, was the only antidote Will could grab on to, and just as it worked at home, so, too, did this state of self-inflicted sedation carry him through his days at the office.

The brief conversation he'd just had with Joe Connelly came closer to linking his job to personal conviction than anything he'd allowed himself since the baby. Since the baby, he'd hardly allowed himself to feel anything at all. Perhaps, it was his father's death that stirred his emotions. Nicholas's explicit role in the baby's drowning invited thoughts that a devoted son could not permit himself. Was it that very desire for condemnation that had kept his father alive all these months, a need to exist as a walking object of blame that might succeed in freeing the children, Will and Barbara, from their agonizing misery? Did Nicholas will his survival in the hope of provoking their denunciation, their indictment his only chance of redemption?

If this was Nicholas's purpose during his last days, he mentioned nothing, existing in a knotted shroud of silence alongside the children, whose natural family loyalty foreswore blame, and prodded them to exist beside him under the shroud.

Their plates barely touched, Will and Barbara endured the flock of benevolent handshakes and whispered sympathies as the well-meaning visitors gradually filed out. Serving tables thumped closed and dishes clattered in the sink as the Pearsons and Waverlys stayed behind to clean up. Betty peeked her head in from the kitchen: "Did you believe that nest she had on her head?" she asked, trying to elicit a smile from her friend, and Barbara did indeed roll her eyes in a conspiratorial critique of Martha Connelly's hat.

Following a quiet chorus of "Call-if-you-need-anythings," and hugs and squeezes of shoulders, the household was empty. Barbara poured herself a drink and sat in the living room. "They did a wonderful job," she said. "Everything went very well." She looked out the bay window at the evening, which remained sunlit.

"I spoke to your mother yesterday," Will said. "She and your dad are sick over this."

"He was a wonderful man, your father. It wasn't his fault."

Will sighed deeply. A number of responses crossed his mind—of course it was Pop's fault; he should never have taken it upon himself to bathe the baby. But then he shouldn't have been alone with Junior in the first place. If Barbara had to go out for the prescription, she should at least have told Pop not to get any ideas about giving the baby a bath. Why hadn't she sent him to the pharmacy? Wouldn't that have made more sense?—but instead: "I was telling Joe Connelly how respected he used to be back home, how everyone looked up to him."

Barbara said nothing. Why go into her resentment of the way Martha had treated Nicholas since the day she'd met him? It was amazing how long it stayed light out in June. Not as late as back home; the days were just a bit shorter here in the south. It really was the south, DC, the heat and humidity, the way people talked with just that hint of a twang, the way it was already dark by nine.

"Your mom would like it very much if you came home for a while," Will said.

"Home?"

"I don't know what I'd do without you," Will continued. "The house is so empty as . . ." He didn't finish the sentence.

"Isn't this home?" Barbara asked.

"I'm worried about you," Will said. "You need to . . . maybe being back home with your folks, you know, maybe it'll get you back on your feet. We, well, we have to go on, you know."

Barbara knew that what Will was saying probably made sense, but she couldn't get her mind off the word *home*. She really didn't know what it meant anymore. Home: it should have a comforting sound.

Will continued talking. "You can take the train. I'll have Annette arrange everything." As he articulated a string of words having to do with Barbara going back to Iowa, Will half waited for her to object: of course home was here with him, she couldn't think of leaving, words to that effect. But his wife just sat there, looking out at the fading daylight. Maybe she would go, after all.

Although she didn't eat more than a morsel herself, the next morning Barbara cooked a full breakfast for them: eggs and pancakes and bacon, orange juice and toast and her incomparably strong coffee. They didn't say more than a few words, and even though Will's appetite was no match for the bounteous meal set before him, he felt that if he did his best to eat as much as he could it would be like telling her he hoped she would stay. He'd still been in kind of a trance when he'd spoken to Millie, and Barbara going home for a while sounded like it could be a good idea, but as soon as it'd come out of his mouth, he knew that being here without her might be more than he could bear. Barbara drank a glass of orange juice, and he prayed that that was all she had in her glass.

After a week of hearty meals and days that just folded quietly one into the other—they took a walk on Wednesday or Thursday; Barbara pruned the hydrangea one afternoon—Will broached the subject of returning to work. He knew that one day soon, they'd have to clear out the baby's room. The door had remained closed since February, Nicholas sleeping on the couch since the baby. He didn't say anything about the room to Barbara, though, nor did he allow himself to imagine what she would do with the hours that she'd be here by herself, beyond shopping for dinner and cooking. "That will be fine," she said, and since that was all she said, he felt it was safe to assume that the idea of her going to Iowa was just a little bubble of conversation that had evaporated, and he couldn't deny his relief. He'd talk to Betty about inviting her over for a game of cards, maybe mah-jongg. She did enjoy playing those games once upon a time, so he'd do what he could to make sure she got out of the house.

Ten days after his father's death, Will boarded the bus that took him to the massive Labor Building on Fourteenth Street and Constitution Avenue. As he stood across the street from the building waiting to cross, he couldn't help but acknowledge a kind of gratitude: the wheels of government rolled on, and being back within their indomitable will to proceed restored to him, however tenuously, a sense of context.

Annette had tidily prepared his desk for him, thoughtfully having reduced the number of files that must await his attention to a manageable few. He knew that stacks and stacks must be tucked away somewhere, and that she would discreetly place them on his desk in meticulous accord with the rhythm he established for getting through them.

"I thought I'd call Mrs. Brown, see if she'd like to go for lunch," Annette said, never calling her boss's wife by her first name when they were in the office.

"That would be very nice," Will said. He didn't put much emotion into the remark, but a discernible smile amply communicated his appreciation, which ran deep. He could count on Annette for so much.

After loosening his tie, he opened the top file sitting on his desk. It belonged to one Samuel Orovitz, a Lithuanian here since '28. According to the papers completed by the legal inspector at the port of New York, the man had stated his age as twenty upon arrival; his employment papers at the Detroit auto factory where he'd worked since then had him two years older. His lie probably would have gone undetected if not for his activities with the union, his boisterous behavior on behalf of which called him to the attention of Ford's security personnel. In the way of routine harassment, they demanded to see his U.S. entry papers, noted the differing dates of birth, and fired him. They also referred the matter to the INS, where, unfortunately for Mr. Orovitz, the paperwork and its discrepancies fell into the hands of Byron Diana, Will's most assiduous inspector.

Leave it to Annette to place this open-and-shut case right on top. It was part of her job to peruse, organize, and arrange the files so that the more complicated cases were placed on top for Will to consider at the start of the day; in his current situation, she didn't have to be told that it made much more sense to start his workday with a case that didn't demand much analysis.

Will uncovered his typewriter and opened a desk drawer to find a blank Form 585, whose title read: "APPLICATION FOR WARRANT OF ARREST." Typing in the necessary file and documentation numbers and the date up on top, he filled in after, "The undersigned respectfully recommends that the Secretary of Labor issue a warrant for the arrest of alien(s)" the name: **SAMUEL OROVITZ, aged 20 or 22, native of Lithuania.** And in the center of the page, he entered:

> **From information contained in the attached report of Inspector Diana, it appears the above named alien is in the United States in violation of the immigration act of 1924 in that at the time of his entry he might have been older than required for entry as a nonquota immigrant.**

He signed the warrant application and put it in the box of papers to be sent to Turner Battle, Perkins's assistant secretary, for his consideration. Obviously, Orovitz would be arrested, have a hearing if he could afford one, and most likely be deported if, as Will suspected, he'd lied to the federal government about his age. Will only wished they were all this easy.

He stretched out his fingers before reaching for the next file.

Poland

As he sat looking out the window of the train taking him from Warsaw to Lukow, Harry realized how used to a black-and-white world he'd become. During his years in America, he'd marveled at the grandeur of the George Washington Bridge, the elegance of Fifth Avenue and Rockefeller Center, but carried along here, in a landscape of trees and meadows, he felt as though the senses that operate in a countryside were rousing from a long sleep, and that the world once again existed in color.

Fields spread from the windows of the train like a quilt of inter-woven greens: the light shades of the wheat, the somewhat darker small grains, and the deep rich greens of the corn. Stocky rows of apple trees lined up every now and then like seams of the blanket, a multi-colored tapestry welcoming him home.

Harry fiddled with the Panama hat resting on his knee, spinning it by the brim. He'd put on his new suit this morning and suddenly feared that its stylishness might set him apart from his countrymen. His fellow passengers wore Polish military uniforms or short-sleeved shirts more appropriate to the weather. Maybe he should at least remove the plaid beige tie, loosened now for the ride, but intended to be cinched tightly to make a smart contrast with his white shirt. He'd purchased the outfit—the beige summer suit, matching tie, and white shirt—not only to make a good impression on Regina and his son, but for the appearance he intended to make later in the summer at the visa office in Warsaw. He wanted to look as American as possible when he asserted his son's American citizenship; a passport was one thing, but it would be even more persuasive to look like a real citizen of the United States.

"*Wuku*," the train conductor trumpeted in a thick Polish accent as he passed through Harry's car. He must have dozed, for already he could feel the train slowing down as it made its approach. He swept his fingers through his hair, buttoned the top of his shirt and tightened the tie. Placing the hat just so on his head, he sighed deeply and watched as the agricultural vista faded behind wooden structures and signposts. Any minute, they would pull into the station. The train would stop, and his eyes would find her.

With the screech of the brakes, Harry curled his fingers around the handle of his suitcase, adjusted his hat once more, and stood up to make his way toward the exit.

The platform was dotted with small clusters of waiting people. Harry's eyes surveyed the station until his gaze landed on two of them, a petite but thickly set woman in a white dress and a boy in a light brown suit. The woman's arm was draped over the shoulders of the boy, as though she meant to protect him, but one of the boa-like feathers that cascaded from her white hat seemed to be tickling his ear so that he kept his head tilted awkwardly away from her.

Harry would remember these details later when he pictured the scene, and marvel that he had managed to observe all this in the few seconds it must have taken for him to descend the steps onto the platform and walk toward his wife and son.

His face broke into a smile that almost hurt; he could feel his skin stretching beyond its natural capacity. But look at them: so lovely, so expectant, so visibly staunch in their determination to present a dignified welcome.

Sure enough, Regina's proud demeanor gave way as he neared, and she lowered her head. Harry tucked his finger under her chin and raised her lips to his. After just a moment's hesitation, he kissed her, gently, first her mouth, then her entire face. His lips brushed her cheeks, her eyelids (yes, the eyes were light green), her forehead, and the bridge of her nose, softly assuring her, he hoped, as well as himself, that he was here, they were together, and things were as they should be.

Finally, Regina spoke. "It's a very nice hat you have on," and Harry thrilled to the sound of her voice, realizing only then that all the letters and photographs in the world had yet deprived him of this sound. For eight years, he had not heard the sounds Regina's voice made.

"From a professional, I take that as the highest compliment," he said with a smile, and he kissed her again.

The boy, Yakob, stood stiffly, his hands at his sides, watching this man he knew only from pictures cover his mother's face with kisses. Harry turned to him and shook his hand, as he'd told himself he must do so as to convey a manly respect, but the rehearsed gesture gave way immediately to a flood of desire to embrace the boy, and Harry pulled him tightly to his chest, kissing the top of his head, warm from the sun, and then cupping his face in his hands, studying it, seeing himself in the boy's green eyes, himself and his Reizele in what had to be a scientifically perfect blend.

"Welcome home, Father," Yakob said in heavily accented English.

"You are a good boy, I can tell." Harry beamed at him. He swallowed the knot of emotion that had gathered in his throat and put his arms around his wife and son. "You can handle the suitcase?" he asked the boy, indicating that he'd like it if Yakob took on that task. "Yes, sir." Yakob hoisted the somewhat weighty piece of luggage, and together, the newly constituted family walked through the stately Lukow train station, out into the tree-lined sidewalks of the town, and made its way to Staropijarska Street.

After a welcome from his in-laws that was as warm as he could have wished, Harry took a place next to his wife at the bountifully set table. Between the seasonal heat and the cooking that had preceded his arrival, the air was quite close, but he ate with relish the elaborate meal Regina had prepared. It had been a long time since he'd enjoyed *kreplach* soup, freshly baked challah, and *flanken*. The aromas and tastes were savory beyond compare, and though he knew he was overdoing it, the pleasure not only of the food but also on his wife's face as he placed each morsel into his mouth kept him from stopping. Moreover, he wanted to set a good example for his son, who, while he was a beautiful child, could stand to put on a few pounds. His cheeks were really more gaunt than ideal for an eight-year-old boy. Harry couldn't help noticing, however, as he started to place a well-proportioned forkful of meat and potatoes into his mouth, that his son was staring at him, wide-eyed with amazement. He put the fork on his plate, leaned back, and laughed.

"Your daddy is a big eater," he said to Yakob.

The boy straightened in his chair, embarrassed.

"Food like this they probably don't give you in America," his father-in-law observed. The Lanskys had entrusted the store to their assistant for the afternoon meal, an unheard-of lapse in their stringent work ethic that further communicated to Harry their endorsement of his presence. Yet, as he took this brief pause from his delectation of Regina's meal, he silently acknowledged that another explanation for his hearty consumption might be that it postponed the necessity of embarking on one of several conversations he'd rather not have. As long as his mouth was busy chewing, he didn't have to say anything, and many topics swirled unspoken at the table, among them the visit he would soon have with his own family, and the matter of telling them that he was a married man. He put the temporarily resting forkful into his mouth.

"Do all Americans eat like this?" Yakob asked. He, too, sat thinking about family matters and the future. Utmost on his mind loomed the other end of this homecoming: his own departure from home, to a world he could barely imagine.

Wanting to deflect serious discussion, Harry attempted to answer both his father-in-law and son with, "You're right. If I take another bite, I'll explode." The observation hardly responded to either of the previous utterances, but it did serve to prompt Regina out of her chair to begin the clearing of the table.

"Let me do it," Mrs. Lansky said to her daughter. "You and Yankel, you go outside, take a walk together. Me and Yakob will take care of the dishes. Right, my sweetheart?" She smiled and winked at her grandson.

Yakob rose obediently. He loved his *bubbeh* so. Would they be coming, too, to America: his *bubbeh* and *zeydeh*? His mother had told him no, that their life was here. But how could that be possible, that he wouldn't see them anymore?

"When we come back, I have a surprise I'm going to give to you," Harry said to his son. "Something from America that you're going to love." How many times when he had been throwing the ball back and forth with Saul had he imagined having a catch with his son! But would the boy appreciate, the way an American boy would, the gift of a brand-new baseball glove and hardball?

Harry and Regina held hands as they walked the few blocks to the town square. Before they'd sat down to eat, he had removed his suit jacket, and she, her hat, and gradually they were feeling their way toward being comfortable with each other. Once, their time together had been characterized by insistent desire; just the touch of the other urged toward intimacy. Ironically, pregnancy and marriage had introduced stiffness and formality into their relationship. Now, with eight years of absence and a son between them, each knew the importance of reinvigorating their former connection.

"You look very well," Harry began as they found a bench under an elm tree in the square. He held on to her hand, stroking it tenderly. "And you should take sometimes pictures without all those hats. Your beautiful curls, it is wonderful to see them."

Regina nodded with a shy smile. "I'm fat," she said. "Not the little mouse you left behind. After I had the baby, I'm sure you could tell from the pictures. I've tried, but taking off the extra pounds has been very hard."

"More of you to love," Harry said, and they both laughed wanly at his little joke, while the word *love* lingered in the air around them.

The bench began to feel like an island of silence as neither of them could think what to say next. People milled about on the warm summer day, children climbing on the rock formation in the middle of the square, mothers looking on as they chatted with their friends. Harry noticed one little girl run crying to her mother because she'd gotten dirt on her dress. The mother tried to comfort the child, but she seemed inconsolable.

"You've raised for us a beautiful son," he said.

"He's a good boy," Regina agreed.

Had her mother known with her apparently simple suggestion how difficult this would be, the two of them being alone together? She looked down at her new white sandals and decided they were very unattractive and old-fashioned. She crossed her ankles and tucked her feet out of sight.

Harry watched the people in the small neighborhood park. He realized that it was less awkward to be with Regina if he perceived the two of them as part of a group, even if the only group available to them right now was composed of strangers. Still, there were things that must be said. "I'd like him to get to know me a little better before I take him to meet my family," Harry said.

"So you'll stay here a few days, and then we'll go," Regina replied.

Harry smiled. "You think my mother won't have a fit if I don't come tomorrow? It's all arranged, Yitzak is meeting me at the station."

"I see. So if you're not here, how does your son get to know you?" Despite her earlier resolve, Regina stretched her feet out in front of her; they made a good object of focus, even if the sandals had entirely too many straps.

"You're right," Harry said. "When you're right, you're right." He knew he was just stringing words together, trying to avoid the grossly uncomfortable topic of the secret he'd made of his marriage for eight years. He would confess to his mother, but he didn't want to just spring his wife and child on her, appear with them out of the blue before having the opportunity to explain to her first. Despite the shade of the tree, his forehead broke into beads of sweat. "They think I'm coming straight from the boat. I didn't tell them about this stop first."

"So, you have a lot to tell them."

"I'll go just for the day, two at most. Sit down with my mother, have with her a private word, like they say, tell her everything. She knows, by the way, through your uncle, that you have a child. She . . ." Harry looked down, the unnecessarily scandalous implications in his next words embarrassing him as they came out of his mouth: "She just doesn't know who the father is. I mean that I am the father, that the child is mine."

Regina didn't say anything, and when he raised his head to finally look at her directly, he was not surprised to see the tears filling her eyes. They just puddled there, two round wet orbs, as though she willed the tears not to overflow or follow the pull of gravity. Harry kissed her eyes, taking the tears from them with his mouth and tasting them on his lips. "We'll go tomorrow," he said softly, "together. Not one more tear will I cause you. I promise, not one."

Regina blotted the area under her eyes with her fingers. She had prepared Yakob for meeting his other grandma and his uncles and aunts and cousins. She herself had no sisters or brothers, and the stories about his other family had, over the years, been the subject of many happy hours and a source of anticipation. Sometimes, he would ask why he couldn't meet them now, play with his cousins in their house in Stawki, but always she said to him, "All in good time, when Daddy comes home."

Harry bought three ice-cream cones on the short walk back to the apartment, Yakob's melting messily by the time they entered the store. Regina's father chided them for being near the merchandise with dripping *lody*, food of any kind being strictly forbidden on the premises, but he was glad to see the playfulness on both their faces as they hurried upstairs.

Despite its watery state, Yakob accepted the ice cream and drank it out of the cone. "It's like ice-cream milk," he said, making his mother laugh with delight. His tentativeness around his father continued, but to see his mother so childlike and happy meant that this must be a good man. For Harry's part, the smile in his son's eyes suggested that this would be the right moment, so he scooped from his suitcase the baseball paraphernalia he'd brought.

Yakob thought at first that the oddly shaped leather glove must be the wrong size; as large as it was, he could barely squeeze his hand into it. But Harry explained that only his fingers needed to fit inside and, with Regina's ready permission, father and son tumbled down the stairs and back to the square to have their first catch.

Checking in the kitchen, Regina saw that her mother and Yakob had done an adequate job cleaning up—she wiped down the sink and stove more to her standards—and then she decided it would be good if she took Harry's valise and unpacked it. His clothes in the closet would convey to all of them that they were a family, living together in one place. Soon, yes, that place would be America, but for the summer at least, their home was here in Lukow, with a night here and there, possibly, in Harry's village, God willing. *And Mrs. Himelbaum willing*, Regina reminded herself, stealing a glance toward heaven for support.

As the train rumbled between Lukow and Wlodawa the following day, Yakob listened intently to his father's stories about the Dodger team, clearly a very important institution in America. Once he'd gotten used to the way the strange baseball glove fit his hand yesterday, he'd actually enjoyed throwing the hardball back and forth, and didn't even mind being the center of attention as many of the people in the square stopped what they were doing to watch his father teach him how to catch a high fly ball. He must get under the ball, Harry repeatedly instructed, as it came slowly, slowly toward him from high in the sky; cup it in the pocket of his glove, and use his other hand to cover the ball so that it didn't pop out. This was a very complicated process, this catching of the baseball, and as Harry recited the many rules and regulations of the game, Yakob could understand why the players were so respected.

Wearing the same white dress as the one she'd worn for Harry's arrival, Regina rubbed the fingers of her left hand nervously. She looked up at the storks' nests on the telegraph poles and rooftops dotting the landscape and prayed they would bring her luck, as superstition said they would—bring all of them luck, really. This was a big day. She'd put a few things in a shopping bag in the event that they were invited to stay overnight with Harry's family and, of course, that's what they all hoped for. If his mother reacted to her son's secret marriage and fatherhood with misery and anger, a very realistic possibility, the change of clothing would not be necessary.

They had rehearsed the night before how to go about making the revelation to Elke: she and Yakob would remain outside the gate and let Harry walk by himself to the front door of the house. Only after he'd told his mother about them would he come and invite them in. They agreed that would be better than just materializing, before the woman had a chance to absorb the information.

Sitting alone at the table once Yakob and the Lanskys had gone to bed, the two had even managed to find humor in the various scenarios they envisioned: at one point they imagined Elke seeing the three of them and jumping to the conclusion that Harry had met an American girl and come home with her. "Not if I wear these stupid shoes," Regina had said. "What American girl would be caught wearing these?" She'd felt only a little badly when Harry hadn't disagreed.

Today she wore black shoes with a little heel, not quite right with a white dress, but all she had, and she'd taken Harry's advice not to wear a hat. "I want them to see your face," he had urged her. "Who can do anything but love you if they see that face?" If he didn't like the hat she'd worn to meet him yesterday, which she herself had designed and taken a lot of time with, he didn't say anything. For her part, Regina was quite proud of the hat, having seen something just like it in an article about a debutante ball that she'd read in one of the fashion magazines from abroad. Well, he had said already how much he liked her hair, so, maybe the hat she would do without. Hats. Shoes. From head to toe, she was trying to please him. And he, too, was trying very hard. She could see that.

What with Harry communicating to his son every single thing he knew about the game of baseball—which wasn't all that much, but he had clearly captured the boy's attention with the subject and therefore wracked his brain to recall every baseball-related conversation he'd ever had with Saul, or overheard between him and various customers at the store—and Regina focused on appearances and the upcoming encounter with her in-laws, both of them managed to avoid thinking about last night's awkwardness in bed. The bed itself was small for the two of them, and Yakob slept just a night table's width away. Regina's mother had suggested weeks before that the boy sleep with his grand-parents in their room, but Regina had vetoed the idea, not wanting her son to feel that his father's appearance meant his own banishment. If either of the reunited couple allowed themselves to think about last night, however, and did so with honesty, they would admit that it was neither the size of their bed nor its proximity to Yakob's that accounted for the palpable lack of physical desire between them. And they would be forced to contemplate the possibility that this marriage that had taken place as the result of an intense sexual attraction, which had in turn produced a pregnancy, might very well have to proceed in a manner more closely akin to a respectful friendship. But as long as

Yakob sat spellbound with baseball stories, and Regina worried about how her role in Harry's story would sit with Mrs. Himelbaum, the questions at the center of their own story need not be considered. And what, after all, was there to consider? They had a son and they were married. They would live together in America, and the way Yakob was drinking in every word his father uttered—with a concentration familiar to Regina, whether the boy was telling her about that week's lessons at the boarding school he attended, or watching his grandfather sew a seam—they wouldn't do too badly as a family.

When they disembarked from the train, Regina didn't recognize Yitzak at first; he looked older than she remembered, heavier and more full in the face, but then it had been a long time. He ran over and clutched his younger brother in a bear hug, fighting back tears and beaming over how well he looked. "A real American. You don't even see that suit in Warsaw. Look at that hat." He grabbed the Panama hat from Harry's head and put it on his own, where it didn't fit at all, looking more like a piece of a costume than a fashionable accessory, the way it did on Harry. Harry grabbed it back as Yitzak turned to Regina. He extended his hand to her, and his face spread with a warm smile. "About time," he said, and then he shook his nephew's hand with affection. "About time for both of you. I'm your Uncle Yitzak, and I'm very glad you're here."

He had brought a buggy with two horses, borrowed from a gentile neighbor with whom the Himelbaums were friendly. Harry nuzzled the horses before climbing in, saying how much he'd missed being around animals, and how he couldn't wait to take a ride out in the fields. "The river and the horses; aside from my family, this is what I've missed the most," he said. He sat up front with his brother as Regina and Yakob settled in the back. Yakob asked if he could practice with the baseball mitt, just throw the ball up a little bit to develop his feel for catching it in the pocket, and Regina was about to tell him to put it away when Yitzak looked back and said, "Let him play. He'll teach my Moishe. They're the same age, no?" The reference to the time of her pregnancy made Regina feel uncomfortable, the distraction making her forget her objection to Yakob and the baseball, and so his rhythmic throwing and cupping of the ball became a downbeat to the *clip-clop* of the horses as the growing new family rode out of the bustling town of Wlodawa and turned onto the narrow road that led to Stawki.

"Storks on every pole, it's a wonderful thing," Harry observed.

"They say the storks themselves are Poles," Yitzak quipped. "That's why the government even builds special platforms for them. They do better by the storks than for the people. But what else is new?"

"And Mama?" Harry asked.

"She's been counting the days since your letter arrived. The house is fixed up like for a prince. And the cooking? I hope you brought with you an appetite."

"*Nu*, that I never forget to bring." After a few minutes of silence: "Of course, I'm nervous about telling her. Chava hasn't said anything?"

"One thing I can say about Chava: she's very good at keeping quiet. The woman speaks to the children; otherwise her lips are closed like with a vise."

The brothers caught up on Hershel and Leah and the children, the Hondra family, who had loaned Yitzak the buggy and comprised the only people in Stawki who treated the Himelbaums and the Kaminskys—the only Jews in the village—with civility. They talked about the growing influence of Hitler and about Buchenwald, the forced labor camp recently established in Germany.

Soon, however, the conversation about anti-Semitism and the threat from Hitler and the Nazis faded into a remote harbinger. Such talk had no place here on this soft, sunny morning, colored by the fields of green in all its hues and the hovering storks on high, accompanied by the padded thud of Yakob's baseball landing in the leather pocket of the glove, and the steady, rhythmic pace of the horses. The sights and sounds of the open meadows lulled the foursome as the time went peacefully by, until they came, at last, to the dirt road on the right that led home.

In accord with what he and Regina had agreed the night before, Harry asked Yitzak to stop a few yards before the house. Regina and Yakob would wait in the buggy so that Harry could appear before his mother on his own. After the hugs and kisses and tears, he would sit down with her and tell her, explain. Yitzak saw the sense of it and tied the horses' reins to one of the posts on the newly installed and painted fence that bordered the property. Harry mussed Yakob's hair as he leaned into the back of the buggy and assured his wife and son, and himself, that everything would work out fine and that he'd come very soon for them.

As he entered the familiar path to the house, Lody, the chocolate-colored mutt named after everyone's favorite dessert, came running toward him and jumped on him playfully. The sounds of the dog's spirited barking brought Elke to the front door. She stood a moment in wonderment at the sight of her son. So handsome, so stylish, so grown up. Her hand went to her mouth, but after that it didn't seem that any part of her body was capable of movement; she felt stuck to the spot at just the sight of him, her Yankele.

The smell of freshly cut wood and wildflowers filled the front yard as Harry walked slowly toward his mother, placed his hat on the bench under the neatly pruned cottonwood tree, and scooped Elke off the ground, twirling her and holding her to him. Elke was not a small woman, so her high-pitched entreaties to put her down—"You'll hurt yourself!"—were heeded rather quickly. Retrieving his hat, he bowed deeply before his mother, and she wiped her tearstained face with her apron. "Ach, you came so unexpectedly, I was looking for the carriage, I didn't even take off my apron," she groused between tears. A web of fine lines drew the years on her face, time recorded there as surely as on the cottonwood, its branches reaching well beyond the pediment above the front door.

"*Nu*, without your apron, would I even recognize you?" Harry beamed, and it was then that he noticed the family that had gathered behind her on the small front porch. He hugged his brother, Hershel, and Leah, she looked so lovely. The husky little boy beside her must be their David, a little uncomfortable in the *Shabbes* shirt and knee pants they'd made him wear.

Holding fast to his mother's skirt stood Moishe, skinnier even than his Yakob and throwing toward the unknown American uncle a look of suspicion, a look matched by his mother's stern visage. Chava's ramrod posture reminded Harry of Miss O'Rourke from the night school, the image coming to him as though from another reality. He shook Moishe's hand, and pecked the cheek of the mother. "Velcome," Chava said in English in her deep-throated voice, and Harry wondered if this was as near as his sister-in-law could come to sounding glad to see someone. But then behind her, he saw the dark, curly hair of the most beautiful little girl. "Sarahle." He smiled as he lifted his niece into his arms. "You know your uncle Harry?" he asked. "You write letters," Sarah said, expressing quite honestly the sum of what she knew about her uncle, except for: "And we made the house all pretty for you. Moishe taught me how to make a broom."

"Quiet already." Chava took her daughter and placed her back down on the ground. "You'll tell him later about the broom. Come, we'll go inside and stir the borscht, make sure everything is nice on the table." But they weren't ready to leave just yet, the spectacle of their long-absent relative too compelling, even for Chava.

"You look like a regular movie star," Leah said, and Hershel, like his brother before him, took Harry's hat to try on.

"Nah, on you it doesn't look so good, either," Yitzak observed. "No one but the American can wear the hat. But come, let's all go in the house, let Mama and Harry sit themselves a while, talk for a minute." To mild protestation, the clan disappeared into the house, and Harry, taking his mother's arm, led her to the bench, where both of them sat, cooled by the generous shade of the old tree.

Harry took both his mother's hands in his and began: "Mama," he said, "you may remember, for a time before I left, there was a girl."

"Oh, my Yankele, I'm so sorry to tell you. Yes, I remember. The niece by Shmuel, of course I remember. But Yankel, I wrote already to Rifka . . ."

"I know, Mama, she's married."

"So you know. They say the child is seven, eight years old. She must have found someone right away. I'm so sorry, my darling."

How to emit the words that would convey the information in such a way as not to produce shock, betrayal, anger? How to stun a person gently?

"Mama, please try to understand, I'll explain everything. It's true that Reizel is married, Mama," Harry took a deep breath. "She's married to me."

Again Elke's hand sprang to her mouth, not before a yelp of astonishment escaped from her lips and echoed through the yard.

Harry held tight to her other hand as he told her that he and Regina had been married just before he left for the United States, when he learned that she was pregnant; that they had a son, conceived out of wedlock, yes, but in the purest and deepest love and respect for each other. He told her, too, his reasons for keeping it a secret. His marriage would have barred him from entering America; the visa clearly stated he must not be married. The burden of holding such a secret would have been too great, on Papa and on her.

"Icko didn't know?" With each drop of information, a shade of color drained from Elke's face.

"I was afraid if they questioned him, I don't know, I didn't want he should get in trouble on account for me." The emotions of the situation tripped up Harry's syntax; he found himself speaking in a mixture of English and Yiddish, the latter more familiar to his mother and therefore coming more readily from him as he sat there doing nothing other, he realized, than begging her to forgive him.

Not apologizing this time for remaining in her apron, Elke freed her hand from Harry's grip and sobbed pitifully into the garment.

Seated in the buggy just a few yards away, Regina had stiffened at the sound of Elke's startled utterance. Following that moment, she heard no voices coming from the yard, so perhaps it wasn't too much to hope that the conversation was proceeding peacefully.

The rhythmic *thwap* of Yakob's baseball was beginning to tear at her determined equanimity, however, so she suggested that he pick some wildflowers to bring in to his new grandma. The boy, as anxious as his mother about meeting his father's family, and eager to keep busy, climbed from the buggy obediently and set about gathering the yellow and lilac blooms that grew in profusion along the road. Watching him filled Regina with a sense of calm, until she noticed a group of children approaching. There were four of them, and they were older than Yakob, and as they came up beside him, in his new suit from yesterday, the children looked soiled and ragged. "Dirty Jew," the tallest boy spat at Yakob. "Get away from here, you dirty mouse. Your family is so poor they had to borrow my father's horses."

With one swift movement, Regina jumped from the buggy, but Yakob, clutching the wildflowers he'd picked, just stood there and looked at the children. "Come away from there," Regina called to her son; yet, while her impulse was to run to his side and shoo away these monsters, there was in Yakob's manner something that stopped her. Her son stood there looking at the offending group, unemotional and unyielding. Of course, no Jew living in Poland was a stranger to these kinds of epithets, so that Yakob seemed utterly capable of handling this himself. Did this make a mother proud? A flood of mixed feelings coursed through Regina as she witnessed her son's capability. Yes, she was proud of the boy's bravery, but at the same time, was it not appalling that her child should be so unmoved by this kind of hatred? She studied Yakob; there was no sign of trembling. Her child just stood there stolid, rigid, and if he felt fear, it was a feeling familiar enough to be controllable.

Gathering whatever she could muster of courage to match her son's, she approached the group of belligerent children as slowly as she could. From the field that separated the Himelbaums' house from their neighbors', she saw a man running over. He was a tall, strapping man, ruddy from the sun, and he forcefully threw down the scythe he'd been using to cut the crops. Despite the likelihood of embarrassing Yakob by impinging on his manly conduct, she pulled him to her chest protectively. But instead of adding his voice to an ugly anti-Semitic altercation, the man angrily chastised the children and told them to apologize. Without uttering a word, certainly offering no apology, the four ran back toward their house.

The man took off the brimmed cap he was wearing, held it to his chest, and bowed his head to Regina and Yakob. In Polish, he said, "You must forgive my children. They are growing up learning terrible things."

But how did he know what they were saying to her boy, Regina asked the man, whose face emanated kindness.

"A father can recognize hatred in his children," he answered. "My wife and I try to teach them...."

The farmer's remorseful words were interrupted by Harry. "There you are," he said as he came around the side of the house where Regina and Yakob were engaged with the neighbor. "I want to introduce you." To Yakob, he said, "Your grandma is dying to meet you. Oh, look at these flowers, her favorite. Hello, Mr. Hondra," he said, extending his hand. "I don't know if you remember me. Yankel, I went to America years ago."

Hondra wiped off his hand, soiled from working in the field, and shook Harry's. "Sure I remember. You were only a boy when you left. There's been a lot of excitement over at your house, everyone getting ready for your visit. I remember you were quite a horseman, so any time you want to ride."

"I see you've met my wife and son," Harry said.

Hondra looked confused. Regina had spoken Polish to him, so she wasn't from America; when had the younger man acquired a family? But there were more important matters to attend to than something that was none of his business. He put his cap on and pulled Harry aside confidentially. "My kids said some bad things to your boy. He'll tell you what happened. I apologize. The way things are, well, I don't want to ruin your homecoming, but if you can see your way to helping them all get to America, the whole family, it would be for the best."

Harry understood what Hondra was talking about, and he was sorry to hear that Yakob had been the butt of what must have been anti-Semitic bullying, but the relief of having told his mother about Regina and his marriage easily superseded anything that might have transpired out here. At long last, the truth was out; other things he would think about at another time.

"Very good to see you, Mr. Hondra," Harry said, returning to where Regina and Yakob stood and wrapping his arms around them. "You know I always remembered that cap of yours. They wear them just like that in America. Recently, I lost mine. I looked all over, but no luck."

"Well, that's a pretty fancy hat you have on right there," Hondra said, referring to Harry's Panama. Without missing a beat, the farmer removed his cap and tossed it to Harry. "Take it. You going back to America? Take it with you. A little piece of home."

Harry's hands weren't free, but Yakob reached out for the cap and grabbed it, like a boy who'd been practicing his catching skills. Harry beamed at his son and thanked his neighbor. "Even better than the one I lost," he said, "I'll wear it all the time," and he led his young family toward the front of the house and through the gate for introductions a long time coming.

Given the scorching embarrassment of meeting her mother-in-law as a woman who had obviously had sexual intercourse before marriage, Regina could not have asked for a more hospitable welcome. Harry's mother could only bring herself to shake her hand, but she did hug and kiss Yakob. Once they were all gathered inside, Hershel and Leah, having been apprised of the circumstances by Yitzak, greeted both of them warmly, and even Chava granted them a smile.

All the warm feelings momentarily threatened to dissipate, however, when Yakob was introduced to his cousin, Moishe, upon whom he fixed a stare even more intense than was his usual habit. Regina swatted him softly to stop, reminding him that it was rude to stare, to which Yakob said, "I know him. From school. He cries all the time. I tried to be his friend, but he doesn't talk to anyone."

The double indignity of hearing her child criticized and picturing him in tears in front of his schoolmates provoked in Chava an instant dislike toward Harry's child. She did little to mask it; in fact, now that she thought about it, she remembered this boy, sitting on a bench and staring at her Moishe that first day.

"Are these beautiful flowers for me?" Elke asked her new grandson, in the way of deflecting the acrimony. Smiling, she thanked Yakob for the flowers and placed them in a vase on the table, and instructed everyone in a no-nonsense way to find their seat.

She had set up a little area in the corner for the children to eat their meal, so that the grown-ups could pepper Harry with questions about New York and everything American, and soon, a sour note averted, the large kitchen area was filled with the joyful atmosphere of reunion—but for Moishe, nuzzled close to his mother at the table with the grown-ups.

Chava's resentment sat as nothing more than an insignificant shadow over the festivities, food and conversation in ample supply to eclipse her pinched expression. And when Regina glanced over at the children's table, she was glad to see that Yakob fit in nicely with his new cousins, enjoying the meal and the company, and sufficiently involved and at home not to be staring at anyone.

As bright sunlight ebbed into the soft colors of dusk, Harry patted his stomach and said he would wait not one minute longer to walk out to the river. He looked around the room at his brothers and their wives and children, at his wife and child, and at his mother, and said that his only regret was that Irene—Rifkale, he corrected himself— wasn't here with everyone. "But just a minute," he said, and from the shopping bag Regina had brought, he pulled a small camera, a piece of technology the likes of which the other Himelbaums had never seen. "It's everyone's hobby in America," Harry said. "Everyone's taking pictures with these. I saved up to buy one for just this occasion. They come from Germany, I'm sorry to say, I hate to give that *gonif* even a penny. But come outside, everybody, let me take a picture to take to Irene."

As the family reluctantly got up from their comfortable and well-fed positions at the table and made their way outside, Harry slipped Mr. Hondra's cap onto Yakob's head. It was too large for the boy, but somehow Harry felt that that was where it belonged. He had caught it, after all, and soon enough, he'd grow into it.

The gentlest breeze rustled through the leaves as the family posed for several pictures. Harry dismissed the suggestion that he should be in one of the shots, saying Irene knew what he looked like. "Sure, she'd recognize you, but we don't," came a voice from over his shoulder. Harry turned around to see his two oldest friends, Carl and Ruby, obviously there as part of a planned surprise visit. The three young men wrapped their arms around each other and appraised how the years had treated them. Elke, seeing her son with his old friends, had to brush away another tear and swallowed the emotions with a brusque reminder, "So go, already, you said you were going to the river." "Yeah, go walk off the meal," Hershel put in. "You should have room for the cake I made you."

Flanked by his two friends and his wife and child, and Hershel's little boy, David, who had clearly made of Yakob an idol, Harry started toward the meadow of wheat and hay and wildflowers, the ground rutted beneath his feet, the colors and air and fragrances soft as a whisper, and he thought again of the image he'd had on the train the day before—was it only yesterday?—of the quilted blanket welcoming him home.

Yet "home" was at the same time the site of the most brazen betrayals. For mixed in with the array of flowers and the air's fragrances, came Carl and Ruby's reports of epithets and violence that had become an almost daily assault. They spoke to him of vandalism and venomous slogans slung across storefronts and between neighbors. This Poland, this amalgam of beauty and beastliness, existed two-faced, the starkest form of cruelty. Reaching his beloved Bug River, Harry tried to make sense of it: How could this golden expanse of river, this most enchanting spot on earth, meander through a land so rife with hatred? The sun sliced low through the trees, producing gleaming bands of light on the water, yet his own son had this very afternoon been the target of racism not two kilometers away. How could a Jew feel a love for this land? The word *homesick* suddenly struck him in all its myriad facets.

He looked over at Yakob and David playing with the ball and glove Yakob had brought along. Mr. Hondra was right: he'd have to get them all to America. From his pocket, he took the camera and handed it to Regina. "Take a picture of us, will you?" he asked, and he drew his friends around him. "Be sure to get the river in the picture," he instructed his wife, for he knew that, despite everything, he would always want to be able to revisit the Bug, even if only on a piece of glossy paper. He settled the Panama hat snugly on his head, put his arms around his friends, and smiled for the camera.

"How long you here for, Harry?" Carl asked. "Will you have time to go riding?"

"I'm here at least six weeks," Harry said. "Of course, we'll ride. The neighbor next door, he'll lend to us some horses." He wasn't entirely thrilled with the prospect of asking Hondra for a favor, the way his children had treated Yakob. On the other hand, the man seemed nice enough, a good neighbor, and Harry couldn't be back in Stawki and not go riding with his friends.

While the boys ran friskily ahead of the adults, Harry wanted to take his time heading back to the house, savor this walk, this field. He stopped to take in the swaying rows of wheat, the gently fluttering flowers. They planned to be here only a few days before going back to Regina's family in Lukow.

He had looked forward to this trip for a long time, being home in Poland with his family. He had waited and saved for so long. Yet the very home he had mused about and missed, he must now dismantle. Of course, he'd known that his trip would include making arrangements for Regina's and Yakob's emigration; now, it appeared equally urgent that he persuade the rest of his family to come to America, as well. Maybe not tonight, but very soon, he decided, he would talk with his brothers. Yitzak: he knew he had a woman in Warsaw. But surely that wouldn't deter him from doing the right thing by his wife and children. Poland was beyond broken for the Jews; it was looking to break them.

As contemplative a mood as the walk had produced in Harry, the scene waiting inside the house swept plans and second thoughts and melancholy from his mind. The table had been covered with a red velvet tablecloth that Leah had decorated with delicate embroidery, and laden with wine, *schnapps* from Yitzak's store in Warsaw, fruit juices for the children, and a cake that looked more like a piece of artwork than something to be eaten. Hershel didn't hide his pleasure as the party oohed and aahed over the intricate pictures he had designed with herbs, berries, and dough. There were birds and flowers of different varieties, hands interlocked with other hands, and even a boat with two flags, Polish and American, to symbolize Harry's return.

All at once, it hit him, the efforts his family had expended in anticipation of his visit. And the money they'd spent, which they clearly didn't have. They'd had to borrow the horses from neighbors; according to Yitzak, only one milk cow remained. Yet look at all this! Thoughts or talk of visas, passports, immigration had no place in this house, in this room, at this table.

Yitzak poured the spirits and handed a glass to each person. One and all they raised their arms and their voices in a heartfelt "*Le Chaim*," and drank to their gladness.

"*Nu*, are we going to get to eat it, or just keep admiring it?" Yitzak inquired with good-natured gusto. The others wouldn't allow Hershel to cut the cake, however, until Harry snapped a picture of it. That accomplished, and as the baker carried out the careful apportioning of his masterpiece, Elke approached Harry and nudged him from the group. "Don't worry, I won't cry; I have no more tears left," she said. "But now that you're here, I don't know how I will bear saying good-bye to you again. Especially now, you bring to me a grandson." She looked with affection at Yakob, waiting with his usual serious expression for his slice of cake.

"Maybe we won't have to say good-bye, Mama," he said, kissing the top of her head. "There's no use talking now, I just got here, but maybe in a week or two, we'll sit and have a talk."

Elke grasped her hands in front of her heart, as though she'd just heard words she hadn't even dared pray for in the privacy of her conversations with God. "You might stay?"

"Mama, I'm an American citizen. And my boy, he's a citizen, too. It's the best place on earth, Mama, to make a living, raise a family." But he didn't want to have a serious discussion or broach the subject of her coming with him to America. "You like my Reizel, Mama? A beautiful girl, no?"

Elke raised a dubious eyebrow. "I hear the father thinks he's better than everyone," she said, repeating what she'd heard in

Wlodawa about Regina's father and the disagreement he'd had with his brother, Shmuel.

"He's a very nice man, Mama. Soon, you'll come to Lukow, they'll come here. We'll all get to know each other."

"So, we'll get to know," Elke said quietly, the momentary fulfillment of her unrequested prayer dashed. "We'll know each other and then we'll lose each other again. You think it's easy? It's not so close, Lukow to Stawki. Closer than New York, that I can't deny. And to think this whole time I had a grandson so close." She still wasn't saying much about Regina. The young woman's trespass on decency, her stature as wife, not to say daughter-in-law, would take time to assimilate.

Harry was sorry to see his mother's head so riddled with worries, judgments, and contradictions. What she'd implied about visits, though, was of course, true: the joy of a visit was by definition fringed with the painful knowledge of ensuing separation. Maybe this would be the very fact that would turn the conversation he intended to have with her toward a favorable outcome. Maybe she would agree to come with him to New York.

The plentiful wine and *schnapps* had made his brothers and Carl and Ruby a little bit tipsy, and the sugar in the cake lifted everyone's spirits. Little Sarah had her uncle's masterwork smeared around her mouth, with the purposeful Moishe wiping it away with a napkin Chava handed him. Off in a corner of the room, Leah and Reizel talked like old friends, and Yakob came over to offer his new *bubbeh* a piece of cake.

"You're a good boy," Elke said to her grandson. "I'm happy to have you in the family. Come, sit with me a minute, tell me what you like to do."

As Elke and Yakob repaired to the small entranceway where Elke slept, Harry joined the merrymakers around the table and held out his glass to Yitzak for a refill. "I know this must have cost a pretty penny," Harry said to his brother. "I don't have to tell you how much I appreciate it." He gestured around the room. "All of this."

"So don't tell," Yitzak acknowledged. "It means the world to everyone, having you home." Harry was about to say that they still shouldn't have spent so much money, when Hershel came over to offer him a piece of cake.

"I saved this one for you," Hershel said, "with the American flag. Believe me, the stars took a lot of work."

"To who did you give the Polish flag?" Harry asked, taking a big bite out of the slice of cake.

Hershel shrugged. "I don't know, I think maybe Yakob took that one. I wasn't really watching every piece."

Harry couldn't say why, but he hoped Hershel was wrong. He didn't want Yakob to have gotten the piece with the Polish flag. He wanted to be thinking of his son, and for his son to be thinking of himself, as an American; nothing must cloud that single, important fact.

"Can Yakob sleep with me, Papa? Can he?" Curly-haired David was pulling on Hershel's pant leg, then lovingly hoisted into his father's arms for the effort. "Mama says he can. Can he?"

Harry was proud of his son for making such an impression on his little cousin; maybe the boy was a leader. More to the concerns of the moment, however, he and his brother agreed that Yakob could stay in the room with Hershel and Leah, sharing David's bed.

Chava, who had been silently grousing for weeks about having to make room for Harry and his family, felt differently catching the hurt on Moishe's face when the sleeping arrangements became known. Not that Moishe had made the slightest gesture of friendliness toward his new cousin, but the prospect of Yakob bunking in with David underlined once again Moishe's perennial position as a loner. Even with a cousin exactly his age, a schoolmate, he could not forge a bond. And that David, never had he shown the kind of reverence for Moishe that he'd been showering on Harry's son since they'd arrived. The obvious slight only caused Chava to pull her boy closer to her. "Here, *tatelah*," she said, exercising precisely the wrong and frequently chosen maternal tactic, "let Mama give you another piece cake."

As for Yakob, he was less than sanguine when informed that he'd be sleeping here and his mother somewhere else. Despite her tepid response to her daughter-in-law, Elke had found time during her busy day to ask her friend Ruthie whether Harry and his wife ("Yes, he's

married," she'd said tersely in response to her friend's astonishment)
might spend the night together in the available bedroom. The two old
friends, who didn't always require explanations, had arranged it so that
Harry and Regina could slip into the house without the necessity of
greetings or conversation. Yakob did not go along with the plan so
unquestioningly. Yes, he had learned to swallow his homesickness in
the dormitory at boarding school, which hadn't been easy, but aside
from those necessary weekday separations, he'd never slept farther
from his mother than the two-foot floor space between their beds. He
was proud of the way he'd behaved during the past twenty-four hours
as he adjusted to the various new facts in his life that came in the form
of a father who actually existed in the flesh, a household he'd never
been to, and most recently, a group of people that everyone said was
family. But his mama wouldn't be sleeping in the same house—not
to mention, the same room? He'd been trying all day to behave like a
grown-up, but this? Regina pulled him aside. "It's just next door we'll
be, *tateleh*. And look how your cousin David begs to sleep with you. You
don't want to disappoint him."

"Please," the cherubic little David pleaded, standing beside Yakob
by now and clutching the baseball glove as though it were the most
valuable artifact imaginable.

Amidst the small agonies of young boys and their sleeping arrangements, Harry ducked outside to say good-bye to his friends. They'd
ridden their bicycles from Wlodawa, and despite the alcohol intake,
mounted their vehicles with easy confidence.

"In a week or so, I'll come back," Harry said as he walked alongside
his friends pedaling to the front gate. "I'll find you in town, we'll go
riding."

As the whirring wheels of the bikes faded into silence, Harry stood
for a few moments in the dim light of a quarter moon. In the morning,
he would make a careful inspection of the farm. He knew that for his
arrival the family had fixed up the house itself to nail-perfect condition. But with Yitzak away for weeks at a time, Hershel remained the
only man on the place. He did what he could with the chickens and

dairy cow, but what about the land? Who was cutting the wheat, harvesting the grains with which Hershel made his cakes and challahs?

There was a lot to go over, but there was also tonight: he and Regina would be alone for the first time in eight years.

By the time he walked back inside, the dishes had been washed and the kitchen nearly returned to its customary tidiness. Regina, seeing Harry, took Yakob to the front door to show him how close the Kaminskys' house was, and, gradually, an accepting fatigue overtook lingering protests after the hours of meeting and merriment and the making of impressions. Yakob hugged his mother bravely before taking David's hand, and now it was time for Harry to take Regina's.

A golden light emanated from a small window of the house to which Harry led his wife. Entering the house, they followed the light to a simple bedroom and closed the door. It creaked only slightly as it clicked shut. Harry and Regina stood at the closed door, arms at their sides, looking at the bed.

After a minute or two, he spoke. "It's funny how you can dread something for such a long time and then when it finally comes to pass, it's not so bad."

"I guess 'not so bad' is not so bad," Regina tried to quell the insult taken. "Like I said, I know I look a little different."

Harry smiled at her mistaken inference. Turning to her, he said, "I didn't mean you, Reizele. My mother, telling my mother about us, that's what I meant." He took her hand, "Come, let's sit."

They sat down on the bed, thigh to thigh, like two teenagers left awkwardly alone at an arranged meeting. Regina looked down at the floor. Tenderly, Harry lifted her chin with his finger and turned her face toward his. The kiss that followed was soft, delicate. Harry felt his desire for her stirring, not with the old insistent passion that he remembered, but persuasive, nonetheless.

Perhaps that is why he could unbutton her dress and slip it from her shoulders with a dexterity unmarred by urgency, and say no quietly when she requested that he extinguish the light. "I want to look at you," he said. With an aficionado's appreciation he gazed upon the elements of his wife's body, stroking them, her neck and chest and shoulders, before sliding one and then the other brassiere strap from its mooring, cupping each breast in his work-hardened hands. Regina took his hands and kissed each palm, anointing his fingers with her lips and granting them permission to continue their exploration. She stood for a moment to allow her dress to fall to the floor.

Then, with barely a sound, they lay beside each other on the bed and Harry found her knees, her thighs, the acquiescent band of her underwear, and the wet, pulsing center of her. He got up on his knees to remove his own garments, never losing his fixed attention on her nakedness. His eyes and hands studied and adored her, until, when he entered her, their lovemaking culminated with two voices lifted in a sustained and grateful sigh.

"Not so bad," he whispered moments later, and they dropped off to sleep.

Regina dimpled his cheeks with kisses the next morning, before slipping out of bed and into her clothes so that she could be there when Yakob awoke. Within an hour, Harry was walking around the property with his brothers.

The fresh morning light shone on the dewy grass and the peeling frame of the barn, which there simply had not been money to repair. As with his walk to the river the previous night, contradictory impressions of beauty and despair bumped Harry's awareness at every turn.

"Why didn't you let me know?" he asked as they entered the barn. The cow was terribly skinny; the structure itself, a shambles; and they were down to two chickens. How many eggs could two chickens produce? The once-pristine barn needed a complete overhaul; sunlight came through the splintered rafters.

"What could you do from New York?" Yitzak returned. "With all the money you've been saving, and sending, what were you going to do?"

Hershel broke the momentary silence that followed. "Look, there may be an answer," he said. And then he informed Harry of what Yitzak already knew: that Mr. Hondra had approached him; he was looking to buy a portion of the property. The brothers hadn't wanted to pursue

Hondra's proposal until Harry returned home, but, as he could see, there really wasn't much choice. "You were the farmer in the family," Hershel said. "The rest of us? For a while, my baked goods brought in a little something, but lately? You know what has been going on here, I don't have to tell you."

Harry regarded Yitzak, who didn't try to prettify the situation. "The marriage to Chava is in name only. You know as much. I bring home *zlotys* enough for the family to have what to eat, keep up the house. Believe me, your secret was better kept than mine. At least, Chava knows. Not that we talk about it, but anyway. Mama, if she suspects anything, keeps it to herself. If she knew I was in love with a gentile, well, you can see why it's better not to bring it into the open."

In New York City, Harry functioned as a worker, an employee who did what he was told and came to know what was expected. Here, at the end of an eight-year absence, he, the youngest brother, was once again in charge. "In love you are?" he asked as the three men walked from the barn out into the field of small grain crops. In the distance, Hondra and his oldest boy, Wladyslow, were cutting and gathering rye and wheat, while the Himelbaum crops stood untended. Harry had already forgotten the question he'd put to Yitzak, so when his older brother said yes, the word floated meaninglessly in the air.

"I'd go live with her altogether if . . ." He couldn't finish the sentence; the clause that came after the "if"—if Ava would allow it— was a fact he didn't want to acknowledge out loud. He'd said enough, though, to stop his brothers where they stood.

Hershel thought this was a good time to change the subject. Though his news would also come as a surprise to his recently returned brother, at least it was news, he hoped, that would please him.

"I've started the paperwork for us to leave here," he said, "Leah and David and me. The writing is on the wall, every other week I can't go into Wlodawa without witnessing another scene of vandalism. The first time it was Feldberg, the bakery; that was bad enough. Last time, the hardware store, Welkowitz's place, burned to the ground. You know about the new law they passed, they make all the storeowners put their name on the window. It's not hard to put two and two together: this way the *goyim* can identify the Jewish owners, and believe me, those are the shops that are being desecrated. This is no place to live anymore. By the end of this summer, fall at the latest, we're getting out."

"And Mama?" Harry asked. He certainly understood, and whole-heartedly endorsed, Hershel's decision to leave. But what about their mother? What about Chava and the children? Did his two brothers just plan to leave them to chance? Two women, one of them getting on in years, and two young children?

"We haven't told her," Hershel said. "Leah and I, we try to bring up the subject of going to America, but you know her: she won't listen. So, for now, we haven't told her we're going. That's why I'm telling you now, so quickly, maybe you can convince her. Isn't she, through Papa, a citizen? Maybe it won't be such a *megillah* getting her in."

"Papa's dead. He's no longer in America," Harry said tersely, though Hershel's assessment was probably correct. But too much was coming at him, too much information and change, and he knew that in many parts of Europe governments were making it increasingly difficult for Jews to travel or obtain visas. Nobody wanted them. Even the British were rumored to be working on a plan to restrict Jewish immigration to Palestine; running out of land, they actually asserted. Sure, he could understand Hershel feeling pressed to get himself and his family out of Poland. But what about Mama?

Looking squarely at Yitzak, he said, "I'll talk to Hondra about selling."

"I didn't plan to fall in love," Yitzak said. "It just happened."

Harry continued: "But first I'll talk to Mama. We're going today to the cemetery. I'll talk to her then." He plucked a strand of wheat from its stalk and turned toward the house, patting his brother Hershel on the shoulder.

That very afternoon, over his father's gravestone, Harry once again took inspiration from the parent who had always been his model for what it meant to be a man, and began the many negotiations in which he would be embroiled that summer.

First, he needed to persuade his mother to come to America. He wanted to do this without frightening her about the growing anti-Semitism in Poland, and he also felt that it should be Hershel who informed her of his plans to leave. Without the strength of these two arguments, however, (with Hershel's departure, and Yitzak rarely at home, all her sons would be gone) he quickly ascertained that leaving Stawki was as alien an idea to his mother as bringing *treyf* into the house. To all his claims, she had a ready retort. When, for instance, he noted how much he and Rifka could use her cooking, she suggested that they come home. Besides, she pointed out, his wife was a very good cook, from what he said, so she'd prepare their meals, and teach Rifka in the bargain. When he described all the nice Jewish women in his building, she described her lifelong friendship with Ruthie. Nothing can compare, she said mistily, with a friend you've known for a lifetime. Thus, the conversation at the cemetery meant to persuade his mother to look favorably upon joining him in New York did not go well. Even to himself, Harry sounded like a not very persuasive salesman. "Potatoes and apples, all the produce you need, sold right at the same store," Harry said, adding with a playful wink, "and I'll give you a discount."

"I can go outside and pick my potatoes and apples," Elke pointed out.

"And a kosher butcher, Mama, right around the corner. You know we have meat almost every night?"

"*Nu*, so what do you need your mama's cooking?"

If Elke understood the seriousness of her son's purpose, she didn't let on, but as she had a counterargument to Harry's every enticement, both would have acknowledged that she was the victor in this first round of talks.

As each of them placed a small stone on Icko's grave to signal that they had paid a visit, Harry felt no closer to gaining his mother's willingness to consider emigration than when they'd set out that afternoon.

His negotiations with Mr. Hondra would have to wait, for Regina and Yakob were eager to return to Lukow. The boy missed his *bubbeh* and *zeydeh*, his newfound fondness for Harry's family notwithstanding, and since even more dramatic changes and absences were imminent for the child, Harry agreed that they would be on the train the following morning. In a week or two, he'd return to Stawki on his own, have that ride with his friends and, while asking for the loan of Hondra's horses, approach the offer the man had made. How much of the Himelbaums' eight hectares did he have in mind?

As Harry and his young family set out on foot for the train station the next morning, he was glad to see his brothers working on the barn. Yitzak would be home for several more days before returning to his job, and his nefarious love affair in Warsaw, and they had all agreed that the place should look its best before Harry entered into negotiations with the neighbor.

Sarah and David ran alongside the Himelbaums as far as the main road that led into Wlodawa. Looking back to see that they'd safely returned inside the gate, Harry caught a glimpse of Chava and Moishe waiting for them under the cottonwood tree. If his mother could be persuaded to go to America, what would happen to Yitzak's family? Just Chava and the two children in the house, with Yitzak likely returning ever less frequently? Was this an outcome to be working toward? He looked up at the two storks' nests that sat on the poles framing the house. With God's help and the birds' blessings, maybe he'd figure things out for everyone.

Walking through Wlodawa toward the train station, which was not nearly as imposing or decorous as the one in Lukow, Harry was surprised at the number of people he knew to say hello to. Welkowitz already had his sons rebuilding the store, and they exchanged a few words; Feldberg, sweeping the cobblestones in front of his repaired bakery, shouted a greeting. And there was Rabbi Braun, sitting with a book at the entrance of the Great Synagogue, as the temple in Wlodawa was known. If the train station amounted to only an amalgam of intersecting tracks, Harry's pride in the beautiful Baroque temple, which dated back to the eighteenth century, surged within him as he decided to approach the rabbi. Sometimes, with all the open hostilities toward them, people could forget that there were nearly six thousand Jews in this town—sixty percent of the population, Rabbi Braun often reminded his congregation. Maybe he was sitting here, not an outdoor-loving man, to lend his blessing to the rebuilding efforts going on around him.

The rabbi looked up from his book to greet Harry as though he'd seen him just the day before, when they'd been in the middle of a conversation. "The child must never know, but it's not too late," he said in Yiddish. He then glanced over at Regina and Yakob standing outside the menorah-shaped gates that surrounded the three-winged masonry building. The rabbi's soft, deliberate manner of speaking, matched by the remarkable slowness with which he turned his head, gave Harry a chance to recover from the shock of the man's statement.

"What are you talking about, Rabbi?" he asked, foregoing any niceties that might attend a greeting after eight years of not seeing a person.

Rabbi Braun went on to explain, calmly, knowledgeably, that he'd had occasion over time to ponder the *ketubahs* he'd drawn up in his capacity as religious leader, and realized years ago that the one uniting Harry to Regina, produced in unfortunate haste owing to circumstances, did not conform to Jewish law. In brief, the customary money exchange had not occurred and therefore the marriage was not binding. "Did you give to her even a ring?" the rabbi asked as if, knowing the answer, his conclusion spoke for itself.

"I didn't have time. You know how quickly everything happened. But you came to us, in Lukow, you yourself insisted that we marry under civil law, and so that's what we..."

The rabbi interrupted, raising a judicious eyebrow and pointing a finger. "The delicacy of the situation necessitated a civil union. At the time, I was caught up in the possible scandal and felt you must be pressured to marry the woman in the eyes of the state. Realizing the error with the religious contract later, I can only thank God that He urged me to take that train to your wife's village. At least, Poland thinks you're married."

This complication over the authenticity of his religious marriage to Reizel was one of the few complications Harry had not envisioned.

"What do you mean, 'It's not too late'?" He sat down beside the old man, waving to Regina and Yakob to assure them he wouldn't be long.

"You give to your wife a ring, all right maybe it's five, ten years late, but at least, then, you have given her something of value, the marriage is legal."

"I sent to her years ago, as soon as I saved up a little money, even before the child was born," Harry said quietly, drained by the endless uncertainties that seemed to be pulling at him. This encounter with the rabbi had seriously deflated his mood.

The information about the ring, however, had the opposite effect on the rabbi. He turned to Harry and gripped him in a rhapsodic hug. *"Mazel tov!"* he cried. Leaning back like a man relieved of a burden, he adjusted his glasses and looked over toward Regina and Yakob, still standing by the fence. "So? Aren't you going to introduce me?"

Hours later, in Lukow, the church bell tolled the hour as weary passengers exited the train. Harry perceived the authoritative peeling as a reminder: despite the many Jews who lived here, it was the large Catholic church across the street from the square that set the tone of this small city. At least in Wlodawa, with all its anti-Semitism, the synagogue dominated the landscape. Harry chided himself for the meaningless comparison. What was the difference, this kind of building or that? Jews weren't wanted anywhere in Poland, period.

Reaching Staropijarska Street, he saw the Lansky name printed large on the display window above the drawing of a feathered hat and realized, as he hadn't when he'd first arrived, that the name had been magnified not owing to pride of ownership, but by decree of law. Regina's parents were compelled to announce their identity on their beloved store so that discriminating shoppers might decide whether the purchase of a fashionable hat sewn by hand was worth the distaste of doing business with Jews.

"What is it, Harry? You don't look well," Regina asked as she noticed her husband's pale expression. Why was he just standing there, not coming inside? "Come, let's put Yakob to bed." She nuzzled up to his ear. "Maybe he'll sleep and we can, you know." The lovemaking of the last two nights had freshened her demeanor; she actually looked younger, and very smitten.

An hour or so later, and at intervals over the course of the summer, Regina's mother succeeded in persuading Yakob to sleep with his *bubbeh* and *zeydeh*, and the younger couple enjoyed those opportunities to be alone. But more and more, Harry's attention leaned toward the tolling of the church bells rather than the romantic bells ringing in his heart. He must provide a safe home for his family—another requirement of the Jewish marriage contract—and that home existed in the United States. Whenever he thought forward to their appearance at the American consulate, and a twist of anxiety threatened his confidence, he slapped it away. He must, he would, get them out. His son, Regina assured him more than once, had learned how to ignore the anti-Semitic epithets of Christian children, and this was not a skill he wished for his child.

Father and son spent much of their time during the month of July honing the more desirable skill of catching and throwing a baseball. They appeared at the square in the center of town so regularly that other neighborhood families came to expect them, little boys asking if they, too, could play. In this setting, and with Yakob the bearer of the coveted sports equipment, religious differences temporarily blurred. Around the most American of pastimes, and the thrill of catching sight of fly balls in the afternoon sun, Harry and Yakob were building a relationship, and their growing proficiency in the game of baseball acted as much as anything else to solidify in Harry's mind their identity as true Americans.

Owing to their respective schedules and obligations and unspoken hesitancies, the meeting of the *machetunim* never occurred. Harry did little to foster such a gathering of the families in light of the more pressing issues weighing upon him. On his several trips between Lukow and Wlodawa, he relished the time and privacy, both essential as he planned the future of the Himelbaums in both cities. The last thing he wanted was for Regina to be aware of his anxieties. She was so excited about the three of them embarking for the United States, she spoke of little else. In fact, with that goal in mind, she had even succeeded in sticking to a diet that helped her to shed a few pounds. "I shouldn't look like a greenhorn straight off the boat," she'd say. Harry laughed with her and encouraged her as she showed off her new "svelte" figure, appreciating with each passing day the character of this woman to whom his youthful passions had bound him. He had only been a kid, attracted but hardly discerning of the things that matter in a person. Sometimes, he felt he hardly deserved her, so patient and kind and playful and disciplined she was. Having to emit confidence for all of them, he kept to himself the quiet uncertainties about the emigration that visited him from time to time. About Yakob's easy admission to the United States there could be no question: the boy was, by virtue of Harry's citizenship, himself a citizen of the country. Would the same untroubled entry be granted to his wife? Surely, there would be no problem; surely the U.S. government wouldn't separate them.

Yet the rabbi's quibbles with the legitimacy of the marriage contract brought doubts to the surface that Harry had managed to repress for the last few years: the lie at Cherbourg, the lie at Ellis Island. His American citizenship was based on those lies.

"Married?"

"No."

He forced himself not to think about the discrepancy between his answer to the authorities and the truth. He should get from Chava, in any event, the Polish marriage certificate. Why had he given it to her in the first place? Had he suspected that Regina would travel to Stawki and reveal the marriage? He trusted Yitzak and Chava more than his own wife? Maybe. He couldn't remember anymore. Nor did he know what he would do with the official document once he had it. Burn it, maybe, so his lie couldn't be exposed? Or would he need it as proof of the legality of the marriage? He rubbed his forehead as if to rub the looming difficulties from his mind. At least with Yakob, there'd be no problem, he told himself over and over again. Harry had his U.S. passport; how could there be a problem?

The more immediate concerns, he felt, were those related to the financial and family situations in Stawki. Working with pencil and paper on the sticky nap of the upholstery in the third-class car bound for Wlodawa, he thought long and hard about working something out with Mr. Hondra. If they were to hold on to the family farm, which, for practical as well as sentimental reasons was the outcome Harry wished for, the land required men to work it. With Hershel leaving and Yitzak barely around, there was little choice but to enter a serious negotiation with the man. His family of six had outgrown its small cabin, barely more than a room, and Harry calculated that offering them half the Himelbaum house, along with two or three hectares of their eight, would enhance the deal sufficiently to garner an agreement. Of course, this discussion, and hopefully amicable resolution, depended upon Elke's emigration to America, for Harry was well aware that there was no way on earth that his mother would abide sharing her household with gentiles.

They are not the only ones guilty of prejudice, Harry thought, gazing out the window at the intersecting colors of the summer crops; to share her kitchen with a *shiksa* would scandalize his mother beyond reasoning. From their brief exchange on his first day in Stawki, he had a fair idea that Hondra might consider living with Jews, but the other way around held no possibility whatsoever. For his financial agreement with Hondra to materialize, he must persuade his mother to leave Poland, which, he knew, was tantamount to leaving Icko. Moreover, Elke spoke barely any English; convincing her to take on the necessary acculturation of a whole new country, a whole new way of life and language, would demand all his powers of logic.

With Hondra's name in one column, and his mother's in another, Harry's ruminations went back and forth between the various contingencies necessary to making everything work, until he finally decided that somehow, when trying to persuade his mother to emigrate, he would have to subtly inject the possibility of the Hondra family moving in. Maybe this prospect, which he would explain as the only way he could think of to keep the farm, would make Elke see for herself that staying in Stawki would be the worst of two evils: at least in America, whether she lived with him in Washington Heights or with

Malka in the Bronx, she could be assured that she would be sharing a kitchen with Jewish women.

Thus he reasoned and plotted as the local train jolted its way to the city of his birth, a place imbued with golden sunlight and the soothing sounds of prayer emitting from open windows, but that held in its shadows the unmistakable signs of menace.

On his first visit to Stawki, after all the hours of thinking and figuring, Harry decided to keep his calculations to himself. He owed it to his mother to just enjoy a few days in the comforts of the family home. Why should she associate her son's appearances with unexpected news and information that shattered the simple truths she'd come to count on?

A few weeks later, however, on his second trip home, Harry determined that he must broach the unsettling topics; it was time that the family respond to Hondra's offer. Waking early on the first morning to meet Carl and Ruby at Hondra's barn—the man only too happy to grant the three friends the loan of some horses for the day— he suggested that they might talk some business later on, and Hondra readily agreed. By late afternoon, when he returned the horses, he arrived with a stronger hand than he'd counted on, for during their robust horseback ride Ruby mentioned that his income was running low; couldn't the Himelbaums use another man to help out on the farm? Thus, by the time Harry trotted to Hondra's barn that afternoon, he was able to put on the negotiating table not only a more spacious dwelling for the man's family, but a strong hired hand to contribute to the day-to-day upkeep of the land and animals.

"Half of a beautiful, well-kept house I'm offering you," Harry said after the two men had unbridled the horses and stood facing each other just outside the barn. "You and your sons and Ruby work the land, and we each own fifty percent, split everything down the middle."

"We could certainly use a larger house," Hondra nodded. "But your friend, I'm not sure we could afford . . ."

Harry politely interjected: "This is why it might be better that, even at the same price, we keep two-thirds of the land. In exchange, Ruby's pay comes out of our share of the profit."

The tall, sun-browned farmer took a few minutes. And then, in the time it required to scratch his head, look out over the fields, and extend his hand, the deal was finalized.

And then another favorable turn awaited him: Elke, apprised of Hershel's plans, and told that Adele Hondra would be inhabiting a portion of her household, agreed with a heavy sigh to relocate. Even New York, New York, looked less distasteful to her than the vision of a *shiksa* at her stove. Harry returned to Lukow after that second visit more than satisfied. Having made a fair and viable arrangement for saving the family farm and getting his mother to agree to emigrate with Hershel in the fall—for she was indeed a citizen based on Icko's naturalization—he could focus with a clearer head on his own small family, and the bright future upon which they would soon embark. Things were going so well, he persuaded himself, there'd be no problem getting all of them to America.

Yet one more difficult encounter remained, and for this Harry made his third trip to Wlodawa, in late July. Chava. He must sit down with her and discuss the arrangements he had made.

The betrayed wife and fiercely devoted mother quite simply could not believe the conditions she was being asked to accept. It was worse than that: no one had asked her anything, nothing at all about the new arrangements. "I am to live here with the *goyim,* alone with my two children?" She fairly tore at Harry's shirt when he finished describing the plans. "This is what they teach you in America? How they defile your thinking? That my children should live in a household with those, those . . . ?" She couldn't find the word to describe the Hondra children, whose taunts had already brought Moishe to tears countless times and even upset little Sarah.

Harry tried to reason with her. "Hondra is a good man, Chavaleh, a hard worker. We'll hold on to the farm, the land, and Yitzak—"

Chava spat on the floor. "Don't say his name to me. If my parents were alive, I'd walk out of here this minute." The mere image of her mother and father, whose lives of toil and poverty had come to nothing but an early death, sent her into a paroxysm of tears. She wept openly and long at the kitchen table, her agony so deep, so bitter and hard, that it mattered not whether her brother-in-law or her children or anyone on the earth witnessed her suffering.

Risking her remonstrance, Harry gently covered her tightly clenched fists with his hands. "My brother has not been a husband to you or a father to his children," he said. "I know this; we all know it. I am doing what I can, Chavaleh, to make it better for you. This way, you keep the farm, only a few hectares I sold to them. If you want, I'll sign a paper, put the Himelbaum land in your name. I'll talk to Yitzak, pressure him to agree."

He could see that his proposal did not entirely displease her, so he continued. "When I have Mama settled in New York, and Regina and Yakob, I'll save up, send for you and the children. With the money you make selling the property to Hondra, it will be enough. We can all be together."

Bringing Chava and the children to New York had not been something Harry had contemplated during his hours of calculating on the train, but the spectacle of her misery brought the truth of her situation into sharp relief: she had been abandoned by her husband, and to leave her alone here for any length of time was unacceptable. He would talk it over with Yitzak, who might even be grateful to Harry for freeing him from a woman for whom he felt little more than a superficial attachment. If they had to sell the farm outright, well, at that point, what would be the difference? There'd be no Himelbaum in Stawki to cultivate or live on it.

As Chava's misery cooled to a manageable level, Harry brought up the subject of his marriage license. Did she have it? Could she please get it for him?

Wiping her face with the heel of her hand, Chava responded, "You think I know where a piece of paper is? That was so long ago, before the children. You've seen the little room we share? I'll look for it, maybe I'll find. I'll bring it with me to America."

Thus did Chava strike her bargain with her brother-in-law. As long as she remained the only Himelbaum on the land, she would hold the deeds to the family farm and to his marriage.

Harry didn't press her for the document. Maybe, for all the trouble it might get him into, it was better off lost in the disarray of Chava's room.

Leaving the house the following morning, kissing his mother good-bye, hugging each family member, pulling a leaf from the cottonwood tree, and breathing deeply of the fragrance of home as he clicked shut the front gate, Harry tried to look to the future. But he realized that with each day he'd been in Poland his responsibilities upon returning to the United States had multiplied. He had left New York living the life of a more-or-less single man, and would return with the welfare of generations on his shoulders.

"Sure, go ahead, take her to America," his older brother said when, a week later, Harry met him at the American Consulate office in Warsaw. The day had come to file the necessary papers for passage to America for his wife and son: Regina would be filing a petition for a nonquota visa as the wife of an American citizen; Yakob would seek an American passport as the son of a naturalized citizen. Both were there, excited and apprehensive on this momentous occasion. Yakob, dressed in his light brown suit and never having been in such a big city, had assumed the serious, militaristic posture that Harry remembered from the first day they'd encountered each other at the train station. Regina proudly wore the white dress from that day—taken in two seams to hug her new slim figure. And perched at a jaunty angle on his wavy blond hair, Harry's Panama hat topped off the all-American tableau that the young family hoped to convey.

Given the growing mood of hostility infecting the nation of Poland, from its largest cities to the most far-reaching of its countrysides, and the hundreds of anti-Jewish attacks during this summer alone, lines in front of the consulate had increased to nearly post-World War lengths. Like most of the families seeking refuge in America, Harry's brought along a small suitcase for the three of them, into which Yakob had insisted that morning on squeezing his baseball mitt. A slight bulge popped from the center of the valise, the three of them laughing on the train that their luggage looked pregnant. They needed the change of clothes for the several days they'd have to be in Warsaw while their papers were processed and steamship passage secured. HIAS, the organization that helped Jewish immigrants relocate, arranged room and board for the duration. Ava had offered the apartment of a neighbor who was currently vacationing at the home of relatives in Budapest, but out of loyalty to Chava, and his own undeniable disapproval of his older brother's involvement with the woman, Harry had declined, stating that Yitzak's affair was his own business, but there was no reason for Yakob to meet his uncle's "friend," which would only arouse unnecessary curiosity about the relationship.

"You could say good-bye to them that easily?" Harry asked. "Your wife and children?"

Yitzak just looked away, knowing that any explanation he offered would open a conversation he didn't want to have. Was he proud of his love for another woman? Did he understand the cruelty of his abandonment? He wasn't a monster; he was simply in love.

Inching their way inside over the course of several hours, and on their own after Yitzak left for work, their turn came at last. Harry could feel the moisture on his palm as he took Regina's hand and they stepped toward the blonde-haired woman behind the long counter. She looked at Harry barely hiding her disdain. This, he thought, was the person the United States hired to represent the government? The din of anxious voices reverberated in the high-ceilinged hall as he cleared his throat to address her.

"I am seeking the appropriate papers," he said, "for my family." He took his passport from the breast pocket of his suit. "I am an American citizen, and I want for my wife and son." He knew the words hadn't come out correctly as he gathered Regina and Yakob in his arms as if to present the requisite exhibits. Regina nodded politely and instructed Yakob to remove his cap, the one he'd caught from Mr. Hondra that day in Stawki. Regina's father had offered on several occasions to fix it so that it would fit him properly, but Yakob preferred the idea of growing into it.

The woman looked at Harry's passport and handed it back to him, saying, "It seems to be in order." She opened her palm on the counter. "Petition?"

Harry handed her the form. The woman read and glanced up at the prospective immigrants several times before repeating, "It seems to be in order." Harry relaxed at the same time that his heart started to beat more quickly. This would happen: he would have his family with him in New York. The woman spread her palm in front of him again. What was this?

"I'm sorry," Harry said, "you say it's all in order?"

"I'll have to see the birth certificate for the boy, and your marriage certificate." She spoke as if affronted by Harry's ignorance.

"Oh, in the suitcase," he said. "Open for the lady, Yakob," he said to his son.

Yakob just stood there, looking straight ahead, as though he didn't understand what was being asked of him. Harry repeated the instruction in Yiddish, which only served to stiffen the little boy further.

"Yakob, *vost vilstu?*" Regina asked, trying to hide her rising confusion. Why was Yakob behaving so strangely? Forgetting her determination to speak in English, to appear poised and unruffled by the life-changing transaction for which she'd come to Warsaw on this day, she abruptly plunked the suitcase on its side and opened it. The baseball mitt sat on top of the modest change of clothes the family had brought. When she'd packed last night, the Jewish marriage certificate and Yakob's birth certificate had sat on top of the folded garments.

"I took them out so they wouldn't get wrinkled when I put in the glove," Yakob said in a mortified whisper. "I meant to put them back, under the clothes." In his mind's eye, which his parents could miraculously gaze into at this highly charged moment, the all-important certificates of birth and marriage sat, unwrinkled, on his bed.

"We don't have the certificates," Harry said in a monotone to the businesslike official who held his future in her empty, outstretched hand. "We'll have to come back."

"It will probably be too late," the woman said, dispensing heart-breaking information with the indifference of a bank clerk making change. "You should get the papers for them back in America. The quota is filling quickly here. Look at these lines. Most of these people, by tomorrow, will be at the French Consulate, or the Dutch. America doesn't have room for everyone."

"We'll come back," Harry repeated, and he turned to take Regina's hand. She was looking down with shame at the open suit-case as though its contents exposed an unbearable failure. Harry tucked his finger under her chin and lifted her face so that he could look into her eyes and reassure her. "Tomorrow. We'll come back and take care of everything. Just one more day." He closed the valise, handed it to Yakob, and walked with his family past the hundreds waiting in line.

Their appearance in Warsaw the following day—with the certificates, with their change of clothes for the stay that would be arranged by HIAS while their papers were being processed, with their hopes and spirits reconstituted after many purposeful pep talks—this appearance went even worse than the first.

Initially, seeing no lines outside the consulate, their determined optimism seemed well founded. Once inside the building, they felt even more encouraged; yesterday's crowds were like a distant mirage. The hall was practically empty, just a few rows of applicants lined up in front of the various clerks. To avoid having to start all over again with his paperwork and explanations, Harry took a place at the end of the line waiting for the blonde woman. Yakob, remembering the stark embarrassment of the day before, sat down on one of the benches, not wanting to face the woman, and Regina sat beside him, telling Harry to go ahead.

When his turn came, Harry placed the two certificates on the counter. "Here are the papers you asked for," he said.

The woman looked at him, trying to place him.

"From yesterday," Harry said. He took his passport from his breast pocket, handed it to her. "Remember? I'm an American citizen? We were missing only the certificates?" He gestured toward his wife and son sitting on the bench. "You remember us from yesterday?"

"You'll have to file in America," the woman said, barely glancing at Harry's family. "We've issued all the visas for this year."

Harry protested, tried to reason with her. "But it's only one day. We were here, it's not even twenty-four hours." He raised his voice in anger, pleaded in despair. "A couple of pieces of paper, that's all we needed. We went and got everything, did everything you told us."

"Go to America, Mr."—the woman checked the passport—"Himelbaum. That will be the fastest way to get the paperwork done. You're a citizen of the U.S., there shouldn't be a problem. Here, there's nothing until next year, nothing I can do for you."

"But the boy," Harry persisted, "he, too, is a citizen. You can see right here." He shoved Yakob's birth certificate closer to the woman, and his own American passport.

Looking them over, she said, "Maybe I can arrange a passport for the boy." Harry looked over at the bench. Regina and Yakob sitting close together, emitted self-conscious smiles.

Turning back to the woman, his voice barely audible: "But not one more visa you can issue?" She repeated the previous information about quotas, but the words fell into the crack of his breaking heart. To take the boy, leave Regina behind, was unthinkable. Unspeakable, and thus he would not speak of it. He knew what Regina would tell him to do, would insist that he do, but three broken hearts he couldn't endure. The boy belonged here with his mother. He, too, would stay.

"Okay, then," Harry said, and he weakly held out his hand for the documents he had placed before her. Perhaps, as the woman returned the papers to him, a trace of sympathy accompanied the gesture, perhaps not; it was immaterial.

Moving slowly and with unmasked dejection from the counter to the bench where Regina sat with her arm around Yakob, Harry didn't tell them the details of what had transpired. Nor did he have to say a word to communicate that things had not worked out.

On the walk back to the train station, describing most of what the woman had said to him, but leaving out the detail about possibly taking Yakob, Harry said he would stay with them in Poland, apply again once the new quotas were opened up. Regina wouldn't hear of it. The woman said he should go back, apply from America. Why sit in Poland when he could set things in motion immediately back in New York? Why waste time? They debated back and forth, waiting for the train, but both of them knew that another separation was inevitable, the best and fastest way to be together, out of Poland, once and for all.

The interminable train ride back to Lukow passed in silence. Harry did little to circumvent the reemerging constellation: Yakob sat close to his mother, his head resting on her shoulder for a while as he slept, and he, slightly apart from them, looked straight ahead, holding his Panama hat on his knees, occasionally, absentmindedly, twirling it.

It was early August. How remote the date had seemed when Ralph had agreed to let him take the summer off. How he'd looked forward to introducing everyone to his wife and son, finally free, with his mother knowing about them, to acknowledge his family. His son would know how to play baseball, a real American, and his wife would relish working with her cousin on a New York theatre production. Oh, he'd painted pictures of how things would be.

Hershel, just a week ago, had managed to get visas and steamship tickets for his family and Elke; they'd be arriving in New York in October. But he, the big-shot American, look at what a mess he'd made. He couldn't blame Yakob for yesterday's mistake. He himself should have made sure the papers were in the suitcase. What an idiot! What a fool!

He looked at the two of them, Regina's head now resting on her son's as she gazed out at the passing landscape, shadows beginning to blur its contours. Her eyes were open just slightly; Harry couldn't tell whether she was awake.

Child Welfare

Two weeks later, Harry returned to Warsaw to purchase his ticket at the Red-Star American line. Once again, he would sail from France on the SS *Normandie*, this time leaving from Havre. Once again, on the day of departure, he held Regina in his arms at the Lukow train station, this time lifting his son to his chest and clutching him there, as he made promises through emotions too thick to articulate the words.

~ ~ ~

PART FOUR

1939

Deportation:

Where is Home?

January

Washington, DC

Barbara radiated glamour in a body-hugging satin gown, her hand dangling elegantly from the lip of the bar. Since the death of her son, she had lost her taste for ice cream, so that her figure slid easily into the fashions of the day. Like a well-oiled machine, alcohol an essential ingredient of the fuel that kept her in working order, she did her duty by Will, and everyone in Washington society agreed that, despite their personal tragedies, perhaps because of them, she and her husband were the model couple. They had borne their losses with grace and dignity, Will barely taking time off from his responsibilities at the Warrant Division long enough for anyone to have to cover for him, and Barbara standing right beside him, after the initial shock, as hostess, guest, and helpmate extraordinaire. People didn't wonder what she did with her days: it was known that she made all her own eveningwear, and her recipes invariably involved the most exotic ingredients. She must spend hours at the various markets around the city just hunting down the herbs and spices for her dishes; the girl was a marvel. Not that she could reasonably be called a girl much longer; she and Will had celebrated their fortieth birthdays just last spring with an outdoor barbecue-buffet that people were still raving about into July. But she carried herself so youthfully and could always be counted on to bring style and friendly conversation to any event. One could hardly think of throwing a party without putting the Browns right near the top of the guest list.

Tonight's extravaganza at the Mayflower Hotel was billed as a New Year's party, even though three weeks had passed since the rest of the world had rung in the last year of the decade. Allowances must always be made for congressional sessions if one wanted the right people in attendance. Even the calendar adjusted itself to the VIPs of Washington, DC.

"Looking gorgeous, as usual," Doug Pearson noted as he handed Barbara the martini she'd asked for. "After you teach Elaine how to cook, I'll sign her up for sewing classes with you if you're game."

"Elaine has raised four beautiful, healthy children, Doug." Barbara smiled before taking a sip of her drink. "Her cooking's good enough."

As Doug caught her up on the latest school projects of his quartet of offspring, and Barbara said she'd just love to help little Joanie with her diorama, Martha Connelly wandered over and started immediately to praise Barbara's stunning ensemble. "Only you and Myrna Loy can tuck a gardenia in your hair without looking like wilted flowerpots," she declared dryly before ordering a brandy Alexander. Doug cleared a space for Martha at the bar and excused himself to "find the men folk."

While Martha Connelly was savvy enough to recognize Barbara's occasional disapproval of her, she continued to regard the younger woman as her own personal discovery. During that terrible period after the baby had died, she frequently thought back to her first encounter with the girl: poor Barbara getting sick in the ladies' room at the Waldorf-Astoria, and yet comporting herself with such grace immediately afterward. Martha saw that initial meeting as a harbinger of what could be expected from Barbara, and assured her husband after the tragedies that both she and Will—the most dedicated employee Joe had ever had—would come out of their misfortune just fine.

"Don't you just love these Gershwin tunes?" Barbara asked, swaying in time as the band played "Our Love Is Here to Stay" and ignoring Martha's compliments. The truth was that Mrs. Connelly had looked foolish with a flower in her hair at the annual Christmas luncheon for the INS staff. Barbara had even felt somewhat sorry for her.

"The good die young, I'll say that," Martha said. She was referring to the untimely death of George Gershwin, but realized immediately the tactlessness of her remark.

"Well, with all the frightening things going on in the world, I feel lucky to have been alive when George Gershwin was writing his songs," Barbara said, rescuing Martha from the awkwardness her thoughtless comment might have elicited. She didn't want the woman's pity, could hardly bear Martha in condolence mode. And her observation about Gershwin was made in all sincerity. Barbara knew full well all the troubling circumstances gathering at home and on the international front. A person couldn't live with her head in the sand, especially being married to Will, who spoke of little else. But even with the Depression, and the ongoing labor unrest here in the United States, and the various invasions one heard about in Europe and Asia, she regarded herself fortunate to be alive at the same time as Gershwin and Cole Porter, Fred Astaire and Ginger Rogers. Surely, the 1930s could be character-ized as much by the music and movies and elegance that adorned the decade as the continuously brewing conflicts that sullied it.

"Well, you mustn't stand here hugging the wall," Martha said. "You, our most beautiful Republican representative. Come on, let's go find the men folk, as Doug would say." She cupped Barbara's elbow and together they wove their way along the perimeter of the dance floor, crowded with fox-trotting power brokers and their expensively dressed wives.

Standing in a corner of the room thick with conversation and cigar smoke, Will objected to a casual remark. "I knew he'd find his way around the Neutrality Act," he said.

"Come on, Will," one of the men in the circle chided, "even Governor Landon backs the president. We can't just look the other way while Japan marches into China. I'm not saying we should enter the fray, but we have to convey in no uncertain terms that we disap-prove of that kind of aggression."

"I'm disappointed in Landon," Will said. "And I'd call sending in tankers more than disapproval. Roosevelt wants to take us into war, mark my words."

"Well, you've got Italy in Ethiopia, Japan in China, Hitler in Austria. I'd say it's those other countries stoking the fires, not us."

"Exactly: other countries," Will retorted. "None of our business. We've got enough foreign entanglements here at home, without going thousands of miles across the water. What with . . ."

A gravelly voice insinuated itself into the debate. "Looking for William M. Brown?" Congressman Tim Barkley said. "Listen for the words *foreign entanglements* and you've got your man." He held out his thick hand, "Happy New Year, Will," and proceeded to extend his well wishes to everyone gathered. Planting his hand on Will's shoulder in a manner that conveyed seriousness, he leaned down, "Talk to you a minute?"

Despite Barkley being one of his least favorite people, Will agreed to a brief interlude away from his friends and followed him out to the hotel lobby. "What can I do for you?" he asked, placing his hands in his pockets. On second thought, he removed them and stood up straighter. Barkley was a big man, and Will didn't like being towered over, especially by a political rival.

"Relative of one of my constituents," the congressman got to the point. "I told you I stand by my people, and I meant it. You got your army out after this fellah, harassing him with threats of deportation, he never hurt a fly."

"This is hardly the place," Will started.

"I'm telling you to call it off."

Will shrugged his shoulders, "I don't know who or what you're referring to, but I'm sure you're not trying to threaten me here."

"Like you and your ilk threatened Secretary Perkins?" The attempted impeachment of Frances Perkins in 1938, on the grounds that she might be a Communist sympathizer, had done little to endear Republican lawmakers to their Democratic counterparts. "You may think you took the bite out of Frances, but I've still got all my teeth," Barkley continued. "And I'm telling you I'm going to stand by this man with everything I've got. Make a federal case out of it if I have to."

"I'm sure if the department has recommended deportation, there are grounds, solid evidence," Will said. "And now, if you'll excuse me,

I'm here to have a good time with my friends. And I'd like to dance with my wife, while I'm at it. Give me a call next week if you're so determined to get involved. Give me a name, so at least I know what we're talking about."

"He's from Poland," Barkley said. "A Jew. You're going to deport him? Where're you going to deport him to? Where's he supposed to go? Or haven't you heard? The Polish government announced in October that anyone who's been living outside of Poland for more than five years is no longer a citizen. They're revoking their passports. Where's this Polish Jew who's been here for ten years supposed to go? Maybe you want to send him straight to Hitler? Or should we just kill him ourselves, save the passage?"

"I don't appreciate your insinuations. If this man is here illegally, it's my job to investigate and take the appropriate action."

"That's the problem with you, Brown, you only see things from one perspective, never consider the nuances of your actions. That's the only explanation I can think of for how you manage to sleep at night—if you do." Barkley turned his back on Will and strode into the ballroom.

"Imbecile," Will muttered. He walked back toward the party with the strident gait of a person wrongly accused, nearly knocking Barbara over as their paths crossed under the majestic door frame.

"Will! I've been searching everywhere." She could see that he was upset. "Is something wrong?"

"Just a little disagreement with the other side," Will said, straightening his tuxedo jacket. "What else is new? I look okay?"

Barbara tucked her arm through his. "Of course. I was hoping we could have a dance."

Will really was a more than satisfactory dancer, and as he led her onto the floor and swept her into the breezy rhythm of "Embraceable You," Barbara leaned into the comfort of being at home in his arms. She'd long ago grown accustomed to tucking her head just so into the crook of his neck, and with such beautiful music, and the reliable lubrication of alcohol, she found the wherewithal to enjoy the dance, to keep going. Life wasn't perfect, after all, nothing was, and especially in

this wonderful country, a person could cope with loss and even marriage to a man whose thoughts on just about every issue she could
think of ran counter to her own. She had learned not to question Will
or confront him because it wasn't necessary here in this great land,
where the truth of one's opinions could be recorded where they really
counted, in the privacy of the voting booth. It was true that every now
and then she had to grapple with just the slightest pang of guilt, for
it might about kill Will to know that, two times now, she'd pulled the
lever for Roosevelt.

By the time the party wound down, well past two in the morning,
Barbara wasn't the only woman in the hall whose feet were pinched to
agony. But as she and Will waited in line for a taxi, she was the only
one who felt no compunctions about slipping out of her toe-cramping
shoes. When all was said and done, Barbara's poise in her stocking feet
represented just what her Republican friends admired most: heartland
roots and a small-town upbringing interwoven with city sophistication. She was a woman with a simple background, who, even barefoot,
carried herself with regal deportment, the quintessential symbol of
the Republican ethos.

Once they were back home, Will and Barbara divided like two disengaged magnets pulled to their customary sites: he to his desk and
files, she to the kitchen cabinet, where a bottle of bourbon and a shot
glass were easily located. "Can I get you a nightcap?" she called. Will
said he was done in for the night, no thanks.

"So why are you standing there with all that paperwork?" she
asked, coming up beside him. Sexual activity had long ago ceased
to play more than an intermittent role in their marriage, but after a
party of some kind, Barbara knew she could anticipate a suggestive
gesture, and she didn't object to their occasional intimacy. In fact, this
was unusual following a gala evening out, Will doing anything more
than briefly perusing his paperwork before turning off the desk lamp.

"Oh, it's nothing," he said, giving her a peck on the cheek. "I just
wanted to check something." He was leafing through some files, as
though trying to locate something in particular. He pulled one to the
top, mumbling that this might be it, and then nuzzled closer to his

wife, breathing in the alluring scent of the gardenia. He slid his fingers down her arm and tucked his hand in hers, gently coaxing her toward the bedroom. "You go ahead," Barbara smiled. "I'll be right in." When Will had disappeared upstairs, she swallowed the bourbon and went to turn off the lamp. Her eyes caught the label on the file Will had just indicated as "it." HIMELBAUM, it said in uppercase letters. "Himelbaum," Barbara said aloud. Why did that name sound familiar?

New York City

The hiss of the radiator fought against the icy cold seeping through Harry's bedroom window. Inches in front of the window sat the small desk he had recently fashioned from crates that accumulated at the fruit store and an old medicine-chest door that someone had left on the sidewalk. He needed an easily accessible surface now for all the paperwork; the Florsheim shoe box in the closet no longer sufficed. Photographs and letters, and, for the last two years, petitions and government documents, spilled out onto the closet shelf before he'd admitted to himself last spring that he must organize the part of his life that existed on paper. And every night, using the foot of his bed as a desk chair, he sat here, reading and sifting, shuffling and rethinking. The openings of the crates to the left held the photographs and letters from Poland; those on the right, the ever-increasing official communications regarding, initially, his requests to bring over his family, and, more recently, the question of his own right to remain in the United States.

Could he honestly say that any of his tribulations came as a surprise? Of course not. He had lived day-to-day since he'd come here, aware of the deceit at the heart of his citizenship and the contradiction at the heart of his dream: to claim the concomitant citizenship of his son. The presumptuous Panama hat sat on the closet shelf where the shoe box used to be, as Harry sorted and sifted, calculated and reconstituted his options. He tried not to think about the blonde woman at the American consulate in Warsaw. Somehow she had become the face of all his problems, with her advice that he apply for his wife and son's passage once he returned to America. It would be faster, she had said, easier. Instead, the procedure here was so much more complicated. He tried not to think of her, but her mocking glance was stamped on each and every sheet of paper. The voice he heard was his father's, admonishing him about the very thought of lying to the United States government.

Soon after reentering the country in the late summer of 1937, Harry had begun the process of petitioning for Regina's and Yakob's visas. With the crucial birth and Jewish marriage certificates that Yakob's baseball glove had so egregiously displaced now in his possession, he obtained the document entitled, "PETITION FOR ISSUANCE OF IMMIGRATION VISA" at the downtown INS offices and set about doing everything as carefully and deliberatively as possible. Every night after work for weeks, he studied the application with all its empty spaces and columns and questions. According to the instructions, he must enter the required information with a typewriter and mail it to the Department of Labor in duplicate. Accompanying documents must be submitted in English. Of course, Harry was fully capable of translating the Polish birth certificate and the Hebrew marriage license, but the instructions stated that they must be translated by a third party and authorized by yet someone else, someone designated as a "notary public." What kind of official was this, and where to locate such a person? And where find a typewriter, a copy machine? His head spun with the puzzlement induced by two pages of fine print, and his heart would occasionally thump in his chest as he contemplated his position. For, far more daunting than the pages of instructions and requirements and directives, were the words in boldface printed right on the front of the petition: THIS FORM TO BE USED BY U.S. CITIZENS ONLY. Harry must present himself as a citizen, but he must also acknowledge the discrepancy so baldly apparent in the dates of two of the requisite accompanying documents: his nonquota immigration visa, issued in Warsaw on April 4, 1929, identifying his status as an unmarried minor; and his marriage certificate, dated a few weeks later, but before his departure for the United States, and his arrival, and his lies.

During one period of extreme self-doubt, he thought seriously of applying only for Yakob, whose status as his son did not entail any illegality that he could think of. He had rejected this possibility while he was in Poland, but would it be such a sin to at least get his son into the United States, since neither his existence nor paternity could be held up to legal dispute? It was only his marriage that he had lied about; should he try to erase it?

The prospect ultimately sickened him. How could he even consider such a desperate act, such a cruel notion, leaving Regina in Poland? He paced and worried, trying to think of another way.

And then, late one night in the fall of 1937, soon after all the excitement attendant to his mother's arrival in the country with Hershel's family, and getting them all settled—Elke moved in with him, sharing Irene's room; Hershel, Leah, and David moved in with Malka—he returned to his lonely strategizing and remembered his encounter with Rabbi Braun. Why hadn't he thought of it sooner? Here, he felt sure, was his solution. He wouldn't erase his marriage, but alter the date of its occurrence!

That very night, he wrote to Yitzak, asking him to seek out the rabbi and persuade him to put in writing the illegality of the date on his Jewish marriage certificate owing to his failure to give something of value to his betrothed until he had been in the United States for several months. For all his brother's moral faults—Harry addressed the letter to Warsaw, where his brother continued to live with the gentile woman—Yitzak promptly complied with Harry's requests, and within weeks, he had the disavowal of the date on his *ketubah* in hand. "Only once he gave to her the ring," the rabbi wrote, "could the union be recognized by Jewish law." There, he could now state honestly that, according to Jewish law, he hadn't been married when he entered the United States. That left only the Polish marriage license to deal with.

Chava, however, to whom Harry had also sent an appeal, did not reply as swiftly or as helpfully. In his letter to his sister-in-law, he had implored her to send him his Polish marriage license. Of course, he made no mention of his plan to destroy the document so as to simultaneously destroy evidence of the civil ceremony, but it was the end of the year before he received her letter postmarked from Wlodawa, and its contents established his eventual realization that he had no choice but to accompany his visa petition with the truth.

> *Brother in law,*
> *You know your brother. He is guilty and blackens us all. I live here with the two children, he never comes. We know where he is, what his choice is. If not for the kindness of Michal Hondra I cannot even think what would become of us. You have all left us, and we depend now on these strangers. Your mother, your brothers, everyone has left us. And you ask now for my help so that your precious wife and child may also join you in America.*
> *You ask and I already told you, the marriage license that you request is lost, like your*
> *Sister in law,*
> *Chava*

Harry had a feeling that Chava knew exactly where she might locate his marriage license, but what was the use? Why should she help him? Why should she have a drop of sympathy for him? Of course, it was thoroughly unlikely that she would in any way use the document against him, but the sheer existence of it made him uneasy about trying to alter the date of his marriage. The absence of the piece of paper sealed the necessity of telling the truth about what it said.

In January of 1938, the various options having been considered and decided upon, Harry set out in earnest to fill out the document that would bring both Regina and Yakob to the United States. He would present himself as an American citizen, but directly address the fact that he had been married when his papers said that he was not. He folded Rabbi Braun's letter, of no use to him now, placed it in the shoe box, and wrote over and over again on sheets of airmail paper drafts of the letter he would include with the petition.

For three months of Sundays, he could be found at the local offices of Congressman Tim Barkley in the Bronx. "Go to him," Malka had urged, once she and Jack knew all the details of his dilemma. "He helps all the time with everything. Every day of the week, you should see all the people, standing with their papers taking turns typing and filling out. He will help you, Yankele, his people will help you. Go."

And, indeed, buoyed by the patience and encouragement of Barkley's staff, who worked in the Grand Concourse offices even on Sundays, Harry had slowly filled out the two-page petition, made copies of it and the accompanying documents, located a translator and a notary public, had everything stamped and dated. Only the letter, the letter in his own words that must acknowledge the deception, remained to be completed before the paperwork could be placed in an envelope and mailed. And even with this, a young lawyer assisted him, telling him how to address the letter, giving him pointers on wording, agreeing wholeheartedly that Harry must acknowledge the contradiction that leapt only too conspicuously from his paperwork.

On the first day of spring in 1938, he attached to his petition the typed plea for consideration. He stamped it and mailed it and hoped for a sympathetic reading in Washington, DC.

> **Honorable Commissioner of Immigration, United States Department of Labor, Washington, D.C.**
>
> **Dear Sir:**
> **In submitting the enclosed Petition for Issuance of Immigration Visa to my wife and son, I wish to submit the following explanation.**
> **I had received my immigration visa from the American Consulate at Warsaw, Poland, on April 4, 1929, as is evidenced**

by the enclosed Immigrant Identification Card. At that time I had been engaged to my present wife, Reizel Lansky, and soon afterwards, through human weakness or indiscretion, I learned that it was necessary that I marry her before I leave if I wanted to bestow my name on my unborn child, therefore, I married her in April of that same year before I left for the United States in June, arriving at New York in June 1929.

My son was born on August 29, 1929, about four months after our marriage, which should indicate that I was honor-bound to act thus before leaving for the United States.

Therefore, dear Commissioner, kindly take the above facts in consideration and allow the necessary approval in behalf of my wife and son.

Thanking you for the necessary attention in this matter and anticipating an early reply, I am

Harry paused here, for he had to use the name by which the government recognized him, the name on all of his official documents:

Very truly yours,

YANKEL HIMELBAUM
454 Fort Washington Avenue
New York, 33, New York

```
Documents enclosed:
1. Issuance of Immigration Visa
   petition.
2. Immigrant Identification Card/
   Nonquota Visa.
3. Certificate of Marriage, in Hebrew,
   with translation.
4. Birth Certificate of my son, with
   translation.
```

Within two weeks—Harry could not believe how quickly the response came—a letter awaited him when he opened the mailbox after work, an envelope with us department of labor printed in the return address section on the upper left. His hands trembled as he walked up the stairs to his apartment, took out his key, unlocked the door, smelled the fragrance of roasting chicken before the door was even open. Unlike every other evening when he returned from work, he didn't say hello to his mother in the kitchen, but went directly to his bedroom, and closed the door. Placing the envelope on his bed, he vigorously shook his hands to stop them from trembling, opened the window to cool off his body drenched in sweat. "Harry, come, dinner's ready," his mother called from the kitchen. "Soon, soon," he somehow found it possible to call back, though his throat was clenched in fear.

Shaking out his hands one more time—it was no use, they could not hold still—he lifted the envelope, breathed deeply, and opened the piece of mail. Unfolding the sheet of paper, he saw that he held in his hands a copy of the very petition he had just mailed to Washington. They had returned his request! With not even a word in response. He studied the pages, looked everywhere for a note, a sign that someone had read and considered his plea.

And then he found it, down on the bottom of his petition, in a section whose instructions began: (DO NOT WRITE IN THIS SPACE):

Date: **4/8/38**

Considered, and the Honorable Secretary of State is hereby respectfully informed that said **Reizel Himelbaum** is entitled to a nonquota status under Subdivision (a) Section 4.

Harry scoured the words he didn't know how many times, trying to persuade himself of their meaning, not daring to accept the simple declaration in front of him, signed, even, by the secretary of labor. It was all right, Reizel was accepted! They had read his letter and they understood, so quickly, so generously. She could come to America, his Reizele, Regina: she could come and be his wife!

He thought of the young fellow in Barkley's office, all the good advice he had given him, telling him, for instance, never to abbreviate anything when writing an important document, not the month of the year, the street address, anything. It showed that a person considered what he was writing important enough not to cut corners, save time; writing out the word *avenue*, for example, demonstrated respect for the addressee. Miss O'Rourke in the night school had never told him of this subtle, yet apparently significant rule.

He must tell Mama!

But then he realized, after how much time sitting in his bedroom and beaming with relief he could not calculate: what about Yakob? There was not a word about the boy. He peered inside the envelope once more; maybe he would find another piece of paper that he hadn't seen. But, of course, no, he wouldn't have overlooked that.

What about Yakob? Regina and his marriage had been the objects of his concern, the objects of the dishonesty he had perpetrated. And for her, there was approval, right here in black and white. Why was there no word about his son?

After several Sunday consultations with legal aides at Congressman Barkley's office, and in accordance with his own trepidations, Harry decided against writing another letter to the Labor Department to inquire about Yakob's status. It would be counterproductive, the young lawyers counseled him, to bring unnecessary attention to his case. Sometimes, the wheels of government spun quicker than one would expect—as had occurred with his wife's petition—but more regularly, they moved along very slowly. Harry must be patient and hopeful. He had, after all, jumped the difficult hurdle; he should just be patient, and soon enough, word would come about his son.

It was during this time, in the spring of 1938, that Harry noticed that all of the paperwork was spilling out of the Florsheim shoe box, and he decided to build himself a desk. The sanding and painting of its various parts took his mind off the document he most desperately wanted to place inside its makeshift drawers; and though Elke complained about the dust and the smell, her son's industry relaxed her nerves, too. At least this project of his was taking his mind off the mailbox, where it seemed he went day and night, even coming home at lunchtime to check its contents, while he knew as well as everyone that the mail wasn't delivered until late in the afternoon.

Finally, in early May, the much-awaited envelope arrived. Harry didn't even wait to get upstairs before ripping it open.

Dear Sir, (the enclosed document began)
ONLY THE PARAGRAPH(S) CHECKED BELOW APPLIES TO YOUR PETITION

Harry's eyes skipped the lines and lines of fine print, going directly to the paragraph indicated:

√ As your child ("Yakob" was typed in) appears to have been born subsequent to your naturalization he should be provided with certified copy of his birth certificate and available evidence in support of said birth, his paternity and your naturalization, for presentation to the nearest American consul when applying for United States citizen passport. Such documents should not be forwarded to any Government department in this country.

More lines of fine print, and then a signature: **"J. Connelly, Commissioner."**

Harry sat heavily on the steps and sighed and tried to clear his head. After all the months of planning and waiting and writing and hoping, this. His boy would have to make the trip to Warsaw, stand in the line with his papers (Harry would have to copy and mail the necessary documents immediately), present his case to a blonde woman behind a marble counter, and wait some more. What if the quota had been filled by the time he made his application? Another year of waiting. Did he have it in him, did Harry have the heart, to write to Regina and tell her? What choice did he have?

It wasn't until June that Yakob filed the petition and paperwork in Warsaw, and of course, Harry worried about the timing, July being the month that the quotas for entrance to the United States were filled.

The summer went by with no official word from Lukow or Washington. Each day as he waited for news and chatted with the customers in the store, selecting and bagging and ringing up their purchases, and sat with his mother in the evenings over the dishes she prepared in the hot weather—white fish, potato soup, sour cream with fruit—he thought of the corresponding dates from the previous summer: the visits to the park, the baseball games, the English lessons, the nights with his wife. When August came, he gave up the dream he'd had of celebrating Yakob's birthday with a Cushman's cake they'd bring downtown to Rockefeller Center. Last summer, too, they'd been apart, Harry forced to leave before his son's birthday so that he could be back in New York for work; but he'd promised the boy they'd be together in America for every subsequent celebration. "Birthdays, holidays, you name it," he'd said.

Of course, letters and photographs between Regina and himself went back and forth as always, moods conscientiously elevated in consideration of the recipients' feelings. In the year since Harry had been with them, how Yakob had grown; what a handsome young man he was becoming. One picture in particular, Harry loved to look at, his wife and son smiling out at him with such a glow on their faces. He purchased a frame from Woolworth's and placed the photo on his desk.

As summer turned to fall with still no word regarding Yakob's petition, there was other news from Europe: Polish Jews expelled from

Germany, Poland resistant to allowing them in; anti-Jewish riots condoned by the German government; German Jews forced to wear the Star of David; ever-increasing pogroms throughout Poland.

Whether opening the mailbox or the newspaper, Harry tightened with anxiety. He must get them out of there; why was this taking so long?

At the end of November, the official Department of Labor envelope arrived. Harry walked upstairs slowly, opened the door to the apartment and entered his room. In the weak light of the overhead bulb, he opened the envelope. This was not a document of approval like the one he'd received for Reizel. This was a letter.

He perused the print before reading the words it formulated.

> **Dear Sir:**
> **The Department of State has advised that your son Yakob Himelbaum recently applied at the American Consulate General in Warsaw, Poland, for a United States passport, claiming to have derived American citizenship through you.**

Harry took off his jacket, hung it up in the closet. He didn't like the tone of the words he was reading. He was frightened, felt his heart beating much too insistently. He combed his fingers through his hair and regarded the sheet of paper he had flung onto his desk, with those words, "claiming to have derived" embedded in it. How could he find the strength to once again lift such an object, which held within itself such power, such authority?

He didn't lift the letter, didn't touch it, just sat at the foot of his bed and leaned his head toward it so that only his eyes interacted physically with the words.

Date by date, identification number by identification number, the piece of paper recounted his father's naturalization and then his own. At the end of the dates and numbers, came the two concluding paragraphs:

In view of the fact that at the time of your admission to the United States on June 23, 1929, you were not the unmarried minor child of a U.S. citizen, your admission on that date may not be regarded as legal. Therefore, since you did not derive U.S. citizenship through your father, your child may not be considered a U.S. citizen under Section 1993 of the Revised Statutes of the United States, and your wife is not entitled to a nonquota immigration visa.

Under the circumstances set forth above, the approval given on April 8, 1938, to accord Reizel Lansky a nonquota status under Section 4 (a) of the Immigration Act of 1924, is being revoked.

With a coldness and cruelty Harry could not fathom, the letter ended, "Cordially yours." It was signed by someone named "D. Pearson, Legal Assistant to Commissioner." Did all the officials in Washington withhold their first names, using only an initial to issue devastating information? "J. Connelly"; "D. Pearson": what were they afraid of, these big shots, that a person such as himself would find them and complain? Or did they just consider themselves too high up to share their first names with the beseeching multitudes vying for their acceptance?

Harry's anger passed quickly, dissolving into a state of helplessness from which he seriously wondered if he would ever be free. ". . . since you did not derive U.S. citizenship"; "Cordially yours": The words, which he read over and over again, mocked him. He went through the drafts of the letters he had written and the one he had finally sent, the petition, Rabbi Braun's letter. He unfolded and read and reread, and refolded each document, his head bent over his paperwork, his hands and eyes busy with the shuffling of it, the reconsidering of the steps, for to raise his head would be to see the framed photograph of his wife and son, and he couldn't, he just could not, bring himself to look at their faces.

Two weeks later, in mid-December, as New York bedecked itself with lights and bells, and radios streamed with music wishing everyone good cheer, the next official envelope came to Harry's mailbox. He didn't have to wait too long for this one, and he'd known to expect it. "NOTICE TO APPEAR," it read. The date filled in was January 17. The place was Ellis Island. This particular document was signed by a W. M. Brown, assistant commissioner of the Warrant Division.

On the eve of his hearing this icy night in January, Harry sat at his makeshift desk, surrounded by his paperwork. The yellow onionskin carbon copies of the various drafts of the letter he'd written left smudges of print on his fingertips as he sorted through the pages looking for the documents he'd been instructed to bring. The very nice young legal aide from Congressman Barkley's office, the one who had told him never to abbreviate, would, at the Congressman's instructions, meet him at the hearing room, just to lend moral support.

It should be a straightforward "Q and A," Al Kansas, the young lawyer, had told him during their preparation session. Obviously, Mr. Himelbaum's case had come to the attention of the Departments of Justice, Labor, and State; they'd picked up on the discrepancy between the dates of Harry's marriage and his entry as an unmarried minor, and while they certainly had the discretion to let it pass, recent events back in Washington over an activist union organizer whose citizenship had been brought into question, and Labor Secretary Perkins's support of the man—a role which had prodded her enemies to bring impeachment proceedings against her—well, all this intra-agency, interpolitical infighting was probably, Al Kansas postulated, the grease that had spurred the powers that be down in Washington to make a deal out of Harry's case. It was happening all over New York, immigrants being challenged on their citizenship. "But it's just a hearing," Kansas told him. "They haven't issued any warrants yet, and we have to look at that as a positive, Mr. Himelbaum. That's very important, sir, that you think positive."

The word *warrant* had been clanging around in Harry's head since that talk with Mr. Kansas. It was there at the fruit store, there at the kitchen table with Mama and Irene—and Saul just about every night— as he did his best to eat the suppers so lovingly prepared. It was there when he wrote his reassuring letters to Regina, and when he tried on his beige suit with the contrasting white shirt and plaid tie bought to match. He'd have to wear the summer suit, because that was the only one he owned. A summer suit that hung on his narrowed shoulders, the pants baggy at the waist, owing to the weight he'd lost since the trip to Poland. At the supper table, he made light of the upcoming "meeting" at Ellis Island, but Elke knew her son was worried. She herself had adapted quite well to her new life here—between her darling sister, Malka, and the nice neighbors in the building, and living again with her daughter and getting to know this very nice boyfriend of hers, she couldn't complain—but her Harry, always the confident one, the cheerful one, when he wasn't running to the mailbox or squirreled away in his room, he certainly wasn't eating. A mother didn't have to be a detective to figure out the mood of her child. The food left on his plate was all the evidence she needed.

Harry got up before the others on the morning of the seventeenth. The kitchen was dark as he stood at the sink, trying to at least finish a cup of coffee. He had no appetite for anything else. "You've led an honest, hardworking life over here," Al Kansas had said to him. "That's all you have to get across. I'll be right there with you. Don't worry. Just answer the questions honestly." Harry reminded himself over and over of the lawyer's reassurances. Maybe Kansas was right; if he persuaded them that he deserved the citizenship they were now questioning, then he would be able to reapply for Regina and Yakob. Maybe it was true, everything would work out.

The beige summer suit provided hardly ample protection against the predawn January morning as Harry descended the steep flight of stairs into the 181st Street subway station. But the heavy winter jacket he wore to work looked foolish on top of the suit, the overcoat Saul had offered to lend him was missing several buttons, and Harry felt sure that the image he presented at this "appearance" was far more important than his comfort. "You'll freeze your *tuchis* off on the ferry," Saul had said. "Come on, take the coat, I'll find some buttons you can sew on." But Harry stood firm. So he'd catch a cold, so what? He should only not get into trouble at this hearing, that was all that mattered. He hugged close to his chest the manila envelope into which he'd stuffed more documents than he'd probably need, bought his token, and waited for the train.

On the thirty-minute ferry ride from Battery Park, he kept moving to stay warm, and laughed to himself thinking of Saul's warning. All in all, Saul was a nice kid, he had to admit.

Arriving at Ellis Island, it wasn't hard to locate the hearing room, for the bustling crowds that had once filled the Great Hall had dwindled to just a few incoming hopefuls ineligible for entry at the harbor. Otherwise, the building was used for deportation hearings, and Harry had only to follow the muted hum that droned through the hall to find the group of people waiting in front of the small courtroom. Like him, they had arrived earlier than the eight a.m. appointment times stamped on all their notices and, like him, they wore their finest clothes, and carried their hopes of exoneration in swollen manila envelopes.

Not wanting to wrinkle his suit, Harry remained standing, as he had on the nearly empty subway car and the ferry, and he continued to circle aimlessly against the cold. There were benches lining the area just outside the double doors that led into the courtroom, but only a few people chose to avail themselves of the government courtesy. A large clock indicated that it was five past eight when Mr. Kansas arrived wearing an overcoat and scarf, and carrying a briefcase. Harry felt proud to have this professional-looking man stride right over to him and shake his hand, but on close perusal, he couldn't help observing that the tall, lanky Al Kansas was terribly young, this person on whose official presence Harry was counting to make him look like a credible American citizen with important allies.

Kansas took off his gloves and unbuttoned the coat. "Come on, Harry, you want to have a seat?" he asked. "We should go over a few things before they call you." Harry explained about not wanting to wrinkle the suit, but said it would be fine if the lawyer wanted to sit down. "No, that's all right," Kansas said, placing the briefcase on a bench and snapping open the clasps. He ran his fingers through a neatly aligned row of file folders. "Remember, this is all very pre-liminary, just a formality. There's nothing to be worried about. They won't be shipping you off today, or anything like that. No definitive decisions will come out of this, I promise you." "Shipping you off": Harry marveled at how the younger man always managed to insert into his reassurances a word or a phrase to jump out and knock him in the jaw. Of course, it wasn't done intentionally, but the fact was that he had a lot to worry about. A lot. "Worse comes to worst," Kansas said, pulling what must be Harry's file from his parade of paperwork, "they'll refer the matter up. But let's not even consider that possibility. Just, like I said, be forthright, honest. Try to look relaxed, like you know there's nothing to worry about, but be respectful. Let the judge see you for what you are: a hardworking man who's kept his nose clean all these years. Oh, and be sure to mention night school, your dedica-tion to learning English. That'll be significant."

Up? Harry thought. *What does that mean: Refer the matter up?*

A while later, his stomach grumbling, Mr. Kansas asked if he'd like to get a bite, but just then, at 9:30, the double doors were pushed open by a short, gray-haired man in a suit, and Harry heard his name called: "Yankel Himelbaum." Mr. Kansas indicated that he should go in first, and Harry took a deep breath and entered the hearing room. The hunger he had been aware of just moments before balled into a knot of fear. The ceiling was so high that to enter this room was to feel immediately diminished. Rows of pews, maybe for bigger cases—for when they referred the matter up?—sat empty, so that his eye went immediately to the robed official sitting behind his elevated desk. *The judge,* Harry thought.

"Swear in the witness," the balding jurist instructed the clerk. A man hardly older than Mr. Kansas sat at a small table to Harry's right as he swung open the grated wooden partition and approached the bench. Kansas took a seat in the empty front row.

Tucking his manila envelope under his left elbow after an awkward moment of not knowing what to do with it, Harry raised his right hand and swore to tell the truth. The young man who had been sitting at the table stood up, introduced himself, "Donald Url for the government, Your Honor," and approached the witness chair. "For the government": it was Yankel Himelbaum versus the government. He forced himself to sit up taller and cleared his throat to dissipate the fear that seemed to have collected there.

A woman seated at a small desk in front of the judge's bench typed vigorously as Mr. Url for the government began the questioning.

```
Q: What is your full and correct name?
A: Yankel Himelbaum.

Q: Have you used any name other than the one
   you have stated?
A: Since my arrival in this country, I am using
the name of Harry.

Q: Where do you reside?
A: 454 Fort Washington Avenue, New York City.
   Apartment 2B.

Q: What is your age and when and where were you
   born?
A: I am 30. I was born in November 1908. Maybe
   the 10th, maybe the 12th. To tell you the
   truth, I'm not exactly sure of the exact
   date. My mother only knows it was cold out.
```

Harry smiled, hoping his attempt at humor would insert some human feeling into the proceedings. Seeing quickly that Mr. Url for the government just stood looking at him impassively, he continued: "In Wlodawa, Poland."

Q: Of what country are you now a citizen and of what race are you?

Harry felt glad at this juncture that he had nothing to wear but a summer suit. He was sweating under the lightweight jacket and shirt as he answered.

A: I am a citizen of the United States, of the Hebrew race.

Q: When, where, and in what manner did you last enter the United States from a foreign country?
A: August 30, 1937 at New York from the SS *Normandie*, third class, and I was discharged as a citizen of the United States under my own name.

Q: Have you ever been married?
A: Yes.

Q: How many times?
A: Only once.

Q: When, where, and to whom were you married?
A: April 30, 1929 in Lukow, Poland, to Reizel Lansky.

Q: Lansky?
A: Yes. That was her name before, her maiden name.

Where is Home?

Harry wondered why his interrogator made a point of Reizel's maiden name. He shifted in his seat during the sustained silence the prosecutor had obviously orchestrated for his mysterious purposes, and watched warily as he walked back to his table and leafed through some papers. Looking up, he continued:

Q: Do you know any other Lanskys, Mr. Himelbaum?
A: Well, of course, her mother and father.

Q: I see. Have you any children?
A: I have one son. His name is Yakob. He was born August 29, 1929, in Lukow, Poland.

Q: What is your business or occupation?
A: I am working in a fruit and vegetable store, California Fruit Market, 1456 St. Nicholas Avenue, New York City, as a salesman. I earn $30 to $40 per week.

Q: Had you been in the U.S. before you came in as a citizen in August of 1937?
A: Yes.

Q: When, where, and how did you first enter the U.S. from a foreign country?
A: June 23, 1929, also on the *Normandie* at New York as a third-class passenger.

Q: How long did you remain in the U.S. after your arrival in 1929?
A: Until 1937.

Q: Since your arrival in August 1937, have you remained in this country continuously?
A: Yes.

Q: Did you appear before the American Consul in Warsaw on April 4, 1929 and obtain a nonquota immigration visa as the unmarried child of a U.S. citizen?

A: Yes.

Q: After the issuance of this visa, were you married in Poland?

A: Yes.

Q: When were you married?

A: April 30, 1929.

Q: After your marriage, did you depart for the United States?

A: Yes.

Q: At the time of your departure, were you in possession of the nonquota immigration visa that you had obtained from the American Consul in Warsaw on April 4, 1929?

A: Yes.

Q: Upon your arrival in New York, were you admitted upon the presentation of this visa?

A: Yes.

Q: At the time of your arrival, were you questioned by an immigration officer?

A: I don't remember.

Mr. Url for the government paused in his questioning to look meaningfully at the judge.

Q: Did the immigration official ask you your name?

A: I don't remember exactly if he asked me any questions. I just know that I gave all the papers to a certain man on the ship. He gave me back a card.

Q: Did you conceal the fact that you were married from the immigration officials both in Cherbourg and New York upon your arrival in the U.S.?

A: I don't remember that question.

Q: But you do admit that you were married at the time of your arrival in the U.S. in June 1929.

A: Yes.

Q: Mr. Himelbaum, you are advised in view of the fact that at the time of your admission to the U.S. on June 23, 1929, you were not the unmarried minor child of a U.S. citizen, your admission on that date was not legal. Do you understand this?

A: Yes.

Q: What have you to say?

As Mr. Url for the government returned to his seat behind the small table at which he had been located when Harry entered the hearing room, and leaned back and stretched out his legs and crossed his arms waiting for an answer, Harry rustled through his manila envelope and, there was no way to avoid it, though it flouted Mr. Kansas's advice to "look relaxed," blotted his forehead with the handkerchief he had neatly folded in his breast pocket.

A: I have to say this. I didn't know exactly the American law. I did not know if this marriage would abolish the nonquota visa which I got from the consul on April 4, 1929. Also, my marriage was through human weakness. I had been in love with her for over a year. Before leaving for the United States, she told me she was in a family way. Therefore, I wanted to protect her honor and give a name to the unborn child. Therefore, it was necessary I marry her. But, as you can see, there may be another way to look at this.

Here, Harry looked apologetically at Mr. Kansas, and then held out a piece of paper to his interrogator. This was not something he and his kind legal advisor had rehearsed, and Harry had decided only to use it if things were not going well, which, at this point, was his considered opinion. As Mr. Url for the government got up from his table and took the proffered sheet of paper to examine, Harry continued:

A: I have it both in Yiddish and translated to English. A notary republic, is that how you say?, has stamped the translation, as you can see.

Q: A certificate of non-marriage?
A: You see what the rabbi says. By Jewish law, the union could not be recognized until I gave to her something of value, the ring. And that was afterwards, I was already here for a while.

Q: This is extraordinary, Mr. Himelbaum. You are asking this court to nullify the date

of your marriage based on some, excuse me,
some ancient tribal custom?

Al Kansas stood up. "If it please the court. Alan Kansas, your Honor, attorney at law. I've been advising Mr. Himelbaum, Your Honor, in an informal way. May I speak to ..."

The judge cut him off with a swift strike of the gavel. "This is a hearing, not a trial—Mr. Kansas, is it? If the witness wishes legal representation, that's for another venue. Please, be seated."

"I would just object to the word *tribal*, Your Honor." Having said this, Mr. Kansas knew he had no alternative but to sit down. He mopped his own troubled brow and threw Harry a cautionary look.

Q: Mr. Himelbaum?
A: I'm sorry. What are you asking me?

Q: This document, sir.
A: It's not that complicated. According to my
   rabbi, we weren't married until I gave to
   her the ring, that's all. So even if I was
   asked the question when I got here, as a
   Jewish couple, it wasn't until later.

Q: Was there no civil ceremony, Mr. Himelbaum?
   In Poland? Where is that marriage certificate?
A: I speak the absolute truth when I tell you
   I don't know. I can't remember.

Q: Can't remember if you were married under the
   law by the state of Poland?
A: The marriage certificate, I don't have it.
   But yes, yes, in Lukow we were married. But
   as a Jew, I . . .

Q: Married in Lukow before your departure for
   the United States?
A: Yes.

Q: When was the child born?
A: August 29, 1929.

Q: Are you the father of the child?
A: Yes.

Q: Did you have sexual relations with your wife
   prior to your marriage?
A: Yes.

Q: Has your wife been married on any other
   occasion?
A: No.

Mr. Url for the government cast a dismissive glance at Rabbi
Braun's sworn declaration of Harry's non-marriage as though deciding
whether it was worthy of placement in his folder. Setting it down as
one would a piece of lint taken from a dark sweater, an intrusion best
left ignored, he proceeded:

Q: You are further advised that inasmuch as you
   were not lawfully admitted into the U.S. at
   the time of your arrival on the *Normandie* on
   June 23, 1929, you did not derive U.S. citizenship from your father's naturalization.
   Therefore, your child cannot be considered
   a U.S. citizen. Do you understand this?
A: (Several moments of silence.) Yes.

Q: Have you anything you wish to state?
A: What can I say?

Where is Home?

Q: Inasmuch as you were not legally admitted to the U.S. in 1929, your arrival on the *Normandie* in August of 1937 as a citizen of the U.S. is not a legal entry and therefore you are subject to deportation. Do you understand this and what have you to say?

A: I wish to say that I have been in this country for ten years. If there is any way that I can, I would like to straighten out this situation.

Q: Have you ever been arrested or convicted of any crime in this country or in any other country? Any encounter with the law?

A: Never. Maybe a few times a policeman got mad at me for selling apples. But together—this was a long time ago, mind you—we worked it out.

Q: Mr. Himelbaum, I'll ask you again: have you ever been arrested?

A: No. That's why, when I realized I was in trouble, believe me, I am not that kind of person.

Q: Have you ever been a recipient of public or private charities?

A: Never.

Q: Have you ever been confined in any hospital or public institution?

A: Never.

Q: Since your arrival in the United States have you contributed toward the support of your wife and child?

A: Yes.

Q: When did you last communicate with your wife?

A: About two weeks ago, and I received a letter from her about two weeks ago.

Q: What relatives have you in the U.S.?

A: I have a brother, sister, and my mother.

Q: No one else?

A: My aunt and uncle, my brother's wife, his son.

The interrogator took several sheets of paper and some photographs from his folder, handling these with much more regard than he had the rabbi's letter.

Q: Yes, you mentioned all of them on your petition papers, Mr. Himelbaum. Everything matches up, except . . . what about Miss Reva Lansky, Mr. Himelbaum? You never seem to mention her anywhere.

A: Reva? She's Reizel's cousin. I suppose you could consider her a relative. To tell you the truth, I haven't thought of her for a while, or seen her.

Q: Well, you used to get together with her quite frequently, isn't that correct? May I approach the witness, Your Honor? Do you affirm your relationship with Miss Lansky?

Url handed Harry a photograph.

A: This picture, what is this?

Where is Home?

Q: You met with her quite frequently, isn't that correct? This cousin of your non-wife? Or wife, it's hard to keep track.

Al Kansas rose to object, but the judge gaveled him to be seated.

A: You were taking pictures?

Q: Did you know that Reva Lansky is suspected by the government of subversive union activities?

A: She sews dresses, that's what I know. But yes, we met sometimes.

Q: And exchanged a great deal of information, from the look of it, wouldn't you say? Papers going back and forth in several of those photos, right?

A: We exchanged Reizel's letters to me, and pictures, that's all. I don't know what you're getting at. It's true, I thought it would be better my father shouldn't know. That I was married. This much is true. You were watching us? Taking pictures?

Q: With due respect, Mr. Himelbaum, I'll ask the questions this morning. Here, I'll take those back if you're done examining them. Your father, Mr. Himelbaum, a Mister Icko Himelbaum, he was a citizen of the United States?

A: Yes, my father was naturalized in the U.S. District Court, Brooklyn, New York, on June 2, 1927.

Q: It's reassuring to find, Mr. Himelbaum, that you're very certain about that date.

A: Of course, it's a date to be proud of. Whereas, my birthday, well, it's not such an important thing.

Q: If you were granted an opportunity to depart from the United States voluntarily at your own expense without a warrant for your arrest being issued, would you be willing to accept such an offer?

A: I'm sorry?

Q: The government is giving you an opportunity, Mr. Himelbaum, to declare your intention of voluntarily leaving the country. Do you accept such an offer?

A: But there are certain difficulties. Will Poland even take me? I hear they no longer recognize someone as a citizen who's been out of the country. Where should I go?

Q: You are free to go anywhere you like, Mr. Himelbaum. If Poland won't recognize your citizenship, well, you are free to go anywhere, as I say. What would be the maximum period of time you would require before departing from the U.S.?

A: (Unintelligible)

Q: Please speak up, Mr. Himelbaum.

A: Six months.

Q: If you were granted this six months' time within which to depart from the United

States, would you at the expiration of that
time apply for further extension?

A: No.

Q: Have you understood all the questions?
A: Yes.

Q: Have you anything further you wish to state?
A: All I want to say is about my mother. At
the present time my mother is 60 years old
and I am the only one who supports her and
it would be a terrible thing if I would be
deported and leave my mother without any
funds to live on. I have been living here
10 years and I like very much the system
of this country and of the government. I
have gone to night school and still go when
I can. My teacher put me in the advanced
class.

Washington, DC

Barbara sat curled in a chair reading the Himelbaum file. It was nearly dawn and her heart was breaking. The snifter of brandy she'd poured for herself sat untouched under the lamplight as she realized that that nice Mr. Himelbaum had gone through all this just four days ago. And already, there was an application for an arrest warrant! She held it in her hand, and the man who had filled it out had within the past hour made love to her.

Typically, after intimacy, Will would fall asleep instantaneously, with a smile on his lips, and Barbara would tiptoe into the kitchen for a nightcap. She'd been curious, on this particular night, about that familiar name she'd spied earlier and, snuggling into Will's easy chair with the file, it hadn't taken more than a few minutes to satisfy her curiosity: coming on the words, "I am working in a fruit and vegetable store," she'd put together the name Himelbaum with that awfully nice man who had been her first friend in New York. Well, not "friend," exactly, but that's how she'd thought of him at the time, someone who seemed always glad to see her, and with whom a few moments of conversation first thing in the morning had become something to look forward to. HIMELBAUM AND SON, she'd read the lettering on the cart every morning for years. Now, she found herself reading this! Who was this horrible Donald Url, promising Mr. Himelbaum he'd have six months to leave the country voluntarily and then, not twenty-four hours later, recommending to Will's office that an arrest warrant be issued? And accusing that poor man of illicit union activities—that's what Url was getting at when he'd questioned Mr. Himelbaum about his wife's cousin and their meetings, shoving photographs in his face.

Barbara knew very well how Will spent his days and what his title, "assistant commissioner in charge of the Warrant Division," meant. She knew how he earned his paycheck, where the money came from for their affluent lifestyle, the house, the new carpeting when she felt they needed it, the furniture and fabrics for her gowns and groceries for her ballyhooed cooking and every last drop of alcohol that silenced her misgivings. William Matthew Brown presided over a staff of investigators whose job it was to dig up dirt on people, poor, working people, mostly; and then he studied their reports and decided whether or not the subjects of the investigations deserved to remain in the country. *He* decided! And if his opinion went against them, he rolled a sheet of paper into his typewriter, filled in the blanks, and sent off the sheet of paper recommending that a warrant be issued for their arrest. Will was a professional harasser, the school-yard bully; her barely five foot five husband, whom she'd known since they were children together, had found his niche in the world: hounding the little guy.

For years, Barbara had understood her husband's feelings about immigrants, and how his intelligence and education and willingness to work around the clock had translated his beliefs into an important title in the echelons of national government and a sizeable weekly paycheck. Because they shared a childhood, and a child, and the excruciatingly painful death of that child, because she'd grown up with Will and promised to be his wife, and because he loved her so, she overlooked his opinions—something the recipients of his recommended arrest warrants couldn't do. In her hand, she held the application for Mr. Himelbaum's arrest; he'd probably hear from the assistant secretary of labor next week. She knew before he did that the federal government was ready to indict him!

"APPLICATION FOR WARRANT OF ARREST," the document was headed, and it was, sure enough, signed by Will, and dated January 18, 1939.

The undersigned respectfully recommends that the Secretary of Labor issue a warrant for the arrest of alien(s) **YANKEL or HARRY HIMELBAUM, aged 30, native of Poland, ex Normandie at N.Y. as a passenger on June 23, 1929.**

> **From information contained in the attached reports of Inspector Diana and NY District Director Donald Url, it appears the above named alien is in the United States in violation of the immigration act of 1924 in that at the time of his entry he was not a nonquota immigrant as specified in his immigration visa.**

Her head suddenly weightless, spinning, Barbara bolted from the chair and reached the bathroom just in time. She hadn't eaten much at the party, so it was mostly liquid that emitted from her heaves of nausea. Bracing her hands on the toilet, she couldn't stop the gagging, though there was nothing more to produce. Weakly, she swept the back of her hand across her mouth, and forced herself to take some deep breaths before she found the energy to push the flusher. "Barb, everything okay?" Will called from the bedroom. "Fine, Will honey, go to sleep."

"Will honey," Barbara repeated, her voice coming out like a low growl. Even in the thickness of anger toward him—she dared not think of it as hatred—and with all the alcohol wrested from her body, the habit of affection maintained its grip, like a reflex.

She stood up to rinse the horrid taste from her mouth and examined her face in the mirror above the sink. Vomiting in the bathroom didn't wash off as flawlessly as once it had. She thought of that time at the Waldorf-Astoria, when the kind attendant had helped her and she'd swept into the elegant vestibule as though nothing had happened, to be embraced by Martha Connelly. That night had been the start of Will's career. *Dear God,* Barbara thought as she gazed at the sallow image in the mirror, *I've been drinking for a long time.*

She brushed her teeth, rinsed her face, and crawled into bed beside Will. As usual, he was snoring lightly; it was a contented kind of sound, nothing so disquieting as to prevent Barbara from succumbing to her exhaustion.

Light poured into the window when she awakened the next morning. From the high angle of the sun, she realized it must be close to noon. Her instinct to dart up from the pillow was immediately overridden by a splitting headache. Will must've been up for hours.

When finally she managed to put on her robe and wash up, she found Will sitting at the kitchen table, his hands cradling a cup of coffee. "Sorry, honey," Barbara said. "I'll scramble some eggs."

"I'm not hungry," Will said. He was looking straight ahead, didn't even have the newspaper spread out on the table, Barbara noticed.

"Something wrong, Will?" she asked.

He still didn't look at her. "I'd say so."

"Well, what is it? What's happened?"

"That's what I'd like to know," Will said. "What did happen, Barbara?"

Barbara shook her head in bemusement, the slight gesture sending a shot of pain through her temples.

"See, here's the funny thing," Will said. "I was going to get the newspaper, and . . ." He didn't finish the sentence. "Well, maybe you can explain the mess you made in there."

Barbara had no idea what he was talking about. She walked into the living room toward the front door, and there it was: Mr. Himelbaum's file of paperwork was scattered on the carpet near Will's chair. In her rush to the bathroom, she'd obviously sent everything flying and had forgotten all about it, until now. Will stood behind her as she went to retrieve the tossed-about pieces of paper. "I'm sorry, Will. I didn't mean . . ."

"What didn't you mean?" Will asked, his arms crossed angrily as Barbara, on all fours, picked up and tapped into alignment at least thirty sheets of paper representing years of investigative work.

"Are the pages numbered, Will?" Barbara asked. "I'll get them in the right order, don't worry." She sat on the chair and started to leaf through the pages.

Will took the folder from her. "Will you tell me what you were doing, reading one of my files? And when, when did you do this? At what hour of the night were you in here snooping into my business?"

"I had just come out for some brandy, you know, after . . ." The snifter sat on the table next to Will's chair, untouched. "I didn't even drink any of it." She managed a thin smile.

"Well, there's a miracle," Will said. "You must have found the reading material very engaging. Why, Barbara?"

"Harry Himelbaum. When we came in last night, and you put it on top of the pile, I thought the name sounded familiar."

"And?" When Barbara didn't answer immediately, Will asked, utterly bewildered, "You know this person?"

"Back in New York. Remember when I used to get those fresh apples every day, when we lived in the Village? Mr. Himelbaum was the vendor. He was a very nice man, Will, a decent, nice man. And I don't see why you have to hound him."

"Oh, is that what I do? I hound people? Is that how you see what I do?"

Barbara rubbed her head. It was hard to keep her eyes open in the glaring sunlight. She walked past Will and into the kitchen to pour herself a cup of coffee. Will was right behind her. "This Himelbaum has a lot of people interested in his case. But I never thought that my own wife . . ."

"Will, please. My eyes are burning, please stop hounding me."

Will heaved a truculent sigh and left the kitchen. A few minutes later, Barbara found him at his desk, putting the pages of the

Himelbaum file in order. "I just don't see why you have to arrest him," she said. "Even if he did, well, it does look like he lied to get into the country. But, for goodness' sakes, Will, did you read the transcript? His girlfriend was pregnant; what was he supposed to do?"

"I can't worry about the particular circumstances, Barbara, I have a job to do." Will said. "Do you know how many of these people find excuses for cheating their way into the country?"

"'These people'? Do you mean immigrants? God, you sound so nasty, like some kind of, I don't know, some kind of bigot or something."

"Oh, is that what I am?!" Will was clearly offended. "Well, maybe you should join forces with Barkley, become a champion of the underdog. The foreign underdog, because what I'm doing here, Barbara, is watching out for the American underdog. If that makes me a bigot . . ."

"Oh, Will, I don't know." Barbara didn't want to hurt her husband, call him names. Underneath it all, he was a good man; she was sure he would listen to reason. "Congressman Barkley? Weren't you talking to him last night? What does he have to do with this?"

"Isn't it in the file? One of his legal aides assisted with your precious Mr. Himelbaum's hearing. And he threatened me last night, Barkley did. All up in arms about this guy. You know, I hadn't filed this application for a warrant, notice that? This is the original." He found and held up the document that had so sickened Barbara the night before.

"Oh, Will, that's wonderful. Can't I just this once exert some influence on you? He was such a nice man."

Will regarded the sheet of paper and then replaced it in the file. "I have no choice now. I can't let Barkley hound me, to borrow your terminology. That's just the right word for him, too: Barkley the Hound. Well, he's going to find that this time, he's barking up the wrong tree. I'm sorry, Barbara, I really am."

"You're going to file the application," Barbara said quietly. "You're going to have him arrested."

"Your fruit salesman entered the country fraudulently. He lied to the United States government. If that's the kind of thing Congressman Barkley wants to advocate, I'll see him all the way to court."

New York City

Carrying a bag of potatoes and onions for that night's meal, Harry trudged up the 181st Street hill against the swirling snow. This lunch-time trip home with provisions for supper had become his excuse for coming home in the middle of the day to check the mail. Rarely was it delivered by 12:30 in the afternoon, but once or twice, especially in inclement weather, the mailman's schedule varied, and how could Harry be expected to wait until the end of the workday to find out what news awaited him, good or bad? Lately, it was mostly bad, culminating with the hearing two weeks earlier.

On the ferry from Ellis Island afterward, Mr. Kansas had let him have it, about the rabbi's letter. "What were you thinking, Harry? You never even told me about this idea of yours, claiming that the Jewish marriage certificate was meaningless because you hadn't given your wife anything of monetary value. I mean, no offense, but that's a, that's a religious practice, Harry. Almost a superstition, with all due respect. It didn't help your case, I'll tell you that much."

"Well, I told about the night school," Harry had tried to defend himself.

"Yes, that was good, very good," Kansas had acknowledged, but then he chewed him out about Reva. Why had he never mentioned this cousin?

"I didn't think to mention everyone," Harry said. He had been completely taken off guard by those photographs. So, Reva hadn't been crazy; they *were* being watched. A "subversive" she was? Harry wasn't even sure what the word meant.

Kansas spent the duration of the ferry ride glued to the newspaper. When the two men said good-bye at the subway station, he hurriedly shook Harry's hand. "Let me know if you hear anything," he'd said before starting down the stairs.

"What should I hear?" Harry called. "They said six months I have." But the young lawyer had already disappeared into the crowd.

Mr. Kansas's remark about hearing something stayed with Harry, lingering the way his other mysteriously inserted, seemingly insignificant comments always did. Thus, Harry's daily trips home at lunchtime continued, on the terrible chance that the promised six months were about to be cut short by a piece of mail, and the off chance that the mail had been delivered.

On this snowy afternoon, he wasn't surprised to find his mother sitting on the steps in the lobby with two of the "lady friends" she'd made in the building. They gathered here every day, exchanging gossip and recipes, remembering the old country through reminiscence and the very act of sitting together, allaying, as much as they could, the gnaw of alienation in this new land.

"*Nu*, so here he is," Elke said in Yiddish to her friends. "You brought for me some cabbage?" she asked Harry.

"I thought you were roasting a chicken tonight," Harry said. "Potatoes and onions I brought."

"*Nu*, so I'll roast a chicken."

"I'll bring everything upstairs," Harry said. "Irene home?"

"What are you talking? She went to work."

"On a day like this?"

"What, a little snow should stop the lessons?"

"It's more than a little," Harry said. Bidding a friendly good day to the women on the stairs, he made his way past them to the mailbox.

Since she'd graduated from high school, Irene had been teaching ice skating in the winters at a rink in the Bronx. At first she had balked when Harry told her about the job he'd heard about through one of his customers. "A bunch of children laughing at me on the ice, just like Moishe," she'd said. But upon further consideration, she'd concluded that being a teacher, even if it wasn't in a schoolroom, had a very nice ring to it, and it was high time, anyway, that she gave up basing her decisions on old memories. In the summers, she did temporary office work.

Opening the mailbox with the hand that wasn't holding the produce bag, Harry found it empty. But later that day, when he came home from work at six, the lobby a warming olfactory blend of onions, cabbage, and dill, he took from behind the narrow brass door a modest stack of envelopes. Smack in the center of one of them was that most alarming of postmarks: Washington, DC.

After a time span that he could never bring back to consciousness, as though he'd actually blacked out, Harry found himself seated on his bed and holding in his hand a document that read as follows:

WARRANT
FOR ARREST OF ALIEN

United States Of America
DEPARTMENT OF LABOR
WASHINGTON

To: **DISTRICT DIRECTOR OF IMMIGRATION AND NATURALIZATION, Ellis Island, N.Y.H., Or to any Immigrant Inspector in the service of the United States.**

WHEREAS, from evidence submitted to me, it appears that the alien:

YANKEL or HARRY HIMELBAUM

who entered this country at New York, NY, ex SS "Normandie," on the **30th day of August, 1937,** has been found in the United States in violation of the immigration laws thereof, and is subject to be taken into custody and deported pursuant to the following provisions of law, and for the following reasons, to wit: **The immigration act of 1924,** in that at the time of his entry he was not in possession of a legal **immigration visa.**

I, by virtue of the power and authority vested in me by the laws of the United States, hereby command you to take into custody the said alien and grant **him** to show cause why **he** should not be deported in conformity with the law. The expenses of detention, hereunder, if necessary, are authorized payable from the appropriation, "**General Expenses**, Immigration and Naturalization Service, **1939**." Pending further proceedings, the alien may be released from custody under bond in the sum of $500, or upon his own recognizance if you are satisfied that he will appear **when wanted**.

The document was stamped "**MAILED, JAN 26, 1939.**" It included two lines on the bottom that read:

For so doing, this shall be your sufficient warrant.

Witness my hand and seal this **26th day of January 1939**.

> **TURNER S. BATTLE,**
> Assistant to the Secretary of Labor

Harry was too numb and terrified to recognize the breach in protocol inherent in his holding this sheet of paper in his hand, in its having been delivered to his address. Nor, before running to the kitchen to phone Congressman Barkley's office, did he turn over the wretched document, where he would have found these lines, written in a rounded hand:

> *Dear Mr. Himelbaum,*
> *You probably don't remember me, but I used to see you at your fruit stand every morning on Fourth Street. I especially loved the fine apples you sold.*
> *I mail this copy of your arrest warrant not to frighten you, but so that you may have advance notice of the ordeal that awaits you. I believe that if you contact Congressman Barkley, he will help you. Please know that you have the sympathies and prayers of*
> *Mrs. Barbara Brown*

No one answered at the congressman's office, Harry's portion of roast chicken went uneaten, and it was not until the following day that Al Kansas, bewildered by the warrant having been mailed to the subject of the arrest, turned the document over and saw Barbara's note. "You seem to have more than one friend in Washington," he said, handing the sheet of paper over to Harry to read.

Of course, Harry remembered the beautiful Mrs. Brown. He even thought about her every now and then, quickly whisking the thoughts away. But she remembered *him*?! This was the extraordinary thing. He remembered now that one of the many documents he'd received in the last several months had been signed by a person named Brown, another one of his persecutors who preceded his last name with initials. (He'd read all the papers so many times, he'd committed the names to memory.) Could Mrs. Brown be married to this man? Is that how she knew of his "ordeal"? Her husband's work, Harry seemed to recall, was somehow related to immigration. Well, it could be. But she remembered him? He was holding in his hand a single sheet of paper whose one side contained the starkest rebuke, and whose other, the kindest, most unexpected affirmation. This was very nice of her, very, very nice, to remember, to care. But a "friend in Washington"? Even with this remarkable letter in his hands, and a United States congressman's aide by his side, Harry could not imagine a feeling more closely akin to utter friendlessness.

"She was right to send it to you," Kansas was saying. "It gives us an opportunity to prepare for the hearing. You'll probably get a notice any day now. I doubt they'll take you into custody, but in all likelihood you'll be required to surrender your passport."

~ ~ ~

April

Washington, DC

"I'm really proud of you, honey," Will said as he and Barbara settled into the luxurious compartment of the passenger train bound for New York. Along with their friends, they were headed for an advance walk-through of the World's Fair, set to open at the end of the month, and Barbara had just declined the cocktail offered by the porter.

It had taken a while for them to get over the argument begun the morning after the Mayflower party; Barbara had said things too disrespectful for Will to accommodate easily. He almost had the feeling his wife didn't like him, a very hard feeling to shake off. But, when he thought about it, Will realized that it was also from that date that he hadn't seen his wife with a drink in her hand. Barbara had stopped drinking! And it wasn't until he could acknowledge the fact of her sobriety that he could simultaneously acknowledge the decade of daily concern he'd suppressed over her consumption of alcohol. Only once the problem no longer existed, could Will admit to himself that there'd been one. Maybe he just knew that she'd get over it, he told himself, so he hadn't really been denying anything. He knew he could count on his girl, and he'd been right.

The house had remained pretty quiet, and relations strained, for weeks following Barbara's incursion into that file. Will could understand that she might feel sympathy for a man she'd known, however peripherally, who now found himself in an unfortunate situation.

That was one of the things he loved about Barbara, her empathy for people. But her immediate siding with this veritable stranger, who, even she admitted, had broken the law, against her own husband and in such belligerent tones, well, any man would find that hard to digest. While it was going on, the silence, the distant courtesies, Will had even wondered if the marriage would survive. Yes, there'd been other periods of tension over the years, but this was different; this time it felt as though a chasm had widened beyond crossing, with neither one of them willing to do the repair work that might narrow the divide.

Whenever she wasn't preparing or serving the well-cooked meals that indeed continued, Barbara sat at the kitchen table drinking coffee. Her capacity for the hot beverage seemed endless. Normally—and it was here that Will started to privately take note—under this kind of strained condition, she'd be sitting there nursing a drink. Although he tried to crush the thought, her switch away from alcohol felt initially like an odd kind of rejection. The change scared him. She looked so resolute, sitting there. So alone and determined, and not at all well. It was as though she were sweating out an illness; her hands trembled slightly, and a damp pallor sat like a veil on her face. Will knew it was probably silly, but he couldn't help fearing, day after day as she sat there, that he himself might be one of the noxious elements she meant to cleanse herself of.

Gradually, her vigil at the kitchen table gave way to more routine pursuits. He found her at her sewing machine, felt relief when she agreed to go to the Waverlys for their daughter's birthday party, and things could be said to have righted themselves. So as not to arouse friction, he decided to continue bringing his files home and placing them, as always, on his desk. He felt quite sure that he'd made the point about her looking through his work, and not another word passed between them regarding Mr. Himelbaum or any other aspect of Will's job. When this invitation to Washington "dignitaries" came in the mail for a preview of the World's Fair, Barbara was planting seedlings in the garden and, hearing the news, she leapt up and threw her arms around him. For the first time in Will couldn't say how long, he could see that color had returned to her cheeks. "New York," she exuded. "Oh, Will, won't it be wonderful to be back there?" He didn't remember Barbara having a great affection for the city, but it was wonderful to hold her; she'd even put on a few pounds, not so bony as when last they'd touched.

Sipping a ginger ale on the plush seat of the train, Barbara giggled and chatted with Joanie Pearson and the Waverly girls. They adored her, the one out of all their parents' friends who seemed to have an endless well of patience and ideas for their school projects and appreciation for their jokes and consolation for the little daily dramas that might tear at their confidence if not for Barbara's sensible suggestions. "Oh, he's just pulling your braids because he likes you. I'll come by early tomorrow morning and put your hair into a bun, that'll nip the problem in the bud." For the weeks of her self-enforced detoxification, everyone, especially the children, had missed Barbara, and they were excited to hear that she'd finally gotten rid of that nasty flu.

"I hear the Fair is very futuristic," Sally Waverly enthused. "There's even a spaceship."

"Can you ride it?" Joanie asked.

"I'd be much too scared to ride into space."

"I'm not. They wouldn't let you ride it if it were dangerous."

"I think maybe we'll just walk around inside," Barbara said.

"But if they do let us ride into space, will you go with me?" Joanie asked, turning a superior glance toward Sally.

"We'll see, sweetie-pie. There's so much to do in New York, you know. I'm not sure I'm going to spend every single minute at the Fair."

Barbara had already told Will that she'd like to visit the various stores on Fifth Avenue, see what they were showing. The department was putting them up at the Waldorf, with its convenient access to the bridge into Queens, the site of the Fair, and it shouldn't be too tricky to find her way uptown from the hotel. "Oh, don't worry," she'd assured Will, "I won't get lost. You remember how everything in Manhattan is arranged in this perfectly perpendicular grid, except for where we used to live. The Village is the only tricky part, and I don't expect to be going down there." When Will had suggested that it might be fun, for old time's sake, to stroll around the old neighborhood, see if that old candy store still existed, she responded with a distracted "Mm-hmm."

"Hey, if I can tear you away from the younger set, let's go to the dining car," Betty Waverly leaned into the compartment. "I hear they serve a mean martini, their way of fooling us into thinking the trip is going quickly. We'll make it a ladies' lunch."

Barbara's friends were too tactful to articulate their collective and unspoken observation, even among themselves, that Barbara had clearly sworn off alcohol. That "nasty flu" that had kept her locked in her house for weeks just seemed to have resulted in coffee being her beverage of choice when she finally emerged. Everyone was genuinely fond of her, admiring of her in so many ways; certainly, intimate friends didn't have to trespass into each other's personal lives to believe in the existence of the intimacy.

"Can't we come?" the little girls pleaded.

But no, Betty and Elaine concurred, this was grown-up lady time. They'd bring the girls back some sandwiches. "And no sulking," Elaine added, "or I won't let you take that ride to Jupiter."

"See?" Joanie said to outer-space travel-phobic Sally. "I told you."

Barbara took her ginger ale and kissed each of the children before joining her friends making their way to the dining car.

"It's not that I'm not really looking forward to the Fair," Elaine said after the women had ordered their salads, two martinis and a coffee, "but if you could show us around Manhattan, Barbara, Macy's, and all the dress stores, that would be my world of tomorrow." She referred here to the theme of the World's Fair. "I'm sure we'll be able to find an afternoon, let the guys take the kids for a day."

"Maybe," Barbara said noncommittally. "Mm-hmm, that would be fun."

"Maybe you have some things you want to do, old friends to see while you're there. Don't worry, we won't take up all your time."

"Oh, don't be silly," Barbara laughed. She raised her cup: "To New York," she said, and the three friends clinked in a good-humored toast.

New York City

In the months since his confrontation with the United States Government had begun, Harry had gone from feeling outright fear to outraged indignation, to humiliation, acquiescence, and the thinnest possible filament of hope. He had also gone, for solace, to the Bible, where he read and reread the story of David and Goliath. It was an imperfect comparison, he knew, for he didn't want to destroy the mighty giant, which, in this case, was the country he revered. But in taking on his adversary, all he had in his quiver were the sticks of his honorable residence and the stones of the consequences of ejecting him. What he also had was the outcome of David's story, and it was this more than anything that infused him with the sense, however fragile, that he would prevail. It was simply unthinkable to believe that the government would deport him.

His tactic was to keep his head down, work hard, earn his money, put food on the table and dollars in the mail to Regina and Yakob, and pray that these simple acts of honest labor would see him through. Yes, he had "friends in Washington"; Al Kansas had been right. There was no question that without the assistance of Congressman Barkley's staff, guiding him and preparing him and speaking for him when the situation called for it, he would have been on the boat long ago. Bound for where, he couldn't even say. He lived in the United States with no passport, no birth certificate, no documentary evidence of his nationality. Poland was dead for him; they wouldn't let him in and he didn't want to go. He didn't want to find himself anywhere in Europe, where just in the last few months Hitler had dissolved Czechoslovakia, and then occupied it; where he had already taken Austria and held Poland in his pocket; and where he had announced to wildly cheering crowds his intention of "exterminating" all European Jews.

About his wife and child, Harry tried not to think, for it would overwhelm him, render him useless, and he must stay focused. He did send money, which he knew they needed more than ever now that the hat store was one of the Jewish businesses being boycotted by Polish gentiles. Regina had written to him about this new unofficial policy, how he shouldn't worry (always, he "shouldn't worry") but what with the general attitude taking hold ("attitude" she called it, not "hatred"), an attitude that surely would pass once economic conditions improved, people weren't coming in so much as before. Of course, he had to get them out, that was at the center of his every effort, but he couldn't even try to reinitiate the necessary procedures to get them here until it was established once and for all that he could stay. To do everything he had to on their behalf, he must put them and the terrifying consequences of failure out of his mind.

So Harry packaged the apples and turnips and onions, selected the just-right pears for Dainty Doris, listened at the supper table to Saul's theories about the young baseball season—this Ted Williams was all mouth, he'd never amount to anything—and avoided thinking, as much as he could, about the realities gathering against him.

In the three months of 1939, there had been that many hearings at Ellis Island. At the first, he was asked all the familiar questions—name, address, occupation; whether or not he was married, the date of that marriage; whether or not he had had sex with his wife prior to the marriage: questions meant to shame him and to besmirch the image of his wife. At this hearing, there was the added invasion of his privacy when he was required to produce his savings account records. "Twenty-seven hundred dollars I've saved up. That plus the furniture, that's what I have. What's the furniture worth? Maybe two hundred dollars." At this hearing also, he was relieved of his passport and released from custody on his own recognizance, pending "final determination" and delivery of a five-hundred-dollar bond. With Al Kansas at his side as legal representative, he agreed to leave the country if ordered deported, and agreed, as well, to appear whenever requested to do so.

He was requested to do so twice more. In late February, the repetitive, mortifying, invasive litany of questions was augmented by

District Director Url for the government proudly submitting proof of Mr. Himelbaum's having knowingly perpetrated a fraud upon the government when he brandished with a burst of bravado the 1929 Certificate of Admission of Alien that his investigative team had tracked down. The Certificate of Admission, executed and signed by an Inspector Wright, and dated June 23, 1929, contained hard black-and-white evidence of Harry's duplicity. "'Question:,'" Mr. Url for the government read, "'Are you married? Answer . . .'" He paused for full effect. "'No.' Thankfully," the district director observed, "the court need no longer depend on Mr. Himelbaum's memory for its consideration of this case."

At the third hearing, Harry was asked to take the witness stand so that he might assure the government that he understood the conclusion reached on March 17 by the Washington, DC Board of Review, which Mr. Url for the government patiently set before him.

"It is very true, sir, as your counsel has tried to emphasize, that upon your application for your nonquota visa in April of 1929 that you were indeed, unmarried. It is true that you came into possession of the visa in a proper and legal manner. But your representative fails to take into account the illegality of your entry into the United States, by which time the information on the visa was false, as was your answer to the inspector at the port of entry. Do you understand, Mr. Himelbaum?"

Harry understood.

"It is therefore ordered by the Department of Labor after considering the recommendation of the Board of Review that you be deported within ninety days of this notification. Is this clear, Mr. Himelbaum?"

It was clear.

Mr. Url then displayed on an easel for the edification of all present a poster-sized calendar. With a pointer, he tapped on the current date of March 24, and proceeded to literally count out the ninety days, including weekends and holidays, which brought the date by which Mr. Himelbaum must no longer be on these shores to Thursday, June 22.

"Passage is to be paid by the steamship company," he punctuated his presentation lest anyone accuse him or the government he so faithfully represented of insensitivity to the alien's plight.

"Passage to which country?" Harry quietly ventured.

Mr. Url was slipping the pointer into a thin sheath, when, with his back to Harry, he said, "Anywhere you like, Mr. Himelbaum. As we've said, anywhere you like."

Ninety days. But here it was, April, and Harry was doing everything in his power not to count, anything, that is, but onions, pears, nickels in change to hand to the customers. "Don't worry about it," Al Kansas had told him that day of the calendar, "Congressman Barkley will work it out."

What it was exactly that Congressman Barkley was working out, Harry couldn't say. But at least during that last encounter, Kansas hadn't inadvertently injected into his summation of the situation any troubling phrase or looming eventuality for Harry to worry over. Mr. Url with his pointer provided enough of an image to blot out of his mind every day. And so, his thoughts adamantly turned away from the calendar and its dissolving days, Harry woke up every morning, put on his work clothes, showed up at the store and tied on his apron. He pleased the customers with his friendly manner and the employer with his sales. He did all this and prayed for the best, and had a congressman on his side. Maybe he had fifty days, maybe sixty, he wasn't looking at the calendar, he wasn't counting. Maybe, God willing, he had a lifetime. Like Al Kansas said, he must think positive. That was all a man could do.

One thing he felt positive about was the flexibility and understanding of his boss, Ralph Weiss. So what if he had made Saul assistant manager? With all the days Harry had missed owing to the hearings, Ralph had not only kept him on, but had docked not a penny from his paycheck. "We're a family," Ralph had said, patting Harry on the shoulder when the string of court proceedings began. Harry, in his gratitude, swallowed his reflexive objection. The assertion about being family no doubt included Saul's relationship with Irene at least as much as the years of steady hard work Harry had put in at the store. *Nu*, Mama liked the boy, Irene definitely liked him, Harry himself could say nothing against him; so, yes, Ralph was right, they were family. Harry never more questioned or challenged, even in his own mind, the romantic attachment that from all appearances would soon be a familial one and about which he'd had such pressing reservations. His Irene with her head in the stars and the movie magazines was, after all, just little Rifkale from the old country, content to be cared for by a simple, unsophisticated fruit man who was, Harry had to give him credit, very good at mathematics, and now, an assistant manager.

It was late afternoon and Harry was concentrating on straightening out the Idaho potatoes so they'd look nice for the pre-dinner customers, when a woman came up behind him. "Do you have any ripe McIntosh?" she asked.

With his back to her and still focused on the potatoes, he said, "Just a minute, I'll take a look. This time of year, though, you may be better off with Red Delicious."

He walked over to the display of the proud and shiny bright red apples and handed one to the woman. He didn't recognize her, not a regular customer.

"I only just got here, Mr. Himelbaum, to New York, I mean. The train just pulled into Penn Station, why, it can't be more than an hour ago." She spoke quickly, nervously.

Harry looked at the attractive blonde woman standing inches from him and it was like peeling the rind from a piece of fruit to find the face that went with this voice, this faintly self-conscious, but friendly, open voice. "Mrs. Brown?"

She was holding the apple he had handed her, and with her other hand, she tucked behind her ear a wave of hair that had fallen out of place. "I'm sorry for just coming up on you like this, appearing out of nowhere. I knew the address from, well, you know, the file. But listen to me going on and on. I have to admit I'm feeling, well . . ." She forced herself to slow down. "I hope it's okay."

Harry could do nothing but stand there and stare at her. The poor woman was as red as the apple she was holding, and yet she exuded glamour in her fitted jacket and slacks; her face simply stunning. A fragrance like wildflowers emanated from her, and her skin, even these years later, and bathed in embarrassment, radiated such delicacy that it seemed it would bruise from even the barest touch.

"I see that you're very busy. It's probably the worst possible time," Barbara said.

"Excuse me one minute, please," Harry said. He walked over to Saul, who was ringing up a customer at the cash register and, removing his white apron, explained, "A woman about my case. I have to go."

"But just before supper, Harry, they'll be pouring in any minute. Can't it wait?" Saul looked toward where Barbara was standing. "Well, all right, I can see it looks important. Go ahead."

Ashamed of the sawdust powdering her shoes, Harry guided Barbara from the store and, not knowing exactly which way to turn, directed them toward the bustling hill on 181st Street. "You've probably never been up here," he said. "It's a lot of us up here. Like the old country." He'd never seen the neighborhood in quite this way before, but walking beside Mrs. Brown, the familiar streets were suddenly a kaleidoscope of scarves and second-hand coats, shopping bags, and weariness. "But we have a very nice park, I'll take you." And they turned right on Fort Washington Avenue toward Fort Tryon Park.

"I can't stay for very long," Barbara said. "I just wanted to stop by and say hello." She realized this sounded foolish and disingenuous. One didn't arrive in Manhattan and within moments of checking into a hotel, make excuses for "just wanting to take in the city a bit," and leave her husband and friends wondering why the immediate side trip, if all she had in mind was a casual "hi-how-are-you?" It hadn't been her intention to seek Mr. Himelbaum out quite so immediately, but no sooner had her feet touched the concrete of New York City than she knew she must make her way to him. She'd be back for dinner, she'd promised Will after hanging up a few things, and then rushed out to Park Avenue and into a taxi.

Mr. Himelbaum's case and Will's role in it had become terribly important to Barbara. She couldn't say why, exactly, yet she didn't feel she needed to find a reason. She hated to think that there was vengeance involved, despite how hurt she'd been by Will's refusal to allow her to exert some influence in the case. It had stung, but that awful morning had had its positive outcome, as well.

Barbara couldn't say for sure that it wasn't the haggard mirror image from the night before their confrontation that had spurred her decision to stop drinking, but she mostly attributed her fervent resolve to the moment that Will had rebuffed her plea on Mr. Himelbaum's behalf and trivialized her opinion. The alcohol willfully soaked up for years to dampen her awareness must be expunged. To help Mr. Himelbaum, and herself, and maybe even her marriage, she had to think clearly. Thus, she slipped a copy of Mr. Himelbaum's arrest warrant from his file while Will took his Saturday afternoon nap, and asked that nice boy at the 5 & 10 to make a duplicate—he was so taken with modern gadgets and they had a Photostat machine right there at the store—and she mailed it without Will noticing a thing. Studying the file every night—What statement was Will making by continuing to bring home the file? That he trusted her? That he thought her interest in the case fleeting, inconsequential?—she focused not on the inherent betrayal of Will, or the crushing headaches that threatened to bury her resolve, but on what she could possibly do to insure against the deportation of this man. This one man who was one of thousands similarly harassed by her husband's "work"; this one man who was asking so very little and whom she just might be capable of helping. When Will came home with the news that they'd be going to New York, she'd seen it as a sign that she was doing the right thing. The trip would give her a chance to let Mr. Himelbaum know in person that she was on his side.

"Mr. Rockefeller himself paid for all this, that they should develop this beautiful place," Harry said as they wended their way through a blossoming pathway of Fort Tryon Park. "Up ahead, there's a new place they opened just last year, with a lot of art and tapestries from the Middle Ages. But it's getting late, it's better to see it in the daylight." After his initial self-consciousness upon seeing Mrs. Brown in the context of his neighborhood, Harry was surprised at how comfortable he felt, walking beside her.

In the soft purples of dusk, they sat down on a bench overlooking a panoramic view of the Hudson River. "It's beautiful," Barbara said. Mr. Himelbaum had been wise to bring them here; she was feeling calmer.

"You know I love it here very much, this country," Harry said after a few minutes. "It's true, your husband and his friends are right, I did lie to get in. I knew it all along, that I could get into trouble. But this was a chance I had to take, you know, maybe like that Edward, for the woman I love." Harry laughed at himself, and blushed with the extravagant comparison. Still, Mrs. Brown's gesture of friendliness and concern emboldened him. He felt sturdier, more like an American, just sitting beside her. Funny that it should work like that, he thought, that her poise and beauty should extend to the person she sat next to, rather than make him feel diminished. This was a gift she had, he decided.

They sat looking out at the vista. After a while, Barbara broke the peaceful silence.

"It looks like it will work out for you, though. The congressional hearing has been scheduled for the end of June, past the date they gave for your deportation, the ninety days. That's a good sign, Mr. Himelbaum; it gives you more time. You must be very relieved."

Congressional hearing? Harry didn't know what she was referring to. "I don't know what you mean by a congressional hearing," he said.

Barbara was confused. "Hasn't Congressman Barkley told you? He's introduced a bill. For your relief."

"I'm sorry, I don't understand."

"Your case is going to be heard before a congressional committee."

"In Washington?" Harry couldn't put it together, what she was telling him. She must be mistaken.

"That's where congressional committees usually meet to consider House resolutions." Barbara smiled. "I'm sorry, I don't mean to make light. I'm just surprised you don't know about it."

"You know how sometimes they say, 'The husband is the last to know'? I'm a husband, that's what started all this."

Barbara tried not to think about her husband. How was it possible that the subject of the hearing didn't even know about it? She'd seen the memo just last week, stating that the "enforced deportation within ninety days of notification would be held in abeyance pending the outcome of the bill during the present session of Congress." Why hadn't Congressman Barkley told Mr. Himelbaum? Was he that insignificant, even to the man who was championing his cause? What if he took it into his head, out of fear, helplessness, to leave the country not even knowing that he'd been given more time?

Maybe when you came right down to it, the ways of Washington were just too complicated for even her clearheaded, sober self to understand and navigate. Surely, when she'd flown from the hotel earlier, it hadn't been her expectation that her congratulatory visit, meant to reassure him, would add more confusion to Mr. Himelbaum's situation.

"I'm sure you'll hear from Barkley's office any day now," Barbara said, her indignation at the treatment of this man spread now to the congressman. After a few more moments: "It's getting dark. I should be going."

Despite the calluses and hardness of his hands, he reached for hers as they rose from the bench; it just seemed as natural and inevitable as the river flowing before them. Her face flushed again, but she didn't withdraw her hand as they retraced their steps from the wooded oasis back to the northern tip of the perpendicular grid of the city. Once on the street, she buttoned the top button of her suit jacket to counter the sunset wind that had kicked up, and both of them put their hands in their pockets.

"On 181st Street, we'll find a taxi," Harry said as they walked down the Fort Washington Avenue hill. "It was a wonderful surprise, I don't have to tell you, your coming to see me. No more redhead, you've got your hair now blonde, but it's good, it looks very good. A wonderful surprise you coming like this."

"Will you be going to the World's Fair?" Barbara asked. "That's why we're here, Will and I, and a whole group of us from DC." As soon as she'd said it, she hated the sound of it, the image of "the group from DC": the insiders, the powerful and comfortable and solidly ensconced.

"The World's Fair? Sure I'll go. Not right away, it'll be here a while. Maybe, with some luck, I will be here, too, for a while. This is very interesting information you told me. A hearing in Washington, this I didn't expect."

Harry saw several yellow taxis approach as they walked down the hill, but he wasn't ready to say good-bye. He let them pass. When they reached the corner of 181st Street, he just wanted to stand with her—Mrs. Barbara Brown, imagine!—in front of Cushman's Bakery.

"You'll call the congressman's office, Mr. Himelbaum, find out why they haven't told you."

Harry knew he should flag down a taxi. He saw one and held out his arm.

As he opened the door for her, she didn't make a move to get inside. She stood so tall, stately, practically his height. Her face was inches from his, her eyes watering, probably from the wind.

"*Nu?*" she said softly.

Harry felt the heat crawl up his face, hoped she didn't see. It would take barely any movement at all for their lips to meet, which they did.

Barbara found the group from DC at a large round table in the hotel restaurant. Everyone wanted to know where she'd been, not least of all Will, who, in any event, was relieved to find no alcohol on her breath when she kissed him hello. He couldn't remember when he'd seen her so buoyant, regaling all of them with the fabulous displays she'd seen inside every department store window and the fashionable people everywhere. Why, New York made Washington seem like a small town, she told them; you just couldn't beat this city for sophistication and flair. Yes, she promised the Waverly and Pearson women and their daughters, she'd be happy to take them around, show them the sights. But, good Lord, she was hungry, a person could work up quite an appetite walking around Manhattan, and just look at this menu! Barbara chattered and exclaimed, she charmed and held her captive audience spellbound as Will couldn't help feeling swollen with pride that she was his, and she did everything humanly possible to silence with her words and pronouncements and enthusiasms the insistent voice within her pleading for a drink.

Later that night, under the luxurious Waldorf bedspread, she allowed her husband to make love to her.

Stawki

"You have a nerve coming here. I already told him, I don't know where it is, your precious marriage license." Chava spoke to her unexpected visitor from outside the front door of the farmhouse, which she had pulled closed behind her. At her side, Moishe stood glaring at Yakob, who had grown taller since he last saw him nearly two years before, making him more than ever an unwelcome presence.

"We came all this way," Regina said. "Sister-in-law, can't you even offer to us a place to sit down? A cup of tea?"

"I am not a relative to you," Chava said, "except when you need something."

"Yankel asked me. He says we should have it."

Coming out of the barn to the right of the house, two of the Hondra children made clucking noises at the Jews standing at the front door. Regina, remembering the insults Yakob had suffered at their hands, pulled her son closer to her.

"This is how my children live every day," Chava said. "Tormented by these *goyim*. The parents, yes, they are nice enough—why not? They get a nice piece of land to go with their tolerance."

Chava had to admit to herself that Yankel's wife looked not so good as before. Thinner, tired. Dark crescents circled her eyes.

"Don't you think that is why we should stick together?" Regina asked.

"Will you stick with me when you get on the boat for America?"

Despite the want of an invitation, Regina sat down wearily on the bench under the cottonwood tree. "You think I'll be on such a boat? Ten years now it's been since Yankel has lived there. The boy, maybe, maybe if Yankel doesn't get in more trouble. I don't even know anymore, I can't keep track of all the problems they give him. He says we should get from you the Polish marriage license. I don't even know why."

"Wait a minute," Chava said, and she disappeared inside the house.

"Do you still go to the school?" Yakob asked his unfriendly cousin.

Moishe didn't answer, just followed his mother and shut the door.

"I don't think he likes me," Yakob said as he sat next to Regina on the bench. He still wore the cap that Mr. Hondra had given to his father. It remained a tad big for him, covering his ears.

Chava came out carrying an envelope with United States postage. "Maybe you can read for me," she said grudgingly as she handed it to Regina.

It was from the United States Department of Labor, addressed simply to Himelbaum, 43 Stawki, province of Lublin, Poland. Inside, a sheet of paper read that **"anyone residing at this address who might know a Yankel Himelbaum and be in possession of his marriage license to Miss Reizel Lansky is to return said document in the enclosed return envelope. This is an official document being subpoenaed by the United States government. Failure to provide this evidence is tantamount to a criminal act."** It was signed by W. M. Brown, assistant commissioner of the Warrant Division, Immigration and Naturalization Service, United States Department of Labor.

Regina's heart tightened in her chest. Her poor Yankel, she thought, this is what he's up against. As if her worst fears required further proof, this piece of paper deflated whatever hope she might have that she'd ever get out of Poland. And from what she heard, Yankel wouldn't even be allowed back in. She looked at her child sitting beside her and knew that even with all this, with all this working against them, they couldn't give up hope. If the three of them were ever to live as a family, if there was any chance on earth that they might succeed, she must do everything in her power, as scant a crumb as it was, to thwart the United States government's determination to deport Yankel.

She handed the letter back to Chava, thanking God her sister-in-law couldn't read English. "It is hard to make out," she said. "But I beg you, Chava. I don't have my husband, my son doesn't have his father. At least the piece of paper, the marriage license, you could give to us, the only thing we might have of our connection to Yankel."

"And what do I have of my husband? My children's father?"

"You have at least your home here."

Chava emitted a derisive sound through her teeth. "Since his mother left, he doesn't even come to see us. We might as well not exist. And that's all I can say for your piece of paper that you want. It doesn't exist, either."

Chava did relent as far as to offer Regina and Yakob a cup of water from the well. After they disappeared on the road back to Wlodawa, she walked into her room and took from the trunk beneath her bed the smudged and crumpled Polish marriage license of her brother-in-law. She didn't know why he and his wife wanted it so badly, but she held it close to her face and cried into it as she had many times before, wept into it like a tissue that gave her the only thing she had of power in a relationship that had long since dissolved.

Holding her son's hand as they made their way on the dirt road back to the train station, Regina clutched with her other hand the return envelope that she had slipped into her pocket. It was minimal consolation, but at least she could rip it up and toss it to the wind. The following day she would learn that even this small, meager act of defiance was without consequence. At the Lukow Office of Records, they would confirm what W. M. Brown's letter had already led her to suspect: a similar "subpoena" had been received at their offices, and the request that a copy of the document be mailed to the United States Immigration and Naturalization Service had already been complied with.

New York City

Along with their spouses and children, clusters of dignitaries from all branches of government—federal, state, and municipal—listened intently as their guides for the day introduced them to the wonders of the World of Tomorrow. Fifty to sixty million paying customers over the next two summers, they were told, would have a similar opportunity, for only seventy-five cents admission, to ogle the Trylon, a 700-foot needle-like obelisk piercing the sky, and its neighbor, the Perisphere, a gigantic globe that weighed in at over four million pounds. Here on this vast converted wasteland, previously used as a garbage dump, Flushing Meadows splashed the architectural, not to say political, marvels represented by the Italian, British, Japanese, Russian, Polish, and United States pavilions, coexisting alongside the Court of Peace with its waterfalls and lagoons, flowers and fountains, and ubiquitous denial of the nine and a half million United States citizens still out of work and the bellicose madman looming over Europe.

Peace and Prosperity were everywhere trumpeted; the future demanded it, and science and technology guaranteed it. Lining up for their turn on General Motors' "Futurama," one of the Fair's most popular attractions, visitors finally took their seats in armchairs for the fifteen-minute ride along a conveyor belt from which they could see for themselves the buildings and expressways and coast-to-coast radio towers that would facilitate trouble-free movement along 100-mile-per-hour traffic lanes. By the year 1960, no one need concern themselves if life presented some bumps in the road. One could always, and with ease, move to a new location, start fresh: find a job, welcoming neighbors, bounty, and harmony.

Wending their ways among the attractions, how could anyone doubt that these promises existed not only in America, but everywhere on earth? In a restaurant attached to the elegant tower of the Polish Pavilion, for instance, visitors dined on scores of varieties of hors d'oeuvres and a plenitude of vodka, and in the Pavilion itself they were encouraged to enter an essay contest that opened with the line: "I would like to visit Poland because . . ."

Nor were the endless possibilities limited even to Earth: children like Joanie Pearson, accompanied by her parents' friends, Will and Barbara Brown, could take a simulated voyage to the moon.

The Browns' good-natured willingness to go along with their friends' children on just about every attraction the 1,200-acre fantasy emporium had to offer eventually ebbed at the end of the day as they looked up at the highly touted Life Savers ride, a 250-foot parachute jump. "I like my stomach just where it is." Barbara hugged the adventurous Joanie to her. "And anyway, haven't you been listening? Tomorrow is another day." With the light waning on the late afternoon, she and Will couldn't remember when they'd been so thirsty, and they treated everyone to a round of Coca-Colas. Little carts with the brand's logo could be found everywhere. "Here you go, Lannie," Barbara said, reading the somewhat unkempt vendor's name tag and handing him a dollar. She hoped she was wrong, but she could swear she smelled alcohol on his breath.

"I don't know about everyone else," Barbara said as she and Will and the others followed signs toward the exit, where a bus waited to take them back into Manhattan, "but I'm exhausted. Thank goodness we can come back tomorrow to see all the nighttime attractions."

"I'll bet the fireworks are something," Betty Waverly said. "And they say all the buildings light up with tremendous colorful displays."

"It should be beautiful," Will agreed. "It's something, what people can do when they set their minds to it." He didn't say out loud, for fear of injecting a critical note into the general euphoria, that it bothered him, some of the philosophies being put forward here. That message about escaping one's difficulties with a car ride, for example. Was that the planners' vision of tomorrow: that people should just move on when things got tough? What kind of character would such rampant escapism instill? And sure, it was all well and good for people to get along with each other, but the world wasn't just one harmonious, homogeneous band of humanity. Nor should it be. What about national identity and national pride? No, Will couldn't help feeling uncomfortable with the Fair's philosophy. And it didn't surprise him one bit that none other than FDR, the past master of both foreign entanglement and shirking individual responsibility, would be officiating at the opening ceremonies. Looking around at his colleagues and friends, though, as they gazed out the windows of the bus or fell into gentle dozes, he knew it was best to keep his reservations to himself. Fortunately, he was someone who could inject his worldview into his work.

He stroked Barbara's sweet-smelling hair, spread out on his shoulder as she slept, and noticed the lapel pin he'd clipped onto his jacket, the little button they handed to everyone as they left the General Motors exhibit. I HAVE SEEN THE FUTURE, it said.

Hm, Will wondered about that. He toyed with the idea of removing the pin, but then reminded himself not to be a killjoy.

"That's right, Harry," Al Kansas said on the very Sunday that Franklin Delano Roosevelt, Albert Einstein, and scores of other luminaries officially opened the World's Fair to a crowd of an estimated 200,000. The young lawyer had stopped calling Harry by his last name months ago. "The congressman introduced a House Resolution with your name on it. We don't know the number of the bill yet, but the hearing is scheduled for some time in June. Something, huh?"

Still, Harry didn't understand: There was going to be a bill named after him? Was that the same as a law? And the hearing in June: Was he going to be questioned at this hearing? In Washington, DC? Why hadn't they told him anything about this resolution?

Harry knew he had countless reasons to be grateful to Al Kansas and the entire Barkley operation, but sometimes, as now, he bristled at the way they made him feel like an incidental player in his own fate. Didn't he have the right to understand what was going on?

The opportunity to air his grievance passed, however, as Mr. Kansas excused himself to advise a woman from Lithuania on how to make a copy of her visa.

Nu, they were good people here. He was going to complain?

~ ~ ~

June

Washington, DC

Ten years to the day since Yankel Himelbaum had first set foot on United States soil and changed his name and answered no to the question of whether he was married, he got off the train at Union Station checking his pocket to make sure that another all-important government-issued card was in place. It wasn't a visa he was checking for this time; today, June 23, 1939, Harry made his way through the unprecedented heat tapping his pocket every few minutes to ascertain the safekeeping of his Member's Pass to the United States House of Representatives. It had been handed to him by Congressman Barkley himself the previous Sunday. Barkley had enjoyed a self-satisfied chuckle pointing out to Harry that the date of the hearing exceeded by one day the date by which they'd wanted to deport him. "We are definitely on top of this situation, Harry," he'd said. "Don't worry about a thing."

To represent Harry's interests at the hearing in Washington, Barkley had assigned none other than his personal legal counsel, Jonathan Kellogg. The other side was mounting an all-out campaign to get Harry out of the country, and if that's the way they wanted to play, the congressman would join the battle with his most potent weaponry. Of course, when he'd told that zealot Brown back in January that he'd make a federal case out of the Himelbaum matter, he hadn't honestly expected the little coot to take him up on it, but if war is what they wanted, let the combat begin.

The humidity was fierce, no cooler outside the train station than it had been on the platform, but despite the damp suit of clothing clinging to his skin—and the circumstances that had brought him here—Harry couldn't get over it: he was in Washington, DC! Even the grandeur of this building, a mere train station, conveyed importance, with its high archways and enormous statues and waving flags. True, he couldn't see any of the famous monuments from where he stood, but he could make out the dome of the Capitol building, just a few blocks away. Soon enough, he'd be inside.

A series of broad, tree-lined boulevards seemed to converge in front of the station, and Harry could easily imagine the king and queen of England, who had just made their famous visit to the United States, riding in their motorcade with President and Mrs. Roosevelt along one of these very streets. For weeks, Irene had spoken of little else, the excitement of the first royal visit. She'd even persuaded Saul to accompany her to the parade route when the couple had come to New York.

Harry stood under the center archway of Union Station's main entrance, as Mr. Kellogg's secretary had instructed him to do during a brief, businesslike phone call the night before. Harry had started to ask how he would recognize the man he was supposed to meet, but the woman had hung up before he could pose his question. A little worn and showing the neglect of sitting on a closet shelf for years, Harry's Panama hat at least provided him with something to hold in his hands. He fanned himself with it, making sure to keep his fingers over the frayed rim. Any of several hundred men walking past could be his Mr. Kellogg: everyone here was well dressed in a suit and tie; everyone looked as though they might hold a very important government position. Even the women, they moved with such grace and purpose, had an air of authority. Several times Harry thought he might have spotted Mrs. Brown, though he'd promised himself not to think of her. That kiss, he must never think of that, either. Maybe one day he would tell Reizel about it, confess his transgression and beg forgiveness. Yes, he would do that.

Standing there, Harry wished he'd thought of telling the woman on the phone that he'd be carrying a hat so that there'd be some way of distinguishing himself on this sweeping boulevard. Judging by the numbers of people standing under the archway, this must be a popular meeting place. How would the lawyer identify Harry any more successfully than Harry would be able to pick him out? The committee hearing was scheduled for one o'clock. It was only a little before noon, but after twenty minutes of waiting, his stomach started to tighten with the anxiety that the prospect of being late induces.

A tall, handsome man with a pockmarked face perused the assembled crowd as he walked confidently past. "Harry Himelbaum?" he was addressing no one in particular. "Harry Himelbaum?"

"Yes, yes, that's me." Harry rushed over to him. Without thinking, he tucked the hat on his head; it felt awkward holding it as he introduced himself to the man.

"Jonathan Kellogg." The lawyer held out his hand and shook Harry's firmly. "Come on, I know it's only a few blocks, but in this heat, I thought we'd both be more comfortable in a cab."

He led Harry to a curb of waiting vehicles. "We've got plenty of time. Congressmen don't like to rush through their lunches. This will give us a chance to go over things." He gestured for Harry to climb in, and all the uncertainties about how they would recognize each other seemed embarrassingly naive in the light of Kellogg's know-how.

"Ever been to Washington, Mr. Himelbaum?" Kellogg asked when they were settled in the spacious backseat, his slight southern twang making the last syllable of Harry's name come out as two. He removed his suit jacket and arranged it neatly on a hanger dangling from a hook, suggesting Harry do the same. "It's ungodly hot and muggy during the summer months, but Jefferson wanted to be near his plantation to pursue his happiness, so here we are. There's a hanger there for you."

Harry had awakened before dawn that morning to find Elke at the ironing board in the kitchen, giving his white shirt one more going over so that her son should look spotless and perfectly groomed in front of the committee. Her efforts had been thwarted hours ago, Harry feared, as the closeness on the train folded into the conscientiously pressed fabrics of his clothing. Stepping off the train, he had felt sweat seep from every pore, and to remove his jacket might very well expose embarrassing stains under the arms of his white shirt.

Saying he was comfortable with the jacket on, he declined the lawyer's casual invitation.

"Well, suit yourself." Kellogg laughed. "Well, there's a pun for you, ay? I'm sure you'd like to see the White House before we proceed on to the Hill," he said, and he asked the driver to take a little detour to Pennsylvania Avenue.

The man could not be more gracious, yet his very breeziness made Harry feel out of place. Everything sparkled white here, the buildings, the sidewalks. Even Mr. Kellogg's apparent lack of apprehension regarding the case—he'd mentioned it only in passing, as though it were little more than an errand they had to run in the middle of a fine, albeit humid, tour of the nation's capital—served to intensify Harry's sense of isolation.

"There it is, Mr. Himelbaum, the official residence." Kellogg pointed to Harry's right. And sure enough and despite his roiling preoccupation, Harry lurched backward, and his eyes did well with tears at the sight of it. "Stop for a moment, will you?" Kellogg said softly to the driver.

The White House! Harry was looking at it with his own eyes. The history of this place, the majesty and potent promise of it filled him with awe. "I forget sometimes, living here, what a magnificent place this is," Mr. Kellogg said. "Never productive to allow ourselves to become complacent." He waited a few moments before asking, "Okay for us to move on, Mr. Himelbaum?"

Harry blinked the tears away and nodded that it would be fine. Clearly, he was in the hands of a kind and sympathetic man.

As the taxi drove closer to the grand exterior of the Capitol dome, Harry felt another wave of reverence, mixed this time with dread. The contradictory emotions churning around his insides might be more than he could bear. To be here in this city at this building for the very reason that the highest branches of government wanted him out: how could one man accommodate such turmoil?

Mr. Kellogg opened his briefcase, explaining that Barkley's staff had done an exhaustive job gathering statements from Harry's bank, his employer, his neighbors and customers, and the fellow at the

Vegetable and Grocery Clerks' Union who'd signed him up and had nothing but good things to say about him. Absolutely nothing incriminating. Even Reva Lansky, about whom the opposition had made such a big to-do, had sworn that the only "documents" she and Harry had exchanged were baby pictures. No, there was no possibility that the government could paint him as anything other than an upright resident of the United States. "It's our job, today, to make that residency legal, and I'm pretty confident, Mr. Himelbaum, that that's just what we'll be able to do. Push comes to shove, we emphasize that you are the sole support of your elderly mother. We have her sworn statement to that effect, as well."

Leafing through the neatly arranged documents inside his briefcase, he pulled out a sheet of paper, and asked Harry if he'd like to take a look at it. "Something to save for the grandchildren," he said, "whom I'll do everything in my power to make sure will be growing up right here in America." He handed the sheet of paper to Harry.

```
          76th CONGRESS  H.R. 3146
1st SESSION _____
```

```
        IN THE HOUSE OF REPRESENTATIVES
                  April 10, 1939
    Mr. BARKLEY of New York introduced the fol-
lowing bill; which was referred to the Committee
on Immigration and Naturalization
```

A BILL

```
    To record the lawful admission to the United
States   for   permanent   residence   of   Yankel
Himelbaum, known as Harry Himelbaum.
```

```
1  Be it enacted by the Senate and House of
   Representatives of the United
```

2 *States of America in Congress assembled,*
That the Secretary of Labor

3 be, and is hereby, authorized and directed to record the lawful admission

4 for permanent residence of Yankel
Himelbaum, known as Harry Himelbaum,

5 New York, New York, on June 23, 1929, and
that he shall for all purposes

6 under the Immigration and Naturalization
laws be deemed to have been

7 lawfully admitted as an immigrant for
permanent residence.

Harry sat looking at the Bill with his name on it and felt that maybe, after all, he had Goliath on his side. He swept from his mind the fleeting thought of Goliath's fate.

Will Brown and his boss, Joe Connelly, stood at the foot of the Capitol steps eating hot dogs. Will was nervous; this was his first appearance as counsel in front of a congressional committee. Joe knew how committed he was to this case and Will appreciated the commissioner's confidence in him. Several of his colleagues in the Warrant Division had taken a more liberal approach to the Himelbaum matter, advising Will to let it drop rather than take it all the way to a hearing, but he had come to see this as a test case once Barkley had become involved, and he'd studied all the immigration law he could lay his hands on to make sure that the department would prevail. Sure, Yankel Himelbaum was a seemingly honest, hardworking man; Will couldn't even pin him on any kind of subversive connection to that Reva Lansky woman. But there was precedent involved here, and the rule of law, and that obnoxious loudmouthed politician, who'd fill the country with Communists and anarchists and all manner of malcontents if he wasn't stopped. Will heard that Barkley's office up in the Bronx resembled the Ellis Island of old, immigrants of every ilk and persuasion huddled inside and lining up out the door to seek help getting around well-established government regulations. Maybe it was Mr. Himelbaum's misfortune that Barkley had chosen his case to bring to the House floor—Will might have let it go if he hadn't had that run-in with Barkley in January—but once he'd threatened to take it that far, Will had no choice but to pursue the matter.

The hot dog tasted delicious, but Will hoped it wouldn't repeat on him or upset his stomach. He'd thought about skipping lunch, then thought better of it. The hearing could go on for hours and he might as well go in without having to worry about hunger pains. Lord knew the committee members were probably right now enjoying a leisurely three-course meal. He might as well be as fueled up as they were.

He was telling Joe about a case he'd dug up from '24, United States v. Tod, in which the court decided that if an immigrant was not dwelling in the United States when his father became a citizen, his questionable entry could not be considered legal, a precedent he thought would definitely apply here, when he saw Jonathan Kellogg getting out of a taxi. The man oozed what they meant by "cool, calm, and collected." He wore his crisp three-piece suit as though it were a mild day in April. The distraction made Will forget that he was holding a hot dog, and with an unthinking bend of his wrist, a dollop of mustard dropped onto his tie. "Damn it," he blurted, "wouldn't you know it." He tossed the hot dog into a trash bin and ran over to the vendor for napkins. He'd need water to take care of this, damn it!

The man walking toward the steps with Kellogg must be Himelbaum. A nice-looking man, quite handsome, much more striking than suggested by the fuzzy Photostat of his visa picture or the snapshots taken in New York. With a self-denigrating reference to his clumsiness, Will tried to sound unperturbed as he walked swiftly past Joe with a wad of napkins in his hand, and explained that he'd just run upstairs and find a water fountain to get rid of the stain.

Stepping inside the sandstone walls of the rotunda, with its pilasters and breathtaking curved windows that flooded the room with natural light, its murals and statues and echoes of the past and of the moment, its encircling panoramic frieze depicting American milestones from

Columbus's landing to the discovery of gold in California, one forgot the sweltering heat outside to feel immediately bathed in the moderating climate of history.

"The committee room is upstairs," Mr. Kellogg said to Harry, "but I thought you'd want to see this. Too bad we don't have more time. Maybe we can settle this business of yours quickly enough so that we can come back in a little while." The clickety-clack of heels on marble and the eerie resonance of hushed voices bounced discreetly throughout the room as the two men climbed the staircase to find the meeting room of the Committee on Immigration and Naturalization. It was just before one o'clock. Mr. Kellogg had suggested stopping for a hot dog, but Harry couldn't even think about food.

The wisdom of his refusal was immediately borne out as Harry entered the dimly lit committee room and his entire torso constricted into the familiar knot of intimidation. Small groups of gray-haired men stood in congenial conversation behind a long table, mildly gesticulating and rubbing their chins as though quietly reasoning with one another, and chuckling amicably. These were the members of the committee, Harry thought, the elected officials who would decide his case. They looked so casual and sure of themselves, while even his legs seemed to have forgotten their function.

After indicating that Harry should take a seat on one of the benches behind a smaller table, the "lawyers' table," he called it, Mr. Kellogg strode over to greet the members of the committee and shake their hands, his gesture warmly received and reciprocated by each of the men. *I should relax*," Harry told himself. This was very good, the way all the committee men seemed to like his lawyer. They must think very highly of him. They would respect his point of view.

As Mr. Kellogg shared an apparent witticism with one of the members, a tall man with a patrician carriage similar to his own came up behind him. Turning around, Mr. Kellogg gripped the man's shoulder, and shook his hand. "Joe, how are you? How's Martha? It's been too long since the four of us went out for a meal."

"Here's the person you want to have dinner with," the man Mr. Kellogg had called "Joe" said. He was holding out his arm and indicating a shorter, somewhat disgruntled-looking man who had just hurried in and set down his briefcase at the small table. "We won't need a restaurant if Will's wife will do the cooking. Jonathan Kellogg, my associate, Will Brown."

Harry's face flushed with heat. *Will Brown.*

He had come to learn months ago that the "W. M. Brown" signing so many of the documents that came in his mailbox to torture him was the husband of Mrs. Brown, Barbara, and he had heard her refer to him as Will. But here he stood, a mere few feet away. Cordially shaking hands with Harry's attorney. Talking about dinner invitations. Cordially shaking hands, alongside the person named "Joe," with the very same bank of men Harry had counted as Kellogg's allies, and hence, his. They all knew each other, spoke in friendly tones. A person could only conclude that they were all on the same side. Which left Harry, where?

"Pleasure to see you, Connelly," he heard one of the committee members say as he shook the taller man's hand. *J. Connelly.* Harry remembered other signed documents. The men with initials were coming into their names today, as well as their faces. At least his face had simmered down, he could tell, no longer boiling with heat, though his insides continued to quiver.

Pulling away from the seemingly boundless good will being exchanged between lawyers and lawmakers, Mr. Brown checked his wristwatch. When he looked up from his check of the time, his eyes perused the room, catching Harry's for a moment, before continuing their sweep. His gaze toward Harry might just as well have landed on a patch of wall for all the sentiment it conveyed. *Maybe he doesn't know who I am,* Harry thought. *Why should he?* Ten or twelve other people had gathered on the benches. Any one of them could be the person whose life he was here to ruin. Yet detachment was not the attitude Mr. Brown exuded. There was the checking of the door, Harry came to notice, along with the checking of the watch, and, too, the man didn't lower his arm after his continual time checks. He kept his left arm cocked in front of his chest, and this led Harry to wonder if the man might be using the wristwatch as an excuse of some kind, as a way of covering something with his arm, especially since there was an unusually large clock mounted on the back wall. It was the oddest pose.

The distracting consideration of his adversary's behavior crashed to a halt under the thud of a heavy hand landing on his shoulder. Harry fairly jumped. "Sorry, didn't mean to startle you," Congressman Barkley laughed throatily, perched on the bench behind Harry's. "Big day, huh?"

Out of the habit of respect, Harry started to stand up, but Barkley immediately stopped him, saying there was no need. "You just sit back and relax, Mr. Himelbaum. Didn't I tell you you're in good hands? Look at him over there," indicating Kellogg in rapt conversation with one of the committeemen. "To the manor born, that's Jonathan. Just wanted to say hello." And he got up to make his way to the long table. He, too, had a warm handshake and friendly word for all assembled. All except Mr. Brown, past whom he strode briskly.

It was hard for Harry to tell whether it was Barkley's snub that did it, but Mr. Brown immediately relinquished his time-and-door vigil, and sat down at the small table, where he unfastened his briefcase. It sprang open with a burst of paperwork, like a plot of earth suddenly giving way to insistent blooms. The contents of Mr. Kellogg's briefcase came to Harry's mind as a comparatively modest array.

Even as he went along with it, Will had little patience for all the glad-handing, and even less for the brazen disregard for punctuality, but in the event, he couldn't deny his relief. Failing at the water fountain and in the men's room to do anything but further implant the mustard stain into his navy tie, he'd phoned Barbara and implored her to get here as quickly as possible with the maroon. He'd spent much of the morning as well as the previous night deciding which of the ties to wear today. Now, thanks to his clumsiness, the decision was made.

Of course, had the subject of this hearing been anyone other than Harry Himelbaum, it would have been Will's dearest wish that Barbara be here throughout, to witness his debut as counsel for the United States government, in the Capitol building no less! Will couldn't help feeling pretty proud of himself, and he always wanted Barbara to be proud of him, too. Instead of strutting the accomplishment, though, he'd had to make light of it, mention only in passing that he'd been given an important assignment, and even then, conscientiously omitting the name of the man whose "lawful admission" he had been cleared to argue against in front of a congressional committee.

It was coming up on 1:30. Even the politicians in front of the room must eventually tire of the jolly-good-fellow chitchat. Will wanted it to start. He'd been pressed to greet the members in his sullied tie, anyway, so the initial impression, good or bad, had been made. He wished they'd get on with it. He sat down at the table and unsnapped his briefcase. Who cared about the tie? Maybe Barbara's presence would make him even more nervous. Maybe she'd see her friendly apple salesman—sitting in the third row, so modest and yet, it ate at Will, so dignified in his bearing—and create some kind of a problem. She wouldn't confront him, of course, her own husband, in any kind of conspicuous way. Oh God, she'd never do that. But what if, after handing him the tie, she spotted Mr. Himelbaum and turned on Will? Decided to stay and sat there quietly disdainful? Rooting for him to lose?

He checked his watch reflexively, since he knew exactly what time it was. He'd phoned her almost forty minutes ago. He'd never be able to catch her before she left the house, tell her to forget about coming. It would be impossibly awkward, anyway, for him to leave the committee room at this point, to try to call her. He'd have to come up with some kind of explanation.

Why didn't they just begin the proceedings? Was he the only person in the room aware that a hearing was scheduled? For one o'clock? How many times could he shuffle and reshuffle the pages and pages of legal proof against this Yankel cum Harry Himelbaum? Make a show of reading and note-taking? Tap the pages and leaf through them once more?

Just as the mutual admiration fest in front of the room began to break up, Barbara appeared in front of the lawyers' table. With perfect discretion, she handed Will the maroon tie. Confident that no one was paying attention, he adroitly removed the navy, handed it to her, and knotted the one she'd brought in.

"Look okay?" he asked.

His wife leaned over and, a bit more forcefully than necessary, Will thought, tightened the knot closer to his neck. "There," she said, and walked off.

Not a word to wish him good luck. No smile. Just, "There." How much smarter it would have been, Will realized in the dust of Barbara's indifference, to phone Annette and ask her to quickly purchase him a new tie and get it to him ASAP. For all his thorough preparation for this hearing, he was certainly messing things up in every which way.

As hard as it was to restrain himself, he didn't turn around to look after Barbara. He concentrated on listening for the swoosh of the back door to signal that she had left, but the attempt was thwarted by the soft yet attention-diverting tap of the chairman's gavel.

"Good luck, Mr. Himelbaum," Barbara whispered as she extended her gloved hand. Harry took it in his. He had seen her at the lawyer's table and immediately turned away. Now it was she who averted her gaze. She looked embarrassed, keeping her eyes directed toward the floor. It reminded him of his Reizele, but he merely accepted her wishes and squeezed her hand, only with his Reizel would he make that gesture to lift the chin. Barbara covered his hand with her other one, lingered only for a moment, and then was gone. In her wake, Harry inhaled the fragrance of wildflowers.

"Good afternoon," Chairman Hillock began. "At this time, having received and considered the various statements and official documents attendant to this case—the bill H.R. 3146 introduced by Congressman Barkley in favor of the relief of Yankel Himelbaum—the committee will hear additional remarks by counsel before making its recommendation regarding the lawful admission for permanent residence of the named alien. Is there any objection?"

Mr. Kellogg and Mr. Brown, both seated now at the small table facing the committee, waved off objection.

The chairman continued: "Let the record show that there appears in support of this bill a representative from the office of Congressman Barkley, serving also as attorney representing the alien. Also present is a representative of the Department of Labor, with the files of the department in the case."

A stenographer diligently typed every word.

Gesturing toward Kellogg, the chairman invited Barkley's representative to begin.

From his chair, Kellogg, sitting a good head taller than his adversary, opened: "Thank you, Chairman Hillock. As you are well apprised of the particulars in this case, I will make my statement in behalf of Mr. Himelbaum brief. We begin, of course, with his father. He came to this country legally in 1922 and five years thereafter applied for and received his citizenship. In 1929, Mr. Icko Himelbaum, the aforementioned father, made application to bring his wife and family over on a nonquota visa. His youngest son, Yankel, was the only member of the family at that time who made the choice to emigrate. Yankel was twenty years of age, and therefore entitled to come to the United States as the minor, unmarried son of an American citizen.

"This young man was very much in love with a girl from his native country of Poland, and after he had received his visa, legally, indeed on the very day in April that he was to depart from Poland, standing at the train station in the village of Wlodawa, he was told by his sweetheart that he was to become a father. Thereupon, unknown to his parents, but pressed by the impulses of decency, he married the girl. Aware of the population quotas about to go into effect that July and determined to fulfill his dream of coming to America, now with the added impetus of building a life for his young family, he sailed for the United States in June.

"By reason of the fact that he was a minor when his father became a citizen, he was granted citizenship as an unmarried, minor child. As an aside, if I may, he was informed of his right to citizenship by none other than my esteemed employer, Congressman Barkley, during a chance sidewalk encounter. In any event, soon after learning of his legal status as a citizen, and with the fervent hope of bringing his wife and child into the country, Mr. Himelbaum applied for a passport as an American citizen. After living a conscientious, hardworking life—all verified and reflected upon in the papers you have studied and so graciously referred to—and having finally saved up enough money, Mr. Himelbaum returned to Poland in 1937, and there applied to the visa officer in Warsaw for a visa for his wife and baby."

Here, Mr. Kellogg was interrupted by his tablemate. "Forgive me, Mr. Chairman, but the boy would have been seven at the time, almost eight years old," Mr. Brown noted, "hardly a baby."

Rather than respond verbally, Kellogg shot a derisive glance at his opponent, sufficient, he felt sure, to point up the loathsomeness of Brown's interjection. Moments later, however, remembering the stenographer, he felt compelled to note for the record that "any parent will concur that throughout its life one's child retains the vulnerable quality and timeless aspect of a babe in arms. Particularly since Mr. Himelbaum had just for the first time met the boy, well, surely, even my esteemed adversary will stipulate. Are you a parent, Mr. Brown?"

Jonathan Kellogg had no way of knowing the dagger his question wielded. Aside from perceiving Will Brown as someone causing an awful lot of bother for Congressman Barkley and poor Himelbaum, Kellogg had only limited acquaintance with the man. If asked, he would describe Will Brown as a department bureaucrat, albeit a particularly tenacious one.

Barkley, however, one of whose primary tenets was to know one's enemy, winced. If there'd been any hope of softening Brown's irritatingly stalwart resolve and clear animosity toward Himelbaum, Kellogg's query had just sunk the teeth in more deeply.

Brown merely commented that he was well aware of the "unique tenderness" of parental connections, and Kellogg continued his statement.

"Owing to the mishaps described in our affidavit—the required documents not being readily available when Mr. Himelbaum and his wife and child first appeared at the Warsaw consulate, etc.—my client was advised to return to the United States and petition here for the visas.

"It was during this petition process, embarked upon once Mr. Himelbaum had been forced by circumstances to leave his beloved wife and child and return alone to the United States, that the Immigration and Naturalization Service learned that the couple had been married prior to Mr. Himelbaum's initial entry as an unmarried minor and, as he himself has so eloquently stated, it was then that he realized he was in trouble. That he was, owing to the vigilance of the INS, deportable.

"But of what worth is vigilance without self-scrutiny? Mr. Himelbaum's father has died, leaving Mr. Himelbaum as the sole source of support for his mother, who has since emigrated to the United States, and his wife and child, who remain as Jews in Poland. I will not take up the committee's time with an explication of the hardship that being a Jew in Poland currently entails. The circumstances under which they exist are well documented in our affidavits, as well as, I'm afraid, in our daily newspapers. I ask only that leniency be extended here, that a finding of forgiveness be entered, and that Mr. Himelbaum be granted legal residency in this most fair-minded of nations."

Mr. Kellogg's heartfelt plea hung in the air with a perfectly calibrated silence that seemed itself to have been orchestrated by the advocate. Several members of the committee jotted notes on legal pads, their pens circling and darting along the sheets. Harry sat impressed, and even moved, by his lawyer's presentation. It must be a good sign, he thought, that the men on the committee were taking notes, no doubt reminding themselves of the persuasive arguments his lawyer had made. It must be good, too, that no one on the committee posed any challenges or questions to Mr. Kellogg's presentation of the case.

He wanted to get up from his seat and shake his lawyer's hand. Thank him. But no one in the committee hearing room stood or seemed inclined to take a break. Chairman Hillock lit a cigarette and looked to his left and right, up and down the long table as if silently polling his colleagues. They nodded: ready to continue. He asked Mr. Brown to proceed, and Harry braced himself.

"Mr. Chairman, members of the committee," Will began, "I find it curious that my esteemed adversary skims over the fraud committed in this case. No one here, or anywhere for that matter, questions the legality under which the alien obtained the initial visa. It is the entry itself, into the United States, to which all fair-minded Americans must take objection. As my learned opponent well knows, it is a deportable offense to willfully misrepresent a material fact in order to gain admission to the country."

"I believe," Chairman Hillock interceded, "that the wording of the law to which you refer states that it is a deportable offense to 'willfully misrepresent a material fact in order to obtain a visa.'"

Mr. Brown stood up. "With all due respect, Chairman Hillock." He walked over to the long table and delivered to each committee member a thick packet of pages. He handed one as well to Jonathan Kellogg. "May I turn your attention to Section 4, subdivision (f) of the Immigration Act of 1924? If you will turn to page four, gentlemen?" He waited during the light crackle of page turning. He himself required no packet or recorded print to articulate his points, having committed the relevant passages to memory.

"As you see, Section 4, subdivision (f) states plainly that 'nothing in this section shall be construed to entitle an immigrant, in respect of whom a petition is granted, to enter the United States as a nonquota immigrant if, upon arrival, he is found not to be a nonquota immigrant.'

"Similarly, and you will find this passage on page three in the papers I just handed you, Section 2 of the same immigration law." He waited once more for the turning of pages. "Section 2 provides the manner of issuing visas and in subdivision (g) thereof provides: 'Nothing in this act shall be construed to entitle an immigrant, to whom an immigration visa has been issued, to enter the United States if, upon arrival, he is found to be inadmissible under the immigration laws.'"

Will Brown inhaled deeply, feeling he must have made an impression here, and returned to his seat.

"On page sixteen of your packets, gentlemen, you will find a copy of Mr. Himelbaum's Certificate of Admission of Alien, dated June 23, 1939. Oh." Will caught his mistake and tried to ameliorate it with a stab at levity. "Forgive me. 1929. A remarkable happenstance, of course, the coincidence of the dates in this case. Here we are, ten years to the day since Mr. Himelbaum committed his unfortunate lapse in judgment." He took a moment, calculated to return everyone's focus to the "unfortunate lapse."

"As you can see, the questions on this certificate were administered by Inspector Edwin Wright, federally appointed officer assigned to Ellis Island inspections. I call your attention to item number 9, where it is asked, 'Married?' Next to which you will see typed in the word, 'No.' Clearly, the alien in this case lied to a federal official, misrepresenting a material fact to obtain entry. As related to the sections of the 1924 law already quoted, can anyone doubt the fraud perpetrated? And therein, lies the irrefutable evidence of the government's obligation to deport this alien.

"Now, if I may . . ."

"Excuse me," Mr. Kellogg intervened, "but I find it somewhat amusing that my opponent refrains from turning our attention to any of the other questions." He waved the packet in the air for dramatic emphasis. "I'm thinking specifically here of question number 4, which asks the immigrant to state his race. Is it not a national embarrassment, gentlemen, that we here in the United States of America willingly type in the man's answer to that question: 'Jewish'?" He threw the packet onto the attorneys' table with unabashed disgust.

"Surely you're not going to try to distract this committee from the case before it by stooping to introduce the matter of anti-Semitism," Will Brown bristled.

Kellogg sighed audibly. "Surely, I am not. Although it is an irony of jurisprudence that all too often the key matters are the ones we turn away from." Not giving Brown a chance to respond, he immediately went on. "If I may contribute to the paper shuffling Mr. Brown seems so fond of, I ask that the committee, and Mr. Brown if he so wishes, turn to the transcripts of the first of the woefully numerous hearings Mr. Himelbaum has been compelled to attend. You will find it among the papers we submitted. It is dated January 17 of this year." He waited while everyone located the record referred to. Displaying that his memory equaled that of the government's attorney, he asked that the committee "turn to page three of that transcript. 'Question: Did the immigration official ask your name?' the District Director at Ellis Island inquires. To which Mr. Himelbaum responds: 'I don't remember exactly if he asked me any questions. I just know that I gave all the papers to a certain man on the ship.' Next question: 'Did you conceal the fact that you were married from the immigration officials both in Cherbourg and New York upon your arrival in the U.S.? Answer: I don't remember that question.'"

"The word no is clearly typed in on the Admission Certificate," Will Brown reminded the panel of adjudicators.

"So stipulated," Kellogg said. "But is the identity of the respondent anywhere indicated on the Admission of Alien Certificate on which you seem to be so assiduously relying?" Visibly irritated, Will Brown located the certificate and studied it intently while Jonathan Kellogg continued. "As we have just reviewed in the transcript, my client has clearly stated that he remembers no such question about marital status being posed. It is possible, is it not, that the inspector merely assumed that the immigrant was not married, as the visa he carried was nonquota. It often happens that printed forms are filled out in a hurry. Perhaps the inspector himself filled in the word no without asking the question."

"As someone who worked as an inspector on Ellis Island, and on the Board of Review," Will Brown said emphatically, "I can assure the committee that no inspector would take it upon himself to just type in an answer without posing the question. Mr. Kellogg's imagination runs away with him."

"Well, I do have an imagination, I'll agree to that," Mr. Kellogg said. "Not a bad quality, if I may take the liberty of suggesting, in an advocate. Very well, without evidence of whom exactly said the word no, and going along with Mr. Brown's confidence that forms are never filled out quickly at Ellis Island, is it not possible that the question was put to Mr. Himelbaum's father, who greeted him upon arrival? As has been plainly averred, Harry Himelbaum had not by that time informed his father of his marital status. Hence, if Mr. Icko, or Izzy,

Himelbaum stated that his son was not married, he told the truth so far as he knew it.

"I'm sorry, gentlemen, for taking up more time than I had intended with this rebuttal, and I thank you for your indulgence, but I cannot emphasize enough that it cannot and must not be assumed that my client, Mr. Himelbaum, provided the answers on the Admission Certificate." He seemed to have made his point before adding, "Oh, and let's give some thought, shall we, to whether we as a nation wish to continue ascribing race to the religious practice of Judaism."

The chairman allowed a trace of annoyance to cross his face. "I must agree with Mr. Brown," he said. "That issue is not pertinent here." He turned to Will, and invited him to continue.

"Mr. Kellogg's eloquence is fabled," Will said, "and he shows us why. Bravo. But since he invites us to use our imaginations, not a practice I, as a lawyer ethically dedicated to facts, normally engage in in connection with my professional obligations, let me indulge his preference for a moment and pose, if I may, an imagined theory of my own. Why did Mr. Himelbaum choose to hide his marital status from his father? And for how long did he do so? By all accounts, they were close, loved each other, lived in the same apartment, even shared a business for a period of time. Himelbaum and Son, I believe it was called. As coincidence would have it, my wife even frequented the fruit stand owned by your client, before, of course, all these legal problems came to our attention. Years ago. I apologize for this tangential information, but you see my point. I'm using my imagination, you see, and in so doing, and in bringing to mind Mr. Kellogg's own declaration, made just moments ago, that the marriage was kept secret from both the Himelbaum parents, I can only conclude that Mr. Yankel Himelbaum knew that his marriage presented legal problems from the moment he married in Poland. Hence, he did knowingly and consciously conceal his marital status because he understood that it would cast an unlawful shadow on his entry into and residence in the United States. A shadow under which, perhaps, he did not want his father to reside."

"While I reject the conclusion, and marvel at the flight of assumptions described by Mr. Brown, I'm glad to see that he concurs that one's imagination can be engaged to useful effect." Kellogg pantomimed a tipping of his hat in Brown's direction and leaned back in his chair.

Inside a swirl of conflicting emotions, Harry sat stiffly upright. Despite the uncomfortable attention his lawyer had brought to the issue of anti-Semitism, which Harry wished he had not done, and despite the fact that Mr. Brown's "imagined" explanation of why he hadn't told his father he was married came jarringly close to the truth, he felt confident that Mr. Kellogg was ahead in the sparring contest unfolding before him. At the same time, he found scant amusement in the fact that the terrifying possibility of his deportation had turned into a sparring contest, and that his future was the object of this swordplay, a future potentially cut off with the swish of a blade. On the other hand, he rationalized, and he had attended enough hearings to accept his impressions as valid, this match between adversaries was an integral and inevitable feature of judicial proceedings. Two sides, representing opposing points of view, stood up to make the winning argument. It made sense that each side utilized its sharpest weapons, and therefore it didn't surprise Harry that here in Washington, the mecca of legal confrontations, the words were sharper and the weapons more finely honed. Notwithstanding his intelligent appraisal of the situation, if he knew the word *haughty*, he might have used it to describe Mr. Kellogg's manner; within the limitations of his vocabulary, he just hoped his lawyer wasn't making a conceited impression. Conversely, he was able to reassure himself that Mr. Brown's recitation of all those sections and subdivisions was equally show-offy.

At this juncture, even with his several misgivings, Harry had to believe that the committee was looking more favorably upon Mr. Kellogg's case, which, he forgot for not an instant, was his own. And yet, he sat in the third row of benches as the argument in favor of his case seemed to be going well, fighting off the most deflating sense of dejection. The mortification had come just moments ago, and what it came down to was this:

Mrs. Brown and her husband had spoken about him.

The apple salesman.

His name had come up between them, in some casual conversation or other. Mr. W. M. Brown, the man who had brought to bear all the power of his skills and office and position and obviously genuine beliefs, held in his hands the one taunting advantage that no amount of silken sophistication nor eloquence in the person of Mr. Kellogg could vanquish: his intimacy with Mrs. Brown, his wife.

Why had he mentioned her if not to put the "alien" in his place? The connection served no legal purpose; Mr. Brown, himself, had referred to it as a tangent.

Perhaps bringing Mrs. Brown's name into the hearing was meant to make Harry feel small. The unequivocal success of this gambit filled Harry with trepidation.

Embroiled in the heated clashing of conclusions warring in his mind, Harry forced himself to listen to Mr. Brown's continuing remarks.

"The term *unmarried*," he was saying, "when used in reference to any individual as of any time, means an individual who at such time is not married. It is very plain from the provisions as outlined that an immigrant must not only have the status that he claims at the time of receiving a visa, but must likewise have that status at the time of applying for admission at a port of entry in the United States. It is likewise propounded that at the time of application for admission to the United States in June 1929, as has been conceded, the subject of these proceedings was then married and was not, therefore, an unmarried minor son of a citizen, and hence was not a nonquota immigrant as specified in his immigration visa.

"On March 17, 1939, the Board of Review of the Department of Labor's Immigration and Naturalization Service did direct that in view of the circumstances, the alien be required to depart from the United States to any country of his choice, except Canada. The specific charge against him is that at the time of his entry, both in 1929 and 1937, he did enter illegally. I trust that the committee will uphold our conclusion. Thank you, gentlemen."

"Thank you, Mr. Kellogg, Mr. Brown, for your carefully prepared presentations and elucidating remarks," said Chairman Hillock. He glanced at the wall clock at the back of the room. "If none object, I'd like to take a ten-minute recess, a comfort break, if you understand my meaning, after which we will reconvene briefly, to hear the committee's recommendation."

Harry desperately needed a comfort break. Etiquette demanded that he thank his lawyer, thank him profoundly for his brilliant representation of his case, but he was spared from choosing between the calls of nature and etiquette by the sight of Kellogg in deep conversation with Congressman Barkley. It wouldn't be necessary for him to suppress his insistent bladder; his lawyer wouldn't even notice his absence.

He looked straight ahead, trying not to meet anyone's eyes as he followed a thin train of people toward the restrooms. Though he had not been identified in the hearing room, sitting anonymously among the observers—indeed, his presence here today wasn't even mandatory; it had, in fact, been offered as an "opportunity" by Barkley—there was no getting away from his role: he was the very reason anyone was here. Still, it might be possible to enter the men's room undetected, and that was his objective, to disengage from his very identity. Yet, pushing in the heavy wooden door, he had no choice but to walk in, despite the fact that Mr. Brown himself stood in front of one of the urinals.

The lawyer for the government, of course, must know who he was. Harry realized he had been mistaken earlier; Mr. Brown must have seen pictures of him. There in his briefcase, there must be more than one. But there was no time for second-guessing. Harry's bladder demanded relief.

From the mirror in front of him, Will saw Himelbaum come in. The proximity bore out his earlier impression: he was a good-looking man. Tall, ramrod posture. Ethnic features, true, but even these were mitigated by his thick, wavy hair, light eyes, ruddy complexion. The suit had seen better days, Will noted; it sat baggy on him, threadbare at the lapel.

Should he let on that he recognized the man? Offer some kind of salutation?

He thought better of it; what purpose would it serve?

Will washed his hands and exited the restroom.

When Harry reentered the hearing room, he immediately approached Mr. Kellogg and thanked him. "We did well, no?" he asked.

"Yes, I think we did well, Mr. Himelbaum," his lawyer said. "A few missteps, perhaps, but overall, yes, I don't think we did anything to hurt our case. Can't count our chickens, though. We'll know soon enough."

These were not precisely the words Harry had hoped for. The unbounded confidence he'd perceived in his attorney, from the cab ride through to his final parry, was somehow absent, replaced by a manner more merely mortal. Had Kellogg heard something during the break to jostle his self-assurance? Maybe he was just being sensible, pulling back on the swagger in order to prepare his client. Maybe this was part of his responsibility, to temper the client's expectations until the decision was read.

"It's time," Kellogg said, giving Harry's shoulder a firm squeeze. The committee was back behind the long table, and everyone took their seats.

"Let it be noted," Chairman Hillock said, about an hour and a half after the hearing had begun and all were gathered following the recess, "that the attorneys in the case and the committee in whole are in attendance. That, while the committee appreciates Mr. Brown's delivery of relevant materials for the convenience of the hearing, all the pertinent acts with which, of course, the committee is conversant"—he looked with some irritation at Mr. Brown—"and affidavits and documents have been in our possession for weeks and duly studied."

There was a brief pause here, Hillock gesturing to a woman in a gray suit who sat behind him. He whispered something to the congressman sitting to his right, then accepted the sheet of paper handed to him by the woman, and read:

"The Committee on Immigration and Naturalization, to whom was referred the bill H.R. 3146 for the relief of Yankel Himelbaum or

Harry Himelbaum, having considered the same, refer it to the House without amendment and recommend that the bill do pass."

For a moment, the statement sounded so unremarkable, so nebulous to Harry, that he didn't know what to feel. The hum in the seats around him told him nothing. But then he saw Kellogg, grinning broadly, throwing his arms high in the air and then resting his hands on his head with his fingers interlaced, a man who had won. And Congressman Barkley actually emitted a whoop.

It was good then, the committee recommendation. He could stay. They weren't going to deport him. He sat quite still, trying to absorb his new situation. It was really over? Maybe, yes, he could allow himself to believe that the ordeal was over. It must be, because for the first time all day, he felt hungry. But Hillock was tapping his gavel, a bit more forcefully than he had earlier.

"Gentlemen, we are not quite through," he said. "The recommendation of this committee will be committed to the Committee of the Whole House and ordered to be printed. The vote will need to be a unanimous one in keeping with the calendar, at which time it will pass to the Senate, where, it is our sincere hope that Mr. Himelbaum's case will find similarly favorable consideration so that he may ultimately receive the relief, which, in the opinion of this committee, he so surely deserves.

"And now, without objection," he waited less than a moment, "I call this hearing adjourned."

Since Barkley and Kellogg were slapping each other on the shoulder and congratulating each other vigorously between the two tables, Harry concluded that the "unanimous vote" mentioned by the chairman didn't pose a problem. It sounded worrisome to him—every single man in the United States Congress would have to vote in favor of his remaining?—but at this point, he figured he would just have to grow used to the idea that things had actually gone his way. If he needed additional evidence of his success, he didn't have to look further than the short man with the maroon tie collecting his packets from the row of committee members barely paying attention to him. Mr. W. M. Brown did not look pleased.

Will tried to maintain a dignified demeanor as he gathered the "relevant materials" to which Chairman Hillock had so mockingly referred. The committee "appreciated Mr. Brown's delivery," Hillock had said, as though the remark compensated for its underlying rebuke: "We know the law, sir; it is this body that crafted the damn thing."

They knew the law, but they certainly hadn't bothered to apply it to this case. What had Will been thinking, considering it possible that these Roosevelt Democrats would even contemplate adhering to the law when they had a simple, hardworking immigrant to take under their wing? Clearly, they'd decided the case before Will had uttered a word. The whole exercise, for which he'd so rigorously prepared, mulling every decision down to the color of his tie, had been just that: an exercise, a hollow maneuver meant to flex their power. Will felt even worse than someone who had just lost a case. He felt like a laughingstock. He felt small.

Carefully stacking and placing into his briefcase the bulky and maligned paperwork, the body of hard law that he'd been foolish enough to believe persuasive on its face, he clicked shut the briefcase and strode from the hearing room.

Himelbaum sat looking straight ahead, as though he, too, might be stunned by the outcome. Or was he already devising his plans for bringing over his wife and child? Well, Will wasn't about to allow that to happen. Not just yet. This afternoon might be construed as a setback, even a serious one, but he still had the facts on his side, and the backing of Connelly, and the weight of the goddamn Immigration and Naturalization Service of the United States Labor Department.

He thought about going straight home, calling it a day. Barbara would like that, Will getting home early. She thought he was too wrapped up in his work, that he should ease up a bit on his all-out dedication. He wasn't ready yet, though, to face her. She'd be noodling in the garden or reading one of her magazines, and ask how the case went; she'd certainly want to know that. And would he be able to bear her response? Even if she didn't realize it was Himelbaum whose lawful standing he had been arguing against, would she be disappointed on Will's behalf or take secret pleasure in the triumph of the "little guy" she always stood up for?

No, he'd go to the office. Still a few hours left in the workday. Annette would have a fresh pot of coffee waiting, and his desk neatly organized, and she'd say just the right thing to refresh his confidence.

Congressman Barkley almost walked right past Harry as he made his way up the aisle to the doorway. "Oh, Mr. Himelbaum!" He held out his hand. "Congratulations. You can unpack that suitcase now. You won't be taking any boat rides."

"I don't know how to thank you."

"Well, you can move to the Bronx and vote for me." Barkley winked.

"And, this vote they talked about, that will . . ."

"Oh, there're a few old codgers we may have to persuade. They prove intractable, we might even have to start all over again, take it to the Senate in a few months' time. I've already spoken to some people over there. But the writing's on the wall, my friend, you're not going anywhere. Give my best to your aunt and uncle, will you? Their son like that job I arranged for him over at the World's Fair?" Not waiting for an answer, he shook Harry's hand once more and disappeared into the halls of the Capitol.

Harry picked up his Panama hat. He didn't know exactly what he should do at this point. He wasn't going anywhere. He had friends in high places, and they would see to it. Mr. Kellogg was up at the long table, smoking a cigarette and laughing with a few of the stragglers on the committee.

He would not be deported, he had to keep telling himself. Did that mean he was a citizen? Or would there be more paperwork, petitions? How long would it take? What if, as Congressman Barkley had said, they had to start all over again? Take it to the Senate?

What about Regina and Yakob?

Regina and Yakob.

"Well, my client is waiting," he heard Mr. Kellogg say across the room. "Thank you all very much."

"So, Harry, we did it," the winning attorney said as he reached Harry's bench. "I wish I could show you around the rotunda. You're welcome to stay as long as you like, but I have to get back to the office."

"Thank you very much, Mr. Kellogg. Thank you."

They walked down the broad hallway to the staircase. When they reached the second floor, Harry looked around at the majestic pilasters and windows, bathed now in the tawny light of late afternoon. Mr. Kellogg checked his watch. "Staying? Going? I can help find you a cab."

"I think maybe I'll stay a little while. Who knows when I'll be back here?" Harry smiled thinly. "Maybe, I hope, not so soon. Myself, I can find a cab. This I can do. But I thank you, from the bottom of my heart. Thank you."

"A good day's work, Harry. You don't mind if I call you that?" And then he waved so-long, and descended a few steps before turning back. "There is one thing I've been wondering about. It's not important really but, well, I'll just spit it out, as they say. And, of course, we have attorney-client privilege here, so nothing you say will be repeated.

"It seems to me that Brown was right in there. That business about your not telling your parents you were married, receiving your wife's letters through her cousin. It's all in the transcripts, but Brown didn't bring up the Reva Lansky material. I'm sure he wanted to nail you as a union agitator. Once he realized it was a bogus accusation, he dropped that whole line of inquiry. Not very good lawyering, but lucky for you, because bringing in those meetings with Lansky, he could have made a pretty strong case for knowledge of guilt. And Harry, that answer on the Admission of Alien Certificate, you did knowingly lie to get into the country, didn't you?"

The two men stood under the mural of Columbus, Indians gathered at his feet as he makes his triumphal landing.

"I can only tell you what I told at all the hearings," Harry said. "I don't remember the question."

Kellogg could do nothing but purse his lips and nod. "Fair enough. Well, you need anything else, any legal advice, it will continue to be my honor to represent you. Remember that."

"My wife and son," Harry said. "When can I send for them?"

"First things first, Harry, first things first. One step at a time."

They shook hands once more and the attorney padded down the staircase.

Harry took several turns around the pictorial representation of American history. He didn't know whether there would be a train back to New York tonight or not. He had a few dollars in his pocket, maybe a hotel. As he wandered around the circular room, he thought every now and then of looking up Mrs. Brown's telephone number, telling her the good news, but then the guard announced that it was five minutes until closing, and Harry remembered how hungry he was. He rushed down the stairs in the hope of finding a hot-dog stand.

Knowledge of guilt, the lawyer had said. Harry swallowed against it as he emerged from the halls of the Capitol into the thick afternoon air. He had been in the country for ten years, and every day he tasted it, that cost of admission. Maybe the battle was over, maybe it wasn't. Either way, he had learned to live with the taste. Ridding himself of it would come only with the safe arrival of his wife and child. Then, maybe everything would be sweet, as he had originally imagined it: life in America.

Had Harry called the well-appointed split-level house in Woodley Park, had Will gone home instead of to the office, neither man would have found anyone there. The phone would have rung indefinitely. Barbara wouldn't be in the garden or reading a magazine. After years of finding one excuse after another to stay with her husband, she had that very afternoon left the Capitol building and taken a cab to Union Station. It was high time she went back to Iowa, visited her mother.

She hadn't with any certainty decided to leave Will. He was her husband. Over the last few days, she'd prepared some of that lamb stew he loved, a spinach casserole, and roasted chicken and potatoes. Enough food in the icebox to hold him for a while, and a note. She'd signed it, "Love," and she suspected she meant it. After a few weeks in Iowa, why, she'd bet she'd be right back in Washington. No use making too much of it, taking this trip; she just needed to get back home for a while.

~ ~ ~

September 1

Warsaw

"Yes," Ava said after placing a cup of tea and a plate of toast in front of Yitzak, who sat at the small table in front of the narrow kitchen window. "I can't sit with you for breakfast," she said. "I'm late for work." She disappeared into the bedroom.

The tea sat at Yitzak's place steaming and tempting, but he followed her into the other room. "'Yes?' What are you talking about, 'yes'?"

Ava stood at the closet in her brassiere and underwear, her robe tossed onto the bed. All these years later, she was still ravishing. He could make love to her right here and now.

"I will marry you." She was stepping into her skirt, buttoning it.

"What?" Yitzak couldn't believe what he was hearing. "Are you playing with me? You mustn't be toying with me. You'll . . . ?" He didn't finish the question, he knew she wasn't making a joke of such a thing. He lifted her up in his arms, kissed her. "You'll be my wife? Now, on a Friday, all of a sudden, you'll marry me?"

"We should probably wait until Monday," Ava said, wanting to hold a serious expression, but breaking out in laughter as Yitzak gently set her down. "It's too late today to take off, but I'll tell them at work I won't be in on Monday."

"You are serious?"

She framed his face in her hands, and looked into his eyes with earnest concern. "Maybe, as my husband, they will believe you are gentile. Your life will be easier."

"You would do this for me?"

"I would, and I will. I love you, Yitzak." She sidled away from him and put on her suit jacket. Though he never complained to her or talked about his fear, his cries in the middle of the night confirmed her own. Now, it was merely uncomfortable to be a Jew in Warsaw. There was menace, snide mockery, news of harassment and destruction filtering in from other parts of the country. Ava didn't know precisely what was coming, but she felt that it was beyond what anyone could know, and that it would find a receptive home in Poland.

"You must tell her, of course. Right away. She will have to agree to divorce you, but in the meantime, I don't care if you're a bigamist. We can go out in public together, be seen as a couple."

"This afternoon, I'll go," Yitzak said. "We close early, I'll catch the train to Wlodawa." He watched as she pinned up her luxuriant black curls, dabbed on a little lipstick. "You've made me very happy," he said.

Stawki

Chava sat under the cottonwood tree knitting a sweater for the coming winter. The evening was warm, making the wool sticky in her damp fingers, squeaky as it slid from one needle to the other, but soon enough, she knew, warm weather would be a distant memory. Every few minutes she looked up to breathe in the satisfaction of watching the children. She got such a kick out of them. *Shabbes* dinner was simmering on the stove, and Moishe, what a devoted big brother, was sitting with Sarah in his garden in the front yard, showing her which tomatoes were ready for picking. It had been Michal Hondra's idea, to designate the area in the front yard to the right of the house as "Moishe's Garden." He had even painted a little sign on a piece of wood and stuck it into the ground. It sat surrounded by the cucumber and tomatoes plants. If only she could meet a Jewish man capable of such kindness.

"What am I thinking?" She interrupted her thoughts.

Then, another interruption.

A deafening explosion. Out of nowhere.

The ground shuddered, plumes of smoke billowed in the distance.

Chava threw aside her needles and raced to the children, and the three of them clung to each other in silent terror.

Wlodawa

The train station barely endured the force of the blast. None of the passengers on the train pulling in from Warsaw just before the moment of impact survived. There was no passenger list, and their remains could not be identified.

Lukow

Regina sat in the square reading for the hundredth time the most recent letter she'd received from Harry. It was six weeks now since she'd heard from him, July 15 it was written, the longest span between letters since he'd been in America. Something wasn't right.

Several times she'd stood in the long line that snaked out of the Lukow post office, to inquire, with the other Jews of the town, about what must be a mistake of some kind. Why weren't they receiving their mail? But they all knew. The Poles were playing mischief; they'd found another way to undermine the daily lives of their hated fellow citizens.

The church bells tolled six times. She and Yakob should go back to the apartment for *Shabbes*. Maybe she'd read the letter one more time. And Yakob, playing baseball with some other boys in the park, with the bat Harry had sent, she hated to pull him away from the one thing on earth that seemed to put a smile on his face.

> *My Dearest Reginaleh,*
> *I was happy to receive the picture you sent of our Yakob in the base-ball cap you made for him. He will fit right in here in America. To a Dodgers game I'll take him, you wait.*

I have to tell you though that the vote in the Congress went as I expected. Not everyone went along with the committee's recommendation. From this one man that I told you about who seems to have it in for me, this Mr. Brown with the INS, I received another deportation letter, so Barkley and the lawyers are taking another bill to the Senate. They will try now to get me in as a quota immigrant, so that the question of whether I was married shouldn't even be part of the case. They are asking that one number be deducted from the Poles who came in during 1929, so that my name can be added.

Don't ask. It's complicated, my darling, but they assure me that even with all the bills and letters and appeals, I am safe here, I am here to stay. And of course, I will never stop with every bit of strength I have to get you and Yakob here, too.

You will find in the envelope a little extra. I am sorry to tell you that Ralph has not been well. They say it is his heart. So he made Saul manager, and me, I am now the assistant manager at the store. 10 more dollars a week I make now, which I will send to you, my darling, with every letter.

There is other news, too. Our Irene and Saul are to be married. No surprise, but they may have rushed the date a little bit so Ralph can be there at the wedding while he can still get around. Irene, the kalleh, I can't get over it, will move in with Saul and his parents, so me and Mama will be here in the apartment alone. But we will not for long be alone here. Soon the house will be full, with you and Yakob. Soon you will be here with us. Please trust in that, my sweetheart.

> *Always, your Loving*
> *Harry*
> *And to my son, forever Love*

Regina's attention to the words she knew by heart was distracted by the sounds of boyish shrieking. Yakob was lying on the ground with his knees pulled to his chest. She shoved the letter into her pocket and ran over to him. To her relief, Yakob was laughing, uncontrollably.

"Look at you, you'll be all dirty for *Shabbes*," Regina scolded him. "Get up from there."

"Oh, but Mama," Yakob said, trying to curb the hilarity, dusting off his pants as he stood up. "Baruch keeps running the wrong way to get home. He thinks it's that stone over there, but that's only second base. He's running all the time the wrong way around the stones." Taking a few moments to gather himself, and feeling badly about his unkind outburst, Yakob walked over to Baruch, who was standing forlornly on the patch of grass the boys called the outfield. Yakob put his arms around his playmate and apologized for not being a nicer friend. Tomorrow, he promised, he would go over the rules with him.

Berlin, Germany

Hundreds of soldiers boarded a black train as night fell. White-painted words glowed in the darkness. *Wir fahren nach Polen um Juden zu versohlen*, they said. "We're going to Poland to beat up the Jews . . ."

~ ~ ~

EPILOGUE

1946

Out of the Shadows

March

New York City

Harry climbs the Fort Washington Avenue hill uptown from 181st Street. He wears his bulky tweed jacket with the zipper. Earlier, he hadn't needed it. It had been one of those first over-seventy-degree days when everyone in the city peeled off their jackets, joining in a collective thaw—of their bones, their skin, those personal dreams and possibilities kept under wraps for winter. Now, a chill has set in, and Harry wears his jacket.

It keeps him warm at the store, except when the weather is bitter. He and Saul became partners after Ralph died, and the brothers-in-law get on well. Irene made an uncle out of him a few years back, naming the baby Icko—Ira she calls him, taking some amount of teasing along the lines of "Ay, ay, ay," everything with an *I*"—but the kid is a solid, burly little fellow, just a little younger than Yakob had been when Harry saw him last and, with a father like Saul, he can already hit and throw and catch a baseball like a real American boy. Yes, he's an American kid, Irene's Ira, going to school in the same elementary school where Harry had studied English.

Those years of night school he had also climbed this hill. To some it may seem like an accident of nature, that the concrete landscape angled upward here, but to Harry it has always felt appropriate, the incline of this particular street. Going from 181st Street north on leafy Fort Washington Avenue, a person was leaving the hustle and bustle and belching buses of commerce and ascending toward a quieter, more serene and self-assured place. The air smelled cleaner here, felt softer on the skin. A calm settled itself on a person's shoulders.

Harry jams his hands inside the roomy pockets of the jacket. In one, his fist cups a small envelope with two Broadway tickets inside. A show she had once told him she was dying to see, *Call Me Mister.* The other pocket holds a letter on onionskin paper, an official government letter from Poland. It will be necessary for her to see the letter before he can invite her to the play. She has been very specific, and of course, he can't blame her. "Please, Harry, I like you very much, but please don't call me anymore unless, you know, unless you can show me that you are free." Those were her words. And now, it has been a while since he made that pledge to her. Almost six months. Through neighborhood gossip, he knows that she isn't seeing anyone else, that she still cares for him.

Yes, this hill has always represented going forward. Night school, and then, of course, he had walked up this same hill with Mrs. Brown that day, the day she'd come to see him, told him about the Bill, that his case was being taken up in Washington. His all-American girl, is how he thought of her. He thinks sometimes about that walk, of how he'd taken her hand as they left the park. And the glancing kiss as he put her into the cab. Could one even call it a kiss, two lips as close as breath, barely touching? He remembers it, smiles on it as a kiss. But it was all of it, innocent.

Mr. Will Brown, it turned out, had had his doubts. At the second congressional hearing in '41, Barkley had pulled Harry aside, and asked with a serious face what exactly had transpired between himself and the prosecuting attorney's wife. It made Harry wonder, was it possible to enter this room without a burning heat spreading over his face? He could feel his face turning bright red.

"He seems to have it in for you, Harry," Barkley had said. "Otherwise, this headstrong determination to make trouble for you doesn't make sense." Barkley had never believed Will Brown would actually insist on another hearing, but here they were, very likely on the brink of war, for God's sake, the Germans doing God knew what to the Jews of Poland, and Brown would really consider sending this man back? Even the disingenuous assertion that he could go to any country of his choice was unconscionable: this was no time to single out a Jew for deportation, just ship him out into a big wide world that didn't want him.

There in the hearing room, Harry assured Barkley that it was just a friendship; less than that, an acquaintance that he had with Mrs. Brown.

"She left him, you know," Barkley whispered. "Walked out the door, right around the time of your first hearing. Brown went out there, to Iowa, tried to persuade her to come home with him. Of course, he didn't confide all this to me, but it's hard for a man to have secrets in DC. It's a much smaller place than people think."

Harry, standing in back of the room as the panel of congressmen slowly found their seats, twirled his hat in his hand waiting for the rest of Barkley's story. Wasn't he going to finish? Barbara had left her husband! Did she come back to him? Wasn't Barkley going to finish the story?

"*Nu?* So? Did he persuade her?"

Barkley peered at him, studied his face before answering. "No, Harry, she stayed right there in Iowa. I believe they're divorced by now, legally and all."

The flurry of excitement that this information stirred made Harry feel foolish, like a teenager with a crush on a movie star, and he made a conscientious effort to suppress it as Barkley continued.

"You honestly didn't know anything about this, did you?" He didn't wait for Harry to answer. "Nah, I can see in your face. And Brown must know it, too. The whole idea is preposterous. But apparently, that hasn't stopped old Will from blaming you for Barbara's disenchantment with him. She took your side from the beginning, and I swear to God, it's as though he is using your case as a way of getting over her, proving her wrong by convincing himself you're the devil incarnate. The lengths a fellow will go to, huh, when he's in love? Gotta hand it to Will for at least that much."

Harry knew he should be focused on the implications of Barkley's words: was Will Brown harassing him as a form of revenge? Some kind of crazy, ridiculous jealousy? Was that what this ordeal was all about? These questions weighed on Harry, but far more pressing, far more insistent, far more final was the verdict Barkley had delivered: "The whole idea is preposterous." Then and there, he knew that it was. It was preposterous to have entertained even one romantic thought about Mrs. Brown, and wrong and inappropriate and the depth of disloyalty. Not for the first time, he silently begged Reizel's forgiveness, until the day he could ask her in person.

It took four more years of character investigations, hearings at Ellis Island, depositions and interrogations, pleadings, deportation orders and suspensions of those orders, votes and recommendations, but at long last, in early 1945, six years after the grinding parade of legal proceedings had begun, Harry won his case. The United States Attorney General himself put it in writing: all future proceedings were to be halted, the matter, dropped. "There is no reason to deport this man or withhold citizenship." Harry's determination had lasted one beat longer than Will's.

And the ordeal had made him stronger. With each legal demand and encounter, he felt more knowledgeable, more justified, more capable. Remarkably, with each challenge, he felt more American. The system had flogged the doubt right out of him.

Preposterous or not, the day he received his naturalization card in the mail, Harry had gone to Barkley's office in the Bronx, insisted on paying for the Photostat, and made a copy to mail to Barbara Brown. He wanted to thank her, show her the outcome of her kindnesses. Barkley had been canvassing the neighborhood that day, greeting voters and prospective voters, and with just a little persuasion, he agreed to ask Annette, Will Brown's devoted secretary, for Mrs. Brown's Iowa address. Will seemed to have come to terms with the divorce, Barkley told him. "Been bumped up to Commissioner of Warrants, seeing some niece or other of his old boss's wife. I should be able to ask for the address without raising any red flags. I'll see what I can do."

When Harry sat down to write a letter to enclose with the copied naturalization card, he drafted and went over it many times before deeming it adequate to be folded and placed inside an envelope. It read:

> *Dear Mrs. Brown,*
> *(I still can't call you Barbara.)*
> *As you can see it took me quite a few years but finally I made it. Nu, I'm a citizen. I thought you would want to know, you were always so kind and helpful.*

He ruminated for days over whether to make reference to her marriage, feelings he might or might not have regarding her divorce from her husband. Ultimately, he decided against trespassing into her personal life, ending the letter:

> *So I hear now you are back in Iowa. You must be happy I'm assuming, because I remember how much you like there the apples.*
> *Sincerely yours,*
> *Harry Himelbaum,*
> *Citizen of the United States*

Weeks later, he received a reply, right in his mailbox in his Fort Washington Avenue building, a letter from Iowa. Coral butterflies floated in the left-hand corner of the page.

> *Dear Mr. Himelbaum,*
> *Congratulations! I am sorry you had to wait so long to find a fair conclusion. Sometimes, I know there are just so many rules. Sometimes, too, those rules are interpreted in ways that unnecessarily delay justice for a good man.*
> *You are right, I am happy to be home. I guess that makes two of us.*
> *Yours truly,*
> *Barbara Brown*

Though Harry no longer had to hide his correspondence in a shoe box in his closet, the habit had stayed with him. What was a person supposed to do with empty shoe boxes? They were too substantial to just throw away. He placed Barbara's letter in his Florsheim shoe box.

Unlike his letter to Iowa, the many envelopes he addressed to Staropijarska Street received no response. Beginning in 1941, a few were returned to him, ADDRESS UNKNOWN stamped on the envelope in German, but more frequently they seemed to just disappear. Like Regina and Yakob. Of course, Harry read the newspaper, heard the rumors; he knew about the ghettos, the roundups, the forced labor camps. He even knew that one of his loved ones had perished. Ava had told him on the telephone call. It was maybe 1940, Harry couldn't keep the years straight anymore. Who could think straight with what was going on?

This woman, Ava, had telephoned him, frantic, in the middle of the night. Several times he had had to ask who she was, there must be some mistake, tell her to calm down, talk more slowly, he couldn't understand. It had been a long time since he had spoken or encountered Polish, and yet, close to sleep, he found the language available to him. "Do you know how much this will cost me?" she had rattled. "How long it has taken me to find out your telephone number? Finally, among his things, I found it. Do you know how many times I have tried to get through? I just thought you should know, his mother should know. Yitzak . . ." Here she paused. "Yitzak is dead. He was on the train that day, when the station was bombed in Wlodawa, he was going to see her, to tell her . . ." Dead space on the phone. When her voice returned, it seemed divested of breath. "It doesn't matter. I went to the farm, to Stawki, to make sure, when he didn't come back to Warsaw. I thought maybe he lived, maybe he went back to her. That's when Mr. Hondra told me (long pause) about the wife and children. They have been taken to Wlodawa, some kind of labor camp they have there. Where they keep them."

And then he heard only static. They were cut off.

So this was the *shiksa*, the "business" that had taken Yitzak to Warsaw so often that it had become his home, much more than Stawki, Chava, and the children. This Ava to whom he had just spoken was his brother's home.

Fury and a sense of betrayal rose in Harry in the middle of the night until he realized that the object of his anger no longer existed. His brother, his *kibitzing*, mysterious older brother—this Ava had called to tell him—was killed on a train. Wasn't that what she said, some kind of explosion? A bomb?

Harry sat slowly in bed, the sheets snarling around his ankles. His brother was dead.

"He was going to see her. To tell her."

Harry yanked at the sheets. His brother was going to tell her. . . .

This woman had never called back, and Harry didn't mind living with the absence of specifics at the end of her sentence. He focused instead on Chava, in some kind of camp in Wlodawa. Would it be safe to write to Hondra, plead with him to do something to help his sister-in-law? How could he ask such a thing? How could he not? What if the letter was intercepted? It could get the man in trouble. He didn't know what to do, but what else could he do? He wrote the letter. And he never heard back, not a word.

He didn't tell his mother about Yitzak until after the war. When he received a card from Chava.

The handwriting was barely discernible as letters forming words, more like tiny scratches on a piece of paper than writing. Her fingers, her legs, those of her children, she wrote, everything was stiff, swollen, atrophied.

> But we survived. Hondra, he snuck us out of the camp somehow,
> the man is so kind. So in the barn he put us. Your brother, from him
> I have no word. Probably killed, like everyone else. Us, me and the
> children, we weren't killed, but you think we're alive, three years in
> a barn without sun, water, the freedom to exist in even one moment
> without terror? No talking, no moving on the straw, we shouldn't

make a peep, no laughing, no crying. He was risking his life, Hondra and his family, that I won't deny. The Germans, their encampment, was just across the river. Every now and then, when he thought it was safe, a bowl of soup he brought for us to share. We drank it silently. This has been our life, brother. You will help us?

There was no signature.

Harry crosses Fort Washington on 187th Street. Along with his brother, Hershel, he has started the process of bringing them over, Chava and the children. They'll live with Hershel and Leah. Hershel's bakery, across from Yankee Stadium, is a big success. Between the two of them, they're arranging the visas, the passports, the tickets, all the paperwork of transport that Harry knows so well.

But from Regina, during the war, after the war, nothing. Harry heard nothing. From her parents, nothing.

About a year ago, after the liberation, he made a telephone call to the mayor's office in Lukow, but minutes dragged by as the person who had answered the phone sought the "appropriate authority" and Harry heard nothing on the other end. The paperwork for Chava started, the full horror of the death camps and Poland's purge seeping daily from news reports, his Reizele and Yakob and the whole Lansky family unreachable, as if wiped from the face of the earth, he knew, even as he searched, that part of him recoiled from finding the answer to his questions. What would he do with the finality of knowing?

Still, on one of those occasions when knowing seemed better than not, he called Reva Lansky. She had heard, she told him, that they were all killed, all of them. "I'm sorry, Harry. It must be true. They say in Lukow the Jews were rounded up, in '42, maybe '43, rounded up and pushed into the synagogue. They burned it down, the Nazis. I never been to Lukow, but that's what they say. A distant cousin who knew Reizel's parents, she told me. The hat store, everything destroyed. And the people, they burned them up in the temple."

Harry wept, yelled: "You don't know this for sure. You repeat things to me, terrible things that you heard from this one, from that one."

"I'm sorry, Harry, I thought maybe you knew."

"There is nothing to know," he said, and slammed down the receiver.

A few days later, he thought about calling his wife's cousin to apologize for his outburst, but he couldn't bear the possibility of hearing her words again, so he wrote her a card instead. A simple note: "I am sorry for losing my temper. It is not your fault. Harry Himelbaum."

And he wrote to the Magistrate of the City of Lukow. Every day hoping not to hear back. This was last fall, late in the year. He had done all this—won his case with the United States government; gone into business with Saul; set everything in motion that he could think of to find his wife and child; started the paperwork to bring Chava and the children over—and here he was, a thirty-seven-year-old American citizen walking on 187th Street, a little thinner maybe than he used to be, but not bad-looking, with a full head of hair, and a woman with whom he might dare to pursue . . . something.

She was a beautiful, sophisticated girl, a redhead. They'd met last summer at a wedding reception where he supplied the fruit platters, and she'd admired the display. She mistook him for a guest (because of course, he'd worn his suit), marveled at the rosy cheeks of the pears, and they began a light but pleasing conversation. She had a head on her shoulders, this Gloria. She was an American, born here; it was a point of pride with her. He found this out when he worked up the courage to call her and she told him that she was accustomed to going out with American-born men. He had already won his case, so he could tell her in all honesty that he was a citizen, and she had, with only the slightest hesitation, agreed to go out with him.

Harry reaches the yellow brick building on Pinehurst where Gloria and her mother live. A very nice apartment they have. She had accepted a second date, finally, despite his foreign birth, because he had said something on their first date that made her laugh. On the subsequent afternoons and evenings that they saw each other, neither of them could remember the joke, but Harry gave thanks every day that the lost witticism had escaped his lips. He liked this girl. She was fiery and somewhat argumentative, true, but he had taken on the United States government, a little zest from a woman he could handle.

Gloria made him feel alive when they were together—watching a movie, sharing a meal, a conversation—and for the first time in America, he felt that it was all right to acknowledge his attraction to a woman. She wasn't married, he wasn't being threatened with deportation, and while he still didn't want to know the answer absolutely, what Reva had told him about Regina and Yakob must be true, he had no reason to believe otherwise. Chava, too, had heard rumors about the Lukow Jews, the synagogue. Surely, he would have heard from Regina by now if they had survived.

Since the previous spring, he had been contacting this and that embassy, refugee camp, department this and agency that, only to learn nothing about his wife and child. How much longer must he approach the mailbox bathed in simultaneous hope and dread that it may hold the answer to the question that had dogged him since his arrival here: Married?

As his relationship with Gloria progressed, Harry could understand that she wanted to be certain about his marital status before allowing either of them to speak of feelings or the future. She realized the turmoil and pain it caused him, the prospect of knowing the fate of his family, but nothing less than an official document proving his status as a widower would do. At thirty-three years of age, and having lost a fiancé in the war, she wasn't getting any younger, and it was simply unthinkable to consider pursuing a relationship with a married man. (She had heard of a girl on 189th Street who found herself embroiled in a bigamy trial. She'd fallen in love with a Polish Jew, married him, and two months later, his wife had appeared at the door!) Before things went any further, she must have tangible proof that Harry was a single man. "Please don't get in touch with me again, unless you're free."

When Harry received the letter on onionskin paper from the Magistrate of Lukow, authenticating with its official stamp his right to once again get in touch with Gloria, he leaned his head in his hands and felt with all his heart that he would never be able to move from this position.

"Your wife and son," it read above the official municipal seal, **"were killed in an anti-Jewish action."**

Why would he want to move? Why believe in words like "future" and "feelings"?

He sat for days, he didn't know how many. He sat, refusing food, his eyes sometimes catching sight as he rubbed his temples, of the pieces of paper spilling from his makeshift desk, so many remnants of futility.

He sat in this same position, with his head in his hands, for he would never know how long. Once or twice, he snapped awake to find himself lying on his bed, but then immediately, he would sit up and resume the customary position, his elbows on his knees, his head heavy in his hands. What was there to see, hope for, imagine, live for? What was there in this world that could hold any interest? For he didn't know how many days, he sat like this. His beloved Reizel. His Yakob.

After a period of time, Harry lifted his head.

After another period of time, he accepted from his mother a few spoons of soup, then a cup, a piece of bread.

It was months before he thought of contacting Gloria with the "proof" she had asked for. Just picturing the two of them together produced waves of self-disgust. What right did he have to happiness, to reside anywhere in the vicinity of happiness?

With the passage of time, he concluded that he had that right.

Slowly, gradually, the waves receded. Harry had fought for years to establish his right to citizenship. Was he now going to expel himself?

Harry gets off the elevator on the fourth floor. The savory aromas of dinner preparations infuse his nostrils, seem even to permeate his skin.

He hesitates for only a moment, adjusts his collar, and stands in his very most straight posture before ringing the doorbell.

As he takes a deep breath, Gloria opens the door. She looks radiant, her smile welcoming, her eyes so glad to see him.

"Harry," she exclaims, "come in."

~ ~ ~

ACKNOWLEDGMENTS

I would like to express my gratitude to:

The late Dr. Gloria Gross for her inspiration, encouragement, guidance and expertise pertaining to all things Polish. As a mentor, scholar, colleague, and friend, she is sorely missed.

Marian L. Smith Senior Historian at the United States Citizenship and Immigration Services, Department of Homeland Security, for her guidance in helping me access materials under the Freedom of Information Act. While this is a work of fiction, its credulity depended throughout on the accuracy of the law and documentation as practiced in the 1930s.

Robert W. Martin, Guide for Military History at About.com, who went beyond the call of duty in clarifying military regulations, circa World War I. "Feel free to ask as many questions as you like. That's my job," he wrote in an email.

Brunye Miller for sharing as much of her story as she could bear.

The late and truly magnanimous Sam Zwass for his incomparable generosity in helping me translate Polish and Yiddish documents. Without his patient help, I don't know if this book would have ever come to be.

Kris Malczewski for his knowledgeable tour of Lukow and Wlodawa.

Krystoff Skabinski, the "ambassador of Wlodawa," for looking at a photograph and saying, "Oh yes, I know that house."

Wladyslaw, Grazyne, and Waldek for welcoming Jeff and me to their farm in Stawki. As inscribed at Yad Vashem, they are truly "Righteous Among the Nations."

Yale J. Reisner at the Jewish Historical Institute on Tlomackie Street in Warsaw for understanding that the search is always valid.

Early readers Dr. Caren Converse, Dr. Jane Rosen, Laurel Bauer, Beryl Elon, Laurie Yehia, Ahmed Yehia, Joni Levin, Kathy Seal, Susan DiLallo, Richard DiLallo, Michelle Katz, Mona Houghton, Betty Lussier, Mickey Glass, and Marilyn Levy for their invaluable insights.

Gadi Elon for always being at the ready to help me turn a Yiddish phrase.

Liz Trupin-Pulli, an early supporter and wonderful friend.

My agent, Peter Riva, for his intelligent analyses and ongoing encouragement as he became a stalwart champion of the book.

Michael Haggiag, who navigated that all-important path to Peter.

Sandra Riva and JoAnn Collins, who are always kind, and always thinking!

Susan Jeffers Casel for her spot-on editing and Andrea Au Levitt for the recommendation.

That ever-magnificent institution, the Sherman Oaks Branch of the Los Angeles Public Library, whose shelves helped me touch the sources.

Jeff, Juliet, and Bobby: my candles and my mirrors.